Praise for *The Wind in the Wheat*

"I can think of no one but Reed Arvin who could have written this book. A story of such insight—full of descriptions to sit and savor, and a narrative that won't let you go. This book should be read by everyone who loves integrity, music, or just great writing."

—Rich Mullins, CCM artist

"I was simply overwhelmed by *The Wind in the Wheat*. It is truly a great book . . . nothing less than sensational. [It] will remind believers of the One to whom they belong. Its authenticity will create a restless heart that can only find rest in Him. I commend it to you."

—Steve Brown
President of Key Life Network and
Professor of Practical Theology
Reformed Theological Seminary
Orlando, Florida

"There is something for everyone within the pages of *The Wind in the Wheat*, but most of all, there are nuggets of truth to those who have ears to hear. To read a great book is truly a joy, but to discover a great author is a treasure."

—Rick Cua, CCM artist

"*The Wind in the Wheat* is a mirror to your soul. It invites you in, and you cannot resist going there. It's about me and untold others who live on the edge of faith everyday. Reading this novel can be an exercise in the service of Christian integrity. It has been for me."

—Dr. George A. Mason, Pastor
Wilshire Baptist Church, Dallas, Texas

"Reed's wonderful ability to capture the imagination pulled me right in. He has written from the heart a warm, artistic and sensitive piece."

—Kenny Marks, CCM artist

"I loved it! Imaginative, entertaining and inspiring. This gifted writer challenges us to seek realness over hype. A celebration of the triumph of small, genuine acts of service over the grandeur of celebrity Christianity. Everyone interested in Contemporary Christian Music should read this book."

—Jenny Gullen, Hoi Polloi, CCM band

"*The Wind in the Wheat* is a stunningly beautiful tale of art and romance. It gives voice to the silent warring of faith and commerce that wearies the hearts of God's children in America and is hauntingly familiar to any of us who profess our faith for a living."

—Billy Crockett, CCM artist

"This is not just a satisfying love story, it is an artist's affirmation of the source of his joy. Andrew Miracle's parents and the land and people of Rose Hill—in fact, the memory of 'the wind in the wheat'—represent for the protagonist what is good, true, and beautiful. That, and the ministry to 'nameless servants of God,' are mighty weapons against the seductive and deadening force of success."

—Marilee A. Melvin
Vice President for Alumni
and Public Relations
Wheaton College

"*The Wind in the Wheat* [is the] story of us all—of vanity and nobility, seduction and awakening, of blind ambition and holy vision. It is a story of the dark, radiant, slippery human soul and the tenacious, tender, laughing love of God. [Reed Arvin] is a gifted writer in a brave search for his own way to be true to his gift and calling. He has succeeded."

—Billy Sprague, CCM artist

The Wind in the Wheat

Somewhere in the world tonight, someone will cook a meal, or play a song, or paint a church for the Lord. There are many such servants. They may feel that in the economy of God what they do is small. They are not famous. They are unknown, except to their small gathering of believers. They simply serve. This book is dedicated to them.

The Wind in the Wheat

REED ARVIN

Publishers Since 1798

THOMAS NELSON PUBLISHERS
Nashville • Atlanta • London • Vancouver

Copyright © 1994 by Reed Arvin
All rights reserved. Written permission must be secured from the publisher to use or reproduce any part of this book, except for brief quotations in critical reviews or articles.

Published in Nashville, Tennessee, by Thomas Nelson, Inc., and distributed in Canada by Word Communications, Ltd., Richmond, British Columbia.

Scripture quotations are from the NEW KING JAMES VERSION of the Bible. Copyright © 1979, 1980, 1982, Thomas Nelson, Inc., Publishers.

Library of Congress Cataloging-in-Publication Data

Arvin, Reed.
    The wind in the wheat / by Reed Arvin.
        p.   cm.
    "A Jan Dennis Book."
    ISBN 0-7852-8146-0
    ISBN 0-7852-7360-3 (mm)
    1. Country musicians—Tennessee—Nashville—Fiction.   2. Young men—Tennessee—Nashville—Fiction.   3. Nashville (Tenn.)—
Fiction.   I. Title.
PS3551.R85W56   1994
813'.54—dc20   94–9961
                                                                  CIP

Printed in the United States of America
3 4 5 6—00 99 98 97 96

— 1 —

The morning after his vision, with the sunlight streaming in through his window, Andrew Thomas Miracle awakened. He opened his eyes cautiously, half expecting to see some kind of vapor hanging in the air, some physical manifestation left over from the night before. But to his relief, everything was normal. His room was filled with the same familiar things, each in its proper place. There was a comfort in the room, in the heavy wood furniture, the blue jeans hung loosely over the back of a chair, his battered work boots standing in a corner. But he knew absolutely that he had not been dreaming. His vision had come to him while he was fully awake.

What had happened that night proved to be the axle around which so many unforeseen stories have turned. It isn't logical. It is inexplicable because of the many cracks in which sin hides, and there is no graceful way to tell it. It went untold for a long time because even as it happened, it seemed that it was intended to be a private thing, not to be shared.

He had been sleeping upstairs in the farmhouse when the Spirit came, and there had been no warning. There was no mighty wind. There was no flapping of curtains and no rustling of leaves. No window crept open, drawn upward by unseen power. The Spirit came from the silence, and it did not ease into the room. It entered the room like a whip, snapping.

Andrew had been praying a dangerous prayer: the prayer to serve the living God. For months he had hurled it out into space like a lifeline, at other times releasing it like a caged animal. Sometimes, at work in the fields, he had just chanted it until it seemed like the words were blown away in the wind, rising into the sky with the scraps and dust off the bales of hay. He had stopped expecting an answer, long before it came. But Someone had been listening.

The whip snapped. Instantly he sat up straight and stared, as rigid and fragile as plaster. He was listening hard like an animal listens to the darkness in the plains. He was tingling and frightened and ecstatic. Then in that taut bowstring of a moment, something preposterous happened. The Spirit leaned His power toward him, a balanced, tipping mountain. He held it there a moment, pressing Andrew down into the bed with the weight. From the silence, exquisitely near, came His Voice.

"You are Andrew," the Voice spoke, not mimicking his parents or friends but somehow defining his very essence. The Voice paused again, and spoke four very unlikely words.

"Andrew, you are love."

The world fell silent. The room and house became invisible. For a moment, Andrew thought he saw what He meant. Then the whip snapped again, and He was gone.

Darkness and silence; then, with the sun Andrew awakened. He got up from his bed and walked to the window overlooking his family's farm. He stared out at the fields, perfectly square and uniform, dark Kansas dirt and yellow and green crops criss-crossing like little soldiers, and the lake of fallow, empty pastureland stretching far beyond. The Miracle farm was large for that part of the country, over nine hundred acres in pasture, wheat, milo, and corn. It was too big to be seen from any one spot, even from the second floor of the house where Andrew stood. He stared out and played back the sound of those words again and again, wondering what they could possibly mean.

The Voice. It was still very much with him. He looked far out into the open countryside, taking in the distance and feeling it all over again. Whatever the message meant, it seemed clear that God would not break every law in the physical universe without some clear purpose.

His name, from which he had received so much unwelcome humor in his childhood, had come with being born into a family of strong farmers that went back generations. They were Midwestern people, farming and dying there in a long line, and he took his place on the farm as surely as his predecessors had. The Miracle family, centered in Kansas but scattered across three states over the years, had been anything but miraculous; they were, rather, steady, enduring, and dependable. But his father had taught him to be proud of his name, and if Andrew had willingly taken some ribbing in adolescence about it, he now had both the physical strength and the wit to put an end to it.

He was twenty years old and too serious to feel like a boy any longer. He had lived in Rose Hill all of those years, and those who have never set foot on a working ranch might have been tempted to call him a country boy, teetering as he was between adolescence and manhood. But he had driven a tractor at age nine, and had worked his way across Kansas for two summers now, rolling from north to south with the traveling harvest crews that cut down a year's worth of growing and praying in a few hours.

He had the kind of lean, hard muscle that comes from growing up working hard outdoors. Six feet and one inch tall, with a good body hidden under plain farm-work clothes, his look fit his life, which was largely outdoors and physical. His arms were strong but not thick, good solid limbs beat into wood by labor and youth. He wore his light brown, sun-streaked hair in a neat, short style that demanded little attention. He was not beautiful, but fine, with an open face and a strong, clean-cut jaw, a characteristic shared by nearly all the men in the Miracle line. He radiated a young, effortless masculinity. His eyes, however, were surprisingly delicate and of an indeterminate color—hazel, but with a motion behind them like a top that never quite stops spinning.

Working the harvest crews required a stout back, strong hands, and a thorough knowledge of Big-8 football. Those were the three badges of belonging, the tools of instant friendship. The shared experience of hard work and hot sun knit friends together, planting them together in the soil they tended. Two could work better than one, and three better yet, so the boys became men side by side, accumulating four or five hard summers together before a few went off to college and left for the beyond. They learned to depend on each other because even as children they knew that drought, sickness, or a burned out tractor hung over their futures like dark, marble clouds. Their friendships were a strong but narrow fit; they knew intuitively that the time would come when each would turn back to the others for the help they had given.

Andrew was as dependable as any and never had to be asked twice to lend a hand. He worked hard, as if by striving with the earth he could achieve a kind of peace. Though his family could stake a claim to the area for generations, he did not fit seamlessly into Rose Hill life. Underneath his hard frame, another, secret man shared his body with him. Sometimes a whole day of cutting wheat would not reveal that other man, and for a moment, or an afternoon, he felt accepted and wholly a part of the life around him. Though he didn't desire it, there were undercurrents in him that set him apart, passions roaming in him that he had never asked for, feelings he would willingly have released.

Sitting high on the combine, he could banter fullbacks and bowl games, lifting high once more the names of Pruitt, Mason, and even Sayers, because history counted for a lot in farm country. He knew well the litany of triumphs and defeats of years past and the names of those who had covered themselves in glory or shame. But the easy, swaggering, camaraderie he saw between many of the others on the crews was denied him.

He was devout and couldn't help showing it, and that held him back. His devotion was a fierce devotion, a possessing thing. The other boys found him moody, and it was true that he seemed to wonder endlessly about things. Most of all, he wondered about God. In Butler County, Kansas, the right place to do that was inside a church, and the right time to do it was somewhere around junior high. As high school passed, so too did the window of knee-bending and humility. Working a field with four or five other Kansas boys just out of high school was very much the wrong time and place, he had learned, unless he tread very lightly indeed. But when it came to God Andrew did not tread carefully. He walked a more dangerous, passionate path. He didn't want to; he longed to take his place as one more comfortable stalk of wheat in a great ocean of a field. There was a comfort in being a part of things, and he wanted that comfort. But again and again, almost against his will, he tread in the worst possible way. He couldn't stop, even though he knew that to speak was once again to betray himself.

Far from humorless, he possessed a quick, self-deprecating wit that he could, when cornered, turn outward and burn with. Once when Cody Hackett had called him a Jesus freak, Andrew had set down a basin of water and soap at Cody's feet and, bowing extravagantly, called him Pilate. The others had roared with laughter, and Cody had kept a respectful distance from then on. But again and again, almost against his will, Andrew would violate the peaceful cud chewing of football scores, love affairs, and grain prices.

Sometimes the boys would break, and they would climb up into the dump trucks, already half-filled with wheat, to rest. They could almost swim in gold kernels up there, and they would lie back, shielded from the afternoon sun by the walls of the bed. There were times when it was so quiet and so hot that they could almost hear each other sweat.

In that perfect silence, the boys would spin lies, telling tales of cheerleaders, prom dates, drinking, and what came after. It was unabashed, masculine, and full of the false bravado of deepening voices and push-ups and basketball. But Andrew lacked the stomach for that kind of talk. Gradually, he would grow restless, his head filling nervously with unbidden thoughts. He would stare off somewhere, feeling words forming inside him, wanting for once just to laugh the loudest and let them keep on bragging. But inevitably, after some time he would stand up, fidgeting, and lean out over the rail of the truck. The boys knew he was about to speak.

They would exchange glances—full, perhaps, of youthful guilt and the wish that Andrew were far away. He saw them do it well enough. It was hard on him because he knew that for a moment he had teetered on the edge of popularity and that if he could just laugh it all off, he could settle down on the safe side of that precipice. But he would always keep on going. These moods had a life of their own. Sometimes, when he had it bad, he would look far out into the half-cut fields, like a prophet, and end up blurting out something unwelcome about the mystical and the unknowable.

God was there, out in the fields, he would say, out where the city noise hadn't drowned Him out. It took hard listening in a day and age like this one to hear Him. But there was a beauty in the silence, in the listening, if we could only hear it. There was destiny. More than anything else in the world Andrew wanted to see Him and to know Him, not like in a book but really know Him, like a person.

He would go on like this for a minute or two, speaking in a lethal combination of poetry and prophecy, and then sit back down hard in the wheat, red-faced. The silence would close back up around him like a felt tomb, and invariably those glistening boys would gape or just wipe their foreheads with a towel and start back in about who was getting what off the girls back at school.

Andrew could feel these moods coming on, closing from

a distance, and they often seemed beyond his control. Sometimes he thought they were a poison, and when he struggled inside himself, the battle was visible and painful. He wished that whatever messages God had for the world would come through some other vessel and leave him alone. At those times, his soul threw pictures up onto his face like a drive-in movie, flashing light and darkness onto a helpless, human palette. At school, he had learned to look down at the floor if there was no avoiding it, and he would stare earnestly at a crack in the linoleum, tense, diminished and retreating. But he had a fire inside and it burned on its own fuel. It was like riding a bus that refused to slow down enough to jump off. He could no more stop his plaintive wonderings about God than he could become a New York stockbroker.

In compensation, he possessed an enormous gift. In the midst of cattle ranchers and farmers, surrounded by dust, corn, and wheat, Andrew Miracle was born with a great ocean of music moving inside of him. When the sea was calm and resting he could bale hay and cut wheat with anyone. But when he sat behind a piano and played, the water would rise up and push the notes out of him, sometimes rushing forward, powerful and focused, at other times frozen and crawling like a glacier. And he would sing. His voice was full of earth, and it seemed to move straight through him into the air. Then, more than ever, the movie would play, his features illuminated and darkened, throwing light and shadows on his listeners. For in this tiny community of less than three thousand, an artist had been conceived.

Andrew, anxious to serve, played his music wherever and whenever he was asked. But to him, church was the real place for it, and Sunday after Sunday, his performances lit up the walls of the small country sanctuary. There, among wooden pews and beat-up hymnals, his wonderings found complete expression and a phenomenal, terrific freedom. His music was electric, of a higher, mystical order. His gift had appeared early and seemingly in full bloom: by his late teens he had already accumulated a kind of unusual celebrity among his townsfolk, and even beyond, to Andover and Mulvane.

To Andrew, all music was about God. Before he played, he would explain that this was so, stepping from one leg to the other self-consciously, looking down intently as he spoke. It was his heart's wish that every fearful soul be turned toward Him, even the coldest and most remote. Speaking in a voice that sounded like shuffling feet, he would say that if a person listened to his heart, then maybe this music would help him see that God is and that there was no avoiding Him. Then Andrew would look up, eye to eye with his listeners for just one moment, and tell his audience that whatever stood between them and God would be, in the end, swept away. It was just a question of time.

Folks would look at each other in wonder that the son of the late Franklin Miracle could talk that way. Maybe they'd seen him that very morning, driving a John Deere in his family's corn field. But then he would sit, breathe deeply, close his eyes, and begin to play.

There is much that remains unspoken between man and God, and for an ordinary man, one without the gift, both the truly fearful and the truly glorious remain unsaid. Like most, the people of Rose Hill had their share of secrets hidden in their darkness. But all of these lived in Andrew's music when his gift was unleashed. This was the place when the forces within him were greeted like friends and ushered into the light.

To Andrew, his music was the place where every secret could be revealed in its entirety. In this way, it was like a prayer, stunning in its purity and sincerity. It contained everything pleasant and unpleasant between himself and God, and listening to it was like eavesdropping in a confessional, or watching a man strip under floodlights. It was the prayer one never had the courage to speak but had always longed to, and Andrew prayed it for all of them. It was the once hidden shouted from the rooftops, and in the end, both he and his listeners were swept away, pushed over the dam of pride and fear in the current of his playing.

Inevitably, the music inside Andrew became the axis around which his neighbors worshiped. Little by little, the congregation in his church grew, until one could scarcely breathe in the Sunday morning service. Some visitors refused to return, grumbling about unconventionality, and propriety. But each week, a few more souls would cram themselves into the Christ's Kingdom Assembly building to be prayed over in this unlikely way.

Like men in combat emboldened by the courage of a comrade, the worshipers felt that something real with God was closer and more possible, while the music played. It was not unusual to see lips silently moving throughout the performance. Andrew didn't make the music but rather released it, sometimes beautiful and plaintive, at other times crashing out, almost grotesque and pained, but always startlingly, penetratingly real. Then, after this revelation, he would finish and become once again shy, a little awkward, and studiously polite.

This morning while Andrew stood pondering the meaning of his visitation, life went on as usual in the Miracle household. Downstairs, his mother went about making their ritual Saturday morning breakfast. Since his father's death, Andrew had been most comfortable with her. She was a true farm woman, and she made meals at the Miracle residence something to look forward to. Saturday morning was as much a statement of ideology and theology as it was a breakfast. Fifty-one hard years had not treated her badly, and if they had shaped her more for comfort than for romance, she was not in any way unlovely. She had a look of consistency about her that Andrew liked, and at least with her he talked easily, unafraid of what might spill out of him. Since Franklin's death they had been a comfort to each other. Her secrets were in her face, which showed the lines of sun and hard work, but the signs of decline and aging she still kept at bay, for a little while. Her jet-black hair was forever pulled back, with little wisps creeping out around the neck. She loved to dress comfortably, sometimes in dungarees but more often in blousy, cotton farm dresses that let her move about.

For all the limitations of her life, she had refused to be narrow. She had filled their farm house with simple but beautiful things that were far beyond the taste of their neighbors. A great lover of music, she had insisted on lessons for Andrew and for his older brother, who resisted them like medicine. Andrew, however, had clutched onto them from earliest childhood with relish, playing far beyond his years and surpassing his teacher while still a young boy. His mother had encouraged his burgeoning, surprising musical talent like a kind of mystical crop that she had planted. The fact that they were on a farm in the middle of Kansas made that music all the sweeter, she would laugh, and then she'd open every window in the house and make him concertize the cornfields with Beethoven and Brahms. Andrew would bang on that piano into the night, and his mother would sit out on the porch, windows and doors flung open, staring at the sunset until it vanished. Her name was Alison. She had been widowed for six years now, and the two of them had lived alone for the last three since Andrew's brother had moved to take a city job in Illinois.

"How'd you sleep?" his mother asked, looking up as he entered the kitchen.

"Like a planted turnip," he replied, unconsciously quoting his father. His mother smiled. Andrew had a great deal of his father in him, in spite of their differences. Franklin may have known nothing about music, but there were times she looked into Andrew's eyes and saw her husband there, staring back at her.

"I've almost got breakfast done," she said. "Grab the O.J. out of the fridge, Drew, and we'll be ready."

Andrew poured two glasses and sat down, his vision gently humming inside him. The Voice. It was still very much with him. He regarded his mother carefully a moment, longing to confide in her. He had never kept anything from her before. But from the moment the Voice had come, Andrew had sensed that what had happened was private. "Was there a storm last night, or anything?" he asked cautiously.

"A storm? None that I know of. But if you know where one's hiding, let me know. We could use the rain around here." Alison looked out the window at the pastureland surrounding the house. It was turning a brown shade, not dangerous yet, but enough to keep a farmer awake if it rained. "What are you going on about? Did you hear something?"

"I don't know, I guess I was dreaming. So you slept through the night?"

"Yes, Drew, I slept fine. Now say the grace."

Andrew paused. Since his vision, prayer would be different for him. "You do it this time, Mom," he said. "I'm still waking up."

Alison took her seat, bowed her head, and recited grace automatically. Andrew helped himself to pancakes, bacon, sausage, and fresh fruit.

"Cy Mathews called this morning," said Alison. "He wanted to talk to you, but you weren't up yet."

Andrew sighed. He knew what Mathews wanted. The pastor had been reminding him almost daily about the upcoming concert of Heaven's Voices at the church. He had agreed to go, of course. He was even looking forward to it. But Mathews had made it clear the real purpose for Andrew's being there was to meet the group's manager, Mathews's old friend John van Grimes. Andrew's nerves rattled every time he thought about that.

"He was reminding me of the concert this weekend, no

doubt?" he asked. "As if I might have forgotten since yesterday?"

"Believe it or not, he didn't mention it for two whole minutes."

"You must have done all the talking."

"Don't be ungrateful, Andrew. You know he's excited about your meeting his friend because he believes in you so much."

"I know. Sorry. So what else did he say?"

"He wanted to remind you about Tuesday night at the old folks' home."

"Pastor Mathews is one of the great reminders in the state of Kansas. I haven't missed playing for the old folks in a year or more."

"And he hasn't missed reminding you for as long."

Andrew smiled. "You're right. I just wish I was a little more confident about meeting Mr. van Grimes. What on earth would I say to a guy like that?"

"A guy like what, Andrew Miracle? I suppose you're as good a man as any city folks try to be."

"A real Nashville music guy, that's what kind. A manager. I shudder to think what pastor Mathews has told him about me. He'll probably show up thinking I'm the next Elvis or something. Cy does tend to embellish when he's speaking about his flock."

"Yes, and it's a charming habit. You listen to me, Drew. Don't worry about what to say. Just be yourself. That's wonderful enough."

Andrew looked at his mother gratefully. In spite of his self-doubts, when she built him up he could almost believe it. He pushed his plate away. "Had enough?" Alison asked.

"Of what, breakfast or your pep talk? Food, I've had plenty. Confidence, I could maybe use another booster shot."

"Andrew, you're going to be fine. Now, what's on the work schedule for today?"

"Well, I'd better start on the fence painting. I'd like to get some of it done while it's still under two hundred degrees out there."

"Good plan. But the really hot days are over for this year, I think. This last spell is just Indian summer." She looked thoughtfully out the kitchen window at the windmill, the well slowly pumping with the wind. The impatiens she had planted around the base of it were beginning to fade. The seasons were changing, in spite of the warm temperature.

"It'll be harvest soon," she said at last.

"Yes, soon. But not just yet." Andrew leaned over and kissed his mother on the cheek. "Better go, Mom. Lots to do."

"Right. Go ahead, I'll get this."

Andrew moved toward the screen door that opened to the back porch, anxious to get to his chores. For a moment, he paused and almost turned to speak to his mother. But when his hand touched the door, he straightened and headed out, grateful he didn't end up blurting out anything about his vision. As he passed out of the house, his mother called to him.

"Andrew?"

He turned and looked back. "Yes?"

"Make that fence pretty, boy."

Andrew packed up his painting tools and hopped in the Ford pickup. His father had bought the Ford a few months before he died, and if a man can love a piece of metal, Franklin Miracle loved that truck. He was a doer and a planter, the kind of man who drives by an empty field and sees perfectly straight rows of wheat ripening in his mind. He had died the way he lived, building. He was struck down, literally, by a collapsing windmill he was helping a neighbor erect. The ground had given way underneath a brace and one huge leg of that tower had slapped him to the ground, crushing the life from him instantly. Andrew still thought of the truck as his father's, and since the accident he had felt closest to him while driving it.

Andrew drove down the road that led to the fields. Once there, he pulled the truck over by the fence, turned off the engine, and rolled down the windows. It was easy to imagine God in a place like that. There was quiet that let a man hear, and after what happened last night, that was what Andrew needed.

The fence split two fields, one in corn and the other larger one in wheat. He rested his arm on the windowsill and stared off into the wheat, watching the waves run with the wind across the tops, a good four feet tall. He watched, but mainly he listened. Wheat that tall and ripe has its own sound in a Kansas wind, pushing across the fields without a single tree to break its flow. The wheat moves in the wind, and it sounds like the sea, only better because there's something of the earth in it and something of man's work as well. It's a strong sound, always changing, and a little wild.

The weather was clear that day, with the kind of impossibly high sky that sits over the fields in Kansas for days on end in August, until a black thunderstorm or tornado interferes. It was dead quiet but for the instruments that God and man played together in the field that morning.

This was Andrew's favorite place on earth. He loved it in the winter when the plowed-under stubble crackled beneath his shoes. In spring it was a lake of green, and he could almost feel the shoots growing, willing themselves upwards. Early fall brought harvest, with the tension of months of weather-watching behind them. But now, in late summer, the plants were nearly grown, maturing within themselves, ready to explode at any moment into fruition.

Andrew unloaded his tools and spent the morning painting, alone with his thoughts. He wondered about his miracle and what it might mean. A world in which God broke all the rules and stepped through a hole in space to converse was a world in which his own plans meant nothing. He must watch and wait. What He had said—that he, Andrew, was love! *Wasn't God alone love?* But there was no denying what had happened. The sound of that Voice did not suffer contradiction.

After some time, Andrew laid down his tools and walked out into the middle of the wheat field. He searched the sky, wondering where the God who had visited him the night before was now. Surely such a visit would be accompanied by some instruction, some explanation of its purpose. He listened again, hearing the wheat moving in all directions around him. He watched the wind run along the roof of the field, picking up speed. He was completely surrounded by an ocean of trembling gold. He began to pray.

"God," he said aloud, "You see me here. You see me standing in this field. You know my thoughts before I speak them. That You are, there can be no doubt."

He moved his hands over the tops of the plants, keeping pace with the wind.

"Forgive me for doubting You. I believe.

"You know perfectly well there's nothing special about me, God. What you have here is someone who knows beyond a shadow of a doubt that You exist, is convinced he's not to tell anyone how he knows it, and is lost in the middle of nowhere with no clue what to do next." He paused. "It does seem You could have picked a better vessel." Andrew stood there in bemused silence for at least five minutes. Finally, he turned his face upward and closed his eyes, feeling the sun burn down on him.

"Give me a task, Lord," he said. "Give me a great thing to do with my life. Show me the way."

— 2 —

The first sin Andrew learned from John van Grimes was the sin of envy. Quite tall, with dark hair that was surprisingly long, he was hardly a man to blend into a crowd. He had a model's face, not chiseled but vulnerable, almost boyish. And he had the sort of body that clothes designers sketch their clothes to hang on, the sort that make pleats hang perfectly straight in one beautiful, unbroken line. His eyes were gray, perfectly symmetrical, and crystal clear. He gave Andrew his start both in music and in ministry, and even now it's still not clear whether it was God or Satan that put them together.

There are few people who have a genuine sense of purpose, and when those less certain encounter such a man, they attach themselves to him like pilot fish to a shark. They know intuitively that such men suck success into their wake, and that there may be a happy few trailing in the backwash. When van Grimes moved his tall frame into a room, the seas parted. Others realized that if they weren't talking to him yet, they were waiting until they could talk to him, and they weren't going anywhere until it happened. There seemed to be around him a continuous informal line of people waiting their turn, pretending to speak to each other in the meantime. But when at last a man's moment arrived, and he tried to appear nonchalant, van Grimes looked right at him, eyeball to gray eyeball. He seemed to have been waiting all night to speak to this one person, enduring a hundred boring conversations until he could confide in his one real friend. All conversations with John seemed confidential.

Like many charismatic men, however, van Grimes was not self-made. He had spent a few years seemingly one job away from success, bouncing from one thing to another, trolling for a match, and making ends meet. He had always been a churchgoer, having been raised in it and fed on it. About a year before meeting Andrew, he had started working in the Christian music business. He started small, managing a struggling gospel group called Heaven's Voices.

Heaven's Voices was a group in which the members were essentially unpaid. Eighteen- to twenty-five-year-olds signed on to play and sing for one year, traveling city to city in vans and ending up in one church or another almost every night. It was bush league, but it turned out to be a training ground for the members, a chance to do some music ministry and to get themselves known. It worked about the same way for van Grimes himself.

The weekend after the Spirit came upon Andrew, Heaven's Voices came to Andrew's church, Christ's Kingdom. Christ's Kingdom Assembly was a lot more than just a building to the people who lived around Rose Hill. They were christened there and had their funerals there, and not much was likely to happen in between those two events that the church wasn't involved in. It was the social, business, and political hub of town, and nobody got elected dogcatcher there without paying their respects. The deacon committee might just as well have been a city commission, and everybody, including Pastor Cy Mathews, knew it. Mathews served at the deacons' good pleasure just like everyone else, and Andrew had often detected a worried look peeking through his habitual affability.

Pastor Mathews had the kind of stocky build that seems to grow a little year by year, until finally it's agreed upon that he is well and truly fat. His black hair was a little too long and always a little disheveled; he was, in short, the kind of man who seemed a little less than the sum of his parts. All the same, he had his value: he knew everything about everybody, told no one, and was as reliable as dry summers. Since his father's death, reliability had counted for a lot with Andrew, and he respected Mathews for it.

For some time now, Mathews had been telling Andrew about his old friend John van Grimes. The two had known each other briefly in college, and Mathews had made the effort to maintain contact with John through the years. When van Grimes called to collect on the favor by booking Heaven's Voices into Mathews's church, Mathews agreed happily. He wanted to see John again, and above all he wanted to introduce Andrew to him. The stocky pastor, limited in some ways, was not limited in his enthusiasm for his flock. He looked on Andrew as a kind of musical genius, and was sure that if he could get them together, van Grimes would see Andrew the same way.

The evening of the concert, Pastor Mathews corralled Andrew the moment he arrived at the church. He flung his arm around him, pulling him aside, and spoke confidentially. "Andrew, my boy," he said, "I've some exciting news for you." His voice was elevated, like it had been torqued upward slightly by a tiny wrench. "I've just had a little chat with John. He and his group pulled in a couple of hours ago, and I've been bending his ear again about you. He's agreed to meet you tonight after the concert. We'll all get together privately, in my study."

Andrew exhaled. Mathews had been threatening this meeting ever since Heaven's Voices had been scheduled to perform, but he had hoped it would never actually take place. Van Grimes had been built up in his mind to mythical proportions. He wasn't sure there was really much point in meeting this Nashville manager, after all.

"I appreciate what you're trying to do, Pastor Mathews," Andrew said. "It means a lot to me. But I wonder what somebody like Mr. van Grimes would see in my music."

Mathews looked shocked. "Are you kidding? Look, Andrew, you've been playing your music around here for what, four years now, right?"

"That's right."

"Well, boy, I'm no music expert, but I figure your stuff's every bit as good as what I hear on the radio, maybe even better. Give yourself a chance, boy. Walk into that meeting and meet the man. He won't bite."

There was clearly no gracious way to decline in view of what Mathews had done to set up the meeting. Andrew smiled wanly and silently shook his head in agreement. He hated his shyness. Each performance began with an agony of fears and uncertainties until he was well under way. Then, at last, the music would take him over, creeping over him from the ground up like honey, covering him and protecting him. In those moments, the audience became lucky bystanders to a personal revelation.

The two figures began to stroll down the hall to the auditorium. Mathews rumbled to a halt in front of a large picture window, and side by side, they looked out on the familiar surroundings, with its buildings that never changed. "Look around you, boy," he said. It was dusk outside but still hot. The grass was turning brown. "Andrew, you've got a gift. And the hard truth is, that gift is never going to grow in Rose Hill, Kansas."

Andrew looked surprised, but Mathews stopped him from speaking. "That's right, Drew. I love this town, but I don't kid myself that it's the center of the world, either. I know this little pond we swim in isn't much." He looked back at Andrew. "Every time I hear you play and sing in our little church, Drew, I can't help but see you down there in Nashville, making gospel records, and reaching out to the youth."

Pastor Mathews always referred to anyone under twenty-five as "the youth." He looked wistfully through the window out into the hot summer dusk, as if by Andrew's going he could in some way escape with him. Then, he put his arm around Andrew, and the two began once again to walk on down the hall. "I've been watching you, Drew," Mathews said. "I'd say that you're a different man these last few weeks. Would I be right about that?"

Andrew thought about his visitation, and nodded his head. Perhaps it was the culmination of something that had started weeks before. The pastor was right. Andrew had been slowly changing for some time. "I guess I've just had a lot on my mind," he answered.

Mathews smiled knowingly. "I can see that, boy. Now, like I've always said, I'm not a prying man, I'm a praying one. But I've known you your whole life, Drew, and it's plain you're carrying a weight around these days." He paused a moment, his red face staring, looking Andrew over. "I've got a feeling you're getting the call."

Getting the call was a phrase no Christ's Kingdom kid needed explained. It was a hallowed phrase, spoken reverently. It was God who was calling, and those who received it walked to the front of the church in a formal ceremony, dedicating their lives to Christian service. Then they were sent out with the church's blessing to a lifetime of pastoring, missionary work, or music ministry. The rest of the church would peer at those who had received the call like near saints, wondering at what must surely be a special relationship with God. The dedication was final, and it was for life. Once called, always called.

Andrew stared back at Mathews, only partially surprised. As strange as it was to hear, his visitation had prepared him for something extraordinary. He had been happily pursuing his music, writing almost every day after his work was done, performing for church retreats and of course for nearly all the Sunday morning services. A few times Mathews had even arranged for him to perform for some surrounding churches. Ever since the Voice had come, Andrew had been wondering where it would all lead. But the implications of "the call" were too much to contemplate just then. He simply nodded and made his way to the auditorium.

Andrew slipped in the back, self-conciously. He was always uncomfortable whenever the church had musical guests. He knew people thought of him as a sort of resident artist, and he could feel them sometimes looking at him whenever a guest soprano hit a particularly high note, as if for approval or criticism.

The church was filling, and as people came in there were murmurs about all the extra sound and light equipment that filled the front. The pulpit had been removed and a small stage built. In the front, six microphones rested on stands, and the back of the stage was filled with drums, guitars, and amplifiers. Off to one side there was room for three horn players, and speaker stacks loomed on both sides of the stage. The group had put up a lighting truss, and a mixing board for the sound engineer took up six seats in the center of the church. It was a long way from the missionary music the church was used to, and the congregation sat in their chairs buzzing and soaking it all in.

Andrew was deep in thought, staring at all the equipment when Pastor Mathews walked to the front of the stage. He grabbed the center microphone, clearly proud of the spectacle he had unleashed. "Well now," he said, "it looks like we're about ready to get started here. Now, I don't want you old folks like me to worry about all this sound equipment. I've been promised there'll be something for everybody tonight, even a slow one or two for the over-the-hill crowd."

The congregation laughed. But then Mathews got his serious look, the one he used when wrapping up a sermon, or to bury folks with. "Brothers and sisters," he said, "I want us to prepare our hearts for a very special evening tonight. As you know, we've got a special concert of music planned by Heaven's Voices. But before they take the stage, I want to introduce you to a close personal friend of mine. We're lucky to have him, because he usually stays in Nashville instead of traveling with the group. But he's here tonight. Give a Christ's Kingdom welcome to the man behind this great ministry, my good friend John van Grimes."

On a cue from John the lights went down, and when he strode onto the stage, a spotlight lit him up in the darkness. As he stood in the center, his eyes seemed to reflect the light back out into the audience, and he smiled the smile of a man who does not doubt himself. In one moment, Cy Mathews was left in the dust.

Van Grimes looked out into the audience, smiling and seemingly making contact with everyone. "Thank you so much, Brother Mathews," he began, "and I want to tell you all straight out how fortunate you are to have a man like him in the pulpit here at Christ's Kingdom Assembly."

Van Grimes sounded as if he'd lived in Kansas his whole life. "I've known Cy Mathews for many years, and he's a good man who cares about people and their problems. Although I will admit I could tell a story or two about him in his younger days." Church laughter rustled through the congregation. "Of course, he was much better looking in his early years. Fortunately, he held onto it just long enough to convince Lois to be his wife. I really never forgave him for that."

Van Grimes was playing the congregation like a stand-up comic. As the familiar chuckles played out over the audience, John winked at Mathews and Lois conspiratorially. Although a total stranger, his approval seemed to land gracefully on the overworked pastor and his wife, making them celebrities. Then his tone changed.

"People, this is a night that could change your life forever. This is a night, if you'll open yourself up completely to what God can do, that can put you on the most exciting pathway you can imagine." Van Grimes smoothed the lapel on his jacket. "I look out on this congregation of folks and I see a lot of happy, buttoned-down people that seem to have it all together. But I know that underneath all that there are folks in this church right now who are hurting inside. They feel far away from the Lord, and they are longing to have their most secret fears and hurts touched by Him.

"I don't believe that there is one person who is here by accident. I think He called everyone that is here tonight because He had something special for them." Van Grimes paused and looked around the room expansively.

"Many of you watch the news every night, and you see what's happening with young people in this country, and I see it, too. But tonight you're going to meet some of the most fantastic young men and women you've ever seen, and your hearts are going to be lifted up together in praise." He began picking up the pace.

"These young people come from all walks of life, but they're united in one common cause, and that cause is to tell the world about Jesus Christ. Ladies and gentlemen, please give a warm, warm, Christ's Kingdom Assembly welcome to Heaven's Voices!"

The church burst into applause, and the band and singers ran up onto the stage, positively beaming. Of the six singers up front, three were men and three women. They looked about twenty years old and seemed to have been plucked, en masse, from the set of a beach movie. They sang the same way that Frankie and Annette danced; flat out, as if there were no tomorrow.

As they performed their first few songs, Andrew found himself thinking about what their lives must be like, traveling all over the country, playing and singing about God. He wondered about how it would feel to perform before hundreds of people every night. He thought about how close they all must be to each other, praying together, winning the world for Christ.

It was clear that the people in Heaven's Voices were quite sincere about what they were doing. But what affected Andrew most was the easy familiarity between them. Growing up on a farm, he had always been a loner, but as the evening went on there reawakened inside of him what he had felt so often before: the desire to belong. The people in Heaven's Voices seemed to be each other's best friends, creating a shared past with each other that only they could understand.

Each of the six singers gave a short testimony during the evening, and Andrew was surprised by some of their stories. Of the six, four came from the kind of strong church backgrounds he expected and understood. They seemed to be right where they belonged, quite comfortable and confident. But when one of the girls came forward, her shyness in speaking was a sharp contrast from her performing style. Her name was Lauren, and she said her stepfather had battered her. The audience winced. She told the audience that social services eventually broke up her home, and she had gone to live with an aunt on the other side of the country. Then her face broke into an illuminated smile. God must have known what He was doing, she said, because this aunt had loved her, taken care of her, and above all had told her about Jesus. God had even enabled her to forgive her stepfather, she said. And now she was praying for him.

Andrew was moved by the girl's story, and he stared at her as she sang her solo after the testimony. He had loved his own father very much. Franklin had been torn from him by a horrible accident. He wondered what it would be like to leave a father voluntarily, because you feared or despised him.

After Lauren's story, one of the young men stepped forward. He had the kind of rugged good looks that made a good college recruitment poster, and several of the high school girls sitting near Andrew leaned forward perceptibly as he began.

"I guess my story is a little bit different from some of the others," he said slowly. "I'm a little older than most of the guys up here, and when I encountered Jesus I had already been singing in nightclubs and bars around my home town for about three years. I was working in a rock and roll band six nights a week, making good money, and dreaming about getting a record deal and becoming a rock star. I might as well admit that I was doing some things I'm not too proud of.

"I was living what I thought was the good life, partying and putting everything else into the band. Sometimes I look back on all that and realize that I was headed down a very slippery slope, and the bottom was a long way down. An amazing thing happened, though. Through a friend, the girl I was dating became a Christian. At the time, I thought this was a major drag."

The church laughed a bit nervously, and for a moment, an awkward tension seemed to settle on the congregation.

"What I didn't know then was that God had another plan for my life, a plan that saved me from that destruction and exceeded my wildest dreams. The truth is, that girl all but prayed me into the kingdom of God right along with her. She nagged me and prayed for me and loved me, and finally I saw so much of Jesus in her that I realized that it had to be true, and I invited Him into my life."

The congregation murmured its approval, and the tension in the air vanished. Then the poster boy smiled broadly, and proceeded to change Andrew's life.

"I'm proud to say that I'm marrying that wonderful woman next month. I've been accepted into Bible college to study church music. God has an incredible adventure in store for me, and I can't wait to get started. I will miss these guys up here though, more than you can imagine. You see, tonight is my last concert with Heaven's Voices."

Suddenly everything became clear to Andrew. It seemed that his whole life had led up to this moment, to those words. God had surely brought him there, and over it all lay the benevolent gaze of John van Grimes. He was right. There were no accidents.

— 3 —

Thirty minutes after the concert, Andrew was ushered into the inner sanctum of Rose Hill—the pastor's study of Cy Mathews. It contained what was surely the biggest desk in town, and the walls were solid bookcases filled with theological books, magazines, and pamphlets of every size, shape, and condition. The room, like Mathews himself, seemed to contain too much. They were both in need of a good shaping up. Behind the cluttered desk, the pastor sat. Two chairs faced it, which, if they could have talked, could have blown the lid off Rose Hill for a lifetime. As Andrew entered, Mathews leapt up from behind his desk, smiling, gesturing, talking, and shaking hands all at the same time.

"Andrew, Andrew, come in, boy. I'm sure your ears must have been in flames, for all the talking I've been doing about you. John, this is the young man I've been telling you about."

Van Grimes, the picture of calm good nature, rose from one of the chairs and greeted Andrew as if they were old friends. "Hello, Andrew," he laughed. "I've been sitting in here with the president of your fan club for the last ten minutes, and it's nice to finally meet the young man himself."

Andrew introduced himself as confidently as he could. The words of the last singer were still ringing in his ears. It suddenly seemed that a lot depended on the next few minutes. "It's wonderful to meet you, Mr. van Grimes. Hopefully Pastor Mathews hasn't been boring you to death with the short list of my musical accomplishments."

"Not at all," he laughed. "If only half what he's told me about you is true, you're a young man I would very much like to get to know."

"I tell you, John, this boy has talent," Mathews jumped in energetically. "I've watched him and watched him, and he's every bit as good as those folks you hear on the radio. Better, I'd say. He'd be just great in your group, I tell you, just great. And there's no telling where he could go from there."

Mathews, though well-intentioned, was dangerously close to babbling. He had just taken in several sentences worth of air when John, in a way Andrew couldn't help admiring, seized control of the conversation without Cy Mathews's ever realizing it. In the future, Andrew would see this talent exercised many times, and he never tired of watching it. There was a different type of social subtlety to the man, a kind one simply didn't encounter in the middle of farm country.

"Cy," he said, "you're a marvel. Here I am, racking my brain looking for talent from Nashville to LA, and you're hiding this kid in the middle of Kansas! You need to be a talent scout." Pastor Mathews beamed and exhaled silently. Van Grimes turned slightly in his chair.

"I understand you're really quite a musician, Andrew. Cy tells me that you're a fantastic singer and pianist, and you write your own songs. He also says, and this means so much more, that you really have a heart for ministry. In fact, Cy was just saying how you always make yourself available and have even started to perform at some of the surrounding churches. That is so great. I mean that's what it's all about, isn't it? Changing lives and ministering to others."

As John talked, Andrew had a chance to get his first close look at him. He wore a dark tailored sport jacket of a lightweight fabric, an off-white shirt open at the collar, wool slacks, and casual leather shoes. All in all, he was a little underdressed for a church service, but it was all in such exquisite taste that it made Andrew and Cy feel a little frumpy. His dark hair was combed back and relaxed down over his collar. He possessed that kind of easy detachment that doesn't threaten but makes everyone want to win him over as a friend. Listening to van Grimes, Andrew felt like he had stumbled into an audition for a major motion picture rather than the pay-your-own-way Heaven's Voices. Van Grimes would have been just as at home at a Hollywood party as in Pastor Mathews's study.

John looked at Andrew and smiled. "Well," he said, "you know our situation, Andrew. Dan is leaving the group after tonight. We have exactly two weeks to find a replacement and rehearse the new person. Then, it's back off to the races. Suddenly, I find I'm fascinated by young men from Kansas."

John laughed and tossed a look at Pastor Mathews, and Andrew realized that he had almost forgotten Cy was in the room.

"Let me give you the basics, Andrew. Of course, I'll have to hear you play, but you'll probably want to have some idea of what you'd be getting into. This is a ministry, pure and simple. No one, including myself, is in this for the money. We don't pay the people in the group; we only provide a nominal twenty-five dollars a week for spending money. We do provide everything you need, including meals."

John laughed and said, "At this point you're probably wondering why anybody in their right mind would agree to work that hard for absolutely no money." He leaned in and looked Andrew right in the eye. "They do it, Andrew, because this is the ministry opportunity of a lifetime. It's a chance to really put your faith to the test, to find out if there's anything down there after all. Andrew, if you're interested in using your gifts for the Lord, we can give you the chance to do it two hundred and seventy times over the next twelve months. You'll have the opportunity to watch people come to know the Lord night after night, and nobody can put a price tag on that. Plus, you'll make fourteen of the best friends you'll ever have."

He paused while Andrew took it all in. Finally, he leaned back in his chair and asked, "What do you think? Are you interested?"

The whole time John had been talking, Andrew had felt his emotions continuously rising inside of him. By the time van Grimes had finished, Andrew was burning inside. He answered without hesitation.

"Absolutely," he said. "The money means nothing to me. I don't expect to get paid to tell people about Jesus. There is only one thing that matters to me. I want to be useful to God more than anything in the world."

"You say that with a great deal of conviction, Andrew."

"I mean it. As far as I'm concerned, you don't have to pay me a cent. To be a part of a great work, to play and sing in front of hundreds of people every night, to do something great for God—I believe that this must be my calling."

Andrew felt his voice begin to tremble. The more he said, the more all of his feelings about his visitation began to flood over him again. He tried to pull himself together for a moment but suddenly found himself blurting out, "This is my mission, Mr. van Grimes. I see that, now. I want to tell people that God *is*. I have to tell them. I must tell them."

Andrew looked at the floor, embarrassed. He hated when his moods came on him like that, at the worst times. He had wanted to pull back and stay in control. He had clearly overdone it. John said nothing, and looked stunned. Cy Mathews gazed at Andrew as if he were trying to figure out who he was. His mouth hung open. At last, van Grimes spoke.

"Well," he said, "I've never heard it put so passionately. In fact, I may never have heard anything put so passionately. That passion could be a powerful tool for God."

Then he laughed, and Andrew looked up, surprised. Van Grimes, at least, had quickly regained his composure. He was watching Andrew carefully. "What on earth has happened to you, Andrew?" he asked. "I mean—has something happened? You certainly have a fire inside you, don't you?"

Andrew returned his gaze directly for the first time. "Yes, sir," he answered firmly.

Andrew and John looked into each other's eyes a long moment, as if reading each other's minds. Electricity seemed to flow between them. Finally, van Grimes stood up and said, "I can't wait to hear you play.

Van Grimes, Pastor Mathews, and Andrew walked across the hall into the empty sanctuary. Only a few lights remained on, and Cy moved to turn on the main ceiling banks. John reached out and grabbed his arm. "That's okay, Cy," he said. "Leave the lights down. Let's create a moment here."

Andrew walked to the piano while Cy and John found seats about ten rows back in the church. The church piano was a magnificent instrument, an estate gift from the Dean family, who were good friends of the Miracles. Andrew had always liked to think part of the reason old lady Dean had willed this incredible nineteenth century Bluthner to the church was that she knew he would be playing it. He loved making music on it more than anything in the world. It was shiny ebony, enormous, and one note on it spoke more than whole songs on a cheap upright. Andrew sat down, opened the keyboard, and took a deep breath. Then he began.

There is a great divide between good playing and great playing. The worst musicians are unaware that this distance exists, and they fumble their way through magnificent literature, oblivious. Most players sense this divide, however, and they know which side of it they are on. A few of these determine to struggle their whole musical lives to reach the side of greatness by practicing and working harder and harder. They end up impressing their friends and colleagues with their machine-like mastery of difficult pieces. But they know that they are not great. They know it because for a few moments, moments that they will remember and cling to for the rest of their lives, they have actually crossed that divide. For a shining moment they understood, and they wept and played and believed in their greatness. But they were cast out again, and no amount of struggling would bring them back across.

No one crosses the divide by struggling, and no one passes through it by practice. There is only one bridge across. It is the bridge of abandonment, and it is built of helplessness, and of courage. Great playing is given over to the music utterly and completely. It is abandoned and willing. It is calm and it is shrieking. It is weeping and laughter, and more than anything else, it is love.

That night Andrew closed his eyes and began to play. He gave himself over to his gift, and let one note follow another. He let whatever music roamed within him play itself out, go where it would go, with no thought to cloud or filter. It was soft, and it hurt; it was loud and impregnable, like a fortress. It was the proud dance of a peasant girl. It was his father, dead. It was the wind, for a frightening moment, blowing up the skirt of a classmate in fifth grade. It was drought. It was his first kiss. For a full half-hour Andrew rode the piano like a horse. He cajoled it and caressed it and pushed through it because it fought him, and he would not be denied its secrets.

At last, he began to sing. He sang softly, singing stories of his father, of the fields, and of solitude. He sang of thunderstorms and of God.

That night Andrew floated across the divide and held it in his hand like a captive bird. It was his to own until at last he released it, exhausted. Then, the spell was broken, and Andrew looked up, astonished to see Pastor Mathews and John standing not five feet away from him. At some point they had left their seats and silently moved toward the piano.

Pastor Mathews had tears streaming down his face, but John was standing with his eyes closed, as if deep in thought. Andrew looked at John, and said, "Mr. van Grimes, can God use that?"

John just smiled. "Oh, yes," he said. "Oh, yes."

4

The next morning, Pastor Mathews brought van Grimes out to the Miracle farm for breakfast and to talk over John's plans for Andrew. Alison, completely in character, was up at six-thirty, cleaning house, making breakfast, and setting the table on the covered porch behind the house. She arranged a centerpiece of fresh flowers on the table and smoothed the country tablecloth carefully. The morning was clean and unseasonably cool, as if the start of fall was in the air; a fresh, gentle breeze lightly ruffled the edges of her dress as she worked.

In her mother's heart, she knew the real purpose of this visit. A lot would be said about ministry, of course, and about opportunity and white fields of harvest. But it all added up to nothing more than Andrew's leaving. In spite of her feelings, she kept on working, toiling to make everything perfect. In farm life there is a hierarchy of laws, and the law of hospitality to guests is supreme—above even personal considerations. So she worked in the morning sun, meticulously preparing the table, just as she had prepared herself. At last, everything was perfect, and as she looked at her watch, she heard a car turn off the highway and up the gravel drive to the house.

That would be Cy, she thought to herself, and sighing she turned back into the house.

"Pastor Mathews is here," she yelled upstairs, and she heard Andrew's steps booming through the ceiling as he headed for the stairs. On her way to the front door, she stopped to check herself in the hallway mirror and gazed at her reflection thoughtfully, as if taking stock of the last several years. A lot of changes had taken place since Franklin's death, and she noted sadly that at last, some were creeping into her face. She had learned what it was like to sleep alone again, and she had learned, the hard way, that a woman could be just as good as a man at breaking up sod with a John Deere and a harrow. But she had yet to learn the hardest lesson: what it was to be truly alone. Andrew was still there, and just knowing he would be coming in every evening after work to sit down at one of her carefully prepared meals had kept a true sense of isolation at bay. Now, six years removed from that awful day—the day the phone had rung and she had felt her life ending—she could almost get in bed without thinking of Franklin, without missing him so much she wanted to die as well, and if there were any justice, to find him and be together again.

The farm could function without Andrew—she knew that well enough. Franklin's ample insurance money had made the operation a continuation of a way of life rather than a hard necessity. Hiring a man to do Andrew's work could be easily absorbed. But she couldn't help fearing the loneliness.

Andrew bounded down the stairs looking excited and exclaimed, "I'll get it," as he passed her in the hallway.

"No, you will not," Alison answered firmly, resolutely turning toward the door and placing Andrew behind her. If he was going to be taken away from her, she, at least, would open the door for it. She had had enough of things happening to her, and she resolved not to be merely a spectator to this. She brushed her hair back, planted a smile on her face, and turned the knob to let John van Grimes—and change—enter her home.

Pastor Mathews said hello in his homey, sincere fashion, but unable to conceal his pride, he introduced van Grimes like some kind of celebrity. John, for his part, acted as if he were being presented at court, and actually inclined his head graciously as he said hello. Alison greeted them warmly, and extending her arm into the hallway, she welcomed them in.

Andrew, smiling shyly, stepped from behind his mother, but before he could utter a sound Mathews exclaimed, "So that's where you've been hiding, boy," and clapped him on the back. "We need you right up front and center, Drew. After all, you're the reason we're here."

"Thanks, pastor," Andrew answered, grinning. He reached out his hand rather tentatively to John, and John grabbed it, shaking it enthusiastically and pulling Andrew toward him.

"Good to see you, Andrew, good to see you. I've been looking forward to this ever since last night. That, my friends, was an experience that I won't soon forget."

"Come into the living room, Cy, and you too, Mr. van Grimes," said Alison. She was a picture of quiet dignity, her back straight, her features strong and fine. "I so appreciate you both coming all the way out here this morning."

"Nonsense, Alison," answered Mathews, cheerful and benign. "Your breakfasts alone are worth twice the drive."

"He has been bragging, Mrs. Miracle, all the way out," said van Grimes. "It seems your cooking makes an impression."

"Please call me Alison."

"Then by all means I must be John."

"Of course, John. Now, if you and Cy don't mind a bit of fresh air, I thought we'd have breakfast out on the porch."

Alison led the group towards the back door through the kitchen, where they were engulfed by the smells of home-cooked food. Mathews was stopped in his tracks, seduced on the very spot by a warm loaf of bread cooling on a rack next to the oven. He hovered over it, inhaling deeply.

"Well now, Alison, that takes me back. I could almost be at my own grandmother's." He took another deep breath and looked up, beaming. "You wouldn't understand this, John, living in the big city like you do. City folks just do not understand."

"For Pete's sake, Cy, you'd think Nashville was New York City, the way you talk. It smells wonderful, Alison."

Alison smiled politely, keeping her feelings to herself. If the two men thought that flattery over her cooking was the key to her sympathies, they had badly miscalculated. She knew her cooking was superb, and she never did it for the compliments of men—not since Franklin had died. She took her own pride in her cooking, in not playing the role of a farm woman but actually being one. She was fruitful, and earthy, and she loved the harvest as surely as any man.

"Come along, then," she said simply. "The sooner you get seated, the sooner you can eat. Andrew, take these two out to the table."

Andrew herded Mathews and van Grimes away from the kitchen and out onto the covered porch. They sat down around the big round table while Alison finished getting breakfast. Van Grimes took his place next to Andrew and leaned comfortably back in his chair, surveying the expansive pastureland that began behind the Miracle homestead. The view from the patio opened up panoramically, with gently rolling plains that seemed to connect with the sky miles away. Closer to the house, Alison had created a garden of summer flowers that were still doggedly clinging to their petals for their last few weeks of life. Off to the north, surrounded by oak trees, the windmill was slowly turning, softly creaking out an unsteady stream of water into a little pond about thirty yards away.

"What a beautiful spot," van Grimes said earnestly. He was speaking, as if on cue, in a softer voice. "I didn't really have this in mind when I decided to come to Kansas. I don't remember a place so peaceful."

"Yes," said Andrew. "We get used to it, of course. And I don't recommend it in January. But I'm glad you see the beauty in it. I'm not sure everyone does."

John gave him a warm, fatherly look. "A man would have to be blind, my friend, not to love this place."

The three sat in silence soaking up the quiet, when

Mathews suddenly spoke up, breaking in on the tranquillity, wriggling his large body in the garden chair.

"Drew, you won't believe how impressed John was with your performance last night. You just won't believe. He went on and on. Isn't that right, John?"

Van Grimes's face betrayed a momentary irritation, as if some secret timetable were being rushed, but his expression quickly corrected itself. "That's quite true, Andrew," he said calmly. "I've been thinking about last night ever since we left the church. I was very moved by what you shared with us."

Andrew looked pleased. "I'm glad, Mr. van Grimes. I don't really have anything to compare myself to out here. Pastor Mathews says what I do is good, but he's prejudiced, I'm afraid."

Mathews laughed heartily. "Well," he said, "I hope you believe me now, Drew. I've been telling you that you're special for years. Ever since you were a kid you had something about you. Now John comes along and proves me right. And I knew it all along."

"Yes, Cy," said van Grimes. "I'm going to have to think of some creative way to thank you for introducing me to Andrew. I have a feeling that it will be a very important day in all of our lives."

Mathews was poised to respond when the screen door opened and Alison came through balancing a large platter in each hand. "Here, let me help you with that," said John, and he got up to take one of the trays from her hand.

"That's quite all right," answered Alison firmly. "You gentlemen keep your seats. Everything's ready. Andrew, would you get the coffee?"

"Sure, Mom." By the time he had returned with the pot, Alison had arranged everything and was serving the men with heaping portions of homemade bread, omelets, fresh fruit with a sweet glaze, and freshly squeezed orange juice.

After serving, Alison took her seat with just a trace of

formality. The eyes of all three men were on her, and she raised her hands above the table and held them face up towards Mathews and van Grimes. "Pastor," she asked, "would you bless the meal for us?" Mathews and van Grimes each slipped a hand into hers, glancing at each other self-consciously, and Andrew joined them, completing the prayer circle. Mathews nodded his head gravely, and his face assumed a serious look.

"Our heavenly Father," he intoned musically, "we are indeed mindful of Your presence here this morning as we look out onto the beautiful vista of Your creation. And we are grateful, grateful indeed, for this magnificent meal that Sister Alison has so graciously prepared for us. Remind us, O Lord, that You have plans, mighty plans for us down here on the earth." He paused a moment, and added, "Plans beyond the scope of mankind, O Lord. Amen."

Van Grimes and Andrew answered the amen in unison, but Alison merely moved her lips silently. The group fell to, Mathews contentedly munching on everything at once, van Grimes elegant and restrained, selecting each bite with care.

"Delicious, Alison, just delicious," van Grimes said warmly. "If you'd let me open a restaurant in Nashville with this food, I could make you a very wealthy woman."

"I do appreciate your compliments, John," she replied evenly. "I fear that big-city life might not agree with me."

"Yes, Alison, I suppose you're right." He looked out onto the peaceful plain that surrounded them. "Things do seem much more, let's say, manageable here. You're quite right to prefer it."

"I think so."

Van Grimes looked her in the eyes momentarily and then turned to Andrew. "Let me ask you something, son," he said. "After hearing you play, I find myself wondering about something. I find myself wondering how you see your place in the great scope of God's work."

Andrew looked up expectantly, as if he were considering a new concept. "What do you mean?"

"I mean, where do you see yourself in the world of ministry, say, five years from now?"

Andrew set down his fork and considered the question a moment. "I guess I would have to say I haven't really thought about that too much. Up until now, I've just put one foot in front of the other and hoped for the best. There's been a lot to do around here. I play for the old folks, write songs for our youth group and camps and stuff. And lately I've been playing at some other churches too, sometimes. More and more people seem to want to hear me all the time. I know I love playing at Christ's Kingdom—I guess that means the most to me." Andrew glanced gratefully at Pastor Mathews, who was returning his smile after adding his own considerable wattage.

"It's been our privilege, Drew," said Mathews. "There've been times when I wondered what the good Lord had in mind, sticking you in our little church. But then I look out and see all those faces, and I seem to be able to make some sense of it."

"Yes," said van Grimes. "I can imagine. It sounds beautiful, what you've been doing here. It's obvious that God is using you here, right where you are. I love that. But great things don't happen by accident, my friends. Great things require planning. Great things require a dream. I wonder if you would mind if I dreamed out loud with you?"

"Of course not," Andrew answered. He and Mathews sat entranced, as if at a mystical reading.

Van Grimes pushed his chair away from the table several inches. The sun was well on its way up the sky behind him, and Andrew had to squint through the glare to focus clearly on him.

"I don't play a musical instrument, Andrew. I don't sing or write songs or poetry or anything like that. So you might well be wondering what I'm doing in the music business."

No one answered. "I'm a dreamer, my friends. My job is to dream, to have a vision. A vision for people that I find, people that have enormous potential for success and may not even realize it. People like Andrew." Alison stirred softly in her seat but said nothing.

"Let me explain what I mean." Van Grimes closed his eyes, leaned his head back, and folded his hands before his face, touching them to his lips. "I've been dreaming about Heaven's Voices for almost three years now. Think about the kids in that group, my friends. They were talented, ambitious, but without much direction. That's where a dreamer comes in."

"You might say that's your spiritual gift. Dreams, I mean," said Andrew.

Van Grimes looked pleased. "Yes, I like that, Andrew. I like that very much. My spiritual gift is dreams." He paused, weighing the phrase in his mind, trying it on for size.

"So I dreamed for Heaven's Voices," he went on. "I dreamed that they would have an ever-expanding ministry, performing over two hundred times a year before tens of thousands of people. It may surprise you to know that your church is one of the smallest ones that we will perform in this year."

Mathews shifted self-consciously, thinking of his modest little building, so lacking in modern facilities. "I know, John," he offered humbly. "We've been stuck in our building ever since I've been here. I've been wanting to build for years, but money's tight on the farms."

Van Grimes turned and smiled indulgently. "This year we're playing some of the biggest rooms in the country. I even have a line on the big one." He paused, letting the moment build. "Second Baptist Church, Houston, Texas. Eleven thousand members." Mathews exhaled audibly. "On that night alone, my friends, Heaven's Voices will perform for over four thousand people."

The four sat in silence. Mathews, clearly mesmerized,

picked up a napkin, and wiped a fleck of perspiration off his forehead. "Heaven's Voices was really a dying entity when I took them over," van Grimes went on. "But just look at what we've accomplished. We're currently negotiating for a substantially larger light and sound setup—something totally professional, like what you would see in a rock and roll show. The system has over ten thousand watts of sound. The lights will knock you right out of your seat. First class stuff. You better believe that we'll be using that in our tour promotion. Something like, 'See Heaven's Voices—currently on tour with over two tons of sound and light equipment.' That's the kind of thing I'm talking about. The best stuff. I believe God's work deserves the best. But you've got to have the vision." Van Grimes was hitting his stride now, warming to his task.

"People are a resource, you see. In Rose Hill, there is an Andrew Miracle. In some other town, another person. Each toiling away, each doing well, no question. But what can happen if these people are brought together? And what can happen if the power of the media, the power of radio and television and print—what if all these are utilized to make a bigger, and bigger, and even bigger statement? It's a new age, my friends. Tomorrow is today. Can you see that there is no limit at all to what we can accomplish with the power of imagination?

"That's the power of a dream, my friends. That's the power of a vision. Vision, my friends. Vision is everything."

Andrew started at van Grimes choice of words. *Vision.* His mind snapped back to the night when the Voice had come, leaving him speechless and waiting for answers. *Vision is everything,* van Grimes had said. Of course. Andrew sat musing, playing the words over and over in his mind.

The sound of his mother's voice brought him back to himself. She had long sat silently, listening, and somehow, he had almost forgotten she was there.

"What does all this have to do with my son?" Her voice cut across the table.

Van Grimes also looked as if he had been disturbed from some private reverie, and for a moment he almost seemed surprised to find Andrew's mother sitting next to him. But, as always, he recovered beautifully. "What I'm saying, Alison, is that I'd like the chance to dream a dream for Andrew." He paused, engaging her directly. "Andrew is like a precious mineral, sitting in a mine. A gold mine for God. That precious metal doesn't do anybody any good until it's mined, you see. Otherwise, it just sits there, full of incredible potential but never really used. I would like to be able to mine that precious metal for God."

Alison sat quietly, a stark contrast to van Grimes's brisk and energetic speech. She had intuitively felt this moment impending on her from the time she had awakened that morning and, in a less defined way, from the day Andrew was born. Now, at last, the moment had arrived. She looked silently at her son and, after a moment, back again at van Grimes. It was dead quiet, but for the sparrows nesting in the oak trees behind the house; they could be heard plainly, sounding unnaturally close in the stillness. Her face, normally robust and vital, seemed somehow older and frail. Slowly, as if unwillingly returning from thoughts far away, she looked up, straight into the eyes of van Grimes, and spoke. Her voice, so quiet in comparison to van Grimes's, drew the men toward her.

"Did you know that my husband made this table, John?" she asked. The question, so out of context, startled van Grimes.

"No, Alison, I didn't."

Deliberately, she pulled the tablecloth up between herself and Andrew, exposing the superb birch woodworking. "My husband was quite a builder," she said slowly. "Folks have told me that a table like this would cost quite a lot at a store in the city. What do you think?"

Van Grimes slowly ran his hand over the wood. Every joint was immaculately dovetailed. The table did not contain a single nail, and the finish was as smooth as an ice sculpture. "I doubt very much you could even find such a table in any store," he answered softly.

"You could be right, John. It takes a long time to make something like this. Most folks these days are too busy, I guess." She gestured with her hand behind them. "My husband built this entire house and a good deal of what's in it. And he planted that stand of oak trees beyond us. You might not realize that trees like that don't grow much in Kansas. He planted that stand twenty-six years ago. There wasn't enough water pressure from the pump, so he carried the water to them in buckets the first few summers till they could grow on their own." Van Grimes stared at the trees, forty or fifty of them scattered over two acres or so. It would clearly have been backbreaking work, more so in the Kansas summer heat. "He built the barn at the Grissom's across the way and helped on who knows how many others." She paused briefly and looked out across the field. "Franklin liked to build things. He's been gone some time now, though," she finished vaguely. She looked suddenly tired, as if the day were ending, rather than beginning.

"He sounds like he was quite a man," van Grimes whispered. He was feeling unaccountably self-conscious.

"Yes," she answered softly. "He was a remarkable man." Suddenly, she put her hand on Andrew's arm, and her voice was surprisingly firm. "I would never want to stand in the way of my son's potential, gentlemen. That's the very last thing I want. Is what you're saying that Andrew should be out playing in front of all those thousands of people? Is that what you're saying will happen?"

Van Grimes pulled himself together. He was unsettled, and he couldn't put his finger on why. He wasn't used to feeling this way, but he was determined to see things through. "Yes," he said. "I think he could be doing great things."

"And is that what you want, Andrew, to do great things?"

"More than anything in the world, Mother. I want to be a part of a great work. I want to make a difference in the world."

Alison sighed.

"Yes. Great things. I suppose that's good. Anyhow, I don't ever want to be selfish about Andrew's talent. And I don't claim to know too much about churches with thousands of people in them. But I'd like to say one thing before my boy goes off and lives anybody's dream, Mr. van Grimes, even God's, if that's what it is you're dreaming. Franklin Miracle never got up in front of ten people at any one time in his whole life, much less ten thousand. He was a quiet man, and I don't think he ever even led a prayer at church. But nobody can tell me that man didn't do great things."

Van Grimes, for the first time he could remember, felt thoroughly off balance. He looked around himself, feeling the peaceful quiet and almost letting the warmth of the sun reach down into him. For a moment, he imagined himself staying right where he was, asking for another cup of coffee and another, just listening to the day go by. For an absurd instant, an image of himself working in a garden flitted through his mind. He hadn't felt this way in—well, in years, anyway. But then he saw Andrew, and his mind filled once again with a vision of a young protégé taking the music business by storm.

"I deeply appreciate what you're saying, Alison," he said almost reverently. "But I believe Andrew may have a different destiny. And I would like to help him find that destiny."

"It's not my place to say," Alison answered wanly. "I won't stand between my boy and his future."

"It's just for a year, Mom," said Andrew gently. "Then I can come back home, if that's what you want."

Alison had a feeling that none of them could foresee what

this decision would mean in their lives. Franklin had gone out to build a windmill and never returned. "The question is, is this what you want?" she asked.

"Yes, Mother. I believe it is."

Alison sat up straight, determined not to look defeated. She let her gaze fall on her son for a moment and then turned it out to where she could see the gold wheat absorbing the last bit of strength from the earth before it was cut down to make another year's profit.

Her voice crept out of her mouth. "Andrew may go."

5

Three days later Andrew was on a plane to Nashville thinking about everything that had happened in the last week. An improbable dream seemed to be unfolding around him. At times, it seemed absurd that so much would be arranged to find him, out in the middle of nowhere. But he was happy and expectant. In such a world, anything could happen to anyone. He wanted very much to believe in such a world. He thought of his vision and reassured himself that God was in charge of everything that was happening to him.

There had been a great deal to organize since the meeting with John. First and foremost was working it all out with his mother. He had dreaded that talk, more for his own sake than for hers. He knew that her friends and the church would support her through the transition and that she would not be alone. But all that merely made leaving possible, not easy. In the years since his father's death, however, Andrew had learned to count on her understanding and on her support. In the end she made it easy on him, as he knew she would. She had said, in her dignified, quiet way, that this might well be his destiny calling, and it wasn't in her nature to stand in the way of something like that. But he still did not tell her about his visitation. He felt that he must continue to carry that secret alone.

At the airport in Nashville, he was surprised to find that John hadn't come to meet him. He had counted on that one bit of familiarity to calm his nerves and to help him ease into things. In his place was his assistant, Carolyn Hemphill, who stood at the gate holding a small square of cardboard with his name printed on it. He waved self-consciously to her, and she bubbled up to him like the perfect prom date for a pastor's son. She wore a light blue sundress and seemed to be dressed more for a friendly get-together than for work. She was about Andrew's age, a very pretty brunette with brown eyes and an inviting face—not the high-cheekboned look of a model but open, healthy, and charmingly uncomplicated. She greeted Andrew without a trace of self-consciousness and chatted easily while he collected his bags.

"I'm a transplant from Minnesota," she said. "I came down here a little over two years ago. But Nashville feels like home to me, now. I love it."

Andrew could muster only a few noncommittal words in response; he had never felt comfortable around that kind of pretty effervescence. His quiet answers hardly seemed to slow Carolyn down, however, and she willingly filled in the silences with her own cheerful small talk. He didn't mind, grateful to have a chance to get his bearings. He would willingly have just listened as she chattered amiably on about Nashville and her family and what a lovely summer they were having. As they turned the corner to walk through the outer doors to the parking lot, however, she surprised him by stopping in mid-sentence and gazing up at him with a sudden, evident interest. "You're the quiet type, aren't you?" she asked.

Andrew held the door with the formal, country politeness that is still sometimes practiced in small towns. "Just at first," he answered ruefully. "I guess it just takes me a little while to warm up. Especially around new folks. We don't meet that many of them back home. Seems I've been talking to the same people most of my life, not that I've minded." She smiled gently in response, and they passed through the open door.

"Well," she said, "I wouldn't worry about it. You'll fit in

down here perfectly. Nashville's an easy town to get to know. You'll be fine."

As they walked toward the car, Andrew ventured, "Was it really that easy for you when you got here?"

"Sure," she nodded. "It was so easy to just plug in to things here. The whole Christian music industry is like a little family."

"What do you mean?" he asked.

"You know, just that everyone is so friendly and all. Everybody knows everybody."

He liked the sound of that. It made things seem less intimidating. But the word industry puzzled him.

"What do you mean by Christian music industry?" he asked. "I mean, what's industrial about it?"

"You know, record companies, publishers, managers, promoters. Stuff like that. Anyway, John said to get you settled in at the Hampton Inn by Music Row and then bring you over to the office."

"Music Row?"

"That's the part of town where a lot of the music industry people have their offices. I guess it started with country music, but most of the Christian music people ended up locating around there, too. It just worked out to be more convenient that way, I guess. John's office is over there, so you'll see it later today."

Andrew clearly had a lot to learn about Christian music. Until then, industry usually meant something do to with smokestacks and time clocks. The idea of his gift being a part of some industry was a new one.

Carolyn pulled her car out, and they loaded up the bags. They hopped in, and she pulled out into traffic. "Welcome to Nashville," she said grandly. "This is it."

Andrew leaned back in the seat and began to relax. In spite of his nerves, he wanted to drink it all in. He had traveled very little in his life; he had once gone to Chicago with his father to a large agricultural show, but he had been only a child. As they drove, Carolyn continued chatting effortlessly, and the sound of her voice had a curiously relaxing effect on him. Gradually, he began to feel more like himself. As they drove through town, he began making mental notes of the landmarks as they passed. She noted his interest and asked, "It's pretty, isn't it? Lots of trees."

"It is," Andrew answered. "We have traveled less than five miles, and I have already seen more trees than there are in the entire state of Kansas."

Carolyn laughed and said, "I know. I had to drive across your lovely state on my way to Colorado from Missouri one time."

"You failed to appreciate the serene beauty of the plains, I take it?"

"It was serene, all right. You can drive five hours without moving the steering wheel."

Her quick replies made Andrew wonder if she were really that simple after all. "I suppose that's true," Andrew admitted. "But you've got more than trees here. In those same five miles I've also seen more cars than there are in the entire state of Kansas. At the rate we're going, by dinner I'll have gone into overload."

Carolyn glanced over at Andrew with a smile. She was enjoying the role of tour guide for this small-town visitor. As they drove, she gave him an overview of Nashville geography, and he tried to fix as much as possible in his mind. After several minutes of explaining and answering Andrew's questions, she said, "I can see this city's going to be way too much for you, Andrew." She couldn't resist teasing him about his country background. "Of course, I guess if you can find your way back to the fort after fighting all those Indians back in Kansas, you should be able to manage." They turned into the hotel parking lot. "We're here."

Carolyn took care of everything at the hotel. Van Grimes had an account there, and Carolyn seemed familiar with the desk staff. She tossed Andrew his key. "You're in room 216. Do you need a little while to settle in? If you don't mind hitting the ground running, you could just drop off your bags and we could head on over to the office. I know John's anxious to see you."

Carolyn waited in the lobby while Andrew hurried to his room to get settled. He slipped the key into the door and dragged his bags in after him. He had never stayed alone in a hotel room before. Once inside, he looked around himself, taking in the room's modern, antiseptic perfection. Not a single matchstick or pillow or slip of paper was out of place. Its one redeeming quality, however, was a big, comfortable bed right in the center of the room. He toyed with the idea of moving it an inch or two to one side just to disturb its perfect symmetry, but decided against it.

Briefly, he arranged his bags in the closet without bothering to unpack. He turned to leave but suddenly stepped hurriedly into the bathroom to have a look at himself. The fluorescent light was harsh, and he surveyed himself critically in the mirror, wanting to gain a good bit of city sophistication in the few seconds before he left to face Nashville and whatever this music "industry" turned out to be. His plain haircut suddenly seemed to him foppish, and his dress clothes frumpy and out of date. He stared at himself a moment, feeling vulnerable and inadequate. But there was nothing for it, so taking a deep breath, he pushed his thick brown hair back into place and passed quickly through the door.

Andrew was quiet as they drove the few blocks to John's office. Carolyn turned the car down Music Square South and entered Music Row. The street was lined with large, converted houses, many of which had been extensively renovated. A few conventional offices were interspersed, but homes in the bungalow style of the thirties and forties prevailed. He was shocked to see even the names of huge corporations with offices in these homey surroundings. Carolyn pointed out a large three-story house, which turned out to be the offices of Warner Brothers publishing.

"Who are all these people wandering around the sidewalks?" Andrew asked. "They don't really look like musicians, do they?"

"Tourists," Carolyn replied. "All summer long tour buses unload scads of people to roam around the streets of Music Row. What they expect to see, I can't imagine. They walk around for a few hours and get back on the bus and go home, I guess. The real music business takes place behind closed doors."

The streets seemed filled with wandering people, all with slightly dazed looks on their faces, as if they were trying to figure out where they had mislaid Garth Brooks or Johnny Cash. Andrew realized with a smile that he was no different from them. Until this moment, Nashville had been nothing more than an idea to him, a symbol of the big time that Pastor Mathews had drilled into him. Unconsciously he had supposed that no one could throw a rock in that town without hitting Dolly Parton or somebody. He began to realize that he had been silly to think of Carolyn as simple. By comparison, he was as green as young winter wheat, and he knew he had a lot to learn.

The two arrived at van Grimes's office, a beautiful, old, converted house on 16th Avenue. Here, Andrew had a surprise. Unless John had other sources of income, Heaven's Voices was obviously generating a significant amount of money. A huge enclosed porch had been converted into a reception area, with a darkened glass wall on the street side. "John van Grimes, Personal Management," was inscribed in beautiful calligraphy above the door. If the home was modestly landscaped, it only served to set off the freshly painted dark green exterior and windows perfectly trimmed in white. The effect was one of comfortable affluence. Andrew took a deep breath and followed Carolyn into the office. The reception area housed a desk, where a pleasant girl said hello as they entered. Several gray overstuffed chairs comprised a waiting area, with a table and plants carefully placed among them. Oriental rugs covered the hardwood floors, and primitive Chinese art hung on the walls. There was not a single room like this in all of Rose Hill.

"Hi, Kathy," said Carolyn. "This is Andrew Miracle, the Kansas wonder-boy John's been raving about. Is he ready to see us?"

"Hello, Andrew. So you're the one, huh? Mr. van Grimes said to go right in. I think he has some people in there waiting with him, too."

Andrew nervously smiled in acknowledgment, and they passed down an open hallway to John's office. As they walked, he thought about just how little he really knew about John van Grimes. It was clear the man who moved so easily among Cy Mathews and the folks back home commanded considerable respect from his employees. Andrew hoped that he could really measure up to that one night in Rose Hill. The thought of going home in failure seemed very real just then. He mentally gripped his vision and tried to look confident.

Carolyn knocked on the door and opened it. John stood in front of his desk, speaking with two other men. He looked up and greeted Andrew enthusiastically. Carolyn quietly slipped out the door, leaving Andrew with the others. "You've arrived!" he exclaimed. "Welcome to Nashville, Andrew."

In this environment, John looked considerably more in command than he had when Andrew met him. Andrew had honestly never seen clothes like that before. They were simple and casual but beautifully made and obviously expensive. Andrew felt conspicuous in his slacks and dress shirt. He had agonized about what to wear to his first Nashville meeting, finally deciding on what he usually wore to church on Sunday nights. It took him five seconds to realize he looked ridiculous.

John walked over and shook his hand. "How was your flight?" he asked. "Sorry I couldn't be at the airport when you arrived. Did Carolyn take care of you okay?"

Andrew felt a case of nerves coming on; the reality of what he had done was suddenly sinking in. He was a long way from home, in every way. "Yes, sure," he said. "I'm very excited to be here, Mr. van Grimes. I can't wait to get started with Heaven's Voices."

"Yes, Heaven's Voices," John echoed. "Listen, Andrew, I want you to meet a couple of friends of mine. Andrew, this is Laurence Hill, and this gentleman is Harold Murphy."

Both men appeared to be in their early thirties and were dressed with the same studied casual style as John. Hill was the taller of the two, with a narrow, intelligent face. Harold Murphy was more compact, but he made the stronger impression with a friendliness that could truly be called professional. Harold stretched out his hand and shook Andrew's warmly.

"Andrew Miracle," he said. "Is that really your name? I mean really? Or do guys show up from Kansas already with stage names?"

"Yes—I mean no," Andrew replied, smiling. This was a question he had grown accustomed to. "It really is my name. But I don't see what's so unusual about the name Andrew."

Laurence laughed and shook his hand. "Exactly," he said. "I think Andrew's a splendid name."

John motioned Andrew over to a mahogany and leather chair near his desk. "Well," he said, "now that we all know each other, let's have a seat." Harold and Laurence took their places in two identical patterned wing chairs, and John sat behind his desk. He pushed a button on his intercom. "Carolyn, could you bring in some refreshments, please?" Then John pushed back from his desk and ran his hand through his hair, letting it settle over his collar.

"Andrew," he said, "Harold and Laurence are representatives of Dove Records here in Nashville."

Andrew gave him a puzzled look and asked, "I beg your pardon?"

"Dove Records. Dove is a very forward-thinking Christian record company here in Nashville. I have the utmost respect for them, both for their musical excellence and for their integrity."

"It's very nice to meet you," Andrew said, immediately feeling stupid. He had already been introduced. Harold and Laurence were smiling, perfectly at ease.

John leaned in. "Andrew," he said, "I don't think you realize how talented you are."

"No, I don't," Andrew replied, quite truthfully.

"Personally, I find that truly refreshing," Harold said. "It's so nice to find someone who is a real talent who doesn't think they rule the world."

"Exactly," John said. "It's very refreshing. In fact, I think the more you and Laurence get to know him, the more you will realize that an Andrew Miracle is something very special."

There was something distinctly odd about being referred to in the third person that way, but Andrew didn't get a chance to think about it. What John said next drove other thoughts right out of his mind.

"Andrew," he said, "I took the liberty of playing Harold and Laurence your tape."

Andrew was stunned. "My tape?" he asked.

John smiled. "Of course, your tape. Ah, I beg your pardon. I fear I didn't explain myself at the time—my apologies. You see, I routinely record auditions for Heaven's Voices with a portable, hand-held recorder. It's really the only way I can keep things straight. Otherwise, I can't review my impressions and give everyone a fair opportunity in the process. I hope you don't mind. I thought I had explained all that at the time. I trust that isn't a problem."

"No," Andrew answered. "I guess that makes sense."

"Good. And I hope you don't mind that I played it for Harold and Laurence. If it helps any, they loved it. They more than loved it."

"That's wonderful," Andrew answered numbly. His head was swimming. "But what's this all about?"

"What this is all about, Andrew, is that the three of us think you are a great talent. An extraordinary talent. And the three of us are convinced that this is bigger than Heaven's Voices. Much bigger."

"Bigger?"

"Yes, Andrew, bigger. And that's why Harold and Laurence are here. I want them to explain to you a little about their company, and then we have something very important to talk with you about. Would that be all right?"

Before Andrew could answer there was a soft knock on the door, and Carolyn came in with a cart of bottled water, soft drinks, glasses, and ice.

"Great," John said. "Thanks, Carolyn. Harold, I assume the usual La Croix for you?"

"Right," Harold replied.

"Naya for me," Laurence said.

"Andrew, what about you?" John asked.

Andrew had never heard of most of the stuff on the tray. "Could I have a Coke, please?"

At that, Laurence seemed to enjoy a private joke. "Coke it is," said John.

Carolyn smiled at Andrew on the way out and shut the door behind her.

"Andrew," said Harold, "I know you're wondering what all this is about. But before we get into that, let me tell you a few things about our company. In view of what we want to discuss with you, I feel it's essential you get to know us and to understand some things about Dove Records, the company we represent. Okay?"

"Okay," answered Andrew, trying not to sound confused.

"Good. Andrew, Dove is one of the biggest Christian record companies in the world. We're not *the* biggest, and we like it that way. We believe that we have the highest commitment to our artists of any company, Christian or otherwise. We stay a bit smaller so we can really understand and work with our artists on a more personal level. We consider every artist with Dove Records a priority. You know what I mean?"

"I guess so."

"We make Christian records, Andrew, and we make no apology for that. We view our company as a kind of trust with the Lord, and we take that trust very seriously. Our goal is to glorify Him in everything that we do, and signing a new artist is the biggest decision we make in our company. We look at the money as the Lord's, and we are merely stewards of it." Harold paused. "There is another side to that coin, however."

"What's that?"

"The other side of that coin, Andrew, is that we don't think God has called us into bankruptcy."

John and Harold laughed heartily. Laurence smiled in agreement and explained. "What Harold is trying to say, Andrew, is that part of being good stewards is making records that are successful, records that make money for the company. If we make records that lose money, then the company can't survive, and we can't continue to make records that we hope draw people to the Lord."

"I see," Andrew said. "But really, what does all this have to do with me? I came down here to play with Heaven's Voices."

"Exactly," said John, "and that was very much my intention. Let me be perfectly truthful, Andrew. Heaven's Voices is a very important part of my work, and I have a strong vision for the ministry that the group has. However, and here I just have to be honest, it's really sort of a semiprofessional thing. It can't really swim in deep water, if you understand. Some of the people in the group may well go on to have viable careers in Christian music, but for most of them it's a great experience for now—nothing more. I realized that burying you in Heaven's Voices would be a misuse of your gifts. I thought about it a lot and finally decided to present your tape, even though it's very rough, to Harold and Laurence. Their overwhelming response just confirmed what I really already knew. God has very big things in store for you, Andrew. I really believe that, and I urge you not to limit Him."

No one spoke for a moment, and Andrew sensed that Harold was watching him carefully. "I'm sure this is all a bit overwhelming, Andrew," he said. "Perhaps you'd like to tell us what you're thinking."

"Yes, Andrew," said Laurence, "just speak your mind."

Andrew took a sip of Coke and shifted nervously in his chair. Obviously some response was required, but he was having difficulty processing all the changes in his life. He had no idea where all this was heading. He had cut a lot of ties to come to Nashville, and he felt adrift. Going home didn't seem an option. He was beginning to feel a strong need to clarify his situation.

"Are you saying that I can't play in Heaven's Voices, even if I want to?" he asked.

John smiled. "I'm not sure you understand what we're getting at here, Andrew. I'm asking you to think a lot bigger. We're asking you to consider an opportunity that makes a lot more sense, and I would have a guilty conscience limiting the way God can use you by confining you to Heaven's Voices."

"Exactly," said Harold. "I like the way you put that, John."

"I don't know about all this," Andrew said. "Of course I don't want to limit God. It's just that I don't usually think of myself in this way, as some part of a grand, divine scheme. I think of myself as a singer from Rose Hill, Kansas. Naturally, I'm more than flattered by what you are saying about me. It just feels like you must be talking about someone else."

"Charming," whispered Laurence.

Suddenly Andrew felt what was important reassert itself in him, coming to his rescue. He surprised himself with the confidence with which he spoke. "All I know is why I came to Nashville," he said. "I came because I felt a calling on my life to tell people about God with my music. If you heard something passionate in my music, maybe that was it. That's what is driving me to turn my life upside down and to jump off the cliff of going with Heaven's Voices in the first place. All I want to do is play my music and tell people about God. That's my bottom line. So where are we headed with this? If I'm not going to be in Heaven's Voices, what would I be doing?"

Laurence smiled broadly. "I love it!" he exulted. "Integrity!"

Harold set his La Croix down on the table in front of them and centered himself in front of Andrew.

"What you would be doing, Andrew," he said, "would be recording your first album for Dove Records as a solo artist. What do you think about that?" He leaned far back in his chair, like a deep-sea fisherman.

Andrew sat, stunned into a kind of rigid wonder. He was literally tingling. He looked to John for some explanation, but van Grimes was merely smiling broadly, as if Harold's comments were completely expected and nothing unusual. After an awkward moment, Andrew realized that the others were still waiting for some kind of answer, if only an immediate reaction. He could hardly sit there in silence forever. But try as he would, he couldn't find the words for a response. His mind seemed dazzled. To his consternation, the other three men in the room remained the picture of relaxed self-confidence. Andrew played Harold's words over in his mind. *Recording an album. A solo artist. Andrew Miracle, recording artist*. They were waiting. Then the sound of Laurence clinking the ice in his glass brought Andrew back to himself. He had, after all, come to Nashville for a reason. In spite of his shock, he knew he had a very important question to ask.

"I guess I'd like to know what that would do to my ministry," Andrew said finally.

"It would explode it!" John cried. "It would explode it and multiply it and increase it in every way. That's the whole idea here, Andrew. We see your ministry potential and our business potential as coming together perfectly. Dove Records has the power to present your music and your message to many times more people than you could do on your own or in Heaven's Voices. The more people we can expose you to and get to hear you, the better for everyone."

Harold picked up the ball. "Let me explain something to you, Andrew. I feel like the luckiest man in the world. You know why? Because I have the kind of job where my success intersects with God's success. Think about it. When we sell more records, obviously we benefit. And we make no apology for that. Successful records are essential to the survival of our company and to signing new artists such as yourself. But the great part is, when a record is successful, it just means that God's Word is going out to that many more people and that the ministry outreach of what we do is being multiplied. We honestly believe that when our company prospers, God is glorified by that. And what we at Dove Records are very much hoping, Andrew, is that you will see your ministry intersecting with ours to our mutual benefit."

"Wow," Andrew said quietly.

"Yeah, wow," laughed John.

Something suddenly struck Andrew. "But there's one thing I don't understand, John. You have nothing to do with Dove Records, right?"

Harold jumped in. "Would you mind if I fielded that, John? Andrew, you can probably imagine that we have dozens of people coming to us every week asking us, or I could almost say begging us, to offer them the kind of deal we are offering you right now. Frankly, most of them don't have very much to offer, artistically. I know that sounds harsh, but it's true. Right, gentlemen?"

John and Laurence nodded enthusiastically. "You got that right," said Laurence. "The ones that come in addressed in crayon we usually send back unopened." Andrew didn't know whether to laugh or cringe.

"Anyway," Harold continued, "of course we do get many tapes that are interesting to us. But even for them, it's very hard for an artist to get signed because we feel that each artist has to have the total package."

"What does that mean?" Andrew asked.

"What the total package means, Andrew, is that sometimes you get a guy who has musical talent but isn't appealing on some other level. You know what I mean. Someone who just isn't salable. Or maybe he's just operating in a vacuum. So a prerequisite for anyone to be signed by Dove is to have personal management. This is for the benefit of the artist, because there has to be someone at the helm of a career making things happen, creating opportunities. Someone with vision, someone who can help an artist realize his potential. And, of course, someone to represent the artist in matters of contract. Personal management is absolutely essential. And that's where John comes in."

Andrew glanced at John. Van Grimes was looking at him like an old friend. "That was a pretty nice list, Laurence. I hope I can really be those things for an artist," John said. "Can I get you another drink, Andrew?" Andrew shook his head no.

"Well, like Harold was explaining," John went on, "personal management is really the key to everything. There's a phrase we use in the industry to describe records that get put out without the total package."

"What's that?" Andrew asked.

"Throw it against the wall," answered John.

"Ouch," Andrew whispered.

"Exactly," said John. "That's why this is sort of a package deal, Andrew. Dove has made it clear that they believe in you very much, but they are only willing to move forward if you have a strong management situation. Anything else just wouldn't be good stewardship. Dove and I have a great working relationship already established, which we both feel is essential to a successful career. So you can see this is the ideal situation. We have everything we need in this room to make Andrew Miracle a household name."

"I'm not sure that I want to be a household name," Andrew said.

"I love it," chuckled Laurence.

John got up from his desk, walked over, and put his hand on Andrew's shoulder. It was surprisingly heavy.

"Look, Andrew, I'm afraid we've overwhelmed you with all this. All I can tell you is that the speed that this thing is moving is simply an indication of how much enthusiasm we all have for your project. All of us are convinced that this is a door that God has opened for us, and we're quite anxious to get moving. But you shouldn't feel any pressure, Andrew. We wouldn't dream of expecting an answer right now. We want, and as your manager I insist, that you take some time to think all this over and to pray about it. We will do the same, I assure you. I think I speak for all of us when I say that we want the best for you. The very best."

"I appreciate that."

"Well, gentlemen, I suppose we ought to let the young man have some time with his thoughts, or he'll start thinking we're pushy or something," John concluded. Harold and Laurence just smiled and stood up.

"I'm sure you're tired, Andrew," said John. "Carolyn will take you back to your hotel, and she will be glad to show you the sights this evening if you want. I recommend her tours very highly. Sound okay?"

Andrew rose and stuck out his hand toward John.

"Yes. I appreciate everything you're doing for me, Mr. van Grimes. I can't believe all this is happening to me. Two weeks ago I would have said this was impossible."

Van Grimes closed his eyes. "Nothing is impossible with God, Andrew."

6

Andrew stood in the middle of his hotel room, stunned. He tried to process everything happening in his life but found it flatly impossible. He felt lightheaded and not quite able to think clearly. Sitting down proved impossible, so he paced the room, replaying every word that John, Harold, and Laurence had said in their meeting with him. He felt like an observer to his own life, like someone on an amusement ride with no control over the next spinning descent. It was thrilling, but he was beginning to want to get off.

He was very aware of his sheltered, small-town upbringing at that moment. In spite of his mother's best efforts to broaden him, nothing from Rose Hill could possibly have prepared him for the world he was being asked to enter, the world of a recording artist. It would mean interviews, concerts, tours. His one-year commitment to Heaven's Voices was stretching into a career decision.

Two completely divergent paths stretched out before him, and choosing between them was not easy. He had no idea what lay in front of him if he took the new road that was being offered to him. It was inevitable that he would feel some resistance to the speed things were moving. Folks from Rose Hill were raised to go slow, to think things through. He felt like a small boy on a bicycle cresting a steep hill, only to discover his brakes have failed. He wanted to put his feet out and slow things down.

In the midst of this maelstrom, Andrew's thoughts rushed back home, to the safe world of the farm, his mother, and Cy Mathews. A part of him actually wished to return, and never hear of John van Grimes again. He would paint fence, and play for his Sunday school class. He would sing in church. He would sit on the porch with his mother and watch the sun go down, arms aching from weeding the garden. He would get up early with his Bible, walk down to the lake, and think about the Lord. He would help a neighbor with his planting. He would write a song about the fields, and God in them. He would spill out his heart to a few and go home to his own bed.

But he couldn't help thinking that this desire was born of cowardice. How could he deny what was happening around him? He was being thrust into the spotlight, through no action of his own. Besides, what seemed romantic and appealing about the farm right now might, in the end, prove to be provincial and limiting. Perhaps this opportunity was what the vision had been about, the great thing that it had led up to. He could think of no good reason not to step through the doors flying open around him.

John van Grimes. Harold Murphy. Laurence Hill. His past had no equivalents to these men. It seemed astonishing that people of such sophistication wanted to work with him and were excited about his prospects. This was bigger than Heaven's Voices, John had said, much bigger. Who knew what they might accomplish together? Whatever the answer to that question might turn out to be, it would surely be more than Andrew could ever hope to do on his own, playing for what now seemed a handful of people. Of that he had no doubt. These men understood the gospel industry, how it worked, its secrets. They lived in the real world of ministry, where thousands were reached by a single recording. He couldn't deny that Cy Mathews, slaving away in Rose Hill, could never reach as many people as he could with a single successful record. And what about his own efforts? He saw himself playing at the old folks' home, or banging out one of his songs for his Sunday school class. He could see the four identical walls of the Sunday school room, covered with missions posters and maps of the Middle East. He could hear that beat-up old upright piano in his mind. He could stay there a thousand years and never make the kind of difference John and the men from Dove were talking about. It was, he began to think, a kind of pride to limit God.

Andrew laid down on the bed and tried to relax. It had already been a long day, and it was only four-thirty. It seemed incredible that early that morning he had awakened in Rose Hill. It seemed as though days had passed. The high emotions had taken their toll; he was exhausted. After some time, he drifted off to sleep.

As he slept, he dreamt. With an enormous sense of relief, he realized he was back in Rose Hill. As if none of the last few days had happened, pressures seemed to rush away from him, physically scaling upward into the void. In his dream it was neither day nor night. His surroundings were illuminated only by the light of his own mind. There was no sound, and everything was quiet peace. Suddenly, he realized he was not alone. Surrounding him was a great throng of people; and he felt that he was loved by them, and he was ministering to them. They pressed close to him, drawing strength from him. After a moment, Andrew turned, and it seemed that the throng had grown larger. They were calling to him, still pressing around him. Then he was being moved along some pathway, leading beyond where his mind could reveal. The crowd seemed to grow increasingly agitated as it moved, and he was engulfed by it as it swept him along.

Finally, Andrew was covered in the darkness of dreamless sleep.

It seemed only seconds later when the phone rang. He opened one eye to look at the clock, and was shocked to see that he had slept almost three hours. He fumbled with the receiver and muttered, "Hello."

"Hey, sleepy-head," a voice said softly. It was Carolyn, calling from the lobby. "I hate to wake you, Andrew. Do you want to just forget about tonight? I'm sure you must be exhausted from everything."

"No, no," he stammered, fighting off sleep. "Don't worry about it. I'm glad you woke me. Besides, I haven't had dinner. I don't really look forward to wandering around Nashville by myself looking for something to eat."

"You sure?" She sounded compassionate, and even half-awake, he enjoyed the sound of her voice. "I'm so sorry I woke you up," she said. "Really, don't feel like you have to, or anything. We can go anytime."

"Yes, I'm sure. Look, I'm awake already. Just give me a few minutes, and I'll meet you in the lobby. Don't forget, you're my only contact with reality in this town. I'd be lost without you."

"You're sure?"

"Yes, I'm sure."

"Okay," she laughed, her voice suddenly full of life. "If you're really awake, Andrew Miracle, then hurry up. Your contact with reality is starved."

Andrew had learned his lesson about the lack of Nashville formality. This time he just threw on some jeans and a casual shirt. He grabbed a light jacket on the way out the door and went downstairs to meet Carolyn. He was determined to live down his country-boy mistakes.

Carolyn smiled when he stepped out of the elevator. Her hair was pulled back now with a simple black bow, and she had changed into blue jeans and a dark green sweater. As they left the hotel, Carolyn held open the door. "Wow, reverse discrimination," Andrew said. "The girls here open the door for the boys."

"When they're lucky," she replied. "Sorry again about waking you. I'm glad you wanted to go, though. It's a beautiful night. Much too beautiful to spend cooped up in a hotel room."

She was right. They stepped from the air-conditioned lobby into a perfect, southern summer evening. The lingering dusk revealed the trees beginning to turn; the heat of the day had eased, and there was a softness in the air absolutely unknown to Andrew.

"Let's head to the Cooker," Carolyn said lightly. "It's classic southern cooking, and a real industry hangout."

Carolyn's convertible was the perfect way to travel that night. The air rushed past them as they drove, gently animating their conversation. Sunlight was fading fast, and everything seemed curiously outlined in the remaining light, framed against the coming darkness. Rose Hill seemed far away.

They pulled into the Cooker, a large, bustling restaurant nearby Vanderbilt University. Carolyn didn't bother putting the top up when she parked. "I feel like trusting human nature tonight," she said.

The noise from inside seemed to rush out to meet them when they opened the door. They stepped through the entrance into a cavernous, open restaurant that seemed to contain the equivalent of the population of Rose Hill.

"I know it's a little noisy," said Carolyn, "but eating here is almost a rite of passage." They squeezed their way through the entryway and gave their name to the hostess. "Everybody says they hate this place, 'cause it's so see and be seen, but then we all end up going here anyway. It's too fun to avoid, and it's the perfect place for you to have your first Nashville dinner. Once you do dinner at the Cooker, you're official."

For the time being, Carolyn had broken Andrew's homesick spell. There was simply too much to look at and take in for him to miss home. In their wait for a table, Carolyn introduced him to half a dozen people, not dutifully but with genuine pleasure. She had a gift for graceful inclusion, as if in each conversation she was not introducing strangers but starting new friendships. Andrew felt like a wallflower in the face of so much easy familiarity, but he loved watching her weaving in and out of conversations effortlessly.

She had described the music industry as a kind of family, and there did seem to be a sense of community there. Like all families, however, there was an unspoken but unmistakable hierarchy of power hanging over the relationships.

That night, she approached one person in particular with a greater sense of caution. A rather short man, he nevertheless had an aura of authority about him. He was older than the others Andrew had met, around fifty, with just the slightest trace of corpulence in his face. He reeked of wealth, but not self-satisfaction; indeed, there was something vaguely disquieting in his expression, as if he were somehow fatigued inside. He looked like a man to whom others constantly catered and who had grown perfectly accustomed to it. Carolyn carefully waited for a definite break in his present conversation, and she spoke only when he turned to face her directly.

"Carolyn Hemphill," he said with a tone of practiced friendliness. "How nice to see you."

"Hello, Michael," Carolyn answered politely.

"How's old John? I haven't seen him in forever." His voice left little doubt that he considered John van Grimes several rungs below himself in the industry power structure.

"He's fine," Carolyn replied. "You know John, always working us hard."

"Yes, he certainly is a . . ." He paused for a moment. "A go-getter," he finished. He smiled in Andrew's direction.

"Michael, I'd like you to meet Andrew Miracle."

"Hello, Andrew," he said, shaking Andrew's hand. "What an extraordinary name. How ever do you live up to it?"

"I don't, I assure you," Andrew replied. "In fact, I'm thinking of having it changed to Andrew Ordinary."

Michael laughed easily and almost, but not quite, looked him in the eye. He had clearly mastered the art of friendly distance. "I'm sure you're anything but ordinary, Andrew."

"Andrew's in town to work with John to develop his solo

career," said Carolyn. "John's convinced he's full of possibilities."

Michael's interest level seemed to spike upward momentarily, and he gave Andrew a brief, penetrating look. He seemed to be memorizing him for any possible future reference.

"Well," he said, "John always had a good eye for talent. I'm sure he's quite right." Michael glanced at his dinner companions who were talking a short distance away. "It was lovely to meet you, Andrew, and especially to see you again, Carolyn. I'm afraid that's my table they're calling." He moved off with his dinner guests, and the eyes of several waiting patrons moved with him.

"Who was that?" asked Andrew, when they were seated.

"Michael Thomasson is an executive vice president of Atlantic records," Carolyn replied. "Harold Murphy dreams about him at night, probably."

The thought of that made Andrew laugh out loud. "What on earth do you mean?" he asked.

"It's a little complicated."

"Come on, Carolyn. I've got to start figuring this stuff out sometime."

"Well, Atlantic, aside from being this enormous multinational record company, just so happens to distribute Dove product to secular record stores."

Andrew stared blankly in response. Carolyn looked at him skeptically and said, "Say *ah*."

"Ah."

"Good. But there's a catch, you see," she explained. "Not all Dove records get distributed. Just the ones that Michael Thomasson decides merit their attention. Only, say, two or three out of the sixty or so releases Dove has each year. Sometimes none."

"I see."

"No, you don't," she laughed. "But it doesn't matter. Let's order."

"Okay," he admitted. "I don't see. But I'd like to. I know this is all old hat to you, but it's like some incredible new world to me."

Carolyn smiled and sighed like an amateur actress. "Okay, you win," she said. "What else can I tell you? Not that I'm an expert."

"One more thing," Andrew replied gratefully. "What happens when Michael decides to distribute one of Dove's records?"

"It works like this. Normally, Christian records get sold only in a few thousand Christian bookstores that most people never go to. But for those two or three records that Mr. Big over there likes, Atlantic gets them sold in about ten times that many secular record stores that everybody goes to."

"I take it that's good."

"Only if you want to make a great deal of money."

"Ah."

"Yes, ah." She laughed. "Of course, it's not really that simple. Lots of times, they distribute the record and nothing happens. But sometimes, they decide to go all the way and really promote someone like they would one of their own artists. Those people have a real chance. Anyway, once Michael decides to pick up an artist from Dove, he also decides whether or not to push singles to pop radio stations, whether they want to make videos for VH-1 and MTV, that kind of stuff. All that takes a lot of money. Hundreds of thousands of dollars sometimes. So naturally, things tend to get rather serious at that point. Actually, Michael's one of the most powerful men in the music business. He can't take a walk without someone handing him a tape, poor man."

"So even Harold and Laurence have masters, it seems."

Carolyn paused. "Well, I doubt very much that they would put it that way. But it's certainly true that Michael Thomasson can push the button to cross over any Christian artist he wants to. If it crosses over big enough, then that one record can make as much money as the rest of the Dove label combined. So you could say they're interested."

"Who are Michael Thomasson's masters?" asked Andrew.

"I have no idea," Carolyn replied.

The waitress came and took their order, and they started in on cornbread and rolls. They talked about Nashville restaurants for a while; then Carolyn began to ask about Andrew and his life back home.

"So tell me about Kansas," she began.

"I thought you said you'd been there."

"I mean it," she said. "Tell me."

"What can I say? It's flat." Andrew's voice betrayed the fact that he preferred to keep his thoughts in Nashville. Talking of home made his decision seem much more difficult.

Carolyn made a face. "Suddenly you're not very talkative, are you? Or maybe this is just your quiet side again. Is that it?"

"Sorry, Carolyn." He found it difficult not to give in to her. "Okay, Kansas. What do you want to know?"

Carolyn thought for a moment. "Okay, what about this?" she asked. "Tell me what you'd be doing tonight if you were there instead of here."

"But I'm so glad to be here."

"Tell me anyway."

Andrew smiled. "You really can be persistent, can't you? Okay, what day is it? Tuesday, right?"

"That's right. What would you be doing at eight-thirty on a Tuesday night in Rose Hill, Kansas?"

"Ouch. It doesn't sound too good when you put it that way. But, as it happens, I can answer that question. I'd be playing the piano at the Sunrise Retirement Home for a bunch of geriatrics."

Carolyn laughed. "You're kidding! Wait, let me picture that. There's one big room, and it feels like a big living room, right?"

"You've seen it."

"And you're playing one of those old uprights, pushed over in the corner."

"Yep, but you left out one thing."

"What's that?"

"It hasn't been tuned in about fifty years. Anyway, that's what I'd be doing."

"You do it every Tuesday?"

"Yeah. Everybody kind of gathers around the piano, and I play for them. There's this old guy there, about ninety. Every time I go there, he asks me to play the same two songs. Always the same ones. You know what they are?"

Carolyn shook her head.

"One is 'How Great Thou Art.' The other one is 'Melancholy Baby.' He sings along to both of them, at the top of his lungs. I didn't even know 'Melancholy Baby' had words."

"I can't believe you knew it at all."

"I didn't, of course. I learned it for him."

Carolyn smiled. The thought of Andrew surrounded by old people singing pleased her very much. "I love that," she said. "Do you do a lot of stuff like that?"

"Stuff like what?"

"You know, like playing for an old folks' home."

"I guess so," Andrew replied. "I play for a lot of church things, mainly. I do something most Sundays."

"Like what?" she asked.

"It's kind of hard to explain. It's not really a typical thing."

"What kind of thing is it? John told me that what happens when you play is extraordinary." She looked slightly away, avoiding Andrew's eyes. "He seemed to think there was some unique spiritual event happening."

Andrew sighed thoughtfully. It was hard to say just what happened in those Sunday services. He pictured the church in his mind, packed with parishioners. He saw Pastor Mathews, squeezed into his suit, wrapping up his message, and giving Andrew the signal to begin. What happened next was something he had never really understood himself.

"I guess I just minister," he said at last. "When you break it down, that's about it. I sing, and I play, usually after the sermon, but sometimes even in place of a sermon. The pastor kind of gives me the floor, and it gets real quiet in the place. I sort of close my eyes, and . . ." Andrew's voice trailed off uncertainly.

"And what?" Carolyn asked intently. She seemed to be trying to see in her mind what Andrew was talking about.

Andrew looked up at her, uncertainty showing in his eyes. Talking about his gift was uncomfortable in the best of times because he knew deep down that he didn't control the gift and that there were times that it actually controlled him. Those were times of ultimate trust. It was beautiful, but it also seemed wild and unsettling. At those times, he thought about some of the prophets in the Old Testament, how they had ranted and acted almost like madmen with visions. The Israelites had called Elijah a madman, after all. Andrew liked Carolyn, and he had no desire to come off like some mystic freak. It seemed a great risk to reveal this most intimate thing in his life. But as Carolyn gazed back at him expectantly, he suddenly, inexplicably felt safe. He decided, for the moment, to open the door.

"I guess I just pray with my hands," he said slowly, "if that means anything to you. I sit down, and I start praying. Only I don't speak. I just play."

Carolyn was entranced. "You mean you don't know what you're going to play before you actually do it?"

"It depends. Sometimes I do. I write songs, and I play those sometimes, when it feels right. But mostly I just start praying."

"And what happens?"

"To be honest, I'm not sure myself. I just know people end up praying along with me. The music kind of opens them up."

Carolyn was silent. She stared across the table at Andrew, as if she were seeing him for the first time. She could sense that there was something more here, something truly spiritual, if she could only understand it. To be sure, Andrew was a long way from some of the sophisticated men that she had met in the music business. She had to admit that although he was clearly intelligent, he had some rough edges that other artists she had worked with had smoothed away long ago—if they ever had them at all. He was, after all, quite literally just off the plane from Kansas. But she couldn't help being intrigued. Finally, she asked, "What do you mean, they pray along with you?"

Carolyn's inquiries were the kind that made Andrew uncomfortable, and he was growing restless, grappling with her penetrating questions and his natural disinclination to self-revelation. And besides, he wasn't completely sure he wanted to know the answers himself.

"I don't know, exactly. I just know that there's a connection of some kind between us when I play. I can feel it. They come along with me." He paused, afraid he was sounding sanctimonious. "But anyway," he added quickly, "not everybody likes it."

He had meant the statement deferentially, as if to minimize what happened in those services. But it only aroused Carolyn's curiosity even further. "What do you mean, not everybody likes it?" she asked. "Why wouldn't they? It sounds marvelous. I can't imagine someone not liking it." Unknowingly, she was edging him closer to the very secret of his gift, the nexus of its power. He felt constricted, the way he did in those lamentable times when he ended up saying too much. He began to look down intently at the table.

"They just don't," he muttered. "I mean I don't always play sweetly, you know? It's not always a peaceful thing. It's not always exactly safe."

Carolyn was unsure how to respond. After working with various artists for over two years, Andrew was the first that seemed to genuinely dislike talking about his own talent. She could see that he was growing nervous, and she didn't really want to press him. But it was too late. He had already gained his own momentum now. He wanted her to understand.

"Can I tell you a story?" he asked.

"Of course," she answered, "if you want to."

"It's about this old lady at the retirement home, Mrs. Harvey. She's about a million years old."

"But I'm sure she must be lovely, in that way old people have," Carolyn said gently.

"She isn't," Andrew replied, grimacing. "She's not lovely at all. She's all bent over, I mean so she can't stand up anymore. Her spine is like an upside-down U, and even in her wheelchair she can't look up and see anything." Carolyn winced visibly, but Andrew kept on, talking more rapidly now.

"Mrs. Harvey sits in that chair, and when she's at her best, her head is in nearly in her knees. But she gets tired, you see, and then they have to tie her into the chair or she would fall forward right out of it."

Carolyn blinked hard, retreating. Her pretty vision of Andrew sharing his gift with the retirement center didn't include this.

"Why are you telling me this?" she asked, suddenly feeling defensive.

"Because you wanted to know about the gift. Because of what she did one time. Somebody asked me to sing 'Amazing Grace.' It was maybe a year and a half ago. Anyway, I sang it. We all sang it, of course. Everybody always joins in. So we're going along, and I look out at Mrs. Harvey. She's bent over, and her hands are touching the floor like she can't control them. She's leaning way out, and the belt was holding her in. It was pathetic. Then, I noticed something."

"What?"

Andrew looked up and met Carolyn's eyes.

"Her lips were moving."

Neither person spoke. The noise of the restaurant faded away, and they seemed to be sitting in a cocoon of silence. After a long moment, Andrew continued.

"I tried to go on, but I couldn't. So I stopped. But everybody else kept right on singing. They were getting to the last verse, the one about the ten thousand years, you know? So they kept right on going. But I couldn't do it. I got up and walked over to Mrs. Harvey. I don't think she even knew I was there. She was pretty far gone. I knelt down beside her and leaned over and put my face down by hers. She was singing in this high, creaky, breathy voice. She couldn't really say the words too well. I think she was in a lot of pain. But she was singing it. *When we've been there, ten thousand years, bright shining as the sun.*"

Carolyn looked away, afraid that she might begin to cry. But Andrew seemed unmoved, even stoic.

"Sometimes I think about her when I play. I see her strapped into that chair. It's not so sweet, then."

The two sat quietly for some time. Andrew felt his vulnerability accumulate in the silence, hanging between them in the air like a mist. He fidgeted in his seat, already regretting that he had told the story. He wished that he had lied to her, saying that Mrs. Harvey had had a beautiful expression of peace on her face, smiling through the pain. But she didn't. She was just holding on.

"I think she was the most dignified woman I've ever seen," he said at last. "Even bent over, unable to feed herself or even go to the bathroom, I think she was the Queen of England. I read a book one time, and the guy who wrote it said that he thought that heaven and hell were really the same place, but the saved loved it, and the damned hated it. It was a question of perspective, you know? Well, if that's true, I think I know what it would be like. There'd be Mrs. Harvey, sitting in her chair. And there would be some stuck up model from New York City, the kind that watch MTV and get mad 'cause their taxi's late when they want to go out dancing. And the model would be bathing Mrs. Harvey, pouring this magnificent healing lotion over her curved back, rubbing her tired muscles, bathing her wrinkled skin, taking away all her pain. Anyway, I like to think of it that way."

Andrew looked cautiously at Carolyn. He had learned from painful experience that revealing this inner self to a girl normally meant it would be his last date with her. Inevitably, when he called again, they would gently explain that they were busy, and he knew it was only a matter of time before he saw them around town, happily holding hands with one of the strapping, moodless football players he worked with in the summer.

He motioned for the waitress, anxious to pay his check and put Carolyn out of her misery. She was sitting thoughtfully, as if playing back the story in her mind. For a long time neither of them spoke. Andrew counted out the money to the waitress, feeling miserable. He put his billfold back in his jacket and asked, "Ready to go?"

Carolyn leaned back in her chair, appearing to be in no hurry. She had a curious expression on her face, as if she were trying to process something new but important. "I'd really rather sit here a minute," she said. "I want to think about Mrs. Harvey. I want to think about Rose Hill."

"You do?" Andrew asked, amazed.

"Yes, I do," Carolyn answered. "You sound like you were very involved there, in that little town. Like your life really made a difference."

"Yeah, I guess it did," he said slowly. "Everything is on such a small scale there. You really know people. You kind of depend on each other."

"I like that," she said, smiling, and her smile broke Andrew's sullen mood into a thousand pieces. "I think I like Rose Hill very much."

"I guess I'll admit I didn't really expect that," he offered.

"Hmmm. I see that, I suppose. You know something?"

"What?"

"I don't think you were at that retirement home for Mrs. Harvey. I think she was there for you."

He had never thought about it that way. He had only thought of Mrs. Harvey as a dignified, suffering martyr. "What do you mean?" he asked.

"I mean you don't have the right to be angry about it. Things fit together in funny ways."

"Like a story behind a story."

"Yes, like that."

Andrew looked at Carolyn in wonder. What it all meant, he didn't understand. But he felt as though a weight might be beginning to lift from him, and he felt his anger abating. Perhaps a great deal of the world was like that, he thought, a story behind a story. For the first time, he felt gratitude to a woman other than his mother. "Can I confess something?" he asked.

"If you want to."

"I do. When I first met you, back at the airport—I think I kind of underestimated you. I'm sorry."

"What made you do that?" Carolyn asked.

"You know, you were so happy, so carefree."

"And you thought that meant I was shallow."

"I'm ashamed to admit it, but yes."

"You should be," Carolyn said lightly, releasing him from his guilt. "But that's okay. You're not the first."

"I am sorry."

"You said that. And now, I really am ready to go."

The two stood up and made their way across the restaurant. The night had grown considerably cooler, and Andrew helped her put the top up on the convertible. It was only minutes before Carolyn was pulling in at the hotel, and he found himself wishing the drive could have been much longer.

"I appreciate what you said about Rose Hill," Andrew said. "I think it would have been easy for you to think it was just a hick town. But life goes on everywhere, doesn't it?"

"Yes, it does." Carolyn smiled broadly and cast off finally any lingering heaviness that remained between them. It was the obvious moment to say goodnight, but Andrew suddenly asked, "You want to know my favorite thing about growing up out there?"

"Tell me."

He turned in the car seat to face her and said, "It's not what you'd think. It's not a pretty lake, or anything. It's a sound."

Carolyn said nothing and waited.

"What I love most, I mean," he went on softly. "It's the wind, on a dead quiet day, moving through a massive wheat field. There are wheat fields so big back home, you can't imagine. Their size hardly has any meaning, you know? They just cover the earth. So you've walked for hours up to your waist in the wheat, deep in your own thoughts. You've made your way to the center of this dry ocean of living plants, not paying attention to where you are or where you're going. In all directions the horizon vanishes. Then you hear it. It's a rushing, like a million little ocean waves. It sounds like gold looks. It's the quietest power you can ever hear. It's not a tame sound at all. It's like the sound of God breathing."

Carolyn leaned back in her seat, as if she were thinking of something far away. After a moment, she said, "I do want to hear that sound. It must be the loneliest thing in the world. I want to hear it, very much."

Andrew turned back in his seat, and opened the car door. As he was leaving, he turned back to her.

"Maybe, someday, you will," he said.

"Good night, Andrew."

"Good night."

At the door, he turned and watched until her car was completely out of sight.

7

As Andrew passed through the lobby of the Hampton, the desk clerk stopped him with a message. "Just a second, Mr. Miracle," he said. "A courier brought this over just after you left." He pulled out a large, stuffed manila envelope.

"What's this?" asked Andrew, surprised.

"It was sent over from the John van Grimes Agency. He couldn't have missed you by five minutes. I think there's a note, also. Hang on—here it is."

The note was handwritten, on a small sheet of paper with John's letterhead at the top.

Dear Andrew,

Wanted to get these contracts over to you ASAP.
Do you think you can read them by lunch tomorrow?
I understand that's a rush—if you think it's too little time,
I'll reschedule. If so, call. Otherwise, Carolyn will pick
you up around 11:30. See you then. Enjoyed our meeting
today immensely.

John

Andrew looked at his watch. It was already almost ten. "Thanks," he said, with a sigh. "Looks like I've got a little light reading to do."

Once in his room, he sat down on the bed and opened the envelope. Inside were two contracts. The first was a personal management contract with the John van Grimes Agency. The other was an exclusive recording agreement between him and Dove Records. The management contract was thirteen pages long, the recording agreement twenty-six. He sighed, realizing he could never hope to read even one of them before morning. He felt a vague sense of irritation over the scheduling of the meeting and wondered why John would have sent the contracts when he did. John knew that Carolyn was taking him to dinner. Andrew toyed with the idea of canceling the meeting, but he was determined not to let van Grimes down. Perhaps this short amount of time was standard procedure.

Andrew flipped idly through the papers. One page looked pretty much like the others. The contracts were full of technical legal jargon. He tried reading a few paragraphs, but he gave up in vague confusion after several minutes. Much of the terminology was new to him. Many of the sections seemed to be about something he could almost understand, but exactly what they meant somehow remained just beyond his grasp. On the last page of the recording contract, however, something caught his eye. He stared in surprise at his own name, already typed in at the bottom of the contract. A long, empty line above it awaited his signature. It was logical, of course, that his name would be there. But it was something else to actually see it, taking its place so officially beside Harold's, and Laurence's. They had already signed, Laurence with elegant deliberation, and Harold with a scrawl, like an afterthought. Quickly, he turned to the last page of the personal management contract. The arrangement was identical. Van Grimes's name had already been filled in, signed with a florid, grandiose style. A blank line above his own name made the contract look incomplete, like a jigsaw puzzle needing one last all-important piece to complete it.

Andrew Miracle. Ever since his visitation, he had somehow felt differently about his name. *You are Andrew,* the Voice had said. *You are love*. But this was surely the first time that the name Andrew Miracle had ever meant anything to anybody in a legal sense. He had never even borrowed money before. It was staggering to think of the events that he could set into motion with the power of his own name.

Dreams were coming true in that room, dreams that had lived on the outskirts of his mind for a long, long time. The complexity of the contracts served to heighten his sense of excitement and anticipation. The legal terminology gave the day's events an even greater sense of importance. Andrew leaned back on the pillows and spread the papers out on the bed, and across his chest. He closed his eyes, and tried to imagine what his life would be like if, and when, he signed them.

He saw himself at the front of a large church, playing and singing for a vast congregation. He had a great deal to say to them, it seemed. He could sense the profound attitude of contrition and inspiration that his music evoked in them. It seemed that they had never before heard such words, such music, and like his little group at Christ's Kingdom Assembly, they were deeply moved. They were far more numerous, however, and he could see their faces in his mind. He cast his eyes down along the rows upon rows of people listening intently, enthralled. They received every nuance of his music, and no subtlety was missed. He had a great message for them, and they accepted it, like soldiers. He pictured them, marching outward from the concert, anxious to do God's will, rejuvenated with spiritual energy. He saw himself, meticulously humble, speaking with a few after the performance. The Andrew Miracle in his mind was well aware of the dangers of pride and had determined to stay approachable no matter what heights his career attained. He saw himself moving deferentially through the crowd, taking the time to speak individually to each person who had waited. People loved him for it.

Andrew ran his hands over and through the papers, moving them across his body.

"I don't deserve this, Lord," he said. "Help me to never forget that. If all this—the visitation, John, everything—if all this is to fulfill a dream I didn't even have the courage to speak out loud, then truly eye has not seen, nor ear heard. Because you know full well, Lord, that I am not the most faithful."

In that moment, he felt his own sense of unworthiness pressing him down, like a weight upon his chest. He recognized that old poison like a particularly unflattering photograph one refuses to throw away. He had grown accustomed to taking it out to look at it whenever he suspected he might grow beautiful. Without that weight, he wondered if he might float upward, and hover above the bed, effortlessly.

Later, Andrew didn't even remember undressing. He merely passed in a moment from one kind of dream to another.

At nine o'clock the next morning, Harold Murphy and Laurence Hill met in Hill's expansive corner office in the Dove office building. Hill was seated behind his large, black, contemporary desk.

"Well, what kind of read do you get on Andrew?" Laurence asked earnestly. "Do you think he'll sign, with everything as is?"

Murphy, seated opposite, smoothed a perfectly cuffed pants leg.

"Hard to say, Laurence," he answered. "Andrew's a very unusual young man. A little unpredictable, maybe. He wants to, though, I'm sure of it. I could feel him wanting to."

"What do you mean, he's unpredictable?"

"I mean he's a true artist type," Harold explained, "although in an unsophisticated way. There's nothing Hollywood about him, of course. Far from it. But I feel something smoldering just below the surface with that kid. He's very passive on one level, but you feel like he could just explode somehow at any moment. It's palpable. We all heard it on that tape. I thought he was going to crawl right out of the speakers bodily. If we can get that on record, or better yet on video, I think the thing could be huge. Right now, though, there's something more important on my mind."

"You're wondering if he'll think of shopping the deal, or just do what van Grimes tells him."

Murphy grimaced. "Right. John assured me that his management contract with Andrew will be signed shortly, and there's no way to sign Andrew Miracle without him. Andrew trusts John, and that puts John in the driver's seat. But, after all, we have planned for that distasteful contingency. You have our understanding with van Grimes ironed out, don't you?"

Laurence scowled at the mention of van Grimes's name. "Yeah, I ironed it out," he grumbled. "I hate playing pattycake with that guy. It cheapens the whole thing. Van Grimes knows a gravy train when he sees it, though. The second Andrew signs with us, John gets a forty-thousand-dollar finder's fee, about twice our normal sum. He beat around the bush about it, but I knew what he expected for it."

"What do you mean?"

"It was clear enough, only nobody spelled it out. I offered the twenty, but he said no go. At first I didn't know what he was talking about. I mean that's the standard thing, even better. But he's still beating around the bush. Slowly I figure it out."

"So what was the story?" Murphy asked.

"He starts talking about how much it can slow down things to shop the deal, and if they shop it and we still want it, how *expensive* that can be, you know? A lot of dancing around things. About how the whole deal could end up restructured if he throws it open, and then—" Hill drew an angry breath—"he starts talking about what might happen if things drag out and Andrew gets his own lawyer. He says maybe things will get complicated. And he starts talking about forty grand. So it dawns on me: in return for the forty, we work out the deal between ourselves, no other labels, and Andrew's out of the loop."

Harold paused, considering. "I see what you mean. But he never actually came out and said it?"

Laurence scowled. "No, but I knew what was going on. Finally, after about twenty minutes of party dancing, I write down forty thousand on a piece of paper and slide it over to him. The guy smiles this tight-lipped smile, folds the paper up, and puts it in his inside suit pocket. And suddenly, all that other stuff vanished. We had a deal in five minutes."

"So everything's in order," Harold concluded.

"Yeah, he tried to jerk my chain on a few points, but we got it all ironed out. I tossed him a few bones, and he thought he was J. Paul Getty."

Harold tossed an indulgent smile at his business partner.

"Van Grimes is trying to hitch a ride on that boy," Laurence added bitterly. "He's not wasting any time getting started, either. I'd love to see the management contract he concocted for Andrew to sign. The words *indentured servitude* come to mind."

Harold's smile faded. Laurence had a tendency to meddle in other people's affairs. He loved to know the inside details of every deal, and that violated an important unwritten rule. At this point, they didn't need any complications. Good relations were the lifeblood of the industry.

"Come on, Laurence," he said. "That contract is none of our business. John found the guy, and that's it. What kind of deal they sign is strictly between them. We all have to do business with people we don't like."

"Right. But I hate to see wolves around sheep with no shepherd."

"Your concern is touching, Laurence. But let's keep our eye on the ball. What kind of deal did you end up working out with van Grimes?"

"The bones I threw him didn't add up to much. Nothing tragic. It's really our standard first offer with a few meaningless tokens. But with one major change."

"Which is?"

"It's a seven record deal, with our option."

Murphy's raised an eyebrow. "Van Grimes agreed to that?"

"Look, Harold, we ought to be buying something with that extra twenty grand. Van Grimes thought he had worked me over on the contract. Besides, he likes his money up front, no risk. He didn't flinch."

Murphy nodded in acknowledgement. For all his faults, Laurence possessed a keen business mind, and he knew how to construct a skintight artist contract.

"Good, Laurence. Now, about lunch. No matter what John tells him, it's ultimately up to Andrew to sign with us or not. It's a contract between Andrew Miracle and Dove Records. There's absolutely nothing to be gained by rocking the boat now. So let's get our approach straight. Let me handle things, at least at first. I don't expect any problems, but there's no way to predict beforehand exactly how much influence John will have with the boy. The first few minutes will let us know how Andrew's disposed. In spite of John, Andrew may want to ask us some questions directly about the contract. If so, fine. The important thing is, I don't want to upset him right off with a lot of details. Fortunately, it's obvious that Andrew isn't very focused on the business side."

"Okay, then what is he interested in?"

Harold straightened himself up and said grandly, "Andrew Miracle wants to be believed in artistically, Laurence. Listen to how he talks about himself. Listen to how he plays. The guy's a poet, something you don't understand." He paused and added, "No offense."

He needn't have worried. Laurence didn't possess the particular sensibilities necessary to be offended, at least about art. On the contrary, he took a kind of pride in his objectivity about spending Dove Records' money. He never let artistic considerations cloud his sound business judgment, and his skin was absolutely made of rubber.

"Then the first mission is to use that artistic stuff to build a level of trust," Laurence said. "In fact, the less we say about the contract, the better. If it doesn't seem important to us, the less important it'll be to him, get it? Heck, maybe we can get this thing signed without ever discussing the contract in detail. Not that I want to take advantage of the guy. I just want to get the deal done with a minimum of hassle."

"Of course." Harold stood up and headed for the door. He turned and said, "So here's the drill, Laurence. After I set the tone for a few minutes, I'll throw it over to you to lay out the basics. I do mean the basics, Laurence. Keep it simple. Then we both start in again about how much we believe in him. We stress the personal side. No problem."

Laurence's face clouded over. "Is there any chance he'll want to delay, or maybe get a lawyer to represent him?" Laurence hated lawyers, especially when they represented artists. It made everything so needlessly messy. Murphy just grinned in response.

"To do what? The kid's in van Grimes's pocket. If I know John, the second he signs that management deal, Andrew will be waiving legal rights he never knew he had."

Laurence growled. "I hate to see things done this way, Harold."

"I know you do, Laurence. But there's simply no alternative. I want Andrew Miracle. So we play ball for now with van Grimes."

8

At precisely eleven-fifteen, Carolyn's Volkswagen convertible pulled into the parking lot of the Hampton Inn. Andrew was there waiting, standing outside the door looking excited and happy. He was breathing in the late morning air, willingly turning the pages of the very pleasant dream unfolding around him.

He was over his embarrassment about last night, and it felt good to see Carolyn again. She had handled his awkwardness easily, and he was grateful. It made him remember times, painful times, when his sudden outbursts of dark moodiness had left the girls back home uncomfortable and withdrawn. As a result, he had learned to monitor those feelings closely, heading them off with a laugh or a forced silence. Often, however, they would push through and do their damage. In some ways that part of him seemed to have a dangerous life of its own. But it seemed Carolyn didn't frighten easily, and if anything, she seemed drawn in toward the very center of his gift.

It had been a long time since Andrew had thought about being close to a girl. He had cultivated some friendships in Rose Hill but always within strict emotional guidelines. He had been betrayed by what was inside him before, and each time he determined to be more like the sturdy farm boys he had grown up with. But he began to let himself think that Carolyn might be a different sort of girl altogether. Though she never pushed, she always asked the right questions, drawing him out, compelling him to talk about more than he would have dared bring up on his own. She seemed to touch something already moving within him, something already searching for an escape.

Andrew got in the car without fanfare, enjoying the familiarity they felt together after such a short time. He looked at her. She was wearing a lovely print dress, once again something less severe than what he had imagined a working woman would wear. He approved. It showed off her figure very subtly but unmistakably. As they drove, he permitted himself short glances, once even daring to hold her gaze a moment as they talked. Her hair was pulled back with a gold and pearl barrette for the windy ride in the convertible, and it gave her a casual, approachable look. Indeed, he thought, Carolyn was one of those rare women who assumed the formality of their attire; she would look magnificent in formal evening dress, her hair pulled up and pearls around her neck, and equally desirable running through the park with a kite, wearing blue jeans and a pullover. In short, she looked wonderful, and Andrew surprised himself very much by remarking so. For a moment he held his breath, appalled at the liberty he had taken, but Carolyn accepted the compliment with a kind of practiced ease that Andrew ruefully felt could only come from hearing the words often. But as usual, her smile disarmed him, and he let himself ride along contentedly, for the moment feeling as if this new life was as natural to him as the one he was leaving behind. But every block that passed toward van Grimes's office took him farther away from Rose Hill, and everything he had known, and loved. As they pulled up to the converted house, he didn't immediately open the door. Instead, he looked up at the building, feeling once again what would happen to his life once he walked through those doors. He felt as though each step forward was irretrievable.

He thought of the farm, of Pastor Mathews, and of Christ's Kingdom Assembly. He saw his small Sunday school class, and the faces in the church congregation listening as he sang his songs. He saw the retirement home he played for every week. For a moment, he saw his mother, working out in the garden, picking flowers. But the face of John van Grimes quickly replaced these, and he thrust thoughts of home from his mind. Why would God have broken the laws of the universe to visit him if not to prepare him for some greater work, some truly significant mission for the kingdom? How could he compare the tiny things he could do for God in Rose Hill with the unlimited opportunities opening before him? He resolved once again to shake off any doubts. He had the calling. God had made that perfectly clear. Somehow, he had gained God's favor.

Gradually, Andrew became aware of Carolyn's gaze. He shook his head, and smiled sheepishly. "Sorry. I drifted off for a second. For Pete's sake, why didn't you stop me?"

"Where were you?" she asked.

"Rose Hill, Kansas, believe it or not."

"It may be a while before you spend much time there again," said Carolyn. "I know you must be leaving a lot behind." She paused and added softly, "You know, what you said, the wind moving through the wheat."

"Yes," Andrew answered, "the wind in the wheat." But he pulled up the door handle with authority and said, "Let's go."

Once inside, Andrew was ushered directly into van Grimes's office. John smiled expansively upon his entrance and invited him to sit down. Andrew was ready for the usual small-talk, and in fact he was counting on it to steady his nerves a bit. But for a long moment, John just looked at him, smiling and silent. John folded his hands together and slowly touched them to his lips several times. After a few seconds, Andrew began to look self-consciously at the various items on van Grimes's desk, only just catching himself before he cleared his throat, like a cliché in an old movie. At last, however, John spoke.

"Andrew," he said slowly, "you may be thinking this is a big day for you. Would I be right about that?"

Now that he was actually seated in van Grimes's office, Andrew felt his self-confidence slipping away. He had determined to maintain a sense of equality with John, but he found it difficult to do face to face. Try as he might, he always felt like a schoolboy around van Grimes. He just nodded and answered, "Yes, I suppose it is."

John smiled knowingly in response. "Well," he said, "I suppose it is. But I'd say that it's a bigger day for me, my friend. I'm perfectly serious. Because today, I'm ready to make an announcement to the world. I'm ready to announce the formation of a new team, the team of Andrew Miracle and John van Grimes." The words sank into Andrew like a balm on dry, sunburned skin. "I'm ready to announce," John continued, "that Andrew Miracle and John van Grimes have started off on an adventure together. An adventure, my friend, in which I'm convinced the two of us are going to do something great for God. And something great for each other. How does that sound to you?"

For the first time, he met van Grimes's eyes directly. "It sounds wonderful," he answered.

John smiled benignly and relaxed in his chair. His tone lightened. "Good," he said. "That's good, Andrew. You know what? From the second I heard you play, I knew there was something special about you. You have a gift. I know, it's a tired phrase, that. *Gift*. We don't understand it, really. But I do know that I decided right then that I wanted to bring that gift, that talent, to the world." Van Grimes rose from his seat and walked around to the front of his desk, where Andrew was seated. "Can I ask you a question, Andrew?" he asked.

"Of course, John." It was the first time he had called John by his Christian name. Andrew looked up into his eyes, but John seemed to be looking through him, seeing something far away.

"Andrew," he whispered, "do you believe in destiny?"

Andrew thought of his visitation. He thought of Heaven's

Voices. He thought of John, of Harold Murphy and Laurence Hill. He thought of Carolyn. "More than anything in the world," he answered.

John picked up a pen, and held it out to him. "Sign here." Andrew took the pen and signed a five-year management contract. John smiled and shook his hand.

"Andrew," he said, "let's go get a record deal."

Thirty minutes later, Andrew and John walked into the 32nd Avenue restaurant like old friends. Andrew held the door as they entered, and it felt good; there was nothing deferential about it. It was the kind of thing friends did for each other. They spied Harold and Laurence, who were already seated. John put his arm around Andrew as they approached the table, and for the first time, Andrew really began to feel at home in Nashville.

"Congratulations are in order, gentlemen," John said. "I'd like you to meet the newest artist to sign with the John van Grimes Management Agency. Gentlemen, Mr. Andrew Miracle."

Harold and Laurence rose, and the men shook hands all around. "Outstanding, Andrew. Just outstanding," said Harold. He talked like a football coach congratulating a player on a touchdown reception. "I have the feeling that this could mark the beginning of an era," he said.

"Exactly, Harold," chimed in Laurence. "I couldn't be happier for you both."

Andrew found himself seated with three industry insiders, not only treated as an equal but celebrated as a distinctive talent. While they waited for their order, the three men spoke casually about the biggest names in the industry, referring to them as if they were close personal friends. But Andrew resolved silently not to seek stardom or self-aggrandizement. For him, there was a more important task—the task of using his gift to reveal God to as many people as possible. If these people were the key to that task, he would accept it.

Harold and Laurence appeared calm and confident. They were gracious and charming, in the manner of men who don't doubt their position in life but have determined to stay friendly. Nothing in their manner indicated that a contract negotiation was about to take place.

When the moment finally came, Harold broached the subject as if he were merely summarizing the result of a long and satisfying negotiation, one in which both parties had felt deeply regarded and, in the process, had cultivated a lasting friendship.

"In the spirit of our celebration today," he began, "I'd like to put a little perspective on the documents that we presented to you both about Andrew becoming a Dove recording artist." Harold was maintaining eye contact with only Andrew now, focusing his considerable personal energy in a narrow beam that seemed to exclude everyone else in the room.

"This record contract," he continued, "is the codification of a relationship. Without that relationship, Andrew, a contract is useless. Its purpose is simply to express in written form what both parties already feel about each other. It expresses their mutual interests, and it clarifies their mutual goals." Andrew found nothing to disagree with in that description and simply nodded.

"Let me explain something, Andrew. Let me give you a little insight into what it's like to be the director of A&R at a record company. Day after day, you search for a unique talent that you can really believe in. There are times when you get discouraged and fed up with the mediocrity that you are slogging through. But you push through all that, Andrew, for one reason only. Do you know what that reason is?"

In only a few moments, Harold had woven a spell of silence and concentration over the table, and Andrew was clinging to every word. "What is the reason, Harold?" he asked.

Harold opened his arms wide. "The reason, Andrew, is you."

Andrew exhaled audibly. He had no idea how long he had been holding his breath. "You must be kidding."

"I assure you I'm not," Harold answered. "You are the reason we search, Andrew. You can't imagine how exciting it is for us, after plowing through hundreds of tapes and people without merit, to find a great talent we can commit our resources to without reservation. A person that we can invite to be part of a very special family.

"The essence of this contract, Andrew," he continued, "is that we believe in you, in your enormous talent, and in your commitment to God's work. It says that you have the desire, the motivation to do something great for Him. Its purpose is simply to provide a framework for God to use us together for His kingdom, instead of separately.

"Andrew, I can't tell you how much anticipation I feel for what God is going to do in your life. I see your ministry just exploding into the market. My part of this bargain is to be visionary, and I can honestly tell you I see an unlimited future for our relationship. This thing just has huge potential. Who's to say you can't reach out to the broader market-place? I am thinking big, Andrew, very big." Harold paused.

Andrew felt obligated to say something, so he asked, "And what is my part of the bargain, Harold?"

Harold smiled and answered simply, "Your part of the bargain, Andrew, is to be willing to work very, very hard, and to be yourself."

"That's it?"

"That's it, Andrew."

Andrew sat back in his chair for the first time since the meeting began. The pressure of a hundred future decisions was being lifted from him. John, Harold, and Laurence had everything in hand. Then Andrew heard Laurence's voice

breaking through his thoughts. "Well, Andrew, if everything's clear, we would like very much to consummate this
relationship today."

John pulled the contract from his jacket and laid the last
page on the table. "Andrew," he said, "I think this is very
much in your interest. It's the beginning of what I think will
be a legendary relationship for all of us."

The blank line above Andrew's typed name stared up at
the four of them, like a work of art, waiting to be signed.
Harold took out a pen, saying, "Please. Allow me." He
handed the pen to Andrew.

Andrew took the pen and signed a seven-record contract
with Dove Records.

In this unlikely way, Andrew's future found him. Thirty-
five pages of promises and commitments, jerked into motion
with a few irrevocable strokes of a pen. Andrew had stepped
off a cliff and into the unknown.

9

From the moment he signed, the pace of Andrew's life began to accelerate noticeably. John had scheduled a photo session for the very next day in which the actual signing was staged for press photographs. The photographer, a bright little man with an earring and short, spiky hair, posed John and Andrew in a variety of ways for the picture. He shot John with the pen, Andrew with the pen, both of them with pens. He posed Andrew alone, then John alone, keeping up a continual chatter of friendly small talk during the process.

"Okay," he said repeatedly, "BIG smile this time." Then the flash, and a satisfied, "Great. Just great."

But even while he talked he was in motion, preparing for the next shot. Andrew felt distinctly uncomfortable with the whole process. The photographer seemed to him to be some sort of out-of-scale butterfly or hummingbird. Andrew didn't like being fussed over. But John kept his arm around him, encouraging him to just have fun and enjoy it.

"Better get used to it, Andrew," he said. "You'll be doing a lot of this from now on."

To his chagrin, the whole process was repeated later in the day at the Dove Records offices. John drove him over in his Lexus, and a different, but entirely similar, photographer put the whole group through its paces for twenty minutes. Andrew noticed with amusement that Harold had quite a vain streak; he continually maneuvered himself with silly, transparent excuses so that only one side of his face was photographed. It seemed that success was no insulation against insecurity.

There was a lot more press work to be done; Helen, the publicist at Dove, was anxious to put together a press kit, and for that she would need a great deal of information. They needed a bio, more photographs, and what Harold called an "angle." When Andrew asked what he meant by the phrase, Harold just laughed and said, "Let us worry about that, Andrew. We don't want our artists having to do two jobs. Wouldn't be fair."

The next few days seemed to blur past, and by the end of the week Andrew had almost conquered the butterflies in his stomach every time he approached John's office or Dove Records. There was a comfort in not having to make decisions, in being a part of a great force moving forward. All the people involved were part of a common goal, although that goal was never quite articulated; but the busyness and constant motion reassured him that the right things were happening.

The energy was especially infectious at Dove. It was obvious that a highly creative and committed team of people had been assembled, and that they were working hard to get things done. Growing up on a farm, Andrew had never really seen an office environment up close, and he was impressed with the teamwork necessary to meet the production deadlines that seemed to continually hang over them.

During this time two things happened which eased Andrew's mind a great deal: first, he was getting settled at last in his own furnished apartment in Bellevue on the fashionable west side of Nashville, and second, his friendship with Carolyn began to deepen into something far more significant.

Carolyn and he had begun, by degrees, to spend more time together. She had helped him find the apartment, and her knowledge of the city was like a lifeline to Andrew. They had enjoyed searching out his place together a great deal, and it felt oddly, if artificially, to Andrew as if they had been married, going into apartments like that together. He was surprised to find that he didn't consider living anywhere that seemed unacceptable to Carolyn. Her opinion was important to him, and he trusted her taste much more than his own. In the end, they settled on a small two-bedroom with hardwood floors and a fireplace. It was very southern, and it felt somehow old-world, as if its builders had a genetic memory of the way things were done around the Civil War. Carolyn loved it, and that was enough for Andrew.

John arranged for the use of a car, a nice Japanese model that farmers back in Kansas wouldn't be caught dead in. He had to smile at himself from time to time, driving in that little squirt of a car, thinking of the huge American luxury liners that patrolled the roads of the farmland in Kansas.

But more and more, there was Carolyn. The more his life changed, the more he felt that she was his constant in the whirlwind around him. She had gotten into the habit of stopping by after work and looking in on him. Invariably they ended up spending the evening together, although plans were never articulated. Andrew loved having someone with whom he could share what was happening to him, and Carolyn was the perfect comrade. She was an insider; she understood the ins and outs of what he was going through.

Sometimes she made dinner, fussing over the limited selection of pots and pans that Andrew had managed to buy over the last couple of weeks and bringing her own to supplement them. "Men know nothing about kitchens," she would say, and then she would prepare something wonderful as if by magic. "You may be great out in the fields, Andrew Miracle, but you're helpless as a cook. What would you do without me? Eat out every night?"

Andrew had to admit that more and more he didn't know what he would do without her. The more time they spent together, the more he found himself thinking about her when they weren't together. There was a kind of flirtatious friendship between them, an unspoken sense that something more was meant by a little glance, a brush of the arm, a hug hello. But several weeks passed without reaching that moment of risk, when something unretractable and unmistakable happens and friendship changes for better or worse. Andrew knew, of course, that it was his responsibility to take that risk, but he hesitated: there was so much to lose with a misunderstanding. For all his new acquaintances, Carolyn was in fact his only real friend—he was too much in awe of John to call him that—and he didn't want to risk what had become a lifeline for him in this new city and new life. At last, however, he couldn't wait any longer. He wrestled inside himself, fearful of the same old rejection he had experienced so many times before. But Carolyn was making him believe in himself, not just as an artist, but as a man. Her subtle, friendly affirmations drew him toward her until he could resist reaching out to her no longer.

He wracked his brain for how to approach her, and in the end, he could do no better than clumsily sitting her down on the sofa and saying he wanted to talk about something. Once again he was struck by the curious duality of his personality: in his music, his passion revealed an unfettered longing that could make a woman catch her breath. When he had to speak, however, he was often reduced to a schoolboy. He sat opposite her nervously, and she looked at him with interest, aware that his anxiety had risen suddenly. "Carolyn," he said at last, "would you like to go out on a date with me?"

"What?" Carolyn laughed.

"You know," he answered, "a date. A real date."

Carolyn's smile seemed disconcertingly knowing. "Well," she said thoughtfully, "I don't know. A real date. Aren't we having enough fun the way it is? What would you say we've been doing all this time?"

"I don't know," he answered, his country shyness apparent on his face, "but no, it's not dating. I want to have a real date with you, Carolyn."

She reached out and squeezed his hand. "Yes. I think I know what you mean. And I'd like that very much."

Andrew found himself looking into her eyes a long moment, and had to tear himself away to avoid making a fool of himself. "All right," he said at last, "how about tonight?"

"Tonight!" Carolyn laughed. "I guess that would be okay. So how do you want to go on this date of ours?"

"First, you have to go home," he said.

"I beg your pardon?"

Andrew stood up, finally sure of himself. "I mean it, Carolyn. You have to go home. I want to pick you up at your house, like a real date."

"But Andrew," she exclaimed, "we're already together. You want me to go home just so you can drive over and pick me up again?"

"That's exactly what I want to do," he told her firmly.

Carolyn folded her hands together and thought for a moment. "Well, Andrew Miracle, I'd have to say that's about the most romantic thing I've heard of. I'm on my way home. When shall I expect you?"

"No, no, Carolyn. I ask that part."

"Sorry."

"That's okay. Now. Carolyn, is eight o'clock okay?"

"Eight o'clock would be perfect."

That night Andrew put on his nicest clothes, and grinning, drove over to Carolyn's house on Blair Street. He rang the doorbell and caught his breath when she answered the door.

Carolyn had guessed correctly that after everything Andrew had said he would arrive dressed up. She was determined to knock his eyes out, and she succeeded. She had picked out a dark green satin dress that fit her like a glove, high heels, and an antique gold brooch her mother had given her. She wore her brunette hair up, and had, she admitted to herself, gotten her makeup absolutely perfect. It was simple, but effective.

Andrew walked in, trying unsuccessfully not to stare, and

for the moment he kept silent. He had an idea, picked up on the fields of Kansas, that he should be in charge of his emotions. Nevertheless, the longer he looked, the less Kansas seemed to matter somehow. In spite of himself, he muttered softly, "You're beautiful."

Carolyn accepted the compliment easily, and Andrew wished she could have been as off center as he was. He was afraid it was the kind of thing she heard all the time. Andrew felt very alive, with an almost physical sense running through him that this night was important. He could feel it on his skin. But she grabbed his hand and led the two of them out the door, picking up a light jacket on the way.

It was the first truly cool evening of the season, and they both enjoyed feeling bundled up in their jackets, summer now really over. The chill moved them towards each other an extra inch or two as they walked, edging towards the warmth. The inside of the car felt like a cozy refuge, and they instinctively spoke a little lower, as if telling secrets.

As they drove, Andrew kept stealing glances at Carolyn. She seemed as different from the girls back home as Harold and Laurence were from the men he had known. There was an extra measure of life in her somehow. Or was it that he was different? Was he finally coming into his own, here in a place where he could leave his awkwardness behind and really be the artist he wanted to be? But now Carolyn was speaking again, and he wanted to just listen to her voice, letting it soothe him with its familiarity and its gentleness.

Andrew felt his demons at bay at last. Here in Nashville, he could explore his music full-time, working with the most talented people in the business. Here he wouldn't feel out of step with the world; he could actually be rewarded for what he created. His artistic temperament wouldn't be a social albatross around his neck, something to keep hidden except while performing. Carolyn understood, he thought. She understood that there was something moving in him, and that the something was where the music lived.

Dinner was perfect, both the food and the location. As if by telepathy, the maitre'd seated them at the most secluded table, and during the meal the waiter left them alone to talk unless summoned. For the first time, Andrew sat on the same side of the booth as Carolyn. He had always felt uncomfortable about that before, like it was trying too hard, but tonight he wanted to stay near her through the meal, as if having the table between them might break the spell and turn the evening ordinary. But he could do no wrong this night, and his moodiness and awkwardness seemed as far away as Rose Hill.

There were comfortable silences in their conversation, the feeling of togetherness growing quietly between them. Their friendship was like a vine, tendrils reaching out and connecting in a hundred small places. It went on through dinner, and afterward, they just sat together, feeling their physical proximity with the anticipation that is never quite repeated once it is expressed. This was the night for them, the moment in time reserved for Carolyn Hemphill and Andrew Miracle. It held the exquisite emotion of realizing that the person you care for says yes to you. He wanted to stretch that moment out as long as possible, knowing that its promise could never be captured and played back between them, no matter how intimate they became. It was the moment of potential, of expectation, of surprising, impossible affirmation. It proved to them both that they were alive, human, and worthy. From a long silence, Andrew heard Carolyn's voice.

"I know this is your date, Andrew, but I want you to give me a gift."

He roused himself from her eyes and answered, "Of course. Anything."

Carolyn suddenly smiled impetuously, like a young girl with a secret. "I'm not going to tell you what it is. It's my gift, but it's your surprise."

Andrew paid the bill, and the two walked out into the

night air. He was glad for the distance to the car. It was growing colder, and he slipped his arm around her waist after a few steps. She moved toward him, and their footsteps synchronized easily as they walked.

"So what about this gift?" Andrew asked. "You realize you'll have to tell me what it is before I can give it to you."

"Of course—but not yet," Carolyn answered. "I'm afraid you'll change your mind if I tell you beforehand. I don't want you to know before the moment itself."

Andrew wondered what that could mean, but by then they were at the car, and Carolyn took the initiative. "Come on, Andrew," she said. "Play along. You promised."

"So I did. Okay, what do I do?"

"It's really very simple, Drew. First, just take us where I tell you. I'll give you directions as we go."

Carolyn navigated him out of the neighborhood and back toward Vanderbilt. He parked at her direction on a little side street on the edge of campus, in front of a beautiful, small stone chapel. It would have looked right at home in a quaint English country village, with its climbing roses and small stained glass windows set in dark wood surrounded by stone.

"What a lovely place," Andrew said admiringly. It was the kind of church that smelled of antiquity, and it seemed to impart stability to the newer buildings around it. It was nothing like Christ's Kingdom.

"Yes," Carolyn said gently. "It's my favorite place in Nashville." She stuck her hands in her pockets and looked up at the chapel like an old friend. "I discovered it by accident a couple of years ago, and I've been coming here ever since. I always show it to important people in my life. It's silly, but I feel kind of like it's my personal secret place."

"I understand."

"No, you don't, silly!" Carolyn laughed. "You don't understand the secret."

"What secret?" Andrew asked.

"One night, about a year and a half ago, I walked down

here about eight o'clock, and I saw the pastor leaving the chapel. He did the most marvelous thing."

"Which was?"

She took his hand and started to walk toward a side door. "The marvelous thing, Andrew, was this."

Carolyn approached the chapel door and counted five bricks up from the bottom. She reached down, and to Andrew's delight, easily pulled the brick right out of the wall. She reached in, and pulled out a key. "He keeps a key hidden here. Let's go."

The door opened easily and silently, and the two passed directly into the small sanctuary. The stained glass was glowing darkly with rich color, letting in just enough light to navigate the pews and altar. Carolyn led the way, while Andrew picked his way carefully after her, clinging to her hand. Suddenly she stopped short, and Andrew pressed up against her in the darkness.

"This is my gift, and your surprise," she said. With that, she stepped from in front of him, and Andrew could just make out the shape of a concert grand piano looming before him.

"I want you to play for me," she said. "That's the gift. I want to hear what's inside of you. I want to hear what it is I feel you trying to put into words, but you never do."

Andrew silently moved past her, touching her as he passed. He sat down on the bench, and then motioned for her to sit beside him. Carolyn glided up to the piano and sat next to him, not touching him now but close enough to feel his energy.

Andrew drew back the doors to his heart and let the strong waters pass through his hands to Carolyn. Everything he had tried to hide he released in one reckless commitment of risk, one total statement of himself for her to love or to reject.

He had no sense of Carolyn's reaction while he played. The decision was his alone to reveal himself, and no matter how it was received, he would see it through and tell every secret story about himself and lay them all at her feet. Minutes passed, the music crashing out of him, his eyes tightly closed, his face revealing the temperature within.

He had finished. As if she were a therapist, he had spilled it all, and once said, it could never be unsaid. She knew him now. He raised his head, and looked at Carolyn, the two of them sitting in the new, absolute stillness. But Carolyn's eyes had been closed as well, and it was a moment before she opened them. At last he turned towards her, and reaching out, he took her face gently in his hands. He held her gaze there for a moment, and in exquisite, prolonged slow motion, placed his lips on hers. He covered her mouth with his own, and in that moment Andrew felt every no in his life wash away in her yes.

10

John van Grimes headed down 16th Avenue toward Dove Records for a two o'clock meeting. He was listening to Andrew's demo tape and smiling to himself. He had a lot to be happy about. Laurence had just sent over his forty-thousand-dollar check, and he had several good ideas about what to do with it. God was certainly blessing him, he thought to himself. Funny business, though. Where else can a guy nail down forty thousand just for an idea? The record hadn't even been made yet, much less sold a single copy. But this was just the beginning. There was a lot more where that came from.

He had finally found it, the golden goose. He permitted himself a moment of pride. Dangerous, he knew. But there was a time for everything. To have found his meal ticket in a place like Rose Hill, Kansas. It proved a point, though. You have to stay alert in this business. A manager is only as powerful as his artists. You never know when opportunity is going to knock. A lot of the guys in the business would have let this one get away.

John pulled his car into the Dove parking lot and grabbed his briefcase. Maybe a little tattered, he thought to himself. He decided to stop by Henri's and pick up a new one. Check that—better wait until he was in New York. The selection was better up there, much better. Harold had mentioned a place he'd discovered on his last trip with the best stuff, primo. The masses hadn't found out about it yet.

John walked into the elevator and pushed the button for the fifth floor. Executive offices. The elevator doors opened directly into the lobby, and John breezed in, walking straight past the receptionist with a brief hello. He knew that he was the golden boy, at least for now. Favor ebbed and flowed in this business, and he didn't kid himself about that. But for now, Andrew Miracle was where the action was, and he owned him.

John turned the corner and saw Harold's secretary in the hallway. "Harold arrived for my two o'clock?" he asked.

"Yes, John, he's in there," she replied. "Why don't you go on in?"

Indeed, he thought to himself. *I think I will. I think I'll just go right on in. I'm the golden boy, for now.*

Harold was on the phone when John walked in, and looking up, he smiled and motioned for John to take a seat on the couch in the more casual sitting area of the office. John noticed with satisfaction that Harold began wrapping up his current conversation almost as soon as he arrived. Within a few seconds he had begged off the call, and he walked over to shake John's hand warmly. Harold beamed pleasant affirmation as he took one of the padded wing chairs opposite the couch.

"Well, John," he began, "I assume you're in a pretty good mood today. Laurence told me he sent the check over."

"Yes, he did. I appreciate it."

"Good. We think of it as an investment. Andrew's future is very bright. It's a pleasant thought to know that we will inevitably be a part of it."

"Exactly."

John didn't particularly like this kind of talk. It was too public to be so self-congratulatory. He much preferred to keep those kinds of thoughts to himself. "I've been listening to Andrew's tape, Harold," he said, "and I'm convinced that 'Lost Without You' is a career song."

"I quite agree."

"I don't want that song wasted, Harold. We both know a song like that comes along once in an artist's lifetime, if he's lucky. It's time we talked producers."

"I assume by your tone that you have someone in mind."

John realized that Harold was giving him some leeway, temporarily letting him take the lead. He intended to make the most of it.

"In my mind, Harold, there's only one person to consider. David Spenser."

Harold crossed his arms and looked straight back at van Grimes. "That's a very expensive suggestion, John." he said. "David is very hot right now. Michael Thomasson at Atlantic is tagging him for several of their new pop acts."

If this was news to van Grimes, he didn't show it. "I know it's expensive, Harold," he said. "But Andrew Miracle is going to be a very big artist. I don't want this thing farmed out to some journeyman producer. I want the whole shot for Andrew."

"David's a very busy man right now, John. Do you have a B list?" Harold asked.

"No." John didn't flinch.

"I see." Harold took a moment to think, and walked over to his desk. He pushed down the intercom button and said, "Kathy, get me David Spenser's number, would you?"

John sighed with relief. Things were going very well indeed. The golden producer to work with the golden artist for the golden boy. Perfect.

Harold walked back over. "I'm inclined to go along with you, John," he said. "I'll have to talk this over with Laurence, of course. David's involvement changes the financial situation somewhat. But I think this is right. Andrew deserves a great producer, he needs one. He's green, and David understands that kind of artist. Who knows, maybe Michael Thomasson will end up wanting to distribute the thing if David does it."

John had already thought of that. You had to push for the top to end up at the top. There were no accidents. What Dove had in mind for Andrew was significant, but if someone like Thomasson could be persuaded to come on board, the picture could change rapidly. Atlantic had the power to make Andrew a genuine star, and their machine would dwarf Dove's efforts. One thing at a time, but it never hurt to position Andrew for the ultimate. Van Grimes found himself thinking that being in Rose Hill, Kansas, that day to find Andrew Miracle was the very hand of God. Hadn't he slaved, paying his dues in the mission field of Heaven's Voices? Hadn't he endured the misery of cold calling to fill up empty dates on the calendar? He had been biding his time, working hard to show God he deserved the big shot. Faithful in small things. It was easy, it took no effort at all, to just let his mind go in its natural direction, and it filled effortlessly with pictures of himself managing Andrew as a major star, and other stars as well, as his power grew, and then he would be calling the shots for a change. He deserved it, because all that small-change church work would stick with him, keeping him humble. God knew that. But day-dreaming was one thing. Making it happen was another, and he had a job to do. If God was going to let lightning strike, then he wouldn't wait for a second miracle. He would make Andrew happen, no matter what it took.

"I can feel the energy building on this project, Harold," he said. "I have the feeling that this thing is going to make some serious shock waves."

"How's Andrew?" Harold asked, scanning John's face for any unspoken problems.

"Smooth sailing," John answered serenely. "Excited—and a little nervous, of course. But ready to get up to the plate and let 'er rip."

"Lovely, John. Here's to a home run."

"And thank God there's no free agency in the music business."

The laughter in the office lasted a long time.

The next several days were busy for Andrew. He had met with David Spenser and had liked him very much. David had an easygoing style that set him at his ease. David had loved his tape, and he had been nothing but enthusiastic about getting started as soon as possible. Then he went off on a streak of technical talk of which Andrew had no conception. David had churned out a solid five minutes of it before he realized he was speaking to a blank stare of incomprehension. Andrew was ashamed to be so in the dark, but David had just burst out laughing and apologized like a madman.

"You're a purist, Andrew," he said. "You care about the music, and that's it. You aren't jaded, like a lot of guys. Don't worry about being new to this, man. Cherish it. You're going to make a great record. 'Lost Without You' is a major hit."

"Lost Without You." Everybody kept coming back to that song. Andrew began to wonder if any of this would even be happening if his life had been exactly the same but he had never written that one song.

With the recording date looming ahead of him in just a few days, his nerves were in full motion. He and David were getting together every afternoon, finalizing the song list and working out the details of the arrangements. Andrew began to feel the passing of each hour, even each minute, individually. His emotions were like a kettle on a stove, and he felt as though someone was slowly turning up the heat as the clock moved inexorably forward. He found himself driving aimlessly in the mornings, singing his songs to himself— puny songs, terrible songs, he suddenly felt.

The morning of the first session, Andrew awakened early to pray. He seemed to pass from sleep into a kind of anesthetized wakefulness the moment his eyes opened. He pulled off the covers in one motion and stood up, staring. The walls of his small apartment stared back, silently. It seemed incredible that so very much had happened, and had brought him, at last, to this moment, the moment of creation.

Andrew pulled on some blue jeans and walked bare chested to the kitchen. He poured himself a glass of orange juice and set it down before him on the kitchen table, staring blankly at it for a long moment. The sudden ringing of the telephone jangled his nerves to attention.

"It's Carolyn," the voice said. "I called to wish you good luck."

"Thanks," he returned, feeling detached and vacant.

There was a silence from the phone, and Carolyn asked, "You okay?"

"I guess so."

"Well, I want you to be sure you're okay. Can I tell you something, Andrew Miracle? Are you listening to me, listening very carefully?"

The animation in her voice helped to focus his mind, and he felt himself waking. "Yes, Carolyn, I'm listening."

"Good," she said, "because I want you to hear this. I want these words to fly right into your ears and expand inside of you until they fill you up inside like a balloon." Andrew couldn't help laughing at the image, and with his laughter, he felt the weight upon him lighten considerably.

"You're a great musician, Andrew," she said sternly, like a teacher to an obstinate child. "You have a torrent of a gift. What you play touches people. It moves them." She paused a moment, and added more softly, "It moves me."

Andrew thought he heard a catch in her voice. "So you think I can really do this," he mumbled, half statement, half question.

"I know you can," she answered simply, and again, even more quietly: "I know you can."

Andrew sighed, clinging to the sound of her voice. Her voice always had a soothing effect on him, taking the rough edges off his uncertainties. "I'm kind of new at having somebody like you in my life," he said. "You make me feel like I could actually pull this off."

"You never had anyone believe in you?"

"No, it's not that. Mom and Dad and Pastor Mathews, they all believed— sometimes a lot more than I did. But this is different. They were all authority figures in one way or another. I mean, it was their job to believe. You and I are—different."

"That's what friends are for, silly."

Andrew felt his heart pounding, the way he did sometimes when he had given himself over to the music. Friends, yes. But ever since the night in the chapel, he knew there was something more. He wanted to say the words, to say them all, to spill out what his heart was feeling; but for once, just this once, he stopped himself. Like in the restaurant, he wanted to stretch out for as long as possible what he saw beckoning before him. He wanted to give them both the chance to let the sweetness of what was growing between them express itself naturally, slowly, exquisitely.

"I'll call you when I get home, sweetheart," he said at last. The words were sweet in his mouth, like honeysuckle. Carolyn's answer was softer and hurt more perfectly than the sound of any music.

"I'll be waiting."

When at last the time to go to the studio arrived, John drove over to pick up Andrew for the trip. He was committed to walking Andrew through things and felt that it would be more comfortable for his artist if they entered the strange environment of a recording studio together. They pulled up to the entrance gate of Emerald Sound Studios around noon. David had told them he needed the morning for setup, and there was no point in tiring Andrew out waiting while they worked out all the technical things.

Emerald was one of the most exclusive and expensive sound studios in Nashville. David had insisted on recording there, and Dove had indulged him this expense. The guard let John and Andrew in after checking their names off his list, and John pulled into a numbered space with a smile.

"Well, Andrew," he said, "this is it. How do you feel, my friend?"

Andrew looked through the window at the imposing building before him. If he let himself, he could feel very small indeed. But Carolyn's words were still ringing inside of him.

"I feel okay," he said firmly. "This has all happened for a reason, John. I wouldn't have left Rose Hill if there wasn't something for me to get done here. So let's go."

John looked at Andrew with genuine surprise. This was a good sign. Andrew was just a kid from Kansas, after all. But he was showing some confidence, and at just the right time.

"Eat 'em up, kid," he said, and he swung open his car door.

Once inside, the receptionist showed them back to the main control room. As they approached it, Andrew felt rather than heard a muffled sound moving through the floor. She pulled back a thick, heavy door, and suddenly an explosion of sound rocked them back on their feet. David Spenser caught sight of them and rushed over to greet them.

"Whaddaya say, Andrew? Feeling good today?" he shouted over the din.

There seemed to be something exploding in the room, and Andrew could feel the air moving against him like a concussive wave.

"I hope you don't mind, but I like to get my drum sounds pretty loud," David went on, nearly screaming. "I find it's a bit more accurate in the end that way."

Suddenly, Andrew understood. The sound he had heard through the door was the sound of a drummer, coming through two huge speakers mounted in the wall opposite the door.

David motioned for the recording engineer to take a break, and the monitors were turned to a low volume. David laughed and slapped Andrew on the back.

"You were saying?" he asked.

"I was saying I was fine," Andrew answered. "That was amazing."

"Isn't it, though?" David replied. "Let me introduce you to everyone."

David called the musicians into the control room where they were talking and introduced Andrew to them, as well as to the engineer and to his assistant. They were clearly a professional crew. It was obvious they had gone through this many times before, and they projected a casual, competent air that stood in marked contrast to Andrew's jangled nerves. He felt he was vibrating inside, like a tuning fork.

Of all the surprises he was encountering, however, none struck Andrew as more unlikely and implausible than the pronounced atmosphere of deference with which everyone in the room regarded him. The musicians all exhibited a respectful tone when speaking to him, unaccountably acting as if they were encountering a superior. Ridiculously, it reminded him of how he had felt many summers ago when he had worked at the IGA grocery store in Rose Hill. He finally worked up enough courage to ask for a raise from old man Stockton, the grocer, and walked into Stockton's office like a polite choir boy and treated the man like royalty. With a shock, Andrew realized that the analogy rang true; a word from him, he supposed, could remove any one of the musicians from the room, to be replaced with another player more to his personal liking. He was, in a completely new way, both an artist and a meal ticket.

The control room was dominated by a monstrous recording console, in which every available inch had been filled with an impossibly large number of knobs, sliding faders, push buttons, and lights. It appeared to him as an indistinguishable visual cacophony, a kind of field trip to NASA, but the engineer hovered over it confidently, as if the proper position of each control was second nature to him.

Andrew's mesmerized stare was broken by David's voice

calling the players outside to the piano. He handed the musicians several pages of music and said, "I'd like to get going, gentlemen. You all have the music to the first song, 'Lost Without You.' The smart thing to do would be for Andrew to run through the song for you by himself so everybody can get the feel of it."

The idea of playing in front of all these professionals was the first real hurdle of the day for Andrew. He looked sheepishly at the piano, but he forged his way through a mass of self-doubts over to the bench and sat down in front of it, smiling wanly. The studio musicians huddled around quite closely, taking positions behind and on both sides of him. From his seated position, they all seemed to tower over him as they stood, looming, he felt, like teachers before a test, their faces radiating studied, concentrated interest.

"This looks great," one said, looking over his music and back at Andrew. "Can't wait to hear it."

"Yeah," said another, his face in the pages of music. "Looks like this could be fun."

Andrew took a deep breath and played a couple of chords on the piano. It fairly sang; it couldn't have been tuned more than thirty minutes earlier. He decided to close his eyes and just listen to the sound that always pulled him through, the sound of a truly great instrument awaiting his command.

"Okay," he said at last, and he launched into the song, feeling the introduction, gaining confidence before he sang. By the time he opened his mouth for the first verse, he was almost alone again, at home playing his old familiar Steinway, his mother listening out on the porch, the night air flowing through the house, carrying with it a perfect accompaniment of crickets and rustling leaves. By the time he hit the first chorus, he didn't hear the musicians turning pages around him, nor did he notice the silence when they stopped turning them, drawn away from the pages and just listening—brought into the music wholeheartedly.

As he finished, the last chord disappeared into a respectful quiet and no one spoke for a moment. Suddenly, all the musicians at once seemed to explode into a cacophony of backslapping, delighted affirmation.

"Great song," he heard from several directions, and he was shaking hands and looking up into several genuinely pleased faces.

"Marvelous. This will be a pleasure," said another.

"Okay, then," David said. "Let's go to work."

As suddenly as they had gathered, the musicians assumed their positions around the studio, tweaking their instruments and adjusting their sounds.

"Stay where you are, Andrew," David said. "I've got a feeling that we need to get this on tape while everyone's got the feeling in their minds of what you just did. The engineer was working on your sound while you were running through the song, and we should be ready to go soon."

"Okay," answered Andrew, still feeling buoyed by the other musicians' responses. "They really liked it, didn't they, David?"

"Yeah, Andrew. They loved it. You were great, man. This is going to be a great record. Now, can I get you anything? Coke, coffee, anything like that?"

"No, thanks, David. I'm fine. I'd feel weird with you guys catering to me anyway. Seems odd, somehow. If I need something, I'll find it."

"Okay, Andrew," David returned, laughing. "Boy, I can tell this is your first record. But remember, everybody, and I mean everybody, is here to make it happen for you. Anything you want—I mean anything—you just speak right up. That's what we're here for."

As David went back into the control room with the engineer, Andrew put on his headphones and listened to the other musicians running through the different sections of the song. He had never heard anything like it. After playing the song for months by himself, the power of having all the other musicians in his ears was overwhelming. Jay, the guitar player, was playing a part on the verses that Andrew had never imagined—but it was perfect, complimenting the piano part superbly, driving it forward into the chorus like a freight train. Mark, the synthesist, had brought up a sound on the chorus that gave it an air of longing and mystery, and Andrew knew it would make the song hurt like a lingering memory. The drums and bass were supporting the whole structure perfectly, giving the song a dynamic range he could never have achieved alone.

Before he knew it, he heard David's voice in his headphones, sounding unnaturally close, almost speaking from inside of him.

"Okay, gentlemen," he said, "let's see if we can't make Andrew Miracle a star."

The rest of that day was awash in a brilliant haze of experiences that Andrew could never quite remember distinctly. But the feeling of the day he would never, ever forget. The tape was rolling, he was playing and singing, turning his headphones up louder and louder until he could feel every nuance of every part, lifted up by the craftsmen around him to create at his very best. It was a special day, and though many more were to follow in the making of the album, nothing ever eclipsed that first day of discovery as he felt the pure joy of hearing his songs come to life on a scale more grand than he had ever dreamed possible. From time to time he would glance through the large glass window as they recorded, and he could see David, his mouth moving like a silent movie actor as he sang along. He was smiling and moving with the music, obviously pleased.

Van Grimes was there as well, standing with his face almost touching the glass, his eyes shining like a Las Vegas gambler on the greatest winning streak in casino history. As he leaned forward, his breath caused a tiny spot of wet fog to appear and disappear on the window. It was nearly six by now, and van Grimes was sure he had some phone call to return, some base he needed to touch. But none of that mattered now, now that the tape was rolling, and this extraordinary experience was being captured forever. A gold mine was being constructed in the air, right before his eyes.

David had arranged for dinner to be catered in, and both John and Andrew were grateful; they were afraid to step out into the sunshine, fearful that the creative spell of the moment might be broken. Andrew wanted this day to last forever, and when at last it ended around eleven-thirty that night, he continued to sit at the piano, his body and mind feeling the stunning denouement of exhaustion and exhilaration.

Andrew looked up to see John coming across the studio floor, beaming. He sat down on the bench beside him and put his arm around him, squeezing his shoulder.

"Andrew, my boy, that was truly mesmerizing. Mesmerizing! I've been in there listening to the playback, and it's astounding. I can't help but feel that we made history here today. How do you feel about it?"

"I feel amazing," he answered. "I never dreamed what that song could be with all this backup. I never want to leave this room," he finished, laughing. "Can my whole life be like this, John?"

"I don't know about that, Andrew, but there's no question that you took a major first step toward a career here today."

"I can't wait to play this for Carolyn. She'll love it."

"Ah, yes, Carolyn," John answered. "You two are getting pretty close, aren't you?"

Andrew smiled shyly. "Yes, we are." It felt good to say it out loud to someone else for the first time, and he repeated himself, just for the joy of it. He laughed again. "Maybe I should have come to Nashville a long time ago."

"No, son, don't even think it. I might not have had the chance to be the one to discover you if you'd done that. And that, my friend, would have been a tragedy."

"Okay, John. Whatever you say. I guess we're ready to go?"

"Ready and waiting. You hungry?"

"Yeah, I could eat something. I didn't realize this would take so much out of me."

"Good, it's on me."

"Oh, no, John, really. You've done enough for one day. I'll never forget this for as long as I live."

"Nonsense, Andrew. I've got to take care of my artist. You're the man, Andrew, you're the man."

John drove to a nearby restaurant, and they grabbed a booth. Andrew slouched down in the seat, and he ran a tired hand through his hair. Now that the day's work was over, he was beginning to relax, and he felt exhaustion slowly creep over him.

"You look beat, kid," John said with a smile. "It's not all fun and games, is it?"

"No, it's not. It's hard work. But it's incredible, John. Hearing my voice through those headphones with all that equipment to bring it out—I never knew I could sound like that. And the other musicians—it was like being in the center of a great dream, but wide awake so I wouldn't miss a thing."

"You can't," John said.

"Can't what?"

"Can't sound like that," John answered, laughing. "In real life, I mean. But that's okay. Nobody can."

"What do you mean?"

"I mean you ought to sound great in there, my friend. They've got about a million bucks worth of stuff in that studio to make you sound bigger, stronger, more sensitive, more in tune, or more whatever else you want to sound like. At the prices they charge, you darn well better sound good."

"It was amazing. I just opened my mouth, and suddenly I had this super-voice. Can you imagine if you could sound like that all the time? Just walking down the street, with all that reverb and EQ and delays and stuff? You'd get elected president in about fifteen minutes. How disappointing to have to hear my regular voice, after all that."

John smiled at his naive protégé. It was refreshing to work with someone genuinely surprised by what for him was old hat. He did have a point, though. "Maybe the Japanese will invent something like that," he said with a chuckle. "They've thought of everything else. Think of it, your own, portable human voice effects system. 'You, too, can sound like a rock star, even when you're ordering sandwiches.' Which it's time to do."

The waitress had arrived, but Andrew had yet to give his order a thought.

"What'll it be, Andrew?" asked John.

"Whatever you say," he answered. "I'm too tired to think. I'll just have what you're having."

"Good man. Two reubens and a couple of Cokes."

The two sat in their booth munching sandwiches, Andrew asking question after question about the recording process, John answering, tutoring his student carefully. Now that he had actually experienced the recording process, Andrew found that he wanted to know everything about it. He peppered John for the better part of an hour, long after the plates were cleared away.

"Look, Andrew," John said finally, "you can't figure all this out in one night. Besides, why worry about it? That's what David's there for. You just worry about your part, and what happens after."

"After the record's made, you mean?"

"Yeah, after it's made, and after it's out—in the stores. That's when the fun starts."

"I really think I've kind of kept that part of it out of my mind for some reason," Andrew said. "I'm not sure why. It seems like the great unknown—what to do once this part is over, I mean. It's just been much easier to concentrate on this right now. But I know that inevitably, it's all leading somewhere."

"To the top, hopefully."

"To the top," Andrew repeated thoughtfully. He had no

idea what that meant. But he knew that he wanted to make a difference in people's lives.

"Look, John," he said, "I have to keep in the front of my mind the fact that I want to minister. That's what's driving me forward through all this. I want to tell people about the Lord. I can never, ever let go of that. Sometimes it gets confusing when we talk about the career stuff because it kind of takes over everything. Sometimes I go a couple of days without even thinking about ministry. I don't mean to, but there's just so many things crowding into the picture right now. I really don't want that to happen."

Van Grimes looked Andrew over carefully. He had to expect this, he supposed, from time to time. And he respected the kid's sincerity. It was good to know that there was a bottom line for him.

"Andrew, I can honestly say that I wouldn't be interested in this thing if it wasn't for your single-mindedness. I love it—it makes me believe in what we're doing together. It makes me want to make all this happen even bigger, knowing that I'm creating a platform for you to share the gospel. Keep in mind that that's what we're doing here: creating a platform. No platform, no ministry. Understand?"

"I guess that makes sense. Are you saying that bringing all these forces to bear on the record and the rest of it is really a vehicle to express the gospel? Because I think I need to hear that again."

"That's what it's all about, Andrew. Now, I never tried to hide from you that we're running a business, as well. Try to keep one thing in mind: the money that the records and concerts and T-shirts and everything else brings in is the very money that makes the ministry possible. It takes money, man. Look at the televangelists, Andrew. They have to ask for money, beg for it. It's all tears and gnashing of teeth. What we're doing is much more honest than that. We're selling a product. People voluntarily pay money for it, and get exactly what they paid for—not some trumped up Malaysian-made tin prayer cross. That stuff turns my stomach."

"I guess that stuff never really rang true for me, either."

"Okay, then. Stop worrying about it, Andrew. This is a straight up and down situation. It's business. It's ministry. It's the business of ministry. Clear?"

Andrew thought he was clear until van Grimes's last statement. But he was too tired to think it through just now. The exhilaration of the day had slowly released him, and he felt he was reentering the real world at last. Gradually, he began to remember something very important, something he was supposed to do after the session. With a start, it came to him.

"What time is it?" he asked, feeling panicked.

"Uh, let's see. About ten 'til one."

Andrew slumped in the seat.

"Oh, no," he said dejectedly. "I was supposed to call Carolyn after we finished at the studio. I promised. I know she was waiting for the call."

"Already got you on the short chain, huh?" Van Grimes laughed. "Don't worry. I'm sure she'll understand. She knows the score."

Andrew looked up, irritated, both with himself and with John. "It wasn't like that, John. She just really wanted to hear how it went. She cared about it. I blew it. I can't believe I could have forgotten it. I just got wrapped up in everything. You think it's too late to call?"

"Yeah, I'd say so. No point in waking her up on top of everything else. Just set your alarm and call her first thing in the morning. It's musicians' hours, Andrew. It's part of it."

"I guess we better get going, anyway."

"Right. We've got another big day tomorrow."

As the two wandered out into the parking lot towards John's car, Carolyn switched off the light on her bedstand and pulled the covers up around herself closely to go to sleep.

11

There were no florists open in Nashville at eight o'clock in the morning, and Andrew knew that in another thirty minutes or so Carolyn would be leaving for work. He didn't have to be back at the studio until ten, but he had dragged himself out of bed early, determined to apologize in person for forgetting to call. He drove up West End toward Carolyn's place, feeling rotten and wondering how he could have been so self-absorbed.

Suddenly, he remembered that grocery stores sometimes sell flowers, and to his relief he passed a large supermarket on the way. He rushed in and bought a large bouquet of pretty carnations and bounded back to the car to hurry on. He looked at his watch. He had ten minutes, and she lived another five minutes away.

Two cars were pulling out of her complex as he was pulling in, and he had to wait an extra moment for the traffic to clear. He drove into one of the empty spaces, grabbed the flowers, and took the stairs to her upstairs apartment two at a time. At last, he stood before her door. Her car was still in its space, so he knew she was still there. What her frame of mind was, he didn't know. He ran over his apology one more time, as dissatisfied with it as he had been every other time. It all came down to excuses, and he had learned from Franklin at a very young age that excuses and fifty cents got you coffee. Nevertheless, some explanation was in order, and he took a deep breath and knocked softly on the door.

He had to knock again before Carolyn answered. The door opened, and she stood with a cup of coffee in one hand, pulling the last two curlers from her hair with the other. Andrew tried to get a reading on her mood, but she turned away and said over her shoulder, "Come on in. I'm just about to walk out the door."

Andrew stepped into the apartment and followed her into the kitchen. She set down the cup and turned toward him, her face impossible to read. He didn't really know how serious not calling was to her, but he knew he wanted to clear the air before it got any worse.

"Carolyn," he said, "I'm sorry about last night. Really sorry. That's exactly the kind of thing I don't want to start happening, you know? Getting too busy for each other."

"Is that what it was?" she asked. Her voice was neutral and offered no clue to her mood. Nevertheless, Andrew relaxed a bit, noting that there didn't seem to be any reproof in it.

"Before I explain anything," he said, "I want to make sure you understand I'm sorry. That's the important thing, not why I didn't call."

Carolyn allowed a tiny smile. "Okay," she said, "I think I have that. Don't worry, Andrew, you don't have to beg. I just wanted to know how everything went. It was your big day, and I worried about you. The flowers are lovely."

"I know you did. The day just got away from me. We went late, and there seemed something to do every second. Then we went to get something to eat. John and me, I mean. I had a million questions, and suddenly I realized it was too late to call."

Carolyn shook her head. "It's never too late to call, Andrew," she said. "Never."

Andrew moved toward her, and putting his arms around her, hugged her gently.

"I'll remember that."

"Good. Now tell me all about it," she said, "and do it in two minutes."

Andrew sighed. "Impossible. But everything went great. It was the most amazing day of my life."

"Was it really wonderful? What did John and David think?"

"They seemed really happy," Andrew answered. "John seemed to think some moment in music history had happened. Of course, you know John."

Carolyn laughed quietly, releasing him from a bit more of his guilt. "I'm sure he was quite sincere," she said. "I'm sure it was the greatest moment since Beethoven. And I'm happy for you. Don't worry about the phone call. The first day must have been overwhelming."

"I hate John's rule about no guests in the studio the first few days. It seems unnecessary. I wanted you there."

"Me, too. Now, speaking of being too late, I'm going to be late myself if I don't get going. Can we have lunch today? You could tell me everything."

"I'd love that, but I have no idea if we're eating lunch out or not. Yesterday, they brought it in."

"Of course," she said, for the first time letting disappointment creep into her voice. She grabbed her purse and opened the door. "Well, don't worry about it. But you *will* call me tonight, right?"

"Without fail."

He did call. But that day, and in the days that followed, Andrew's time in the studio changed from a glamorous adventure into simple, hard work. David Spenser's approach to recording was a blend of spontaneity and perfectionism, sometimes going for pure emotion, at other times forcing Andrew to sing the same lines over and over, looking for something elusive that Andrew couldn't pinpoint. It was slow going, but little by little the album was taking shape.

Carolyn supported him dutifully, even though the tough schedule meant that their time together was increasingly rationed. It was hard on her, and she often felt that she came last behind the many demands of John, the staff at Dove, and making the record. The tight release schedule meant every day was important; often, after waiting patiently for him, the Andrew she spent time with was tired and emotionally drained. In her head she understood that this was merely a part of his life now, and she rarely complained. But it was no use pretending it wasn't a loss. It had only been a few weeks since Andrew had arrived, but already he seemed vaguely older, more experienced; it was oddly disconcerting to steal a few minutes with him, exhausted after hours in the studio, talking about trying to get the right vocal or struggling with another musician on a song. Increasingly, she felt protective of him, wanting to slow things down, give him a chance to adapt. But the forces converging on him were demanding, and as John's employee she could hardly insist that the schedule be slowed to accommodate her private desires. All the same, she often found herself regarding Andrew closely, mentally comparing him as time went on with the boy she met at the airport such a short time ago, the boy with the gift.

Even while the recording process was continuing, the marketing plan for "Lost Without You" was quickly emerging at Dove. Helen, the publicist at Dove, had already scheduled several interviews for Andrew, beginning the very next week. But first, looming like a dentist's drill, was the photo shoot for the album cover.

Andrew dreaded the shoot. He had never considered himself photogenic and had always tried to avoid being photographed. He had spent considerable effort dodging even school yearbook pictures as a child, his father at last walking him directly into the room where the school photographer lay in wait, hiding behind bright lights and reflective umbrellas. Andrew, perched high on a stool in a suit one size too small, would plaster something between a smile and a grimace on his face until the explosion of light released him back into the real world. When the annual was published, he felt that he couldn't possibly be the creature sheepishly grinning back at him from the page. The idea that soon his photograph would be seen in record stores all over America was something that he had not permitted himself to fully embrace.

On the day of the shoot, Andrew rose, feeling gargoyle-like, a monster being led to a brightly lit sacrifice. He washed his hair and stepped into some jeans and a shirt. John had told him not to worry about his clothes. Mickey Lyles, the photographer, would supply the wardrobe.

On the way to the shoot Andrew drove over to John's office and picked up Carolyn. Over the last few weeks John had supported their relationship, assigning Carolyn whenever he was unavailable to help Andrew through any uncomfortable situation. After work she had become a fixture during the long days of recording, bringing in dinner when time didn't allow a real break or pulling Andrew out for a drive when he felt he could sing no longer.

Carolyn was bubbly and excited as they drove to the photographer's studio, showing none of the dread that gnawed at Andrew. She was wearing an off-white top that flowed over her, draping her shoulders and reaching down to the top of her thighs. Tight pale blue leggings and shoes of the same color completed her outfit. Andrew couldn't help feeling that it should be her photo session they were driving to.

"Take my place?" he offered as they turned toward the studio. Carolyn put her hand on his shoulder and leaned over to peck him lightly on the cheek. She felt she knew what he was going through, and she was determined to support him through it. She wanted to catch him when he wavered, to put up her arms and steady him, enabling him to do what he had to do. She couldn't hide her pleasure that he came to her first when he needed someone, and she was coming to believe that she had a kind of magic touch with him. She felt lucky, wanting to savor the events they were sharing these days. She and Andrew were clearly boyfriend and girlfriend now, snatching every possible moment together whenever his schedule permitted. How many girls, she wondered, had ever driven with their boyfriends to a photo shoot for his album cover? She was happy and made no attempt to hide it. But she knew what Andrew needed to hear.

Looking into his eyes, she repeated the question she always asked when Andrew needed support. It was a question turned into a statement, and it had become a kind of lovely shorthand between them, a secret code that communicated much more than the words themselves. It was the phrase she had used when she called Andrew on the morning of his first recording session, and they had shared it many times since then.

"Are you listening to me, Andrew Miracle," she asked, always the same words. "Are you listening very carefully?"

Andrew knew what she meant. It was like the first line of a song, and completing the verse wasn't necessary. "Are you listening, Andrew Miracle?" she would whisper when she kissed him, willing him to hear with his body. Then he would bury his hands in her long, brunette hair and say it back to her, tracing her face with his fingers, memorizing her mouth, her eyebrows, the underside of her jaw.

"Are you listening?" they repeated to each other, taking comfort in their shared secret.

Andrew relaxed, and exhaled deeply. He took one more deep breath and opened the car door. Carolyn smiled, loving her influence on him, her ability to draw him out when he needed it.

"It's good to have you here, Carolyn," Andrew said as they walked toward the front door. "You ought to give lessons." She squeezed his hand, and he opened the door to the studio.

The entrance opened up into a large, warehouse-type

room with high ceilings and gray, industrial walls. Rows of oversized round lights were aligned on ceiling tracks, and a small army of movable floor lights and reflective surfaces were scattered in various positions around the room. Supplies of various kinds were stacked against the walls: curtains of many colors hanging in a row, stacked plywood, carpentry tools, lighting trusses. This was clearly a room in which work was done. No accoutrements of luxury softened it in any way.

They watched in silence while Mickey worked for a few seconds, letting him continue to prepare the set for the shoot. He was a little man, full of artistic energy that seemed to flow out from him in every direction. His hair was cut short, and a few lines in his face showed he acted younger than he really was. He looked like some middle-aged haute couture schoolboy. He wore tight black jeans, a black T-shirt, and a black, ragged jacket.

Mickey had a reputation for being the best in the business, and he clearly relished it. There was just a trace of effeminacy in his manner, but he commanded his helpers with military directness. He viewed his studio as a kind of fiefdom, a shrine erected to his work. When he spotted Andrew and Carolyn, he bustled over to them, taking several steps more than the distance seemed to require.

"Ah," he murmured, "the star has arrived." He stood back, taking Andrew in. "How beautiful he is." Andrew wanted to crawl in between any two cracks he could find in the floor. Of all possible fussings-over, he realized, today's would surely be the most microscopic and prolonged.

Andrew introduced himself and Carolyn, and Mickey responded by announcing, "I am Mickey," as if resolving a mystery the world had been struggling with for some time.

"Come," he continued, "we will sit down, no? I have a table for this. Do you drink coffee? I have coffee, you see." The three sat down, and Mickey poured coffee into three tiny china cups.

"I have seen your picture, of course. In my meetings at Dove." He was looking at Andrew like a chef admiring a loin, wondering what lovely sauce would bring it to life. "But now I see you in person." He had the habit of saying out loud whatever he was doing, as if to add emphasis to his actions.

"The people at Dove were a little vague about the details of what we were going to do, Mr. Lyles," Andrew said. "I wonder if you could tell us where we're headed with this."

Mickey smiled indulgently at his subject. "You are concerned," he said.

"Yes. I don't really like having my picture taken," Andrew admitted.

"Come. While you are made up, we will discuss."

Mickey rose, and extended a hand to each of them. Carolyn took one lightly, but Andrew stared at the other a moment, and seeing no alternative, took it. To his utter astonishment, he found himself being led by the hand, gliding across the studio floor to a brightly lit makeup area.

With Andrew ensconced in the low-backed chair, the makeup artist went to work on him. Later, he couldn't remember what the woman looked like. His eyes were closed in terror almost the entire time. Then, out of his self-imposed darkness, he heard Mickey's voice.

"Now. You must tell Mickey what you are thinking."

"I'm thinking, Mickey, about how much I wish I was skipping rocks on the lake back home. I'm thinking that I wish I was taking your picture instead, so that the folks back in Kansas could actually believe this was happening to me."

Mickey laughed musically, like a chime, and said, "You find this experience unusual?"

"Yes."

Mickey assumed a thoughtful pose, although Andrew didn't see it through his tightly clenched eyelids. The makeup artist was still carefully brushing powder onto his face.

"You are right," Mickey replied firmly. "Mickey's job is . . . unusual. I must present to the world Andrew Miracle. I must tell a story about him, in one photograph. I must reveal the inner man. I must expose his soul." He gazed lovingly at his subject. "And above all else, I must make the person pick up the record cover and want to take Andrew home with them." He reached out and brushed a hair off Andrew's face. "Now, tell Mickey who is Andrew Miracle."

Andrew felt this was a good question, one he needed to be able to answer. After a moment, he said, "I'm a minister." For some reason, he felt self-conscious about saying this to Mickey. But he went on, and added, "My music ministers to people. In a way, it's not really about me. It's about what I'm singing about. The Person I'm singing about, actually." Suddenly, he opened his eyes. "I have it!" he exclaimed.

"Andrew has what?" Mickey asked doubtfully.

"Put a picture of Jesus on the album cover!"

Mickey took two short steps back, and Andrew heard the sound of makeup containers clattering noisily to the floor. It echoed in the large, open room and ended in a sudden stillness. "Mickey doesn't know how to photograph God," he said slowly.

"It was just an idea."

"Now Andrew will look," Mickey commanded. He rotated the chair so Andrew could see himself clearly in the mirror. Andrew blinked. He looked better. He looked a lot better. He couldn't help smiling, he looked so much better. His hair, which had grown considerably longer since he moved to Nashville, seemed to have been injected with life. His face was perfectly smooth and shadowless. Every line from the sun was erased, and for the first time, he noticed that he had cheekbones. His eyes seemed inexplicably larger and brighter. He glanced gratefully at the makeup artist, who simply said, "You're welcome," and glided away.

"You are the star," Mickey said. "You must look like the

star. That is the first principle. You may be many things after, but first you must be the star."

He reached out and once again took Andrew by the hand. "Now you will dress."

Mickey led him over to a portable stand where several outfits were hanging. He took a pair of loose-fitting teal pants and a shirt the same color off their hangers, and handed them to Andrew. He motioned Andrew behind a screen to change. Andrew stepped behind it, stripped off his blue jeans, and stepped into the clothes Mickey had picked out. The fabric was something he had never felt before, a kind of cotton that was somehow shapeless. The pants fit well around the waist but then trailed more loosely down over his legs than the fit he was accustomed to. There was no belt, and the shirt was of a similar, but lighter weight material.

Andrew stepped gingerly from behind the screen, unsure of himself. Mickey cooed his approval in a voice two notes higher than is perfectly safe in Butler County, Kansas. Andrew looked at Carolyn hopefully, and she was beaming back at him.

"Now, I will finish you," Mickey said.

He pulled a jacket off its hanger, and raising Andrew's arm, slipped it on him. It was a remarkable garment, made of a magnificent light fabric that Andrew had never seen. It was the same color as the pants and shirt, but had a striking beige geometrical design on the front, repeated in miniature on the sleeves. Like the pants, it was quite loose-fitting. At the waist, however, it tapered in noticeably and actually hugged his hips. There was no simple way to describe it other than to say that it was the coat of a star. Mickey reached up and fastened the top button around Andrew's neck.

"Now you are blue, blue like the sky," he said. "You are Andrew Miracle of the blue sky."

Carolyn clapped her hands with pleasure and exclaimed, "You look fantastic! How do you like it, Andrew?"

Andrew looked down at his clothing. "I look like a Popsicle."

Mickey gave Andrew a sharp look and said, "Come. You will see." He led Andrew up two : _ps onto a dimly lit stage, and called to an assistant. "Alexis! Turn on the fan. And Mickey needs a mirror. The big one."

A tall, striking woman picked up a full-length mirror on a stand and set it up a few feet in front of Andrew. Then, she turned on a small fan, and aimed it at Andrew's face. It moved the air gently, and felt like a cool summer breeze. He felt it softly moving his hair, animating the scene. The other two assistants, both young men of roughly college age, approached, conscious that the session was about to begin in earnest. They stationed themselves by the lights, and Alexis retreated to a large control box on the floor off to the side of the stage. The room fell silent. Mickey dramatically backed away from the stage, facing Andrew and holding his eyes as he did so. Then he said triumphantly, "Now!"

With that, Alexis threw a large switch and Andrew was instantly bathed in impossibly bright light. He retreated a moment, blinking, shocked with surprise that he was suddenly standing in a pool of brilliance that exceeded sunshine on a clear day. The world became shadowless, illuminated, and microscopically revealed. The people around him became invisible, lost in the circle of darkness that the light shining on him created. He looked for Carolyn, squinting his eyes and peering, but she, too, was gone, and he could see nothing but the brilliant lights focused on him.

Mickey drifted slowly forward, turning his head slightly from side to side. "Look," he murmured, "now Andrew will look."

Andrew glanced away from the lights, letting his eyes gradually adjust to the brightness. Then he turned his face directly toward the mirror and gazed full into his own reflection.

He was shimmering in the light, remade, a figure floating in the atmosphere of the beige backdrop. He seemed to have stepped out of a novel directly into the picture, bringing a substantial history along with him. The clothing flattered an already good body, and the fan moved his hair and clothing gently, as if he were standing on a beach. Above all, he looked like a man with a story, a story of seeking and of losing. He looked like Andrew, only romantically perfected, and unattainable.

It was hard for Andrew not to imagine how delightful it would be to have a picture of himself like this in his hand, something to look at and perhaps to send to one or two young women he had known in what he called his real life. He turned slightly, self-consciously, looking at himself from different angles. He wished he could be alone with the mirror, letting himself believe he really looked like that. But he felt hurried, knowing he was being watched.

"What do you think, Carolyn?" he asked, to the darkness.

After a moment of silence, her voice came answering back, "I know I want to take you home with me, if that's what Mickey was trying to do. I think you look beautiful."

"Well, I guess if I were rich, lived in a big city, had about a million girlfriends, traveled to Europe frequently, and had never seen the inside of a barn, this is about what I'd want to look like," Andrew mused.

The form of Mickey's face gradually appeared, fading in from out of the darkness as he walked forward toward the stage.

"Andrew's soul does not live in a barn," he said, looking up intently at his creation. "It does not even want to spend one night in a stable with dirty animals." He was clearly visible now, standing just at the edge of the stage. "No one will want to pick you up and take you home, if you look like you came from a barn. Smelly donkeys, and sheep."

Mickey launched himself up the short steps onto the stage, and brandished a light meter at Andrew. He slowly advanced, staring at the needle as he moved closer. At last, he was holding it mere inches from Andrew's face, measuring the light, the perfection of its coverage. He painstakingly took readings of every surface. Andrew flinched backward with astonishment as Mickey waved the meter back and forth under his nose, but Mickey only muttered, "Shadows," and kept on, searching out some dark spot. But it seemed at last that there was nothing to be done, no blemish to be chased away, and after a moment he shouted, "Alexis! Bring me the Polaroid."

Andrew looked surprised, but Mickey said, "First we take the pictures with the instant camera to check for light. Mickey is too expensive to hire twice if there are mistakes." He began to take picture after picture, moving from one place to another around the stage. He circled Andrew, ripping off the film as it emerged from the camera, Alexis obediently picking up the film from the floor. After several shots, he retreated to see the developed prints. Alexis padded silently behind, towering over him like a perfect, pet giraffe.

Mickey hovered at a table for several minutes and then pronounced the lighting perfect. His own internal enthusiasm seemed to increase another notch, and he hurried back over to the stage. He clambered up the two steps and wagged the photos in front of Andrew triumphantly, like a lawyer before a jury.

"Mickey's work," he exulted.

Andrew picked out a picture cautiously, holding it at arm's length. Even after the mirror, he genuinely feared what he would find there, half-expecting to see a grinning nine-year-old boy wearing a bad suit, mocking all their efforts. But Mickey had earned his money that day. The face looking back at him fulfilled in every way the promise of his reflection.

"Can I have this?" Andrew asked softly.

"It is Mickey's gift."

With that, he spun around and, looking at his assistants, asked, "We are ready?" They nodded silently, and one of them rolled forward a cart covered with large cameras and lenses. Mickey approached it like a doctor preparing to select utensils for surgery. He picked up a camera, much larger than Andrew had ever seen, and turned on his heel to face Andrew.

"Magic time," Mickey breathed.

The next four hours were not at all the living nightmare that Andrew had expected. Mickey proved to be a master at bringing him out, cajoling, pleading, tricking, and seducing. At times, Andrew felt like he was sitting on Santa's lap, watching an elf shake jingle bells at him. At other times, the photographer would suddenly grow taciturn, and shake a stubby, reproachful finger at him. Sometimes he almost whispered, and Andrew had to lean in to hear him. He was spinning a story, and for a few glorious, electrifying moments, Andrew could actually believe he was the beautiful, mysterious, unapproachable creation that Mickey was describing.

Gradually, he began to realize that for Mickey's purposes there was no good or bad emotion. There was only impact and attitude. Mickey could use them all, and create a story out of thin air with them.

"You are uncomfortable," he would say, watching Andrew try to pose in an unusual way. "You are afraid. Show me. Use it."

Mickey prodded and sweet-talked the whole afternoon until finally Andrew was beginning to have trouble concentrating. Mickey sensed the change in Andrew instantly, and abruptly ended the session.

"The star is tired," he said. "Mickey has everything he needs." For a moment, Andrew was unsure what this meant, but when he saw Alexis pushing the cart off into the dark background of the room, he slumped down onto a chair in exhaustion. Like a marathoner, he had kept fatigue at bay for the race, but now it had ended, and his body demanded its due. He had felt more tired than this before—ten hours in the fields were far more physically demanding—but this was different. It was a fatigue of the mind, even beyond. Carolyn, whom Mickey had kept decidedly in the background during the shoot, knelt beside him and rubbed his neck.

"You were great," she said. "How do you feel?"

"Don't know," he answered in a tired voice. "Sort of like something on a microscope slide, or maybe an animal in the zoo. I feel—weird. But I lived."

Mickey bustled up, and pulling him to his feet, embraced him. A full six inches taller, Andrew had to bend over or risk smashing Mickey's nose into his chest. Mickey seemed curiously emotional; he acted as if a short-lived but intense love affair was reaching a bittersweet but inevitable conclusion.

For all Mickey's idiosyncrasies, Andrew had to admit that he knew his business. After seeing the Polaroids, Andrew had no doubt that the quality of the final product would be compelling, if nothing else.

In spite of his exhaustion, he was anxious to get out of the clothes for the shoot, and he dragged himself behind the screen to change. The clothes were drenched in sweat, and they hung like lead on their hangers. Andrew stood a moment, shoulders slumped, in stocking feet and underwear, and looked back at them, hanging heavy and lifeless. He turned and pulled on his comfortable blue jeans and shirt. There was a mirror in the changing area, and he looked at himself, in his own clothes now but still made up, his metamorphosis half undone.

He stepped out from behind the screen and searched for Carolyn; she was far away, conferring with Mickey. He hurried over to her. Suddenly, he found that he wanted to leave the studio as soon as possible. He hated to see them together for some reason.

"You can tell John that the proofs will be sent to Dove in about four days," Mickey said as he approached. Mickey acknowledged Andrew and added, "The star has done well. All went very, very well. You will see."

Carolyn ran her arm through Andrew's and said, "Thank you for everything, Mickey. We'd better go. I'm sure Andrew would like to get some rest."

It was clear some response was required of Andrew as well, but he found it curiously hard to speak. In the end, he just stuck out his hand and shook Mickey's self-consciously. Mickey walked them over to the door and held it open for them, and they passed back out into the late afternoon sunlight of the real world.

"Well, that's over," Carolyn said, the door closing behind them. "What do you feel like doing?"

Andrew thought for a moment, and said, "I feel like I need a shower." But even as he said so, he fingered the Polaroid photograph in his pocket, the one that Mickey had taken in the bright light.

12

V an Grimes sat in his leather office chair, staring mood- ily at his appointment book. Scribbled in for lunch that day at twelve-thirty was Harold Murphy's name. John thought, *if it weren't for lunches, the whole music industry would grind to a halt*.

It was nearly noon, and his stomach was churning. But eating was the last thing on his mind. Andrew's record was coming along fine—better than fine, in fact. David Spenser had justified his exorbitant fees by producing a record that would certainly create a splash in the marketplace and es- tablish Andrew as an artist to be taken seriously. It was so good, in fact, that the team had begun to dare to think bigger: Harold had taken the project to Michael Thomasson at Atlantic for a first hearing, and John knew his own future and Andrew's hung on the results of that meeting. From the beginning, they had harbored the dream that Atlantic could be brought on board to market Andrew to the world. Now they were on the verge of discovering if that dream could be a reality. If Atlantic passed on the project, they had themselves a gospel act that, at best, would generate a considerable but certainly finite sum of money. If, however, Thomasson decided that Andrew was a golden boy with crossover potential, the lives of everyone involved could change forever.

Van Grimes was well aware of the great wall between gospel and pop, and he knew as well that it was slowly coming down. The moment for a new, positive voice to emerge was now, and timing was everything in this business. For the first time in years, every major pop label was sniffing around, looking for a viable crossover act to take from contemporary Christian to the mainstream. The labels were worried that people might have finally had their fill of the dark, thrashy bands that had generated so many millions of dollars for them in the eighties. The baby boomers were growing up, and the big companies were hungry, anxious to stay ahead of the trend, and in an acquiring mood. There might never be a more fortuitous time, and John van Grimes was poised with one golden bullet: Andrew Miracle.

He reminded himself of rule number one in the industry: power flowed to the hot. It took only one successful pop act to anchor a management agency, and attracting other, more established acts would be possible only if Andrew was successful. He had no illusions—the way things stood, no major artists would even consider signing with him. He knew the big wheels in town that didn't bother to return his calls, knew every one of them by name and face. He knew the condescending smiles they tossed his way in casual, momentary encounters around town. But if Andrew broke out— that changed everything. It was stunning, sitting there alone in his office, realizing that he was thirty minutes away from finding out if he carried the heat.

There was more than the record to deal with, of course; it remained to be seen if Andrew himself was up to the job. The boy would take some careful handling if he was going to reach his potential. Andrew was a genius, no question, but unpredictable; sometimes he seemed right on target, at other times hesitant, unsophisticated about the realities of the business. Van Grimes thanked his stars for Carolyn—she had a head on her shoulders, and it didn't hurt that Andrew had obviously fallen in love with her. John had to put that down to pure luck, or maybe destiny. He couldn't have planned it better himself, as long as she kept her senses.

Van Grimes glanced at his watch one last time, packed his briefcase, and slipped out the back door of the office to the parking lot behind the building. He didn't feel like small talk just then. Let the secretaries figure out where he went. Whoever might call while he was gone wasn't as important as the meeting he was driving to.

As he drove over to the restaurant to meet Harold, he found himself thinking once again just how messy the music business really was. Such a funny thing, making money with artists. Some of them—he'd seen it from a distance—you could just print money off them. You better believe their managers always got their phone calls returned, my friend. But other artists, you'd nurture them for years and never even get your money back. Messy. Not at all like making ovens or refrigerators. That was so clean, so industrial. But just try to generate a dollar bill out of the artistic temperament. Those boys that dealt in jet planes and widgets would go out of their calculator minds. It was a shame that the artists couldn't somehow be taken out of the loop. Hundreds of thousands of dollars riding on whether or not some kid who doesn't know the first thing about business breaks up with his girlfriend or gets writer's block. It was nuts.

Van Grimes pulled into Faisons, Harold's favorite place for lunch. Harold had already arrived, and van Grimes slipped into the empty chair opposite him, maintaining his cool and projecting, he hoped, nothing but confidence.

Harold shook his hand casually, apparently in good spirits. Underneath his friendly veneer, van Grimes watched him carefully, reading him for signs of how the Thomasson meeting had gone. It was bad form to bring up the subject himself, he knew. Rule number two: never look too eager. Eager meant you needed it, and if you needed it, you weren't hot. Play the fiction, baby. It's deal-making time.

Harold chatted, enjoying himself, well aware that Van Grimes was about to choke on his anticipation. He perused the menu meticulously, even though he knew he would order his usual just like at every other late afternoon lunch he had there. This was too much fun to hurry.

Van Grimes took his time ordering as well, determined to

match Harold minute for minute in the waiting game. But when the food actually came and nothing had been said about the meeting, he cracked.

"So tell me how it went with Thomasson," he said as casually as possible. He prayed he wouldn't begin to sweat. Harold leaned back in his chair, smiling. He had won the first round of the game.

"I believe I may have some very exciting news on that score, John. It's very possible."

Van Grimes was trying to stay calm, but Harold was infuriating him.

"I see. Is there some reason why you can't tell me now?"

Harold looked placidly at his watch and replied, "In approximately two more minutes, Michael Thomasson will be here, and he can tell you himself."

Van Grimes felt his stomach tighten. "I beg your pardon?"

"Michael is very excited about the project, John. But he is concerned that things be handled, uh, properly. He has some concerns. He felt it would be best if he discussed these with you personally, and I felt confident in telling him that you would be delighted."

Van Grimes took a sip of water, controlling his nerves. He hadn't seen Michael for over four years, ever since Thomasson had begun his dizzying ascent to the pinnacle of Atlantic. Michael had stopped returning his phone calls almost as soon as he had stepped off the elevator of the top floor of the Atlantic building. This would be an interesting meeting. John needed to think. Michael had most of the cards, of course. That was a given. But van Grimes wasn't powerless. He had Andrew. Interesting, indeed.

"He's coming here—to the restaurant?" John asked, his voice silken calm.

"He's coming through the door. Now."

Van Grimes spun around a trifle faster than he would have preferred, betraying himself. Thomasson was heading straight for the table, ignoring the waves of eyes being raised by tables of mid-rung industry people wanting to say hello. Van Grimes was surprised again by how small Thomasson was; it seemed incongruous that so much power could rest on such an unassuming frame. But it only took a glance at his face to see that sitting across a negotiating table from Michael Thomasson was like competing with a hungry leopard for a perfect steak. You were likely to lose.

"Hello, gentlemen," Thomasson said as Harold and John rose to shake his hand. "Nice to see you, John. It's been . . . quite a long time, hasn't it?" John knew what he meant. A long time, and Thomasson had made much better use of it than he had. The game had begun.

A waiter bustled up, smiling effusively. Thomasson waved him off.

"Just bring me a Pelegrino with a twist of lime. Thanks." He took his seat and looked over the two men with falcon's eyes.

"Well, Harold, I trust we can start at the beginning?"

"I have made it clear to John that you are interested, but with reservations."

"Thank you. That is correct. Let me get straight to the point, gentlemen, because I know you are both busy men." Thomasson smiled a thin little smile, letting the irony settle on the table. "Gentlemen, Andrew Miracle is a major star." Van Grimes exhaled audibly. "I am telling you that he is a major star," Thomasson went on. "Mickey's given him a great start on a look, and he writes hits. His voice is very exciting. Very exciting. The decision to use David Spenser as the producer was correct. David is making a record that sounds like money to me."

Van Grimes was astounded. It appeared as though Michael was giving away all his aces before the first hand was played. If Thomasson thought Andrew was a star, then power was flowing away from Atlantic and toward van Grimes. Thomasson would need at the very least to establish a good cooperative relationship with Andrew's management. John decided it was time to speak up.

"That's wonderful news, Michael. I was sure you would see the talent that Andrew has. But Harold says you have some concerns. What's the problem?"

"When I say that Andrew is a star, I am, of course, speaking rhetorically. He is a star if everything works. He is a star if the public makes him one. If the public loves him. And above all, he is a star if Atlantic commits what I conservatively estimate to be something over a half million dollars to make him one." He paused. "That is a great deal of money."

"Yes, it is, Michael," van Grimes breathed.

"I have an obligation to the stockholders of my company to make that kind of investment where it will generate the maximum return. Any other position is immoral and improper."

"Of course, Michael," Harold said. "We understand completely."

"Then I must tell you that I cannot commit a single dollar in that cause until we have a meeting of the minds about Andrew's cooperation."

"Cooperation?" asked John.

"Exactly. I could do a great many things with that half million, gentlemen. I could invest it in any one of the existing bands I now have, bands that are out there working extremely hard to sell records. Bands that have brought in image consultants and acting coaches for their videos. Bands that will do anything, and I mean anything, to be successful. To justify the great faith that we have in them. I assure you that they are a delight to work with."

"So what do you want to hear about Andrew?" asked John.

"Andrew has many talents, and two major problems. One, he has a latent but completely undeveloped sex appeal. There's an energy inside him, and it's magnetic. That must be developed and encouraged. I see his target audience as primarily female, eighteen to thirty-five. Second—and I will respect you both by saying this as plainly as I can—he sings too much about God."

Neither Harold nor John answered for a moment.

"He's a gospel artist, Michael," John ventured at last.

"I know that. And I didn't say, if you will notice, that he can't sing about God at all. God is acceptable. Many of our artists are quite spiritual, and we respect that. I fully understand that Andrew has his own agenda. I have no desire to make him deny that agenda. I respect the fact that there is more to the man than meets the eye. I'd love to have him date my daughter. But before I can invest hundreds of thousands of dollars in him, I must be assured that my agenda will be respected as well. I have nothing against missionaries. But I see no reason for the Atlantic Records Corporation to subsidize one at this time. I propose, there-fore, a compromise."

John sighed, seeing the trap laid out at last. He had been foolish to be lulled into thinking Michael would be easy. A half million was a very large card to play, and it was clear that Michael could walk out of the restaurant without a second thought if he didn't get what he wanted. He had to respect a man like that—a man who had learned the abso-lute power of the word *no*.

"I'm listening, Michael," he said, with unconvincing confi-dence.

"I propose, gentlemen, that at least one of the songs on the album be changed."

Silence settled on the table. Harold was watching both players closely but casually, as if the possibility of establish-ing a major pop star through a Dove-Atlantic alliance was just another lunch meeting for him.

"What do you propose?" asked John. "I should warn you that Andrew is kind of a special case. He's quite sincere about his message. He can be slightly intense about this kind of thing."

"I understand," replied Michael. "The artistic temperament is something to be respected. Atlantic has always been a company that places the utmost value on the integrity of its performers. You are talking about a label that has established some of the most important musical poets of the last twenty years, and we have stood behind some very controversial material in that time. However, I'm proud to say that without exception we refused to let our artists be censored by reactionary forces in the industry, even in those cases where the material was personally offensive to the management of the corporation. We consider artistic integrity to be the cornerstone of our company. Our commitment to the first amendment is inviolate. Nevertheless, I believe there is a possibility that need not violate either of our agendas."

"Which is?"

"I refer to the song, 'Lost Without You.' Andrew has a hit there, a big hit. A career-launching song."

"I was in the room when Michael played it for the Atlantic radio promotion staff," Harold interjected. "John, I could feel them salivating across the room to jump on that song. Their eyes lit up like shiny little cash registers."

"Marvelous," John said, feeling worried. That song was a sort of personal cornerstone for Andrew. He doubted that changes would be very well received.

Michael smiled, completely within himself. "The song is perfect for both of us, with one simple change."

John cringed inside, but kept his face calm. "Which is?"

Michael's expression didn't waver. "I should think it's obvious. Simply remove the word *Jesus*."

For a moment, John sat in stunned silence. Then he heard himself gasp, "From 'Lost Without You'?" He looked helplessly at Harold. "Did you know about this?"

It was the first time John had ever known Harold to be

nonplussed. "No, I didn't," he answered. "I'm not sure what to say about it."

"Gentlemen, I ask you not to overreact about this. There are still plenty of songs left on the album that talk about God, albeit more obliquely."

"Then can't we change one of them?" asked John. His heart was sinking as he imagined trying to explain all this to Andrew.

"Unfortunately, those songs are not the hit that 'Lost Without You' is. They have their charm. But whatever happens, that song must be the first single."

John glanced back at Harold, who was looking down at the table thoughtfully. So much for the little game the two of them had been playing between themselves. A much bigger player had come, and he wanted to change the rules.

Michael sat quietly for a moment, his face implacable. After several seconds, he said, "A little background, gentlemen. I don't know about your world. I do, however, know about mine. There is a fundamental reality at work here, one that a great deal of expensive and ultimately money-losing experimentation has established immutably. Many people have attempted to break this law, only to have their bank accounts smashed upon the philosophical rocks of this truth. There is no sailing against this wind, gentlemen. It is Newtonian. It is mathematical. This law, this truth, can be expressed in one simple, unalterable phrase." He paused, at once engaging both his listeners like a teacher lecturing naive, petulant children.

"The truth, gentlemen, is this: Darkness will never pay money to hear about the Light."

John sat up straight, jolted by the pure simplicity of Thomasson's statement.

"I do not seek to reinvent the wheel here, gentlemen," Thomasson went on. "Although people will not pay money to hear that they are going to hell, they will most certainly pay money to feel good. To be uplifted with a positive message, if you will. And by removing the word *Jesus* from 'Lost Without You,' we have the perfect song for the times."

"But that song is very direct. *Jesus* is in every chorus, and more than once. How can we change it that much? Besides, it's still important to establish Andrew in the gospel market as well. We have to establish his credentials there, also." He turned to Harold. "Or am I losing my mind here? Do you really think we can bring Andrew to the Christian market with a love song as the first single, Harold?"

"Times are changing, John. But I don't know if they've changed that much yet— not for a new artist, anyway. He has a point there, Michael. Dove can't afford to let him be damaged in the Christian market."

Michael pulled a sheet of paper from his coat pocket and smoothed it down onto the table.

"This is the chorus of 'Lost Without You,' with the word *Jesus* deleted," he said. "Permit me to read it out loud to you."

I often feel myself fall
But then I hear you call
And I remember
Yeah, I remember, that I'm

Lost without you
And I've been
Lost without you
And I'd be
Lost without you
I wouldn't know what to do

I finally recognized what's true
That I'm lost
I'm lost without you

"The song works perfectly, either way. Like most great songs, it's meaning is in the eye of the beholder. On pop radio, it's about a relationship. On Christian radio, it's about

God. Believe me men, I wouldn't dream of asking Andrew to *deny* anything. That would backfire, in the end. But the words can mean different things to different people. I think it reflects perfectly on the strength of the song. It's even conceivable to have two versions—one with *Jesus* in and another with it out. A different one for each market."

"No, Michael, I'm afraid that wouldn't be wise," Harold interjected. "Not in our market. They would perceive that as double-minded, even manipulative. It has to go out one way."

"Very well, Harold," Michael replied matter-of-factly. "I defer to your knowledge of your market. Personally, I'm not sure I see the difference between being in the manipulation business and being in the music business. Records are only sold one way, gentlemen. People stand up and sing to throngs of adoring high school girls because of hit songs, image creation, and effective marketing. Those are the rules of the game. To get money from their pockets into our pockets requires that the rules of the game be respected. I respect those rules, and they have treated me well. You may have your own personal agenda, which you desire to follow. Fine. But the rules are stronger than our agendas, gentlemen. Remember: you must respect the rules."

John shuddered involuntarily at the detached logic sitting opposite him. But he had to admit there was a lot of truth in what Michael was saying. It suddenly struck him that here, at last, was a man for whom the music business really was as clean and industrial as the widget business. He had broken it down to its component parts as surely as a physicist—or an economics professor. Thomasson's success, he supposed, was inevitable. And he wanted that success as well, if possible. But his world had yet to become as antiseptically perfected as Thomasson's. He had one inevitable question that had to be posed.

"What if Andrew doesn't see it this way?" he asked. "What if he doesn't agree?"

Michael looked suddenly tired, as if other matters were beginning to press into his immediate consciousness, matters that were far more important. Van Grimes wondered if Thomasson had ever practiced that look in a mirror, honing it to perfect effectiveness.

"I have no doubt that your existing distribution at Dove will accommodate his decision," Michael replied. "I, however, have at my disposal the over thirty-one thousand retail outlets currently serviced by the Atlantic Records Corporation. Placing Andrew Miracle in each and every one of them would be a decisive step, I should imagine, in spreading the word that he so desires to express. That, for him, was after all the point." Michael glanced around, instantly gaining the attention of the waiter and motioning for the check.

"Allow me to get this, gentlemen. I have enjoyed our time together very much, but I fear my schedule calls." He signed the bill, telling the waiter to put it on Atlantic's standing account. The waiter nodded deferentially, and vanished as quickly as he had arrived.

Nice touch, John couldn't help thinking, wondering how many restaurants extended such an arrangement to Atlantic so that Michael Thomasson could exit masterfully.

"I trust I will be hearing from you shortly, Harold. John, it's been lovely to see you again." Michael rose, and Harold and John followed suit. Curiously, however, Michael hesitated before leaving, as if some doubt played in his mind. "I trust there's no misunderstanding, gentlemen," he said. "I have no personal axe to grind regarding Andrew's message. This is strictly numbers. And now, I really must say goodbye."

Thomasson moved purposefully toward the door, not waiting for the other two to follow. Harold and John were left stranded, shaking each other's hands self-consciously, left to retreat into the Nashville sunlight in Michael Thomasson's substantial, razor sharp wake. At the door, Harold patted John on the arm.

"Talk to Andrew, John. I don't like it, but Michael's obviously not going to move on this. He's playing hardball. I'm sorry it turned out like this. I had no idea it was going to go this way. But it makes sense. The song works, and Andrew doesn't have to deny anything about his intention."

"Won't be easy."

"That's why you make the big bucks, buddy."

"Right. Call you."

13

Van Grimes sat in his office carefully considering his options. He had a lot to absorb. A few days after their lunch meeting, Thomasson had sent over an agreement-in-principal with a more detailed explanation of how he conceived the Atlantic-Dove alliance. Thomasson's plan was to let Dove release the album first, generating momentum through the Christian retailers and radio. Atlantic would play a waiting game, seeing how much juice Andrew had on his own. Then, assuming Andrew was moving on his own, Atlantic would weigh in with their power. There would, in effect, be two simultaneous marketing plans: Dove, working in the Christian marketplace, and Atlantic, attempting to break him out into the mass media. Under the agreement each marketing machine would work fairly independently, so Dove still had a considerable responsibility to get the ball rolling and, if Atlantic's attempts were unsuccessful, to give Andrew something to fall back on.

It was all just a pleasant dream, however, if he couldn't cross a tricky bridge with his artist: getting Andrew to change the lyric of "Lost Without You." There was no question that it had to be done. Atlantic had the potential of tripling Andrew's sales. Financially, the results of that would be genuinely life-changing. Success like that came around once, if you were lucky, in a lifetime of hard work.

On the other hand, John faced the very real risk of alienating his artist. He could, if necessary, force the change on Andrew. The contract was quite clear on that—to delete a word from a song was well within van Grimes's legal rights—but Andrew was a passionate young man, and to disenchant him at this early stage could have disastrous consequences. It would have to be handled carefully, sensitively.

Van Grimes rubbed his temples, thinking hard. Everything, absolutely everything, had gone right up to this point. Nothing must upset the forward momentum. Van Grimes sat silently behind his desk for a full twenty minutes, at times fingering the flap on his new briefcase, at other times leaning back, eyes closed, as if asleep. But his mind was clicking behind his closed lids, thinking of the way to handle his talented but potentially volatile artist.

Suddenly, he leaned forward and picked up the phone. He pushed the numbers, waited a moment, and spoke.

"How's the star, Andrew?" he asked, his voice upbeat. "How's the golden throat?" Van Grimes sat listening through Andrew's answers, his face blank. "Great, great. You ate 'em up on your photo shoot, Drew. Uh-huh. No, I'm not kidding. Nah, no way, Drew. Those shots are incredible. You look like a movie star." More listening. "Great, great. No, there's nothing phony at all about them. Can I tell you something? There's nothing spiritual about a bad picture, my friend. You look fantastic. I'd buy the record for the jacket alone. Listen, Drew, I've got a little business to talk over with you, if you've got some time. Can you stop by later? Great. See you then."

Three miles away, Andrew hung up the phone feeling decidedly better. His initial uneasiness over the photo shoot had perhaps been unwarranted. It was so hard to know where his feelings came from. Was he sensing something genuinely important at the photo session, or was it just the old uncomfortableness with himself—with the idea of being photographed? The connection between him and the little crowds at Christ's Kingdom was, he knew, dependent on his total honesty before them. That was the very secret of the gift. There was no way to know how tenuous that connection was. On the other hand, the shoot had been hard, but evidently Mickey knew his stuff. Maybe John was right: if you have to be on an album cover, you might as well look great. He picked up the Polaroid that Mickey had given him at the shoot, smiling in spite of himself. The folks back home would scarcely believe it. Andrew Miracle, looking like a movie star.

Andrew hopped into his borrowed car and drove the short way over to the office. He was enjoying himself; it felt good to know his way around a bit. He was cheerful as he said hello to the girl at the front desk and breezed confidently into van Grimes's office.

John greeted Andrew with the perfect sense of inclusion that he had used so effectively throughout his career. He stood, his face in a broad, affirming smile that seemed to say that Andrew was the most important and delightful thing to have happened to him that day. It delivered a lovely sense of belonging that struck a sensitive chord in Andrew, and he sat down expectantly, like he would with an old friend. John, practicing his art, tiptoed through his usual set of affirmations designed to set Andrew's mind at ease, and after a few minutes, he approached the subject at hand.

"Drew," he said, "I've got some very exciting news." He laughed, a fruity, earthy sound. "It's phenomenal, in fact."

Andrew's reaction to John's statement might have seemed, on the surface, understated, but if so, it was not from any lack of excitement. He was, in fact, tingling, tingling most of the time these days, it seemed. He was at a loss as to what the appropriate response to more good news was, the way that a man might be speechless upon learning he had won the lottery a second time.

"What is it?" he asked after a moment.

Van Grimes smiled. He had to take Andrew down the path from the beginning. "Andrew," he asked, "how much do you know about the Christian music distribution system?"

"Not much, really. Just that it's kind of limited, I guess. Carolyn explained a little."

"She was right on that, my friend. *Limited* is the word. Not in what they do, but in their sheer numbers. There just aren't that many of them. But you and I are about to blow all that away, Drew. Right out of the water. We are about to leapfrog past all that into every record store in the country."

"Wow."

"No kidding. From a ministry standpoint, it's a godsend. I mean what good's a message, if people don't hear about it? Not much, right? So here's the deal. Harold played your album for Michael Thomasson—"

"The vice president at Atlantic," Andrew interrupted.

Van Grimes raised an eyebrow. "Right," he said, his curiosity aroused. *How did Andrew know about Thomasson? The kid was a quick study. Have to file that away, it might be important later.* "You get around town, don't you, pal?" he asked, laughing quietly. "Well, the thing is, Thomasson— that is, Michael—heard your tape. And he loved it."

While van Grimes talked, Andrew was replaying what Carolyn had told him about Thomasson that first night in Nashville. "So what does that mean?" he asked.

"Well, basically, it's an incredible opportunity, the kind that comes around once in a blue moon. It's the chance of a lifetime, really. Here's the long and the short of it: Michael loves your project, and he's prepared to market and distribute the record through Atlantic worldwide. Really push it, like one of his own acts, big-time. Do you realize what that means, Andrew?"

"Not really," Andrew answered truthfully. "I still can't believe that he liked it that much. But I assume that it would be very good to have such a big company behind it."

"Yeah, you could say that. Good would be the word. It means that your record will get more exposure in a week than Dove can give it in six months. I couldn't believe it when I found out! It's so rare, I really think it has to be God."

Andrew perked up. "Really?" he asked. "You think it's God?"

"No question!" van Grimes answered. "Look. You've got to understand how unusual this is. Thomasson is prepared to put the entire weight of Atlantic behind your project, and the result of that kind of support could be enormous." He disliked having to exaggerate like that, knowing that Michael's only solid commitment was to release the album; it remained to be seen exactly how much Atlantic would end up committing to push Andrew. Still, he felt he had to put the best face on things, if only to get Andrew to go along. *You have to push for the top to get to the top*, he reminded himself.

Andrew, to his consternation, felt a host of things, but nothing so much as embarrassed. Was he really that good? After a lifetime of feeling like the odd man out, it was a powerful thing to hear, especially from a person like Michael Thomasson. "Of course, I don't know what to say, John," he began, fearing his face was red and revealing. He longed to be professional, not so naive. "I'm very grateful. The idea that my ministry might be so . . . so large, it just never occurred to me. Never at all. It always seemed remarkable that people just came to the church to hear me play."

"I understand, but that's where I come in. That's what I'm here for, Drew, remember? To dream. There you were, playing in the middle of nowhere and feeling like that was the whole world. But it was only the beginning of much, much bigger things. You're not stuck in small town, U.S.A. anymore. Now dream with me a minute. Your record, in every record store in America. Concerts, with thousands of people there, listening to your message. Awesome, isn't it?"

Andrew had to admit it was a very attractive vision. More than attractive—it was almost overwhelming. The idea of playing at the old folks' home seemed right then about as fascinating as working in a factory. But he wondered something nevertheless, his natural midwestern skepticism coming out in him. "Why does he want to do all that, John?" he asked. "Why is he so interested in me?"

Van Grimes smiled. Things were going well so far, but the rough bit was still ahead. Time to get to the nub. "'Lost

Without You,' Drew," he said. "That's the key. He thinks he can make you a star with that song."

Andrew shook his head. "I just can't get over how everyone seems to be responding to my record, John. Especially that song. It's incredible."

"That's right, Drew. They love your project. But you're right about the importance of that song: Michael made it clear that everything, the whole plan, depends on that one song." He paused a moment, and added, "There's just one problem. He can't use the song as it is right now. He has to have one change to make everything work."

Andrew raised his eyebrows. Van Grimes's last statement had an ominous sound. "What's that?" Andrew asked hesitantly.

Van Grimes smiled. He would answer the question in his own way. "There are many kinds of evangelism, Drew," van Grimes answered. "There's a Billy Graham, in your face, on your knees, kind of evangelism. We need that, certainly. But there's room for a subtler, more low-key kind of evangelism, as well, don't you think?"

"Yes, I do. It doesn't help to beat people over the head with it."

"Exactly. You have to get a relationship going first, you have to get people to want to hear what you have to say."

"Sure. But what about my song?"

Van Grimes breathed deeply. It was now or never. "Well, here's the idea. Thomasson wants to make a change to the lyric of the song, because it's the only way to get the song played on the radio. No change, no way it will work. He's very emphatic about that."

"I see. What's the change?"

Van Grimes spoke his next words calmly, his tone perfectly even. "Michael thinks that the song is too overt—not for himself, mind you, he personally loves it the way it is— but to happen on the radio, we would have to take the word *Jesus* out of the chorus."

Andrew was stunned. "You must be kidding, John. That's—" He frowned. "I don't know what that is."

Van Grimes remained absolutely calm. This response was inevitable. He had expected it. It just needed some damage control. "I know it seems like it, Drew, but think about it. That's all I ask. Will you do that for me?"

Andrew looked at his manager. He didn't like where this conversation was going at all. All the same, John had taken him this far, and he supposed he owed him a hearing. But he had no inclination to change the lyric at this point. "Okay," he said at last. "I don't want to sound disrespectful, but I don't want to change the song, John. I really don't."

"And I respect that. Heck, Michael respects it too. He made a real point of saying that. He went on and on about it. But he made another point, too, and it's a powerful one. In fact, it has no answer. Without the change, the song can't make it to mainstream radio. And without that, he can't bring Atlantic on board. So you see he's got a heck of a point there. And there's something else. Look. You aren't just one song, Andrew. That's too limiting. Your ministry goes beyond 'Lost Without You.' So we get people to listen with that song, and then we zing 'em with the other stuff on the album and in your concerts. Follow me?"

"You mean like some kind of teaser?"

"Yeah, like that."

"I never really considered that song to be a teaser, John. That song is probably the most important thing I ever wrote."

"And I think we're both about to find out why, Drew. Look at it this way: Michael isn't asking us to *deny* anything. Not a thing. The song is still about God, it's just that you aren't saying the *word*. You understand. The meaning is implied. People will hear the song, buy the record, and then they'll understand the whole picture. It's very effective, actually."

"I don't know, John," Andrew replied cautiously. "I understand what you're saying, but something doesn't seem quite right about it."

Van Grimes suddenly took a serious look, and his tone of voice became firm. "Look, Andrew. I don't want you to be unclear about this. Everything depends on the change. The Atlantic shot, the distribution, the whole thing. We're not talking about a small change to your career here. We're talking about a completely different planet."

"I'm not sure why that's so, John," Andrew said earnestly. "Why is it so deadly just to say *Jesus* in the song?"

"Because that word is the trip wire of all trip wires on the radio, my friend. It's like a hand grenade. It's as simple as this: without the change, no airplay, or at least no hit. No hit, no Michael Thomasson. No Michael Thomasson, no half million dollars in marketing. No explosion. No mainstream media exposure. We're left strictly small time."

Andrew started. "Did you say half a million dollars?" he asked incredulously.

"Right, Drew. This is very serious. Michael has committed a half million to bring you, and your message, to the world. Dove can't even touch that." He laughed. "Not even close. That money and power will unlock doors for you that you can't imagine. I think this is the evangelism opportunity of a lifetime if we're just smart enough to see it. I really do."

Andrew looked at his manager thoughtfully. Half a million dollars was more than the entire Miracle farm was worth, much more. He was awed for a moment, considering the incredible amount of money involved and the willingness of a company like Atlantic to wager it on his popularity. It was clear that this was very important to the whole strategy that John had put in place. Suddenly, he felt he needed to know exactly how important. "What's going to happen if we don't do it?" he asked, his voice hesitant.

John grimaced. "There would be a lot of disappointment. It would be devastating, actually. We're talking about, and believe me, this isn't hyperbole, the chance of a lifetime. We could work for years, trying our hearts out, and never make this happen. I'm not exaggerating when I say that there are people all over town that *have* worked years to try and get a chance like this. And it drops in our lap. That's why I say it's God. It has to be. I remember something I heard one time, I think a preacher on TV. 'If it's too good to be true, it's probably God.' I think I see what he meant, now. We've got to seize this."

Andrew sat thinking. "Are you saying that the change will actually *increase* the ministry opportunities?" he asked finally.

"Yes, it will. Look, do you think that only people who go to church need to hear the gospel? Do you realize how small the Christian radio audience is? How about all those other people driving down the street, the ones who wouldn't dream of listening to gospel music? Well, how are you going to reach them? With a gospel song? No way. If we can use this song to bring your music to them, then we are doing a terrific thing. Having a hit record will, conservatively, expand your ministry potential by a factor of ten." He paused, looking at Andrew carefully. "Or we can just blow this and go back to beating our heads against the wall trying to get anything to happen. If that's what you want."

Andrew felt John's change of tone like a blow. He found that he had developed a surprising dependency on van Grimes emotionally, and it was hard to disappoint him. "No, I don't want it to seem that way, John," he answered after a moment. He didn't want to let John down, not after everything he had done for him. "What does Harold say?" he asked.

"Harold is sold out on the idea. Completely."

Andrew sat, considering. At that moment, it seemed ungrateful, even presumptuous to turn down what was, he was learning, something that a lot of people worked a lifetime to get and never attained. He looked up at John, who was regarding him earnestly, with a pleading look. "You're sure this is for the best? I mean in the long run."

"Absolutely."

Andrew sighed. To change the song went against his every inclination. On the other hand, surely these men knew what was best. If Harold wanted it too, then Andrew was the only one who had misgivings. It didn't seem likely that he could be the only one who was right. John was saying that this would give them the chance to reach a whole new group of people, the mass of people beyond the normal reach of gospel music. "I guess what you're saying is that it's a tradeoff of a sort, and that we'll look back on this and see that a lot of doors were opened by it."

"Exactly."

Andrew sat, still struggling. "I don't know, John. I can't get a handle on this, somehow."

"Then let me simplify it. If we make this one simple accommodation, then all of our lives have the potential of changing incredibly. If we don't, then we're stuck where we are. And one last thing: chances like this don't come around twice. It's now or never, Drew."

Andrew rubbed his temples. After a long moment, he sighed again, more deeply. "All that you say can happen with this one compromise?"

"Just this one."

Andrew sighed. "Then let's go ahead, if that's what you want."

Van Grimes literally jumped from his seat and clapped his hands. Andrew flinched in his chair, but looked up to see a sparkling van Grimes, beaming down at him. It felt good to see John so happy, and he felt he must be doing the right thing.

"Great, Andrew. I'm so glad we came to terms on this. Now, I've got phone calls to make. We're going to make you a star, my friend."

Andrew rose and smiled deferentially. He still got a slightly unnerved feeling when his name and the word *star* were used in the same sentence. It seemed incongruous.

But he would have been a liar to pretend it didn't feel good. He felt the weight of a thousand real and imagined rejections lift from him as he thought of it. Andrew Miracle. Star.

When Andrew had left, van Grimes pushed the speed dial to call Harold. When Harold answered, John spoke words of almost surreal beauty to him, words of power. It was no exaggeration to say that they opened the door to a whole new life for him. "Green light," he said, exulting. "Andrew said yes."

14

Harold opened the door to the company conference room with purpose. Noting that all the others were in their places, he nodded a quick hello to the group at large and took his seat at the head of a long, rectangular table. The weekly Monday morning staff meeting was about to commence, and today he had a vision to sell. He planned on selling it well. Laurence, he noted with a smile, was sitting blandly in his chair as always, anxious for the meeting to be over before it had even begun. Laurence hated these bull sessions, wanting to get to the bottom line as quickly as possible. He was a chart and graph man, not a process man. But Harold loved the *sturm und drang* of revving up the corps for a big push. He could have been, with his stocky build and bull-headed energy, a successful football coach. Miraculously, he had found himself in the music business, and he was making the most of it. He loved putting plans together, talking about possibilities, and generally acting like the visionary head of a record company. As one of the two guiding lights of the company, he could have the floor whenever he wanted it, and he wanted it often.

He looked down the long table at the team he had assembled to make Dove run. They were young, ambitious, and capable. Like most good employees, they had two speeds. They could do what they were told, or they could put their hearts and souls into their work and the sparks could fly. This time, he needed their creative heat turned up to the maximum. He needed their personal commitment to make Andrew big. If he could get them as excited about "Lost Without You" as he was, that would be a head start on the flashy beginning to Andrew's career he had in mind. He sat silently, letting the murmuring of the others die down, waiting until the focus of each person was appropriately centered on him. When every face was turned expectantly toward his, he began. His approach, he decided, would be direct.

"Ladies and gentlemen," he said to the still room, "I have an announcement to make." He paused dramatically. "I believe that Dove Records is sitting on one of the biggest projects in the history of Christian music."

There was a slight stir in the room as the staff took in his opening statement. Even for those inured to hype, this was a bold beginning. Harold looked around for a moment, reading their faces, letting the opening fireworks fall to earth.

"Last night, at Emerald Sound Studios, I heard the final mixes of Andrew Miracle's record." He held up a small tape. "In my hand, ladies and gentlemen, I am holding the future of Dove Records. It's quite possible that I am holding the future of Christian music. As such, I am holding your futures, all our futures, as well." *Nice touch,* he thought to himself. *Always get the team to feel a sense of ownership.* He leaned back in his chair, and delivered his next comments in a gentler, more confidential tone.

"First of all, I confess that I owe you all a small apology. As you know, I haven't made rough mixes of this project available to you as the record progressed. That's unusual, because I depend so much on you all to be excited about our projects throughout their birthing process. From the beginning, this whole thing has been clothed in secrecy, and I hope you haven't grown too impatient as we went along. But I had my reasons for letting this record grow undisturbed. We were creating something delicate, and it needed air to breath. Perhaps, if we're lucky, the cloak and dagger treatment has given it an attractive sense of mystery, and your curiosity has been aroused. But here, in my hand," he continued, waving the tape in the air energetically, "is the payoff, quite literally, to something that I believe can change the course of our company. Here in my hand, ladies and gentlemen, is the first record of a major star." He paused, letting the hopes sink in. Harold knew that stars were the lifeblood of a record company, and the success and failure of each individual rode squarely on the backs of the organization's big sellers. He knew that he was engaging the personal hopes and dreams of everyone in the room by presenting the project as a blockbuster waiting to happen. Slowly, he turned the tape over and over in his hand.

"So, here it is. Andrew Miracle, 'Lost Without You.' The new record from Dove. Ladies and gentlemen, meet the music of Andrew Miracle."

Reaching behind him, he put the tape in the high-powered stereo system installed in the conference room and pushed *play*. Five seconds of silence passed, and then the emotional introduction to "Lost Without You" poured into the room like a beautiful freight train. Harold stepped aside and let the music wash over his team and do its own selling. He watched their faces confidently, and as Andrew's voice began, he could clearly see the staff's enchantment. When the chorus hit for the first time, there was actually applause. By the end of the song, everyone in the room knew it was a career-maker. Harold reached around and stopped the tape.

"I think you all see what I mean," he said. "'Lost Without You' will launch this project into the stratosphere. When that song comes out there is going to be a major buzz on the street about Andrew. People are going to wonder who he is. I want there to be an answer, ladies and gentlemen. That answer is your job.

"When you return to your desks, you will each find a final copy of the entire recording waiting for you, wrapped in gold foil. It's wrapped in gold because I want this record to achieve gold sales status faster than any record in the history of Christian music. Five hundred thousand sales on a new artist. That's our challenge—pulling together to make sure that the momentum that this song creates is turned into a steamroller of sales. I want Andrew Miracle to be the name on the lips of everybody who buys Christian music, and on a lot more besides." At that, he rose from his seat, and with every eye following him, he began pacing slowly around the table.

"Today, ladies and gentlemen, I am introducing you to this artist, this monumental success story waiting to happen called Andrew Miracle. Now you must start in motion the plans that will introduce him to a waiting market." Once again he held up the tape, shaking it in front of them. "So how will we do it? How will we turn this piece of plastic and acetate into the future of our company? That is the question which you must answer." Every eye was fixed expectantly on Harold, but he merely continued pacing, letting their anticipation accumulate.

"What's wrong with the Christian marketplace today?" he asked suddenly, gesturing upward in a curious, spiking motion. "What's wrong with it is that it's saturated with product that is dry and passionless. But an Andrew Miracle is passionate. The Christian marketplace is saturated with records that all sound alike. An Andrew Miracle is different. The marketplace is saturated with people trying to be sophisticated. An Andrew Miracle is rough around the edges. The marketplace is saturated with product that is predictable. Andrew Miracle is a creative time bomb. He will explode onto the scene because he is what people unconsciously are waiting for. He's unpredictable, he's powerful, and most of all, there's something burning inside him." He had arrived once again at the head of the table, and turning to face the staff, he engaged them all directly.

"I want us all to catch fire, ladies and gentlemen."

With that Harold sat down, his back erect, and laid his hands flat down onto the table.

"The release party for Andrew's record is November first. That's four weeks from today." He turned to Helen Naismith, the publicity director for Dove. "I want to be sure that the press is here en masse, Helen. We know that Andrew is big. We need to convince the rest of the world that he's big. I want a big spread laid out, everything at least one level up from what we normally do. As soon as anyone walks in the door, I want them to feel that this is special, and that we're very serious about Andrew. I want to see all the Christian music press here, but I want to work on the secular press, too." At this point, his tone changed to a softer, more confidential one.

"Obviously, this puts a great deal of pressure on Andrew. If he comes off like corn pone, nobody wins. So Helen, make sure that he looks right," he said. "Buy him some clothes. Talk to him about how things will go, so he's not thrown off by it all. Spruce him up, and get him ready. Work with Mark on it."

Mark Haffner was the director of marketing at Dove. More than anyone else, it was his responsibility to draft the details of the plan that would launch Andrew's career. Like Harold, he was small of stature, but where Harold was a stocky bulldog, Mark was slight, like a small reed. His features were almost precious, with high cheekbones and a small, distinct mouth. He lacked Harold's presence, but he was a genius at his job, and creative ideas flowed out of him. He dressed in a style of impeccable, moment-by-moment trendiness.

"Mark," Harold went on, "you've been brought into things more than the others along the way. That's because you're the key guy, here. I want you to make a presentation at the listening party."

Haffner responded in a soft-spoken voice. He realized that thus far, no one other than Harold had spoken a word, and in a strange way he was breaking a silence. "What would you like me to do, Harold?" he asked quietly.

"My idea is this," answered Harold. "When we've got everybody in there, we hit them with something big. Something flashy. I want them to take something away in their minds, something memorable. We're spending too much money on this thing to let them get away with a few hors d'oeuvres and mineral water. Got any ideas?"

"Well, I'm working on the print ads to run in magazines. Maybe we could blow up a couple of them to a huge size, and reveal them in a kind of ceremony."

"Great. I like that. Maximum fanfare."

"Right," said Mark. "Then we could hand out copies of the tape to everyone, packaged with the print ads."

"I like that. And no bio at the party," said Harold. "I want it to look like this guy came out of nowhere—because that's what he did. Build that part of it up—the fact that he's like a streak of lightning from nowhere."

"Except that we hope he lasts a lot longer," added Mark with a smile.

"Yes, a lot longer," Harold nodded. He stood, and addressed the group as a whole. "If there are no other questions, I suggest that you get back to your desks and get to work. You have only a few weeks to make Andrew Miracle look like the star he's going to be."

Mark Haffner wasted no time getting to work on Andrew's project. He was a professional, and he had a job to do. The key was to try to craft an image for Andrew that seemed real to him, had an authentic ring, and connected to people. And, of course, it had to be something Andrew himself could live with and pull off. Plans like this took time, and even more would be needed to get product out after he had completed the creative work. Printers and duplication services all had to be scheduled, and they had to be watched; colors never came back quite right on the first set of proofs, and Haffner had never settled for average work. Within a week a broad sketch had emerged, and he arranged for a meeting with himself, Helen, and Andrew to discuss the project.

Andrew came to the meeting full of curiosity. He had no idea how marketing strategy worked, but he had determined to be cooperative and helpful. Things seemed to have gone well so far, and if there were things he was uncomfortable with, the competency of the team soothed him considerably.

Mark's office was a curious mixture of art nouveau and business center. All the walls were covered in art, much of it in an oddly disturbing, contemporary style. It gave the room a vaguely counterculture atmosphere. The pictures were the kind that Andrew imagined a college art major at a university would have if he could have afforded it. All the same, the desk Mark sat behind seemed perpetually, inexplicably organized. In this and all future meetings, Andrew never saw a paper out of place anywhere in Mark's office.

Mark rose to greet him as he walked in, and Helen entered the room seconds later. Their small talk was affable and short. Helen wanted to know how he liked Nashville, and was particularly interested in Carolyn, but it was really only a few minutes before Mark had led the conversation back to the job at hand.

"Andrew," he began, "I want you to know that I'm personally very excited about working on your project. It's no secret that Dove has a lot on the line with it, and I like that kind of challenge."

"Good," said Andrew. "I appreciate all your hard work. All this seems pretty amazing to me. I had no idea that so much went on behind the scenes."

"That's what we're here for," said Mark. "Now, Helen and I have been working together on some things, and we thought we would run them by you."

"I really think you're going to like this," said Helen intently. "It's coming together."

"Great," said Andrew. "Fire away."

"Well," said Mark, "You're from Kansas, and that's not really a sellable point, per se. On the other hand, being from the country *is* sellable, but unfortunately, you're not a country artist."

Andrew laughed. "No, I'm not. I never really liked that stuff too much. I heard enough of it, though."

"I can imagine. So I kind of hit a brick wall on that. But then, it hit me. Your music is about what's *inside* you. The thing I hear about you over and over is that you've got a fire inside you. Harold calls your music *electric*. You're an artist. You're a poet. You come from nowhere. And nobody knows where your fire is coming from. All we know is that you're burning inside, burning with a message that you have to deliver."

Andrew listened, thinking. Some of what Mark said was true; there were times when he felt a kind of fire inside himself. But he had never thought of actually defining himself that way. It was odd, being the person with the fire inside, because he was also the person with the doubt inside.

"I suppose that's true," he said thoughtfully. "Most of the time, anyway."

"What do you mean, most of the time?" asked Helen.

"Look, guys," answered Andrew. "I mean yes, I have a message. There are times when it really does burn in me. But there are plenty of other times when I'm just some guy who's wondering about things, you know? Some guy who's wondering if what he's doing is the right thing. Believe it or not, that doubt is a part of me, too."

"Yeah, but come on, Andrew," Helen chided. "I mean there's nothing we can do with that. It might be true, but we have to deal with the real world here. I mean what if we put together an ad campaign that said, 'Andrew Miracle, a guy who pretty much believes in what he's doing, but occasionally wonders what it's all about; and sometimes he has a fire burning inside him, but other times he's not sure why he's even trying. Pick up this confused guy's record today.' I mean, be serious."

"Well, what you just said is the truth. You've described me perfectly."

"Andrew," Mark said gently, "I appreciate that you are a multifaceted person. But my responsibility is to present who you are in one image to the public. I do it in one image because I only have one image in which to do it. If record store owners would let me tell a short story about you, I would. But they don't. By the same token, if I could afford to buy four pages of magazine space to explain your nuances, I would do that, too. But in actual fact I have one small square of space in which to interest people in you, and not just a little—I have to interest them in you about fifteen dollars worth. You can say whatever you want, but that's how it works. It's the nature of the beast."

Andrew mulled that over for a moment. "It's hard to say much that's true about a person in one statement," he answered hesitantly. "Except that I'm alive. Most everything else seems to need qualifiers."

"Nonsense," countered Mark emphatically. "I'm not interested in lying about you. I want to tell the truth about you. Surely you can see that I don't have to tell everything about you to make what I do say valid."

That seemed to make sense, and Andrew agreed, "Yes, I can see that."

"Good," said Mark. "That's all I'm saying. Now look at this."

Mark pulled out the mock-up of an ad under a clear, plastic sheet. It was in pieces, and a large portion in the middle was blank.

"What goes there?" asked Andrew, pointing to the blank spot.

"Your picture," said Helen. "We're having it retouched."

"What do you mean?" asked Andrew.

"We had a picture of you that we liked very much," said Mark, "but your hair wasn't quite right. So we're having it fixed."

Andrew wasn't sure which was more stunning, the concept or the technical possibility of doing it in the first place. "You're fixing my hair? How do they do that?"

Helen laughed. "Andrew, we could give you a completely different head of hair if we wanted to, and it would look perfectly natural. Computers are wonderful things."

"So what did they do to my hair?" asked Andrew, his voice a mixture of apprehension and hope.

"A few things," answered Mark. "Little things, but they help. We made it thicker, and we erased from it a few spots where it was out of place. Also, we lightened it a bit because with the dark colors of the ad we're using, a lighter color sort of comes off the page better. It makes you look more alive."

"How alive can I be?"

"Well, a little bit more alive, as it turns out," Mark explained. "Again, these are all minor things, Andrew. They're really just a matter of course. The real question is how you feel about the whole poet, visionary, burning inside thing."

"Yes," echoed Helen, "that's what we want to find out. How *you* feel."

It was an interesting question, especially the way Mark put it. How *did* he feel about the whole poet, visionary, burning inside thing? It was a question not likely to ever be posed inside the confines of Butler County, Kansas. But he wasn't inside those confines anymore. He was inside the confines of the music industry, and here, apparently, those kind of questions needed answers.

"I'm not sure how I feel about it," he ventured thoughtfully. He was feeling unsure of himself, not just because of the ideas that were being discussed, but because he had no desire to appear ungrateful. Mark and Helen were professionals, and they certainly knew what they were doing. It hardly seemed right to criticize their work. On the other hand, he had begun to feel distinctly uncomfortable with the version of himself he was seeing. He began to wonder if there wasn't some unforeseen end to a beginning like this, an ending that would be even more uncomfortable. It seemed that all the perfecting of his image that was going on created a distance between the people who heard his music and the real him. He remembered something his father had said: If you start out lying, you always end up telling more lies just to cover your tracks. His father's words had a way of proving themselves true. On the other hand, this wasn't strictly a *lie*. What Mark and Helen wanted to say about him was, in some sense, true. It just wasn't the whole truth. But perhaps what Mark had said was right: there wasn't any way to tell the whole story in one shot.

"I don't feel like I should be telling you two how to do your jobs," Andrew said after a moment. "I wouldn't feel right about that. I know you guys have been doing this kind of work for several years, and I can't imagine coming in here and laying down some kind of law to you."

"So what does that mean?" asked Mark. "That you have no problem with the basic direction we're headed with this thing?"

Andrew rustled uncomfortably in his chair. "Maybe I'm just not used to how things work," he said. "Maybe I just need a little time to get used to things."

Mark smiled. "That seems about right," he said. "I will admit that it's a weird business. But I'm glad that you said what you did. Kind of keeps us honest."

"Then you know what I mean," Andrew said, feeling relieved. "You see the dilemma."

"Of course," said Helen. "We work in it. But I'm not sure there's a real answer to it. We have to work in the real world."

"Remember something, Andrew," said Mark. "What it's all about, in the end, is communication. You want to commu-

nicate the gospel. So do we. We're on the same team here.
But if this ad does nothing to stimulate interest in your
record, then you'll be communicating to some cornfield
somewhere. In other words, there's nothing to argue about
here. More effective is better. More effective means that
more people buy the record, and you get your message out.
That's what it all comes down to."

Andrew paused, taking in everything that Mark and
Helen were saying. Their arguments were persuasive, but
a new, even more effective rationale for going along was
raising its voice inside of him: for the first time, he began
to realize that thousands of people were actually going to
see the record and the ads, and he had a natural desire to
look as glamorous as possible. It wasn't unpleasant to think
of the kind of perfected picture that Mickey took being
distributed from coast to coast. Once again he imagined his
friends back home and all the folks at Christ's Kingdom,
whose idea of a photograph was something from Olan Mills.
These people were working on an entirely different level,
and he would certainly reap a very real benefit from their
expertise. Also there was this: he was beginning to see how
many others were depending on the success of the record.
It wasn't just his personal life that was involved. If the record
didn't sell, Mark and Helen's futures were at stake, and
probably others at the company as well. More and more,
he realized that although his name was on the record, he
didn't own it. Each day spread the ownership of it farther
and farther out into more and more companies, each with
a stake in the size of its economic return. First, van Grimes,
and his employees. Now, Dove and its considerably larger
staff. David Spenser, as well, and on the horizon, Atlantic.
He began to wonder how many others would be part owners
of this message before it was all over. It was still early in
the game, after all. The record had yet to released.

"Okay," he said, at last. "I'm sorry if I've been acting like
a child. I can see that you guys know what you're doing,

and it's way out of line for me to tell you how to do your jobs. Blast away, and good luck."

The mood in the room instantly lightened, and Mark brightened most visibly; he sprang up from his desk and, putting his arm around Andrew's shoulders, walked him to the door.

"Excellent, Andrew," he enthused. "And I promise you that you'll love the finished product. I guarantee that you'll look like a million bucks."

Andrew smiled. "Thanks, Mark. You too, Helen. Sorry for the fuss."

"No problem," answered Helen, opening the door. "Now you just call us if you have any questions. Anything at all."

"Thanks. I will. See you."

Mark closed the door behind Andrew and turned to face Helen.

"That was close," he said. "We learned one thing, though."

"What's that?"

"Simple," he answered, taking his seat behind the desk. He began fingering the mock-up thoughtfully, and suddenly looked up again at Helen. "Today's lesson: in the future, don't ask Andrew."

— 15 —

In the country, one day follows another naturally, each sunrise quietly reinforcing the passing of lives and seasons, wordlessly telling the animals, crops, farmers, ranchers, and flowers that the cycle may once again be repeated. There are few alarm clocks in the country. The earth tells the farms when to awaken; later in winter, when the hard ground rejects any tilling, and earlier in the spring, when any daylight hour is an hour that the sun is waiting for seeds to be planted. Both day and night have their harbingers: frogs and insects near creeks and ponds signal the farm to begin thinking about sleep, and birds and cattle rouse with the sun, bringing the rest of the farm to life with them. Clocks, by and large, are for communicating with the outside world of the city—for catching a television program or for meeting a plane.

Andrew was jolted awake by his alarm clock the day of the release party, his head humming with a faint nervousness from the moment he awakened. The days leading up to the party had passed unnaturally, flinging themselves after each other in a rush. The nights, too, were changed; since he had moved to Nashville, new sleep habits had gradually evolved. He was going to sleep later, usually falling into his bed around midnight or later. For a while, he continued to awaken just after sunrise, his body trained through years of habit to come to life gradually, sleep falling away from him as the sun rose slowly over the plains. As his schedule changed, however, he began getting up later and later, jarred out of his sleep in his darkened bedroom by the brazen jangle of an alarm clock.

The alarm woke him at ten o'clock this morning. The last night had been a late one. John and he had met with Harold at Dove after dinner, and the meeting had gone on until nine-thirty. John had drilled him about the release party, teaching him how to handle what was, for Andrew, completely new social territory. He had been released from their lessons to a waiting Carolyn, and the two had shared a late dinner and a long talk about the future of Andrew's career. He hadn't come home until well after one, and then he had lain awake at least another hour, searching for sleep in the midst of a storm of thoughts.

His afternoon was quiet, with John and the Dove staff busily putting the final touches on the big event. Curiously, his time alone had become unfulfilling. It was a new sensation to him. Back in Rose Hill, being alone had been a blessing to him, a time to think and feel without restraint. Here time seemed to slow down when he was alone, and in spite of his trepidation about the party, he tried to will the hands of the clock to move faster.

Around three-thirty he began to dress, carefully laying out the outfit that Mark had picked out for him. Where the money was coming from for these clothes Andrew was unsure; all he knew was that John and Dove were continually debating about such issues, and by reading faces, Andrew concluded that John was winning most of the arguments. He picked up the shirt Mark had selected for the party, thinking once again how distinctly odd it was to be a grown man dressed by others. Since he had arrived in Nashville, there had been a good deal of being dressed and being spoken for, neither of which, he suspected, his father would have tolerated for a moment. It served to underline how different his life had become from what he had left behind. It seemed that the ridiculous became the sublime in the world in which he now found himself.

He dressed quietly, watching the minute hands creep around the clock. Then he sat in a chair, trying to read.

Concentration proved impossible, and he paced his apartment, afraid to lie down on the bed for fear of wrinkling his clothes.

At last, four-thirty arrived. He had intended to leave for the Dove offices around four-forty, but he couldn't wait any longer. Even driving around in his car was preferable to waiting in silence in an empty apartment.

He met John and Harold on the third floor, and they sequestered him in Harold's office as soon as he arrived. "Don't want any early arrivals catching a glimpse of you out of the program," said Harold, and John had heartily agreed. They had bustled him off and within a few seconds had both left themselves, so in the end Andrew was relegated to wait alone after all.

At five o'clock Harold came to get him, his bulldog face smiling like a carved pumpkin. The crowd was filing in, he said, and it was a veritable who's who of Christian music. Virtually the entire music press was there, and an unprecedented number of mainstream press as well. Dove had expended considerable capital in getting the word out loudly enough to get some of the people in the room to attend, capital that would be difficult to get back if they failed to deliver something special. Mark and his crew had seen to it that the food and the ornamentation in the room all communicated that this was a special day for Dove. The hype was there. It only remained for Andrew to come through with a winning performance.

Harold led Andrew down the hallway, and the two met John at the elevator. John had insisted on handling Andrew alone in the crowd, and when the elevator doors opened, he took Andrew's arm, leading him to the expansive conference area on the second floor of Dove's offices.

With a deep breath, the doors of the conference hall were flung open and Andrew was ushered into a scene packed with people, both familiar and unfamiliar. It seemed that the offices of the entire Nashville music industry had been emptied into the room, and although the room was quite large, it was impossible to walk more than a step or two without turning to the side to make way for others. The conference hall was designed for large-scale presentations to the entire Dove staff, including the traveling sales force, a group that, combined, numbered close to eighty. It could accommodate around a hundred and fifty standing, but it seemed to Andrew that a number greater than that had been pushed into the room. He jostled his way through the crowd, and John stayed close to his side as they navigated their way through the mass of people. John looked supremely confident, introducing Andrew to smiling face after smiling face. The mood of everyone they met seemed elevated, as if someone had surreptitiously mixed a small percentage of helium into the atmosphere. Smiles were frozen in delightful affirmation. To Andrew's surprise, he heard his name filter through from other conversations as he passed, his name being called as he appeared and disappeared from view.

In spite of the crush of people, Andrew took a moment to look around himself. The Dove offices had been carefully prepared. A huge banner hung across the front of the room that read, *Andrew Miracle—Lost Without You.* Underneath the banner were two large, dark sheets covering what appeared to be some kind of poster, waiting to be unveiled. Several large photographs of Andrew hung on each wall, and to his horror, Andrew found that one of these perfect pictures smiled back at him no matter where in the room he faced. The stage was set up at the front of the room, and a large grand piano waited for him to play at the appropriate time.

For the next hour, Andrew smiled and said the same several sentences a hundred or more times. He tried to remember what John had told him, but in fact his natural country politeness, more than van Grimes's instruction saw him through the first few minutes of the party. After some time, however, he gradually realized that it really didn't seem to make that much difference what he said. Most of the people he met seemed content to do most of the talking themselves, happily chattering away about the exciting things they saw in Andrew's future. They seemed to already know a lot about him. It was as if he had walked in the room bigger than life, and people talked to him the same way; he was ordained as the Dove wonder boy, and so in their minds he already possessed all the qualities that such a person must have. It was curious, after his tongue-tied adolescence, to be the focus of so much unearned attention. He merely glided from one delighted person to another, receiving approval like Christmas gifts from strangers.

He wanted to check on Carolyn, but her tasks seemed to be keeping her occupied. She was working with the Dove staff, making sure the food and drink flowed seamlessly and that people waiting to talk to Andrew were entertained. He caught her eye a few times and winked at her. She smiled back, but inevitably someone caught his arm and swept him away from her before either of them could say anything.

The people at the party were a curious mix of artist and business; they seemed to be the two sides of Mark Haffner's office decor come to life. Many of the guests looked and dressed like well-to-do artists, with varying degrees of high-dollar trendiness. Others looked like young lawyers, the kind with heavily mortgaged houses and leased cars.

After some time, Mark took the stage and, after some fiddling with a microphone, called for everyone's attention.

"Ladies and gentlemen, I want to formally welcome you to the proceedings today and get started with our presentation. I want to thank you all for coming and for being a part of what we feel is a great day at Dove Records." There was light applause, and he beamed broadly at the crowd.

"Of course, we're all here for one reason, and that's to be introduced to a bright new star on the Christian music horizon. It means so much to us that you are all here, because this artist means so much to Dove. This party is an indication of how much faith we have in this young artist, and I'm sure that when you leave here today, each and every one of you will understand why we feel that way. This young man is very special to us, and we want him to become as special to you. So to move things forward, I want to introduce you to Harold Murphy, president of Dove Records."

Harold took the stage to applause and overlooked the assembled crowd with satisfaction. His team had done their job well. All the important press people in Christian music were there, and there was an undeniable atmosphere of importance to the event. They were halfway home. Now, he would try to knock the ball out of the park.

"Thank you, Mark," he began. "And I just want to echo Mark's statements of gratitude that so many of you could be here today to share what is really a celebration for us." He paused, and passed over the room dramatically with his eyes. "Incredibly, it was only a little more than four months ago that John van Grimes first came to me with a tape. He had been to the hinterlands, you see, back in Kansas, and he claimed to have discovered someone there that was some kind of phenomenon. Well, I'd heard all that before, of course, but I agreed to listen. It was the best decision I've ever made in my life."

John was beaming, and he squeezed Andrew's shoulder. "Well, when I heard that tape I was stunned. I hadn't heard anything like that in my life, and I knew I wanted to meet the boy right away. That's when the begging started."

There was laughter at that, and Harold let it quiet before continuing. "One thing led to another, and we met, and talked, and prayed, and Dove became the place that this marvelous young artist wanted to be. I guarantee you that you will be hearing a lot from this young man. He's got the kind of integrity and commitment that we look for here at Dove. Getting to know him has meant so much to us, and I want you to meet him right now. Ladies and gentlemen, Andrew Miracle."

Andrew climbed the four stairs up to the stage in a dream.

Harold took his hand and shook it heartily, taking the opportunity to maneuver Andrew beside him to face the audience. Andrew's thoughts seemed crowded with nerves, but he smiled out at the throng, trying to look calm.

"Before we hear Andrew play something from the new record, we have a little presentation to make. Mark, would you come back up here?"

Mark came up onto the stage and took the microphone from Harold. "Thank you Harold," he said. "Now, we do have a little something in mind here, if you'll bear with us. For those of you in the press, we wanted to give you a sneak preview of what you'll be seeing in the future. In fact," he said, laughing, "if we all do our jobs right, you won't be able to get away from it. But it seemed appropriate to unveil these today."

With that, he turned, and as he did Andrew noticed for the first time a long cord hung down from each of the covered pictures. Mark walked towards one and pulled on it hard. The fabric came fluttering down, and a nine-foot-square poster was exposed. Andrew's photograph was on it, artfully retouched and looking soulfully out into the distance above the crowd. His face was floating over a desert of desolate tumbleweeds—the kind of place one finds in Nevada or Utah. A setting sun was shooting flames across the desert sky. Superimposed over the bottom of the photograph, in dark red, flaming letters was:

**A strong, new voice
A brave, new artist**

**The soul of an artist who is a burning flame
The voice of a man who is sold out to God**

ANDREW MIRACLE

LOST WITHOUT YOU

The crowd emitted an audible "ah," and then applauded for several seconds. Andrew stared at the poster, unsure how to respond. The words seemed to be about someone entirely different from him. On the other hand, the reaction of the people around him was overwhelmingly positive. It was clear that something marvelous had been done. Andrew, on the other hand, was doing nothing but standing there, staring as wide-eyed as the rest of the audience. Nevertheless, he could sense that, somehow, he had grown in their minds. But Mark wasn't finished.

"This is the ad that you'll be seeing in most music publications," he said. "But I also wanted you to see another piece of the puzzle." Mark walked to the other side of the stage and pulled on the cord hanging from the other picture. This poster presented a very different image; the photograph was not of Andrew at all, but a side view of a beautiful young woman, sitting alone outdoors on a lovely stone bench. She had long brown hair, and she wore a long, flowing dress that imparted a Victorian feeling. In some indefinable way, she looked lonely, as if she missed someone, or was waiting for someone. She was holding a book open on her lap, but she was looking out into the distance across a large body of water in the background. The whole picture was very slightly out of focus, as if viewed through a mist, or in a dream. Below the picture, written this time in a kind of cursive style, were these words:

Andrew Miracle is like no other friend you have.
He's a friend who's seeking the heart of God.
He's seeking your heart, too.
Andrew Miracle
is
Lost Without You

The new release on Dove Records

Again the audience applauded, and Harold walked over toward Andrew, putting his arm around him. The time had come for the big finish. He checked his artist for nerves, but Andrew seemed fine. Harold took the microphone from Mark and, pulling Andrew along with him, took the center of the stage. The pictures above them framed Andrew perfectly, one on each side.

"Well," he said, "I know you're all anxious to hear from Andrew himself. Before I hand over the microphone, I just want to tell you that we have a little gift for you all. After Andrew plays, we want each of you to have a copy of the new record, together with a little token of our appreciation that you were here today. For you radio programmers, by the time you get back home, a copy of Andrew's first single will be at your desk. You people are the key, and we'll all be holding our breath to get your response to it. But now, it's time to let Andrew speak for himself. Ladies and gentlemen, Andrew Miracle."

The audience erupted into applause, and John, giving Andrew an emphatic thumbs up sign from the audience, mouthed the words, "Eat 'em up, kid." Andrew took the microphone from Harold still feeling a bit overwhelmed. He glanced behind himself a moment, taking in once more the finished product that Mark and Helen had created. He had wondered about it in Mark's office, but now he had to admit that they had probably known what they were doing. The presentation had been a great success, and no one seemed to feel that the ads were excessive in any way. He turned again to face the audience and saw nothing but smiling faces turned up toward him. He took a deep breath, reminding himself that John had said to keep it short.

"This is all a bit much for a country boy such as myself," he began. The audience seemed to regard this as a lovely joke, and laughed approvingly. Again, with a shock, he realized that the details of what he said made far less difference than he had expected. The main thing seemed to be that he was who he was. Nevertheless, he wanted to at least say something that brought God into things.

"At any rate," he said, "I want all of you to know that it means a lot to me that you showed up to see us off on our voyage. I hope we go somewhere that the Lord would be proud of. This is a huge adventure for me, and I'm grateful to have the chance to do it."

The crowd murmured its approval, and he decided to quit while he was ahead. "I guess I'm supposed to play something for you, so I might as well get to it." He handed the microphone over to Harold, and walked over to the grand piano that dominated the center of the stage. The audience applauded as he walked, which was a new feeling for him. It was the first time in his life that he had received applause before he played.

Andrew took his seat at the piano, grateful for the sound check that John had insisted on earlier. He felt comfortable there, hiding behind the piano, and he relaxed as he sat on the bench. He had always been lucky in that regard. He could always find his center there, behind the piano. Rooms changed and people changed; the keys of the piano remained the same. Now he insulated himself once more, away from the people around him and especially from the looming, perfected photographs of himself that surrounded him. He retreated back into his gift, sure of it, and needing for his own reasons to visit it once again.

After all the production that his songs had undergone in the studio, it felt oddly refreshing to hear the simple piano version of "Lost Without You" begin under his fingers. It was like the first time he had written it, over a year ago. He let it speak for itself, not pushing, and let the simple lines of the piano spin around his voice with little embellishment. He could hear the silence grow in the room as he played, but he resisted listening to it; he wanted to hear only the music, and he did so, quietly, imbuing the song with a new tenderness. On a whim, he introduced a new element in the middle, playing without singing for a time, letting that tender feeling grow a bit and express itself. But before long, he came back home and finished out the song even more quietly than before. There was a hushed silence as he ended, and he waited a moment before opening his eyes.

He exhaled and looked out into the crowd. In a moment, they exploded into long, excited applause. He was carried away with it, and it lifted him up off the bench and down the stairs into the waiting throng of people. John was smiling his prospector's smile, and Harold was obviously pleased as well. He strode over to Andrew and shook his hand.

"Home run, son," he said energetically. "Home run. Now, a few more minutes of pressing the flesh, and we'll turn you loose from this circus for the day."

Andrew moved through the crowd for some time, John and Harold escorting him through the people waiting to speak with him. The very moment the party began to subside, however, John collected him and moved him quickly out into the hallway. The quiet of the corridor was startling after the noise of the crowded conference room.

"How'd it go?" asked Andrew. He knew the answer, but it felt good to hear it anyway.

"It went perfect, my boy, perfect. In fact, take tomorrow off. You've earned it."

Andrew did feel exhaustion creeping over him, now that the event had ended.

"I'd like to go back and get Carolyn," he said. "We were planning on spending the evening together."

"Uh, going back in's not a good idea. You've already made your exit. Why don't I go back in and have her meet you at your place?"

"You mean I can't go back in?"

"Look, Andrew. Trust me on this stuff. We just went to a lot of trouble to create a moment here. Once you make the grand exit, you can't go back in without losing ground."

"Are you serious?"

"Everything helps, Andrew. Everything. You run on home, and I'll have Carolyn meet you there in an hour."

It went against his grain to leave without Carolyn, but Andrew had to admit that so far, everything he had been told to do had worked out. John knew a lot more than he did about the situation he was in.

"Tell her I'm home waiting, okay?" he asked.

"You got it, champ. You gobbled 'em up today, kid. I mean, you absolutely gobbled."

"Thanks, John. See you later." Andrew smiled, feeling the relief of having done well at a critical time. He knew that everyone had been counting on him, and he had carried his part off well. Nothing remained now but to wait for the returns and to follow the path that lay before him.

After the party wound down, John and Harold met briefly in Harold's office to debrief. John collapsed onto Harold's sofa and took his shoes off, reveling in the familiarity he now possessed with Harold. Harold, on the other hand, seemed as fresh as ever; his stocky physique seemed incapable of stooping.

"Nice job," exhaled John, looking tired but contented. "It's not the physical exertion, you know, that tires you out at times like this. It's the waiting to see if your guy is going to screw up or not. It's like Chinese water torture."

Harold, sitting comfortably at his desk, merely smiled. His self-confidence had always had an unnerving effect on John. He would like to have known where the reservoir of belief in himself that Harold had came from; he would put in an order for himself.

"I think Andrew did very well," Harold said. "Very well. He was short—"

"That was my doing," interjected John. "I told him to keep it short."

"Yes, John. Very wise. Anyway, he was concise, looked grateful but not too grateful, and sang marvelously. The boy really is an enormous talent. At the end of the day, after all the preparations, he just has an enormous talent. It's very gratifying."

"Yeah. So now what?"

"Now, we just wait. In some ways, the hardest part."

"When will we know anything?" asked John.

"Well," answered Harold, "we'll be getting some informal feedback from radio programmers within a few days, I should think. But it will be a few weeks before we really know if the record is headed anywhere. If we're lucky."

"Do you think we did everything we could have? I mean, up to this point? Do you think we left some stone unturned?"

Harold thought to himself once again how much he disliked John's overeager side. Van Grimes could be a very smooth operator, and his good looks and usual above-it-all demeanor could be persuasive to those outside the music community's inner circle. But when the real pressure was on, he revealed his inner flaw: he wanted it just a little too much, just a little too obviously. It came, Harold thought, from the fact that as of right then John had only one significant iron in the fire: Andrew Miracle. Dove was risking a great deal on Andrew, certainly, but for John, Andrew's success meant everything. Without Andrew, he was left with Heaven's Voices.

"No, John," Harold answered after a moment, "I think we did everything we could have. You, especially. You were marvelous. Now get on home and relax. You've earned it. The party was a great success."

John pulled himself out of his slump on the couch and put on his shoes. Maybe Harold was right, he thought. But even as he thought it, he knew he had a lot to do that night. He was getting a head start on a touring plan that would put Andrew in front of thousands of people in the first few weeks of his career. It was a bold move, but if he could pull it off and if Andrew could measure up to the pressure, it would catapult him past a lot of pretenders in the race for exposure. Nothing was going to derail the plans he had for Andrew.

16

It only took a few days for the faith that Harold had put in "Lost Without You" to be rewarded. The radio promotion department at Dove had started telephoning radio programmers the day after the release party, and the response was overwhelmingly positive. For the first time in recent memory, small stations were adding the song to their play lists without waiting for the big stations to lead the way; it was as if hit status was being bestowed on the song wholesale, with little or no warm-up time.

The song went number one in two ratings reports, making it one of the fastest rising singles in Dove history and by far the fastest for a new artist at any label, at any time. In the space of one month, "Lost Without You" was the most played song on Christian radio in the United States, penetrating the marketplace like a gold-plated bullet.

Andrew's radio success solidified the excitement at Dove. It was one thing to hype and push an artist in faith, but now concrete results were appearing. There was something real happening in Andrew's career at last, and the staff at Dove was determined to capitalize on it.

The next piece in the puzzle was to get Andrew performing as quickly and as widely as possible. The number one status of his first single notwithstanding, it was still too soon to book a proper tour under his own name. Concert promoters would still regard him as too big a risk to undergo the great expense of renting a hall, buying advertising, contracting a crew, and all the other expenses associated with holding such an event. The logical approach was to get Andrew to open for an established artist, someone that could bring in large numbers of people. Then Andrew would have access to those people, and the chance to make a personal connection sufficient to selling the record with each one of them.

If Harold had any concern that John would lag behind on this plan, he needn't have worried. Van Grimes was ahead of the wave, and had begun negotiations with a promoter to put Andrew on one of the biggest tours in Christian music. Darren McCloud, the brightest light in Christian music of the previous year, was headlining. Another new act from Darren's label was opening the concert, but the promoter was considering adding a third artist to broaden the bill. Andrew's flashing entrance onto the scene got John's phone call returned. John knew there was a risk involved in being a part of such a big tour; Andrew could win big, but he could also certainly lose big. The part of the marketplace that was willing to pay for a concert ticket was generally the hard-core fan, and over the twenty-night tour Andrew would be performing in front of a significant percentage of that marketplace. He had never played before a large crowd, and if he bombed, it would be very difficult to ever recover the lost ground. In some ways, it made more sense to develop Andrew more slowly, letting him make mistakes in front of hundreds, rather than thousands. But the up side of the tour was unmistakable, as well, and any plan had its risks. Andrew had the chance to leapfrog over years of career building with the Darren McCloud tour, and if he excited the crowds enough, by this time next year he could be headlining his own smaller tour. In the end, John decided to believe in destiny, his and Andrew's, and take the shot. It took work, but John managed to convince McCloud's manager that getting on the front end of the Andrew Miracle train was good sense, and the promoter had agreed to put Andrew in the middle spot. The tour left in three weeks, however, and there would be a lot to work out in a hurry if it was to come together.

John called Harold with the good news, and the two agreed to meet at Dove to discuss the details. John's eyes gleamed as he explained the deal to Harold. Darren McCloud was one of the premier seat-fillers in the business, and getting Andrew on the tour meant that he would be performing in front of six or seven thousand people every night. It was a dream come true for a new artist, and for everyone who owned a piece of him.

"Harold," John began, "I want this thing done right. I want your people to support Andrew in every city with press and product." Harold smiled serenely at John, but was inwardly calculating the changing power structure between himself and van Grimes. Power was fluid in the business, flowing constantly to and from those who carried the momentum of that instant. The bigger Andrew got, the harder John could become to handle. Andrew's rapidly increasing marketability directly affected John's influence on how things progressed. But Dove had its own reasons for promoting Andrew, and Harold hardly needed lecturing from John.

"Of course, John," Harold answered lightly. "We're right with you on this. Our people will advance every concert date to the hilt. And, I want to congratulate you on getting Andrew on board with Darren. It was a bold move, and you pulled it off."

Van Grimes relaxed, and his tone evened out. He was among allies here, he reminded himself. "Yes, Darren is the perfect slot for Andrew. He pulls the mainstream, and that's where the numbers are."

"Exactly. But the tour leaves quite soon, doesn't it?"

"Yeah, that's the hard part," van Grimes admitted. "Only three weeks away."

"Of course, John, my only concern is that we don't throw Andrew to the lions."

Van Grimes grimaced. "I agree. He's got to be prepared for that kind of crowd. We can't just dangle him out there.

We've got to get him ready. But I believe I have that covered."

"Glad to hear it," answered Harold. "What do you have in mind?"

"Andrew has never played the kind of auditoriums he'll be in with Darren. They're completely out of his frame of reference. He's extremely green, after all."

"What's your idea?"

"First, we take him out and buy him four or five outfits. Make him look like a star. Give him some presence. Haffner can take care of that, right?"

"He will be delighted," Harold assured him. "And then?"

"Okay. Andrew only has thirty-five minutes on stage. Thirty-five minutes to do his thing. Thirty-five minutes to connect with six thousand people. Somebody's got to work those thirty-five minutes over with him until they're greased lightning."

"Great. Like who?"

"Me."

Harold raised his eyebrows and said, "I see. You know, John, this isn't Heaven's Voices."

John scowled, irritated. "Are you saying I'm not up to it?"

"Of course I'm not. I'm just saying it's a big responsibility and would take a lot of your valuable time. So this is something you'd like to tackle yourself?"

"Yes, Harold." Van Grimes stared back at Harold. He was feeling protective of his position. "Andrew and I have a very special relationship," he said.

Harold regarded John evenly, trying to determine if this was a battle worth fighting. If Andrew did poorly on a major tour, it could set him back a long way. If he did well, it would catapult him onto the fast track. On the other hand, there might be even bigger battles to fight with John later, and he didn't want to expend capital unnecessarily. Giving no further hint of his reluctance, he agreed.

"Great," he said. "Then that's settled. Who do you have in mind for the band?"

"Got that figured, too. Carolyn's been making calls for the last few days, and we've got everybody lined up. Top guys."

"Glad to hear it. It sounds like we're on the way, John. Go to work on Andrew, and we'll all be there for the first date."

John left happy, and he had Carolyn call Dove to arrange a time for Andrew to go clothes-hunting with Mark the very next day. The next morning, Mark, looking like the cover of a rock and roll magazine, picked Andrew up at his apartment to begin the search.

Andrew couldn't help feeling self-conscious, but this constant off center feeling was growing increasingly tiresome to him. He was beginning to feel that he was always behind the times, always nervous and overly self-aware, while everyone around him seemed to flow effortlessly through the challenges of his soaring career. He resolved that the time had come to just get over his nerves and understand that photo shoots, artsy clothes and smiling receptions were all just a part of life as a recording artist, and to get into the spirit of things. It was uncomfortable always feeling like he was dragging his feet inside, the odd man out while everyone but him enjoyed his success. He realized that by not going along, he was in fact drawing even more attention to himself. He felt as if his shy discomfort was a leaden weight that he dragged around with him, robbing him of the pleasure of enjoying his remarkable life. It seemed that all he needed to do was to cut those doubts away; then he would be free to really begin living.

By the time Mark arrived, Andrew had put himself firmly in a good mood, and he greeted Mark enthusiastically. The two hopped in Mark's car and talked excitedly about the success of Andrew's first single.

"Man, do you realize how big this thing is?" asked Mark. "I mean, the offices at Dove are positively buzzing."

"That's what I hear," answered Andrew, smiling. "Who would have dreamed?"

"You are absolutely the man of the hour, buddy," laughed Mark. "This whole town is talking about your entrance onto the scene."

The notion that people who had never met him would now be discussing him would have been irrational to him just a few months ago, but Andrew was beginning to understand how things worked in the music business. Your career preceded you, and the whole music community was constantly sensing where the action was flowing and ebbing.

"I can't deny I'm excited," he said. "Are people talking more about the single or the tour?"

"Both, man, both. The single was the *coup,* and the tour was the *coup de grace.* You are flying, man."

That, Andrew admitted, was an agreeable sensation. He had come to town a complete unknown just four months earlier, and he was, in no uncertain terms, taking the town by storm. There was no point in resisting this; if he was going to do it at all, it made sense to do it as big as possible. Why start on a path and then hamstring it with doubts about the process? He also had to admit that his talent must be considerable. The pace of his rise was remarkable even to the professionals he was dealing with. There was no point in false modesty; he definitely had something special.

"I can't wait to get to the store," Andrew said. "I want something wild."

Mark stared and then laughed. "Hello, is that Andrew Miracle?" he asked. "Did you say *wild?*"

"Yeah, it's me. And why not? Doesn't anybody think I have it in me? Who am I around here, Mr. Timid?"

"Maybe just a bit," Mark answered, still laughing. "But I like the change. Man, you are going to end this day decked out and ready for warfare."

"Bring it on," said Andrew. "Where are we heading?"

"A little shop called Dangerous Threads," answered Mark. "But don't worry, the name is just a figure of speech."

A few minutes later Mark pulled his car onto Church Street, and they quickly arrived at Elliston Place, a trendy little area of alternative clothing stores, funky restaurants, and newsstands. Mark parked the car, and the two walked toward the store.

"Is this where you buy your clothes?" asked Andrew.

Mark laughed. "Not exactly," he said. "This is maybe one step beyond what I can get away with at work. But it's right on the money for a concert."

Inside, Mark greeted the store manager as an old acquaintance, which comforted Andrew. Evidently this was a common shopping place for artists. He noticed the pictures of dozens of rock stars on the walls, indicating, he assumed, that they had shopped there. A few Christian artists were interspersed with the other, bigger names.

Mark led him around the store for a few minutes, fingering merchandise and talking softly to himself as he did so. He rejected a dozen or more possibilities before finally stopping on a dime, galvanized, looking up at an ensemble hanging above him.

"This is it, man. Look number one for Andrew Miracle." Mark reached up and pulled down a maroon jacket and tailored pants. The jacket was covered with an intricate inlaid design the color of pearl, and was double-breasted with black buttons. There was a black silk shirt to match. "What do you think about this?" he asked.

Andrew stared at the suit. He honestly had no idea what he thought about it. He did know, however, that he had resolved to go along with Mark and see where it led. "You think it's me?" he asked.

"Are you kidding me?" Mark answered. "Do the words tailor-made mean anything to you? This outfit is class, it's music, it's a statement, and above all, it's you."

Andrew swallowed hard. "Okay, then," he said, nodding. "Let's go with it."

Mark called the manager over, and for the next fifteen minutes they hovered over Andrew, fitting the clothes and picking out accessories for the outfit. Andrew stood patiently like a scarecrow, held together with pins and folds.

"*Voila,*" Mark said excitedly as he turned Andrew toward the mirror. The pearl inlay in the jacket reflected the light of the room back into the mirror brightly, scattering color as Andrew moved.

"That will be incredible from stage," said Mark. "When the spotlight hits, you'll be on fire."

"Then I guess we have one down," ventured Andrew.

"One down," echoed Mark. "Let's shoot for one more this trip."

The store manager looked Andrew up and down thoughtfully.

"Tell you what, Mark," he said, as if Andrew weren't there, "I think I have the perfect look. He comes out in this one, right? I mean, it's a sophisticated thing. But then he has a costume change, right?"

"Don't know. It's a short set. But I'm listening."

"Okay. How about this?"

With that, the store manager pulled out an outfit that was so far beyond what Andrew thought he would encounter that even in his cooperative state of mind, he was stunned. Before his startled eyes hung an electric blue jacket with a high, stiff collar that reminded him of something Napoleon might have worn if he had been in pop music. It had a distinctly military flair. The shoulders were flat and covered with gold fringe hanging over the sides. There was formal gold cording in the front, and the cut of the jacket was narrow at the waist. To Andrew's greatest astonishment, however, there was a white lace ascot and white lace cuffs attached to the jacket as well. Underneath the jacket, there was a blue sleeveless vest with brass buttons showing. The pants were black, with black leather leggings opening for black boots. It was absolutely out of Andrew's reckoning. He exhaled audibly, imagining himself being seen by anyone he knew back home in such an outfit.

"You've got to be kidding," he breathed, betraying himself.

Mark was enraptured. "That is the most magnificent thing I have ever seen," he bubbled. "I mean, that is something unforgettable. Andrew, you have got to at least try it on."

Andrew looked sideways at the outfit, as if he were regarding a new and possibly dangerous species of animal.

"I don't think so," he said softly.

The manager looked flustered. "Why not?" he asked. "This outfit is the most incredible thing I have in my store. I guarantee that you will be hearing screams the next day when the lights hit you in this thing."

"I'm sure I will," whispered Andrew. "I'm just afraid they'll be mine."

Mark laughed out loud, which helped ease Andrew's mind somehow. Perhaps he was just taking everything too seriously. Mark seemed to regard it all as a kind of fashion game, something to be played at tongue-in-cheek.

"Andrew," Mark said cheerfully, "I will admit it's a little over the top. But I want to see you in it, anyway. There's something you're going to have to trust me on, and it's this: you keep thinking about these clothes from the perspective of what you would wear on the street. Forget that. You have to put yourself in the place where they are meant to be worn and you have to begin to do it now because, ready or not, in two weeks time you will be standing in front of several thousand people who are going to take about ten seconds to make up their minds about whether or not you are happening. What I'm saying is that the clock is ticking. You have to begin to start thinking like a star because you are either going to go out there and slay those people with an unforgettable performance or you are going to get yawned at and promptly forgotten. I hate to put it so bluntly, but that really is the truth of it. The time is now, and I'm not going to sugarcoat it for you."

Andrew stared at the jacket, Mark's words humming inside his mind. If he walked out on stage and flopped, the idea of failing so grandly chilled him. The outfit seemed absurd, but he had to admit he had no idea what alternative there was to going along with Mark's established track record with style.

"Tell me something," he asked, tearing his eyes away from the jacket.

"Sure. What's that?"

"How do stars think?"

Mark smiled. "It's not so tricky, Andrew. A star knows that he is special, and he's willing to look like it. He's come to terms with all that. He is willing to stand apart from the masses, because he knows that everything depends on that. He understands how the game is played, and he has determined to win."

"So in the end, it's just a game."

"Of course. It's all just wallpaper, really. Everybody's about the same, underneath it all. I'll tell you a secret: I've met a lot of famous people, and other than their talent, some of them can be kind of boring."

Andrew took an odd comfort from what Mark had said. If it was in reality just a game, perhaps playing it didn't have any dire circumstances. Perhaps being a star was a label that he could put on and take off, as necessary. He looked back at the jacket. All the same, the outfit he confronted was a stretch.

"Am I really that special?" he asked. "Special enough to wear that?"

"Are you kidding? You can ask me that, after everything that's happened to you? You are most definitely special, Andrew."

Andrew paused a moment. "I'll put it on," he said at last, "but I make no promises."

The store manager clapped his hands and led Andrew back to the changing room.

While Andrew changed, he resolved not to look at himself in the mirror, fearing he would lose his nerve and emerge again in his blue jeans and sweatshirt. Dutifully, he pulled each article of clothing on, down to the leather leggings that fit, skin-tight, over the black pants. The boots, however, were too small, and he came back out into the store dressed in the new clothes, but in his stocking feet. He noted gratefully that the other customer in the store had left while he was changing. He walked tentatively out of the changing area, arms hanging listlessly at his sides. He turned the corner and confronted Mark and the manager head on.

"My God," breathed Mark. "It's perfect. It's genius. It's unfathomable."

"It's what?" asked Andrew apprehensively.

"It's unfathomable," answered Mark, more loudly. Taking Andrew by the sleeve, he led him to a full-length mirror.

"Look at yourself," he whispered.

Andrew did so. He looked like an officer in a fantasy army, victorious, romantic, unapproachable, and returning from great adventures. He gazed at himself incredulously. He was realizing that to his astonishment, there could be a great gulf between what was underneath a person's clothes and the persona that was projected by the calculated decision-making of professionals. As long as people were kept at a certain distance, he could, to an extent, be manufactured like any other product.

"Are you saying that this would look less outrageous on stage than it does in here?" he asked tentatively.

"Of course," said Mark. "If you wanted to wear this down the streets of Music Row, I'd have you locked up. But on stage, it gives you a whale of a punch."

"And that's what I need, is it? A whale of a punch?"

"That's exactly what you need, Andrew."

"I can't forget about my ministry, Mark. I'm not sure I understand the impact of this stuff on that," Andrew reminded him.

"It helps, Andrew. Remember something: you're competing."

"What do you mean?"

"You're competing with every other group out there, secular and Christian. You're competing for attention. There's a million ways people can spend their money, and if you don't take this seriously, you'll be blown away by people who do take it seriously. Very seriously."

"I just wanted to play my music and say some things about the Lord," Andrew ventured cautiously.

"Well, do you want to have anybody to say it to or not?" Mark asked firmly.

"I want to have somebody to say it to."

"Then get the outfit."

Andrew closed his eyes. There were a great many decisions to be made that he had never anticipated. But so far, everything that John and the people at Dove had told him had worked out just as they had hoped. He hated the idea of letting them down. Somehow, he had the idea that if he failed to cooperate, their enthusiasm for him might fade quickly.

"Let's do it," he said, surprising himself with the certainty in his voice. He repeated, "Let's do it."

Mark clapped his hands. "Make a note, one and all," he said elatedly. "On this day, Andrew Miracle grew up."

Andrew looked at himself in the mirror, letting the new him sink in. Success was definitely better than failure. There was only one road ahead, and that was the road to winning. Losing had become unthinkable. He knew nothing about the person who was looking back at him in the mirror, dressed like a man in a play. But he had decided to come to terms with him, for better or worse. So many people depended on his being able to do just that.

Over the next two days, Mark and Andrew continued to search for stage clothes, finally settling on five outfits that could be rotated throughout the tour. This part of the preparations done, all that was left was to tackle the music.

17

Rehearsals were a grueling, seven-day affair. John had arranged for Graham Heath, an Englishman with a great deal of road experience, to stage manage the tour. Graham had set up the rehearsal hall exactly like a small stage, and he attempted to replicate as closely as possible the stage setup Andrew would encounter on opening night. The last detail, which he had done in good-natured humor, was setting up ten or twelve empty chairs in front of the stage, symbolic of the thousands Andrew would face only a few days later.

For only thirty-five minutes of music, John was determined to find some elusive perfection in each minute of performance. He insisted on running over every element of the songs, leaving no stone unturned. He wanted Andrew to be able to walk out on stage and do his part of the concert in his sleep.

For Andrew, these rehearsals were a new concept. His performances at Christ's Kingdom had always included a certain level of spontaneity, and that had always been an important element of his self-expression, musically as well as spiritually. It had been a conduit for the deepest part of his ministry. Once the album had been recorded, however, final versions of songs had been codified once and for all, and John was insisting that the band stay extremely close to the recorded versions. Andrew resolved to work hard and to stay enthusiastic, however, and the band plowed dutifully along, spending hours on musical minutiae until John acknowledged that his version of perfection had been

achieved. Only then would he release them to work on
another song.

Nothing received more attention than Andrew's personal
performance. His natural tendency had always been to withdraw into the music, rendering himself more and more invisible, letting the Spirit lead. John was convinced that this was
a deadly mistake in a large auditorium, however, and
worked tirelessly to get Andrew to look up and out, "working the crowd," as he said.

It was John's idea that at least twice during each concert,
Andrew would get up from behind the piano and stride the
stage, just singing and letting the band carry the accompaniment. Andrew could make more contact that way and show
a more entertaining dimension to his performance. Andrew
received this bit of instruction like a bad-tasting, but necessary medicine. Try as he might, the farther away he moved
from his piano, the more uncomfortable he became. He
would gaze longingly back at it as he sang, wanting to feel
the keys under his fingers, to withdraw into the solitude of
the music.

On the last day of rehearsal, Andrew pushed himself as
always, but John waved his arms at him for the hundredth
time to project and smile so that people four hundred feet
away could see it. The band ground to a stop, and Andrew
sighed, feeling a bit hopeless.

"John, I'm doing my best to cooperate," he said, "but I'm
beginning to feel like a trained monkey. I'm having a hard
time feeling sincere about this."

"What's the problem?"

Andrew spoke deferentially. "I guess it's just that this part,
I mean the performing part, was where everything was
leading to for me. That's where the ministry has to happen.
I'm not sure how to do it with all this." He gestured around
himself vaguely.

John shrugged his shoulders. He had tried everything,
from cajoling to convincing, to get Andrew to act like an

entertainer. He was running out of ideas. "Okay, Andrew. Just go out there and bomb. What do I care?"

"I beg your pardon?"

"I said, just go out there and bomb. Because that's what you'll do. If you go out in front of a huge crowd and don't project, you'll die out there."

"I thought they were coming to hear the music, and the message," said Andrew limply, already knowing that his situation had already become far more complex than that.

"Yeah, sure they are. But you're leaving something very, very important out, my friend."

"What's that?"

"They paid."

Andrew stood in silence, considering. He had to admit that as obvious as it was, he had never really considered the full implications of those words.

"They've paid big dollars to be there, Andrew," John went on. "You've got an obligation to entertain them. If they had wanted to go to church and hear a sermon, they would have gone to church. But they paid money, and they want to see a show. No show, and they're not happy. And I don't blame them. If you were doing ninety minutes, then fine, take your time, warm up to each other, talk a little while. But with thirty-five, you've got to set the songs up and get to it. I don't see any alternative. You've got to get through as much of the album as you can, and you've got to get people excited about what you're doing. You've got to entertain them."

Andrew found that he had no answer to John's point. It was one thing to look at ministry in a church, but when people buy a ticket on a Friday night and take a date they would reasonably expect a different kind of experience. The trouble was, he had never considered what he did as entertainment per se, and he had one more day to make that transition, a transition he wasn't sure he had wanted to make in the first place. For a moment, he saw the sanctuary of Christ's Kingdom Assembly in his mind, and he realized the terrific freedom that he had enjoyed there.

"Look, John," he said. "I don't know what to say to all this, because I guess you're making sense. But at some point I have to begin asking what I'm doing up there. I'm doing this for a reason."

John's normal upbeat demeanor was rapidly fraying around the edges. "What's your point, Andrew? Are you saying that Christians can't have a good time? Are you saying there's something inherently wrong with entertaining them? Because if that's what you're saying, I'd have to disagree with you there."

Andrew shook his head. "No, John, that's not what I'm saying. To tell you the truth, I'm not sure what it is that I am saying. But I'm sure it's not that."

"Then what is it?"

Andrew looked down, feeling depressed. His head was spinning, and getting a clear thought to emerge seemed a distant possibility. "I'm just saying that I'm very simply confused."

This last sentence was uttered quietly, with a tone of resignation.

John looked at his artist with sudden compassion. Andrew was under a lot of pressure, and he had been hard on him, pushing him faster than he would have preferred. But the McCloud tour was worth it. He put his arm around Andrew and gave him a short, firm hug. The role of father-confessor was a comfortable one for him, and he enjoyed it.

"I understand, Drew," he said slowly. "This is all a whole new ball game for you. But I've explained it to you before. When in doubt, just remember my little phrase: It's business. It's ministry. It's the business of ministry."

Andrew looked up at his manager, determined to understand. He had to understand because so many people depended on him. In two short days, he would walk out in front of thousands of people and sink or swim. Totally apart from any spiritual concerns, he had no desire to make a fool of himself on stage. He was determined to get to the bottom of what he was feeling.

"You say that a lot, John. That business and ministry thing. I can tell it's a touchstone for you. What does it really mean?"

"What it means is this, my friend. You want to reach people, right?"

"Right. I'm sure about that."

"Good. Then draw 'em in. See, people are gonna be drawn by something. Right now they're being drawn by a lot of trash out there. Why not give them an alternative? But why not be the best show out there, and then we sock it to 'em with the gospel."

"Yeah, Mark said something about that. So what you're saying is that this show-biz stuff has nothing to do with the gospel part? I mean it's like a separate dimension?"

"Pure window dressing, my friend. It's like bait on a hook."

"Okay. But explain to me again. Where exactly does the business and ministry part happen?"

"I don't see why this is so complicated for you, Andrew. Look, the show is business. When people come to the show, we profit. Pure and simple. We sell more records, too. We profit again. I have never tried to sugarcoat or hide it for one minute. I don't see why I should. It's totally aboveboard. The ministry is the ministry that goes on at the concerts, and with the recordings. The more we sell, the better the Lord is served. It's mathematical. Get it?"

Andrew scrunched his brows together, struggling. He had heard this reasoning before, from the moment he hit Nashville. On one level it made sense, but now he was a principal player, and he based huge decisions on its validity. That was different. He had to get up in front of a great many people in a very short time and sell the idea himself. The truth or falsehood of this continuous undercurrent was beginning to be very important to him personally. He had to put his thoughts away until later, however, because John was already motioning him back into position to start the rehearsal again.

Andrew sighed and walked back up onto the small stage. He looked out at the back wall, and tried to imagine a huge crowd there in place of the white painted brick. He remembered that most of them would be there not to see him but to see Darren McCloud. If he failed to entertain them, he would experience a level of humiliation beyond any previous experience.

The issue, he realized, was no longer simply who Andrew Miracle was. The moment that John had booked him on the Darren McCloud tour, the issue had also become who people wanted to see when they spent their money on a concert ticket. Being yourself was one thing. Not giving people their money's worth was another. More than anything else, he didn't want to fail in front of so many, and particularly in front of John and all his friends at Dove. In his mind's eye too was Carolyn. For a frightening moment he imagined walking off stage a loser, and he imagined her embarrassment as the bubble of his career was burst before it ever floated off the ground. No matter what, he couldn't let that happen.

"Okay," he said at last. "Let's go back to work."

John clapped his hands and said, "You heard the star, boys. Let's get cracking, and this time I want you to sell this song like it's never been sold before!"

The band kicked into the tune with new vigor, and Andrew belted the lyric out. When the chorus came around, he picked the microphone out of the stand before the piano and stood up. He closed his eyes and pictured in his mind the faces of countless, expectant fans. He imagined that Carolyn and all the people at Dove were in the middle of a huge audience, and that he was the focus of all their attention. It worked. His performance took on a new energy and vigor, and at the same time he began to feel more relaxed, more within himself. It felt good to just let go and stop worrying so much. He imagined people hundreds of feet away from him, and his motions grew more exaggerated as he related to this imaginary crowd. He had watched some music videos on television since arriving in Nashville, and he mimicked some of the movements he had seen in them, cautiously at first, and then more openly and with enthusiasm. As the song ended, John was wearing his prospector's smile again, and the tension in the room had evaporated. All was well.

"Dinner's on me, boys, and you name the place," John said, elated. "This is a turning point in your career, Drew. We'll remember this day for a long time."

Andrew looked out at John, taking in his happy smile and finding a refuge from his ambivalence in it. He was tired after his performance, and there was sweat on his forehead.

"I'm sure we will," he said. "But you guys will have to do dinner without me. Carolyn's got something planned."

John frowned, and took Andrew aside. "I appreciate that, but we leave tomorrow, Drew. This is important bonding time."

Andrew looked up at John. He had given John everything he had wanted, but it seemed that there was always something more on John's mind. "I'm sorry, John," he said apologetically. "Carolyn's already got this thing going, and I really do have to go. You guys have a great time without me, and I'll meet you at the bus at nine o'clock tomorrow morning, as planned."

John was irritated, but there was no way to confront Andrew with so many onlookers. He turned away and said cheerfully, "Okay, boys. Looks like it's just us tonight. Where to?"

To Andrew's surprise, most of the band members seemed to lose enthusiasm for the dinner plans when he announced he wouldn't be coming along. It was as if he was the glue that held them all together, and if he wasn't there, there was no real reason for anyone to be there. Several of the guys muttered about needing to get home. In the end, the rehearsal broke up on a surprisingly somber note.

As rehearsal ended, Carolyn was putting the finishing touches on her little apartment. She was preparing a party, but unlike Andrew's release party, this was an event for only two. It was a going away party. Andrew would be gone for nearly a month on tour, and she had managed to keep her sadness about that fact at bay by being a part of it. She had decorated her apartment with balloons and ribbons, and had set the table carefully.

She dressed for Andrew that night. From the beginning he had been easily pleased in that regard, and she had a half a dozen outfits to choose from that she knew he loved. She liked that simplicity about him. Often she had noticed that he hadn't had a chance to grow cynical and callused about love yet. He was inexperienced with it, and that stood in marked contrast to many of the men she had met since moving to Nashville two years ago. Those men had not been inexperienced in love, and they had wanted to share their experience. Andrew was different—he had little experience to share—and he seemed genuinely moved by all the small things she did for him. That quality was precious to her, and she wanted somehow to guard it against all the pressures that would attack it in the future. That was what made his leaving so difficult for her. He had already changed, subtly, in the few months he had been in Nashville. It was inevitable, she knew. To be the focus of so much attention and praise and remain, not artificially but genuinely unchanged would take a remarkable person. Once he was on tour, the pressures on him would increase a hundredfold. Increasingly, she saw that what meant most about him to her was his humility and simplicity. She began to realize that those qualities were not inviolable in a person, but could, by degrees, be changed.

Carolyn picked out a pretty print dress in a heavy fabric that Andrew had commented on several times. Seated before her mirror in the bedroom she put on her makeup carefully. It was odd, having all these new feelings. It was as if their relationship had been turned upside down: in the beginning, she had felt her power with him, and enjoyed it. Now, she was increasingly feeling like the pursuer, and she found herself worrying about where she stood with Andrew. Dinner was almost finished, and he was due any minute. She was giving herself a last-minute look when Andrew's familiar knock on the door drew her away from the mirror. Turning, she opened the door and let the man who had come to mean so much to her into her apartment.

Andrew's mood was high, full of nervous energy and distracted cheerfulness. He was counting down the hours until he and John made the drive to Knoxville to meet the Darren McCloud tour on its opening night, and his conversation was preoccupied with the details of the tour. Carolyn listened attentively but impatiently; she wanted to connect with his inner man again, the way she had the night he had played for her at the chapel at Vanderbilt. It had only been four months ago, but it seemed like years.

Dinner was lighthearted, and they held their conversation artificially aloft to keep their parting at a distance. When they finished, Andrew pushed back from the table and sighed. "I suppose it will be a long time before I get a meal like that again, Carolyn," he said. "I'll miss that on the road."

"Will you?" asked Carolyn. She looked at Andrew wistfully. "Then tell me something. What's the thing that you'll miss the very most when you're gone?"

Andrew smiled. "Easy. You, of course. I'll miss you the most." He stood, and stretched his legs languorously. "I'll help with the dishes," he said, starting toward the kitchen with a plate.

"Let's leave them," Carolyn said, and he caught an unexpected intensity in her voice. Looking down at her, he realized that his leaving had at last intruded into their evening together. He set down his plate and led her to the couch.

"You know what I think?" he asked thoughtfully.

Carolyn was feeling vulnerable, and found herself not as talkative as she had imagined she would be. "What's that?" she answered softly.

"I think I just realized how much I'm actually going to miss you."

"What made you think of that?"

"I suppose it's just how busy everything's been, and it's been easy to let one thing follow another. There's been a lot of excitement, and John's had his whip out, pushing everything forward. But I just now realized what it means that I won't be seeing you, at least not after the first night. You're still coming up with the office staff, aren't you?"

"I'll be there."

"Good. I'm sorry I've been so absorbed, lately, Carolyn. There's scarcely been time to breathe."

Carolyn smiled. "I understand all that, of course. But I hate to let you go."

Andrew laughed. "You're not letting me go," he said lightly. "That just sounds wrong somehow. I'll be out of town, but we don't need to put it that way."

Carolyn turned her face away, not wanting him to see her. He had become much too adept at reading her face. An uneasiness had been slowly growing in her, a little more each week. It had begun, she supposed, with the release party. The feelings centered on Andrew, and a sense that perhaps his gift was fragile, as well as precious. It could well be far more fragile than anyone realized. Could it endure the changes that were coming? But Carolyn felt that she had no real right to her worries, and she had resisted talking to Andrew about them. The feeling was ill-defined. It came from a feminine place inside of her, a place of nameless, but nevertheless demanding, intuition. As the tour approached, the feeling had gradually grown stronger, and now it was becoming difficult to ignore. She felt it again now, more strongly, but she resisted it. She had never been the possessive type, but this was a different kind of relationship. What seemed like an important intuition could easily just be a selfish need to keep Andrew close, where they could be together. Surprising herself, she suddenly reached out to him and pulled him close.

He came to her easily, and in his arms again she felt that perhaps there was nothing to worry about. It would only be for a few weeks, and then he would be back, the same Andrew she had fallen in love with. The moment passed, and she came back to herself, her old lightheartedness coming to her rescue. Their last thirty minutes together were easy, and the time flew by until they both knew it was time for him to leave.

Andrew moved slowly toward the door, hesitant to go but knowing that the bus would leave early the next morning and the coming day would be an extremely long one. He reached to kiss her good-bye when Carolyn once again held him tightly with a surprising, nervous forcefulness.

She held him silently, and then she whispered, "Don't change out there," her head buried in his neck. "Let them cheer you and love you, but don't let them change you."

Andrew pulled her back, disentangling her arms from his body and looking her in the eye. "Don't worry," he said firmly. "They won't get to me. I'll call you every night."

With those words they kissed once again, a long kiss meant to carry them across weeks of separation. Andrew reached for the door and passed through it, walking out into the city beyond. As the door closed behind him, Carolyn closed her eyes and leaned back against it. She couldn't help thinking that he had passed beyond her protection as well.

18

There is, perhaps, no line of separation more complete than that of the stage curtain. The world is cleanly split in two, the one side where the great mass of humanity resides, fueling the fame and fortune of those few that live on the other, the side of privilege and position. There is a camaraderie there not unlike being at court; the sycophant lord chamberlains and even the lowly chambermaids, by dint of their laminated passes, may come within the castle walls, and there may even be a court jester. The king is the artist, and he rules behind the curtain that hides Neverland from view. There are the lords and ladies, the artist managers and road managers. There are guards, great hulking men in sweaty, identical T-shirts that stand before any entrance to what lies behind the curtain. There are the knights, the musicians in the band, supporting the king, granted access to the inner life of court. There is the counselor of the exchequer, known as the tour accountant, and the various pages and chambermaids and cooks, and indeed the whole of court life as well. All depend upon the king, for they serve at his pleasure. All, including the king, depend upon the curtain. The curtain depends upon no one. It is the boundary, the great wall that gives Neverland its meaning. Without it, laminated passes are so much laminated plastic.

The stage curtain not only differentiates royalty and commoner, it also defines the public and the secret. Life behind the curtain can be as serene as a lake or as frantic as a fire drill without the mass of people on the other side ever realizing it. Arguments are won and lost. The audience can be mocked or respected, never the wiser. The imperfections

of t
is d
poss
mad
into
men
cam
hims
beca
curta
anoth
of he
that J
of con
on. A
the ar
dange

voice call softly, "Ready?" Lysette nodded
seconds, a voice boomed her introdu
There was a sudden whir of mot
bled and pulled back rapidly,
swept away to reveal what la
to expel its accumulated
and whistles. Before t
drummer was co
slammed into it
of the prosc
Instant
her s
ed

...y but latently in the back of every person's mind, even the most humble: he is worshiped. All attention falls upon him. He is as rare and as valuable as a diamond in a museum, or a panda in a zoo, with the incalculable advantage of being able to perceive his status. What is dimmed in most people through disuse and improbability is tickled with a light feather, aroused, and sensitized. Eve is awakened. Long live the king, and Adam can be like God.

Andrew was not thinking these thoughts as he watched from the wings, fascinated, as the opening act was introduced. Instead, he merely positioned himself between two curtains at stage left and peered wonderingly at the enormous crowd of faces turned toward the stage. Behind the main curtain, Lysette's band had taken their places and were waiting silently, staring with blank expressions at the back of the heavy fabric hanging in front of them. There was an undeniable tension in the air, made more acute because it was completely unknown to the audience. The tightness suddenly shifted appreciably higher, and Andrew heard a

..., and within a few
...tion through the P.A.
...rs, and the curtain trem-
...its great folds compressing,
... behind it. The crowd, anxious
...anticipation, erupted into applause
...he curtain was halfway open Lysette's
...nting off the first song, and her band
... as the last fold hid itself away in the sides
...nium.

...y, Lysette was in full motion, full of the rhythm of
...ng, half-walking, half-dancing her way to the very
...e of the stage. She greeted the audience with a shout,
...d spinning around, launched into her first vocal, radiant
in the spotlights trained on her. They followed her every
move, gliding across the stage as she did, capturing her, a
bright spot bobbing on a dark sea.

"Does anybody here love Jesus tonight?" she fairly
shouted, her voice shimmering with energy. The crowd
roared its yes back to her, and she repeated her question
again, even more enthusiastically.

"I said, does anybody here love Jesus tonight?"

The crowd responded in a wave of powerful energy, their
ebullience carried aloft by Lysette's.

"Then let's give Jesus a hand," she said triumphantly.
"Let's just give the Lord a hand."

The crowd applauded, and many stood and clapped, their
hands in the air. While much of the crowd was still standing,
Lysette counted off the next song, and soon the whole crowd
was on its feet, clapping in time to the music.

Andrew watched from backstage, transfixed. It seemed
incomprehensible that in a very few minutes he would face
this same crowd and be expected to send them to the same
level of ecstasy that they were experiencing now. He stood
in awe of the ease in which Lysette moved and swayed,
dipping in time to the music, fairly skipping across the stage.

Her music was only one part of her total presentation. Her every movement was designed to lead the crowd into a specific response. Her first few songs built the audience up; then, for a short time, she let them down a bit; finally, as she approached the close of her set, she began marching them back up the ladder of enthusiasm until, as her final song ended, the crowd was once again on its feet and clapping wildly.

Andrew was jarred back to himself by the whir of motors. As Lysette stood in the middle of the stage locked in a graceful bow, the curtain began closing on Lysette's band. Once again, the enormous felt door trembled momentarily and then swung closed. As the last speck of vision onto the stage was erased, Lysette relaxed, wiping sweat from her forehead, and turned to walk slowly off stage. The window had closed. Even as she left, the stage was being overrun by workers anxiously striking her set and preparing Andrew's. At that moment, Andrew felt a hand on his shoulder. It was Graham, his stage manager.

"Time to go, Andrew," he said. "Ten minutes to places, fifteen to show time."

Andrew followed Graham back to his dressing room, where Carolyn and John were waiting. John was pacing anxiously. When the door opened, he leapt from his seat, exclaiming, "Good Lord, boy, where have you been? But you're here now, so let's get a last look at you."

Andrew looked at himself in the mirror, and John gave him a thorough going over. Everything was in order. Carolyn was sitting quietly on a small office chair, excluded, it seemed, by the sheer pace and frenetic tension of the moment. She sat a few feet away from the flurry, smiling a confident smile in Andrew's direction. He locked onto her eyes, finding for a moment his confidence there. She rose, invited into the circle of energy by his look, and she gave him a quick hug, letting him quiet himself in her eyes, a calm place in the commotion. Andrew felt he would have liked to have stayed there, with her arms around him. He could, in that moment, have simply let the concert go on without him—never to have succeeded, and never to have failed.

"I'm with you out there," she said softly, and kissed him lightly on the cheek. "Don't forget that." She had wanted to say more, to express some powerful support to him. In spite of Andrew's hug, however, she was feeling ambivalent about the next thirty minutes for Andrew. She was afraid for him, she supposed. She wanted him to win, knowing the consequences of a bad performance. But she was also afraid for herself. She tried to push that feeling down, thinking that it was beneath her. She was there to support Andrew and to help in any way for him to walk on stage ready to perform. She wanted the absolute best for him. But she could hear the audience clapping in time down the hallway from the stage, and she couldn't help feeling that the moment he walked through the door of his dressing room, she would be sharing him with thousands of other people that didn't really know him and had no right to him. She stood silently, feeling Andrew's arms around her, willing herself to be content. Then John touched him on the back, disengaging them, and maneuvered him out the door and toward the stage. As Andrew looked back, Carolyn smiled confidently and waved. She gathered her thoughts for another moment before slipping out the stage door to her seat in the audience.

Andrew found himself being pushed forward hurriedly, and he moved quickly toward the stage. His band was already in their places, and they nodded cheerful but tense hellos as he followed John to his place at the piano. He took his place there, reexamining his position relative to the piano every few seconds, as if this time there were something unique and different about the way the keys lay waiting for him. They looked like strangers. He sat there, shaking slightly with nerves, but absolutely determined to do well. Above all things, he felt he couldn't afford to fail. Not tonight, not with everyone there, not with everyone depending on him so much. He had to give the people what they wanted, or John, Carolyn, and everyone at Dove would be the butt of a cruel joke.

John shook his hand warmly as he turned to go, but Andrew could sense that he was nervous too; they both knew that each of them had every bit as much on the line as the other. The two stood silently a moment facing each other, and then John stepped back and said in his confident way, "Eat 'em up, kid." With that, he turned and walked briskly into the darkness, and Andrew was left staring after him, alone with his band. He turned and faced the back of the curtain. It hung as straight and motionless as a stone wall. At any moment it would move back, and there would be nothing but bright air between himself and the eyes of six thousand waiting people.

The background music playing through the huge speaker system stopped suddenly, cut off in the middle of a song. It was time. Andrew took a deep breath. The crowd, sensing the concert was about to resume, responded with scattered yells and clapping. Then Andrew heard the starkly simple phrase that would push him off the fence of waiting, and into the race.

"Ladies and gentlemen," a voice thundered, "please give a warm, Knoxville welcome to Dove Records' recording artist Andrew Miracle!" At that moment, the motors whirred, the curtains pulled back, and Andrew entered a dream. There was a moment of surprising darkness, and then in a flash he could see nothing but three enormously bright lights shutting out all visible sense of the audience. He could hear them, however, their applause rising out of the darkness, and he could pick out voices, yelling from the sides. Then he was awash in sound, as his band began and the powerful stage speakers blasted out the intro to his first song.

There was nothing to do but sing for all he was worth. There was nowhere to hide. There was no thought of the gift. There was only the bright light, and his band thundering out his music, and winning or losing. With so much to lose, he was determined to win.

In spite of the sound check, things sounded different to him now. He soldiered on through the first song, blankly going through the motions, and he was suddenly grateful for all the rehearsal John had insisted on. He was far from comfortable, but he had to assume that he would have felt worse if he hadn't gone through the show so many times. His eyes adjusted a bit, and he could distinguish the faces of five or six rows at the front of the stage. They were far below, staring up at him.

The first song ended. Later, he would have no memory of it. Applause washed over him, but in his state of mind, he barely heard it. He was unable to assess the level of acceptance by the crowd; he wondered if John and the rest of the team would find the applause sufficient. Lysette, after all, had aroused the audience to a fever pitch. Andrew didn't want to seem disappointing in comparison. Time seemed compressed, and the first song seemed to have taken only seconds, rather than minutes. Before he realized it, the second song was underway, and then the third, and he floated through them as well, gradually increasing his awareness, his sense of himself fading in from the numbing, initial rush of nerves.

After each song a wave of applause rushed up to meet him, and he bathed in it, letting it lift him up out of his fear. At the worst, he thought, he wasn't dying out there. He had no frame of reference for what a good audience response would sound like from the stage, but certainly what he was experiencing was not a disaster. As he sang, he could see more and more of the faces in the audience, and he perceived that many were focusing on him with an almost unnatural intensity; they seemed to regard him as a different kind of person, a higher being by merit of his position on stage. It seemed that there was a stream of expectation in the minds of the people there, and he had only to step into that stream, instantly taking on certain desirable qualities merely by being the focus of their attention. He could move to the left, and a hundred eyes moved with him; to the right, and they willingly turned, following him like spectators at a tennis match. To his surprise, many people seemed determined to meet and catch his eye, and he had only to look in any direction to see a dozen faces upturned, eyes searching his own to hold his attention. During the introduction to the fourth song, he let his eyes fall on a plain-looking young girl in the second row. She returned his gaze directly, smiling up at him unwaveringly. Even through the haze of his first concert this struck him; the normal, mutual shyness and decorum of meeting people seemed not to apply while on stage. In his life, he had never stared directly into the eyes of a unknown woman such a long time. He held his eyes on hers, counting seconds, and she did not flinch. Instead, she merely returned his gaze unashamedly, staring up at him as if he were a statue. He sang to her another moment, and pulled himself away to face the huge crowd once again.

Even before Andrew had begun his set, John had made his way to the back of the auditorium to watch. That was always the true test. It was one thing to see excitement in the first few rows. Those people were just glad to be so close to the action—they were almost determined to have a good time. Here, in the back, one could get the real feel of a concert's success or failure. Here, the performer was a small speck in the distance, and his ability to excite the entire hall was transparently revealed.

Initially, van Grimes had been a bundle of nerves, nerves that he couldn't afford to let Andrew see. His mind was churning with thoughts of phenomenal success and abject failure. *Once again, the thing's completely out of my control.* He thought to himself. *The kid will either bomb, succeed, or simply disappear into a yawn, and I can't do a thing about it.* He felt the familiar irritation at the inexact science of the entertainment business. You paid your money, you took your shot. You tried to stack the deck in your favor, but in the end, one temperamental artist met one fickle audience in the dark, and you flew or you fell to the ground with a dry thud.

Van Grimes had been as tight as Andrew during the first song. The kid had looked tense, but he was singing well, and his band was pumping out the kind of energy that brought the people dedicated to having a good time to their feet. Once they were won over, the skeptics would follow. By the time the second song ended, van Grimes had begun to relax. Andrew was doing well. There had been some awkward moments, but by and large he was surprisingly loose, gaining momentum as his set went on. He looked good, even standing still in the early stages. The show would need some refinements, but overall the hard work had paid off. The moment that the lights hit Andrew, the crowd had sensed that something special had been given to them and that Andrew was destined for something bigger than just opening for another artist. He had always sounded like a star, and now he looked like one. The only remaining ingredient would come with time: he needed to act like a star. This first concert was an encouraging sign.

"The kid's gonna make it," John said softly. "He's actually gonna make it." The candy store had been locked, but now Andrew was handing him the gold-plated key. John could see Andrew's confidence growing with every song. Judging from this first night the tour would be a success, and with a successful tour John knew that he would have more power to demand what he wanted from other promoters and from Dove. They would return his phone calls. He would gain bargaining power for signing more artists for his management company. *Power flows to the hot,* he reminded himself grimly as he looked out over the throng of people. They seemed to have forgotten all about Darren McCloud for the moment. *Good,* thought van Grimes. *Let them forget*

McCloud. The guy's history, anyway. Let them only remember Andrew Miracle. And, dear God, please let them remember him all the way to the record store tomorrow morning.

Andrew was approaching a touchy part of the show: the setup for the fifth song. Although John had strictly limited his time to speak, this was the point at which he said the most. John had decided, in the end, to give Andrew a bit of rope after all here, figuring that if he could pull it off, it would give the audience a greater sense of identifying with him. It had been a perilous decision, though, because this would also be the moment of greatest vulnerability, with the greatest possibility of failure. Even at Christ's Kingdom, Andrew had never been much of a talker.

The fourth song ended, and Andrew picked up the microphone tentatively, pulling it from its stand. The spotlight operators narrowed their beams, and he was lit by narrow rays of brightness in a sea of darkness. He took a deep breath and began.

"I bring you a message," he said uneasily, and his voice careened violently around the hall, returning to him nearly a full second later. His voice was enormous, the voice of a deity. There were a few intermittent yells from the crowd, and he realized he hadn't spoken in several seconds. He had simply been standing, an awestruck bystander to the sound of his own voice.

"I bring you a message," he began again, speaking slowly and deliberately. "It's to all of you. My message is this: God is. God knows you. God is calling you to complete sincerity with Him. Complete honesty. Complete truthfulness. Don't just bring your beauty to God. Don't just bring your faithfulness. Bring your ugliness to God, and He will stare at it. Bring your anger to God, and he will calm it. Bring your lies to God, and he will right them."

Andrew breathed a moment, the sound of the air filling his lungs audible through the enormous speaker system. While he had been speaking, it had become remarkably, awkwardly quiet in the hall. For a ridiculous moment, he and the audience simply stared at each other. Then he turned, and the spotlights shimmered off the sequins in his jacket, shooting sparks into the audience. The drummer counted off the next song, and the computerized lighting system sent swoops of light narrowing onto Andrew's still, thoughtful figure. The moment passed, and the concert resumed.

When Andrew paused, collecting himself to speak, van Grimes had squinted at the stage, the darkness of the hall hiding the nervousness playing over his features. *Keep it short,* he thought. Andrew started, but then stopped. He was just standing there. Van Grimes's face tightened. Another second passed, and at last, Andrew began again. *That's right. You're okay, you'll be fine. I wish you wouldn't say ugliness, though. Bad word choice. Makes people uncomfortable. Okay. It's over now, it brought the room down, but you'll survive. Back into the music.*

Andrew's band kicked in, and when the fifth song was nearing its end, the time came for Andrew's costume change. The band continued to play, and Andrew, dutifully waving as he had been instructed, left the stage dramatically, as if his portion of the concert had ended. The audience responded with a wave of sound, and Andrew slipped into the ministrations of a waiting helper to change his clothes. He was appalled at the jacket he took off; it was literally drenched with sweat. Quickly, he put on the leather leggings, stripped off his shirt, put on the silk shirt with the lace ascot, and held out his arms for the electric blue jacket. His perception of time off the stage seemed oddly reversed from his time while on it; offstage, time seemed to slow incredibly rather than speed up. The whole changing operation took only a little more than a minute, but it felt like a lifetime as the band played on without him.

The lights were turned low on one side of the stage, and it was bathed in darkness. Andrew slipped onto it, looking in the dimness for his tape marker indicating the precise spot to stand. He found it, and assumed his pose, eyes closed, arms behind him, chin up. He stood in the dark, frozen, waiting to be illuminated. In an instant, he was bathed in light as three spots and a host of vari-lites hit him simultaneously. Even through closed eyelids, he could sense the extraordinary brightness of the light and feel its heat. The crowd erupted in applause. He heard screams from in front of him. He opened his eyes, and he could see that much of the crowd was on its feet. Everything had worked out just as Mark and John had said it would. Everything was fine. He felt an enormous sense of relief; he had risked a lot in wearing the extreme costume, and in striking a pose that was so far from his natural inclination. In the back of his mind had been the very real fear that the audience would merely stare, or erupt in laughter. But it seemed that life when the curtain was pulled back was very different from life away from the concert hall. What would be regarded as lunatic megalomania in a restaurant or a house or a church was wildly rewarded when lit by spotlights. Emboldened, he strode the stage to the microphone stand and ripped the wireless microphone from its resting place. He spun on his heel and walked straight out to the front of the stage. He was winning, and he knew it now. He let his eyes play out over the audience, his security growing moment by moment.

The band was nearing its crescendo, and then peaked, landing hard on the first chord of the introduction to "Lost Without You." All the instruments but one stopped suddenly on that chord, and only Keith on keyboards played the powerful opening chords to the song that was lighting up radio stations all over the country. It took only a few seconds for the theme to be recognized by the majority in the audience, and as they heard it, they burst into applause. Andrew stood motionless in the center of the stage, eyes closed dramatically. He began singing, not with all the strength he possessed, but with a strong, silken voice that led from one word to another with the smoothness of frosting.

Once again, the song worked its magic. Before the chorus was over, the crowd was swaying as one, singing the chorus in unison with Andrew. It was, he admitted, easier than he had feared. He hadn't anticipated the extraordinary grace that the audience had granted him simply for being on stage; his first awkward moments were largely forgotten now, and he was more and more in the moment, feeling and receiving the affirmation of thousands of people swaying and singing his song together, united in his music and in his presence. It was an experience absolutely out of his reckoning. It filled him up, seeming to heal his every insecurity and inadequacy. He was accepted. The great mass of strangers before him, people that he would meet on the farm or in a mall or anywhere else, were lifting him up above other men. They were revering him. It was a feeling greatly to be desired. It rendered silent the inner screaming that he was a fraud. It quieted the noises that he had heard since a child that he was different, a bad kind of different. In their applause he could no longer hear himself stammer his way through an awkward date in Rose Hill. He had only to look at a girl, and her eyes were sure to meet his own in return. In the wash of applause he was able to hold at bay the awful feeling of aloneness that hides inside of every person, both famous and anonymous. He wanted this feeling to last. He wanted it to grow and grow, and above all, he wanted to be able to take it with him, turning it on and off at will. But he had come to the last line, and as "Lost Without You" ended, he hung his head in the fading spotlight, feeling the crowd explode before him in ecstatic energy. As the music faded, he heard the motors and saw in the corner of his eye the curtain tremble on its huge casters. He would have willed the curtain back, restraining it until he was ready to relinquish his throne. But the curtain ignored him absolutely, obeying, it seemed, a higher power. It moved noisily toward him, and with a start he realized that unless he moved quickly, he would be trapped on the wrong side of it, revealed, and humiliated. He jumped back in the nick of time, and felt the fabric brush against his legs as it moved past him, interlocking and impenetrable. His set was over. He stood trembling a moment, wanting to let every feeling sink into him. But almost instantly he heard workmen moving rapidly toward him, and turning, he saw a union stagehand mechanically reach out and take the microphone from his hand. Without speaking, the workmen began moving microphone stands to different marked locations on the stage. All around them, workers were feverishly preparing for Darren McCloud, the main act. A worker bumped into Andrew lightly as he passed, muttering, "excuse me," a slight irritation audible in his voice. Andrew realized that now, with the curtain closed, he was merely an impediment to the job others had to do.

He started across the cluttered stage, picking his way in the half light across the cables that were being pulled across the stage for Darren's set. He was, he suddenly realized, exhausted. In thirty-five minutes, he had expended an entire day's worth of energy. He was exhausted in mind, he realized, and in his soul.

As he entered the backstage area, he met John, Carolyn, and several Dove employees clapping their hands in applause. He smiled sheepishly, but it felt good. He was still stunned at how quickly his moment had come and gone and with what finality the curtain had closed on him afterwards. Now that it was over, the entire event seemed to have taken only seconds. It was good to have the time prolonged a while by the accolades of his friends.

"A star is born, ladies and gentlemen," John crowed, pushing aside the others to position himself closest to Andrew. "You ate it up, my boy, you ate it up. They were putty in your hand."

Andrew looked up at John gratefully. He had felt he was doing well, but he was longing to get the response from those watching from out front. He wanted to feel the praise of each person in turn.

He wasn't disappointed. Everyone he spoke to after the concert was nothing but positive. He was encircled by seven or eight people, and he stood still while they rained praise on him for a full five minutes. After all his nervousness, it was wonderful to let the fact sink in that he had met their expectations.

Carolyn had been as enthusiastic as any, but after some time, Andrew realized that she had at some point drifted away and was now nowhere to be seen. She had been among the little group around him. He looked for her now, but she had disappeared, apparently vanishing into the darkness toward the stage door. The group moved in that direction and burst into Andrew's dressing room in a happy rush. Andrew found her there, unexpectedly sitting quietly in a chair, alone. When she saw him, she stood up quickly and smiled broadly. She reached out and kissed his cheek, and he hugged her, searching for any telltale stiffness in her body that might betray her attitude. She was compliant, and returned his hug, smiling at him. There was no chance to speak, however, because the group crowded into the little dressing room excitedly, and several conversations broke out at once about his performance.

Andrew turned to the others once again, who began asking how it felt to go through his first big opening night. He talked excitedly for some time, frankly admitting his nerves and laughing as the group relived each song in turn. After several minutes, however, he once again became aware of Carolyn, sitting off to the side, smiling but quiet. She seemed oddly detached from the exuberant party that swirled around him in his moment of triumph, as if watching it from another place. Her behavior hurt him; he wanted her, more than anyone, to share in his exultation. A part of him wanted to take her away and talk, but it was impossible; he was hearing sentences breaking in on each other from all directions at once, each directed towards him. Shutting the group of well-wishers off in order to deal with Carolyn would be unthinkable, as these well-wishers were the very people that had made the evening happen in the first place. He had a very real responsibility to them. And there was another thing: an artist's opening night only happened once, and it didn't seem fair that it should diminished by someone else who didn't seem to understand it. In the end, he put her out of his mind and happily let the congratulations of the others wash over him.

He was just about to describe how it felt when the lights hit him after the costume change when a booming sound came through the closed door to his dressing room. Darren McCloud's band had just started their set, and from the first note, the audience could be heard screaming even backstage where Andrew and his friends were sitting.

Several people hurriedly left the dressing room with rushed apologies, saying that they wanted to see Darren's set. Andrew could see in their eyes that Darren had established a special presence in the marketplace, and even the professionals at Dove left to see his show. John and Harold left soon after the first wave, having a natural interest in observing one of the reigning superstars of the industry. The sound of Darren's band was coming through the walls of the dressing room, and it became hard to talk. One by one, the others left, heading out into the auditorium to hear the show. Andrew showed the last of them out, feeling a bit that his night had been co-opted by the bright light of Darren McCloud. He turned back into the dressing room and saw Carolyn.

She was sitting in a corner of the dressing room, a pale smile on her face. Andrew walked to her and took a chair opposite her, wanting to speak but having difficulty beginning. He felt inexplicably embarrassed before her.

"Some night, huh?" he began lamely. He was searching for some beginning, any beginning.

"Yes, Andrew," she said lightly, "it was a wonderful night. And you were wonderful. I was very proud of you."

Once again he searched her face for a sign of displeasure or resentment, but again, there was none. Her congratulations seemed genuine, but he sensed a far away quality in her, as if she were holding a portion of herself apart. To encounter this attitude on his victorious night was disconcerting. "I'm glad you were proud, Carolyn," he began again. "In a very real way, you know, I was singing for you out there."

Carolyn raised an eyebrow very slightly at this, and its effect on Andrew was to push him even farther off center. She had not uttered a word against him, yet somehow he felt that she was disappointed. There was no accounting for it. She had, after all, been a part of the entire process, literally from the moment he had stepped off the plane from Rose Hill. From the moment he signed until this point, she had been his greatest cheerleader. He had counted on that consistency.

"I'm not sure you're all that pleased, Carolyn," he said—bravely, he felt. "I'm not at all sure that you're with me on this."

Carolyn reached out her hand and took his in her own. She sat opposite him, holding his hand and looking into the open palm. After a moment, she looked up and met his eyes. "No, Andrew, I want you to know that I was very proud of you tonight. You were marvelous out there. I was sitting right up front, and I could feel that everyone was with you from the first note. You did everything you had to do tonight, and I know that the tour will be a terrific success."

"Okay, but I know I'm not imagining this. There's something bothering you. You're not really here tonight."

Carolyn paused before answering. Her own heart was in doubt. The nagging feeling she had been dealing with for some time had come again, and she hated the timing of it. She looked up, and saw Andrew staring at her, obviously feeling a little sulky. She could hardly blame him.

"I can't explain it," she said, "and I don't know that it's fair of me to talk about it when I don't understand it myself."

"Is this about what we talked about the other night? You started to say something, but it seemed you didn't really want to go on with it."

"I don't know. It's not formed in me yet. It may never be. It might be nothing at all."

Andrew was frustrated and made no attempt to hide it. "I have enough pressure on me already, Carolyn. Pressure to do well. If something was bothering you, why didn't you tell me?"

This was the worst possible result for Carolyn; she had tried to hide her lack of peace with a quiet smile, but they knew each other too well for that now. Andrew was probably right to get upset, she thought. How did she know that her feelings were legitimate? She was in a complex situation.

"I was ashamed," she answered, resisting the temptation to look away from Andrew's eyes.

Andrew was surprised by her answer. "Ashamed?" he exclaimed. "Whatever for? We have no secrets."

Carolyn hesitated, but then blurted out, "I didn't say anything because I'm afraid that all I'm really feeling is simple jealousy. I do feel something, but I don't know what it is. What if it's just unnerving to see you getting so much from all those people out there?" She gestured vaguely out past the shut door, toward the auditorium. "Maybe all I wanted to know was that we had something different from all that. Seeing you so happy and fulfilled on stage made me wonder if you would still need me as much when this tour was over, and the next, and the next. I started to wonder if you'd still be the same. Or maybe I was just afraid I couldn't compete with it. I was afraid that all I was feeling was just childish envy." She stood up and kissed his forehead. "I'm sorry, sweetheart," she said, her face opening to him for the first time since he walked off stage. "I'm probably way off base here. This is your night, and your cheerleader has just arrived."

Andrew kissed her gratefully. He didn't want to have to choose between the dreams unfolding before him and the first woman that had ever really loved him. That choice would be intolerable. She was coming around, and everything would work out fine. "Believe that you mean more to me than a hundred audiences," he told her, "because you do."

Carolyn smiled, and once again put her concerns far away. "You want to go out and hear Darren?" she asked cheerfully.

"No, not really. I'll have the chance to do that a lot of nights on the tour. Nights that you aren't around. I'd rather not share you tonight."

"What about all your stuff?" she asked. "And when do you have to be back to go to the hotel?"

"Let's write 'em a note," Andrew laughed. "It's only a few blocks away. We'll meet everyone back there."

"Then let's get out of here," Carolyn said happily. Once again, she had been able to push out of her mind her worries that troubled her. The two of them quickly packed up Andrew's personal effects, and arm in arm, slipped out of the hall through a stage door and into the cold night air of Knoxville.

19

There had been a difficult moment with Carolyn when the band left Knoxville the next morning; it was a good-bye, which was hard enough, but in addition, Andrew sensed that during the night her anxiety about the future was once again preying on her mind. Nevertheless, she soldiered through the parting with a kind of forced cheerfulness that they both found ghastly. He had tried to be kind to her then, realizing that while he was leaving for the greatest adventure of his life, she was returning to the routine of normal existence. It was natural that she would feel the impending separation more keenly. He was off to nineteen more cities, places he had never seen, off to sing his music before thousands of people. Carolyn, he realized, would be going home to her desk at van Grimes's office.

John stayed with Andrew through Orlando, the fifth night of the tour. He had wanted to stay on even longer, worried that somehow the success they were having would prove to be an illusion held together by his presence; he had a tortured feeling that he would return home to find that Andrew Miracle had never existed, that he would wake from the most pleasant dream of his life to find himself planning another low-rent tour for Heaven's Voices. There were pressures mounting in Nashville, however, and he knew that he had to turn things over to Graham and fly home.

Meanwhile, Andrew was discovering life on the road and finding it a remarkable succession of contrasts to his life in Rose Hill. The morning after the Knoxville concert John had led him onto the enormous tour bus that was reserved for the artists and their management. The crew, which was on a different schedule, rode in two other buses scheduled to arrive at each successive city many hours ahead of the artists. The artists' bus was designed to be a kind of portable home, decked out with a microwave, two televisions and VCRs, a stereo, a refrigerator, and a bathroom. The rear of the bus had been converted into a small bedroom with its own entertainment system and a large bed. Darren, as the headline artist of the tour, occupied this room. Lysette, her manager, Andrew, and for the first few dates, John, spread out in four of the eight bunks that were positioned in the center of the bus. The front was comprised of a common area, with two tables, a sofa, and captain's chairs. Huge windows surrounded this part of the bus, and Andrew loved to sit up and watch the countryside roll by mile after mile, seeing places he had never been before.

At first, he was continually surprised by the level of courtesy and even servility with which he was treated when they arrived at a new city. His life in Rose Hill had of necessity emphasized personal responsibility and hard work; here on the road, anything approaching discomfort had been systematically removed, and he never needed to think about where he had to be or what he needed to do. Graham, his road manager, had explained to him that he never had to touch his luggage: all the bags from the artist's bus were numbered and delivered to the appropriate room without attention from the artists. Unknowing, Andrew had bounded off the bus at the first stop and grabbed his bags eagerly, drawing amused stares from the rest of the people on his bus. After being corrected, he had returned to the bus and waited in comfort until the rooms were ready. Then he had walked straight into his room to find his luggage, carefully stowed, a large bowl of fresh fruit and candy, and an arrangement of fresh flowers. Likewise, once he had arrived at a concert hall for the evening, his dressing room would have fresh flowers and a considerable array of food and drink awaiting him. He never ate more than a morsel of that food—his nerves prevented it—and he couldn't help wondering what happened to the rest of it when it magically disappeared at the end of the night.

A routine for travel had already been well established by Darren's efficient touring machine. After each concert, a crew member or security guard led Andrew to a limousine waiting underground to return the artists to the hotel. The next morning, porters would appear at their rooms at the appropriate hour to remove the luggage and store it underneath the bus.

Andrew couldn't help noticing that the others on his bus absorbed this extraordinary attention with a kind of bored detachment. The contrast between this life and his former one back home continually struck him; life on the farm was merciless to procrastinators, and it emphasized above all things the responsibility of doing things for yourself. Seeds never planted were never harvested. Fence not painted got weather damage and had to be replaced sooner. Life there was an endless reminder of the laws of consequence, laws which unobtrusively but firmly formed the character of the people who lived there and laws which seemed to have been utterly suspended for the length of the tour. Only one consequence was of any import now: he had to please the audience. He had to deliver the show to the last row, to get them on their feet and with him every moment of every song. Virtually nothing else was required of him.

Within the glass cage of the bus, he could see normal life going on all around him as the miles passed by. The entourage would pull into a small town, and he could see mothers picking up children from school or shopping. He could see people out mowing lawns in the afternoon or driving home from work. The rolling glass cage split through that life like an arrow and arrived at the next concert site ready to spill itself out into the waiting hall like leaking laughing gas.

The crews would already be hard at work when the artists' bus arrived around 4:30. They, at least, still lived in the

world of consequence. The crew rode all night, sleeping on
the bus virtually every night and getting to the hall by eight
o'clock in the morning for setup. There, they worked like
carneys pitching a circus tent, and Andrew was constantly
amazed at the massive amount of work they accomplished
before the artists arrived each day. More than once he had
stood and watched in admiration as they finished the setup,
recognizing at once the camaraderie of hard work and
sweat. They were a team as a harvest crew was a team,
and to his surprise he occasionally pictured himself working
with them rather than living the strange life in which he
found himself. It was, in many ways, more familiar territory
for him. He found himself overlooking the appalling crude-
ness and base vocabulary that ran through their conversation. He recognized it for what it was: a code of familiarity,
and it gave them a comfortable sense of inclusion. Crew
work was demanding, not just physically but mentally as
well. Riggers started the day early in the morning looking
over architectural plans for the hall to find the proper points
from which to hang the huge speakers. Then they scurried
up scaffolding, stringing audio line, and hung like chim-
panzees from metal cables, supervising others who raised
tons of equipment into the air. The lighting crew worked
hard as well, effectively tearing down, packing, and reas-
sembling enough lights to handle a large-scale Broadway
play every twenty-four hours. Local union men handled a
measure of the grunt work, and the local concert promoters
had armies of helpers as well. They had to print tickets,
purchase advertising time, design ads, as well as arrange
catering. And above all, the personal plans of thousands of
people in each city had been arranged so that they could
attend. All of this preparation for the three hours that the
curtain was open. Once it swung shut again, the whole
incredible, complex process was simply put on wheels and
recreated a few hundred miles away for another crowd of
people.

With the success of the Knoxville concert, Andrew placed himself firmly in the hands of John and the staff at Dove. He still had reservations about the sincerity of his performance, and there were times that he recognized the great distance imposed between himself and the people he was trying to reach; his artificial magnitude and brightness, it seemed, were oddly out of scale with his real opinion of himself. Nevertheless, he wasn't sure there was any point in resisting their advice; they had handled things masterfully until now, and they had been proven right at every turn. Even more important, he found resisting them increasingly tiring. It wasn't possible to go forward continually haunted by doubts; it was easier to agree. He reminded himself of the sense of destiny that had come with van Grimes from the beginning, from the day John had swept into Rose Hill on the heels of Andrew's vision. Just because he was confused didn't mean that God wasn't a part of what was happening. Indeed, how else could he explain the phenomenal success that accompanied their every move? They were golden, and everything they touched turned to gold with them. In the meetings that followed the next few concerts, Andrew listened carefully, determined to incorporate everything that John told him into his stage persona. A raised arm, a dramatic bow, a spinning dance step—all these had a powerful effect when supported by thousands of watts of sound and light. They were tools to be developed and used to enhance the effectiveness of the show. Every evening he grew more familiar with the techniques, learning what worked and what was less than successful, gauging his success by the level of applause and adoration showered upon him after each song.

Meanwhile, "Lost Without You" continued its reign as the number one song in Christian music, and Andrew's name recognition increased dramatically. By the third week of the tour, his introduction was creating a dramatic stir in the audience. The momentum was obviously building for him, and many wheels were turning to enhance his stature as a rising star. The staffs at van Grimes's office and at Dove Records had not been idle. Helen, in particular, had been working hard on Andrew's behalf. She had organized interviews in each city with the local press, starting with the entertainment editors of local newspapers and any local music publications and continuing with short radio interviews taped for broadcast at a later time.

At first, Andrew had found little beyond a polite interest in his presence by the press people backstage at the concerts. They had come to see and be seen with Darren McCloud, and when Darren entered the room Andrew had the disconcerting sensation of being rendered invisible. His own light appeared as a shadow next to Darren's brightness, and more than once Andrew had slipped from the room unnoticed, passing behind a row of people as they turned their backs to him. Helen had been faithfully doing the laborious advance work on his behalf, however, and with each successive concert he found the interest in his presence growing.

In spite of his natural shyness, at first he had looked forward to these interviews with anticipation. He had hoped to find in them a reconciliation between his stage persona and what he regarded as his real self. He felt that by speaking unreservedly in his own words, he could blend the two together and resolve his remaining discomfort. The reality of the interviews, however, was a numbing sameness. It seemed that only twenty or thirty possible questions existed in the minds of all the press, and these questions steered decisively away from philosophy. On the contrary, they circled faithfully around his growing celebrity status like moons around a planet, drawn and held immovably in orbit. "How did it feel to be plucked from obscurity and thrust into the limelight?" they asked him, night after numbing night. "What did it feel like to have a number one record?" "How did he find life on the road?" And most often, "What was Darren McCloud like?"

Andrew was determined in his heart to remain somehow above all the public relations that preceded him from place to place. He felt that as his fame grew, his responsibility to remain humble and accessible grew as well. Nevertheless, it was impossible for him to miss the dramatic change in the way he was treated by others as his notoriety grew, and in its inevitable, self-fulfilling way, he became bit by bit more detached from the people with whom he spoke. He found there was no alternative, because he was rarely presented with a whole human being with which to converse. His celebrity standing changed the people that met him, changed the way they spoke to him, and as his power grew they transformed before his eyes from real people into mere reflectors of his light, their eyes shining, bubbling up before him like newly opened champagne bottles, words popping from their mouths like corks. By the last few nights of the tour, he found that his relationships were increasingly flowing in one direction, and it was impossible to maintain his original, shy demeanor in the shimmering light that came from him, reflected back on him, and dimmed the people around him. He found, for example, that it was difficult to have a conversation about anything other than himself; the shining discs that danced before him were intently lifting him up, almost feverish in their praise. Indeed, in their fashion they almost demanded that he be in all respects larger than life; the magnitude of their own moment of proximity to his light depended on the size of his fame, and they were determined not to be disappointed.

Never was Andrew's detachment from normal life more clear to him than after a concert. On those occasions, when he emerged from the backstage area before the crowd had been herded out, excited squeals of delight greeted his appearance. Likewise, when he walked from the concert hall for a bit of air he would be pursued by well-wishers. Their high spirits seemed ironically to dishearten him; their momentous good will came to symbolize the distance between them. Occasionally, Andrew met a person who, unlike the majority, approached him with a deep sense of gravity. One girl, to his horror, actually burst into tears in the middle of a conversation with him about "Lost Without You." He had stood, rooted and embarrassed, unable to speak before her outpouring of emotion. Not all the people who came to his concerts reacted in such extremes, he knew, but because of the security around the concerts it took considerable effort to reach him, and for this reason most of the fans that he actually met seemed to be involved on some inexplicable level. But he had only to think of the poster-Andrew, and then he understood the reaction of people to him: he was, in a very real way, presented to them in a fashion far beyond normal human experience. The poster-Andrew eclipsed the friends in their normal lives like perfect cut-glass eclipsed plastic. Had they ever had a friend who spoke with a hundred thousand watts of power? Had the girls he met ever dated a boy lit up by spotlights and the drama of the stage? The light of his perfected image, whether he desired it or not, dimmed the light of all around him. It unnerved him to have this effect on people, but he had no idea how to fight it; indeed the effect seemed to be exactly what the designers of his career had counted on, what they had wanted from the beginning. To be made bigger than life was to have the power to draw others to him and make them pay for the experience. He had often spoken to John about his feelings, but van Grimes had, as usual, answered him with a persuasive statement that silenced him but failed to satisfy him. John had reminded him of the impressionable nature of many young people, insisting that they were looking for someone to admire.

"Young people today are going to have heroes, my friend," he had said with his earnest smile. "Just look around you. There are super-heroes everywhere. But who are they looking up to? Gambling athletes and drugged-out rock stars. I just thank God that there's an Andrew Miracle out there for them to look up to. Because, believe me, they're going to look up to someone. Why shouldn't it be someone who believes in Christ? What you're doing is more than just all right, Drew—it's essential."

John's answer made sense, as usual. But Andrew was once again left with his old condition. What was the good of being looked up to if he wasn't sure where he was leading people? He thought back to his music at Christ's Kingdom. It had been so uncomplicated, and above all, it had been absolutely sincere. There had been no stage presentation, simply the unabashed pouring out of his heart. Perhaps, he wondered, he could translate that experience into the concert halls he was playing now. But when he thought of revealing himself that way to so many, his heart froze. How could he play of Mrs. Harris bent over and singing "Amazing Grace" under the fanfare that preceded his every move? How, indeed, could the poster-Andrew tap into the wellspring that his music had come from in the first place?

Ministry. That was what he had wanted to accomplish when all of this started. His ministry, he knew, was a specific one: telling the tales of honesty and simplicity before God. His music was of the wheat fields, of telling God about his love and also his hate. He found that the concerts themselves were the most difficult times of all to actually minister, however. Once Lysette had whipped the crowd to a fever pitch, the concert had a momentum of its own. As soon as he appeared under the spotlights, the crowd was elated and, more important, demanding.

He was becoming, certainly, more professional. Each night his audience response was growing, and he had, at least, the satisfaction of knowing that he was winning on stage. But a curious helpless feeling sometimes gnawed at him. He walked out on stage each night as if he was missing something, but couldn't discern what it was.

In the midst of all these thoughts, Andrew began to feel that on top of his other sins, he must be profoundly ungrateful. At times he felt guilty, sure that God was looking down on him like a petulant crybaby. He tried to keep his feelings more and more to himself, knowing that he would sound haughty and self-inflated to complain. Wasn't he being treated like royalty? Wasn't he instantly getting everything he asked for? If he wanted something to drink on stage, all he had to do was glance at Graham. His dressing room was like a flower shop. He traveled by limousine from the concert hall to his hotel suite. Nevertheless, his uneasiness inevitably worked its way to the surface. Unable to express his true feelings, he found that he was short with people who were trying to help him; unconsciously, he resented their presence. Several times in the last day alone he had barked at a backstage hand who had failed to please him—but perhaps that was the poster-Andrew and not the real Andrew, he thought. In atonement, he redoubled his commitment to do well. There was no excuse not to humbly march forward and do his best to please the people who had entrusted so much to him.

Carolyn, in particular, represented a difficulty for him. She was on both sides of his problem. On the one hand, she knew him well, and she had been the first to sense that something was wrong—even before he had realized it himself. But she was also the hard-working employee of the John van Grimes agency, so he assumed that in her day-to-day existence she spent much of her energy helping John to promote the poster-Andrew. He longed to confide in her, but her allegiance was plainly split. For Carolyn, his doubts called into question not just his life but hers as well. More than once they had nearly quarreled, avoiding it only by doggedly changing the subject.

As the tour went on, Andrew let his thoughts drift back to Rose Hill. He had not talked or written to his mother much lately—she of all people could sense when he was unsettled, and he hadn't wanted to distress her. It was easier to just put off calling her day after day. He missed talking to her; she hadn't been all that well the last few weeks, and he was worried. He had taken her sturdy health for granted so long that it disturbed him that she had been ill. He didn't want to add any concern for him to her difficulties. Inevitably, his thoughts were drawn back to the small tasks that he would be doing if he were there: helping around the farm, playing for the old folks, singing songs for his Sunday school class and, of course, playing for the Sunday morning services that had become so integral to the life of the church. Only two or three hundred souls could hear him there, and in Sunday school, only twenty or so. Still, it seemed that there was some essential ingredient in these small acts of creative service that was lacking in the huge spheres in which he now found himself. As he thought of Rose Hill, his thoughts were wrenched back through time, the weeks flashing before him until he remembered the moment at which it had all begun: the moment of his visitation. Once more, he pondered the meaning of those improbable words:

"Andrew, you are love."

What did it mean? He asked himself the question for the hundredth time. Perhaps, he thought with a start, it hadn't been God at all who had spoken to him. Was it possible that the Voice was actually coming from the darkness, from Satan disguised as the Light? He had never given this possibility any thought, but it might not explain his ambivalence? In his mind, however, he discounted this. The Voice was still imbedded within him, and his spirit gave witness to the love and peace within the sound and fabric of the One who had spoken to him. Then, he remembered what Carolyn had said, something about stories within stories. He had been telling her about the suffering of old Mrs. Harvey, all bent over at the retirement home and in pain. He saw the old woman again in his mind, flecks of spittle on her mouth as she sang. Carolyn had said that perhaps he wasn't just there for Mrs. Harvey, but that in some way beyond human understanding, she had been there for him. It seemed impossible that God would let her suffer for the benefit of another person. But there were stories within stories. Maybe the truth was that they had been there for each other. If that was so, then there was no way out from where he was but through the fire. God hadn't released Mrs. Harvey from her affliction. Andrew wondered if maybe He would release her if he could learn what it was he was supposed to learn. Maybe he would one day know what the words the Voice had spoken to him had meant.

20

Michael Thomasson parked his black Mercedes underground at the Atlantic Records offices. He picked up his suitcase almost demurely, his motions small and restrained. Smoothing his tailored suit carefully, he glided rapidly into the elevator, and appeared at nine o'clock sharp at his office.

Thomasson had a deal to make today. He had been carefully monitoring Andrew Miracle's appearances on the Darren McCloud tour, and the news was good. After a shaky start, the kid was picking up steam. The song was a huge hit on Christian radio, and the album was selling out at a terrific rate for that market. It was time to move.

His legal department had drawn up papers and he had sent them, unsigned, to Dove records for consideration. They spelled out the labyrinthine financial considerations of distributing "Lost Without You" internationally through the retail outlets that normally sold Atlantic product. It had taken seventeen single-spaced pages of legalese to cover all the bases, but Dove had returned the document signed within three days. That had been one day longer than he had anticipated, Thomasson admitted with a smile. The psychological games—the pretense of being pursued and not looking anxious looked distinctly humorous from where he now sat, leaning back in his hand-sewn calfskin chair. Dove had, no doubt, considered that if they didn't respond immediately, any changes they might have asked for would have been taken more seriously, making it appear as if Harold and Laurence were debating whether or not to sign the contract at all. Perhaps they had hoped for a phone call from Thomasson himself to see how things were going. By the end of the third working day, however, they had broken down, and the signed contracts were delivered by courier to Atlantic's offices.

Thomasson glanced over the terms with familiar satisfaction. He had been the architect of the deal himself. It was heavily biased in Atlantic's favor, as he felt it should be: Atlantic was taking the risk, after all, shoveling money into the public relations world to convince them to suddenly find Andrew Miracle indispensable.

Thomasson opened his desk drawer and selected a Cartier pen from his collection. He carefully unscrewed the lid and set it down parallel to the papers. Then, drawing the act out into several small but distinct motions, he picked up the papers, tapped them against the table to align them precisely, set them back down on the table, and turned each page over one by one until he had arrived at the last page. He picked up his pen ceremoniously and assuming a formal air, wrote his name on the document in a long, flowing script, as if he were signing the Magna Carta. Thomasson had always prided himself on his sense of occasion; life was to be savored, and so many, he felt, lived it so tactlessly. As he signed, his mouth automatically formed a smile. When he had finished, he realigned the papers and put them carefully aside. Then, he screwed the top back on the gold pen deliberately. He closed his desk drawer with satisfaction and picked up the telephone opposite him on his modern, tidy desk.

"Karl, would you come in here, please?" he spoke into the receiver. As he waited, he leaned back and looked across the room at the wall covered with gold and platinum records. Each represented a calculated gamble that he had taken and that had paid off handsomely. Each was a tribute to his sense of the market and his business savvy. Each signified, as well, a life changed to its core by stardom. He was ruminating comfortably on his spectacular batting average when Karl Hunter opened the door and entered his office.

Karl Allen Hunter was the director of media relations for Atlantic Records, Nashville. As such, he headed the entire team of PR professionals that were employed there to keep each of their artists constantly in the public eye.

"Good morning, Karl," Thomasson began easily. There wasn't a trace of tension about him, nothing to declare that he was about to unleash a half million dollars worth of publicity about Andrew on an unsuspecting nation. Hunter took a seat opposite him, deferentially awaiting orders.

"I've decided it's time to move on Andrew Miracle," Thomasson said, his voice level. "I'm going to give him the whole shot. The whole thing." Thomasson had an unnerving habit of referring to any work done by any Atlantic employee as his own.

"I don't want to promote him as much as unleash him," he said, warming to his task. "I'm committing to a video right now, budgeted at one hundred twenty thousand dollars. I want a list of prospective directors on my desk tomorrow morning. Be looking for someone who can deliver something young, earthy, and right under the surface, sexy. Call Dove and get the master to Andrew's record. We'll do at least two re-mixes for pop radio formats, at twenty-five thousand dollars each. We'll release those two and the original version simultaneously all over the country. Get Candyman 95 to do the re-mixes."

Candyman 95 was the *nomme de guerre* of the hottest remix man in the country. His job was to take music that had been made with one audience in mind and transform it with his studio genius into something that a completely different demographic group would buy. He enjoyed total freedom to work his magic: he disassembled the master tape of a song and recorded new music around it. Sometimes all that remained of the original song was the lead vocal. He often recorded completely new accompaniment around the vocal, bringing in dance grooves and new guitar parts and mixing it all into a new sound that defied the original recording. The potential payoff was immense: increasingly, radio stations were limiting their formats strictly and only playing music that fit into a very narrow category. Candyman 95 had established an impressive record of transforming music that had been written in one narrow vein into various versions that everything from dance clubs to rock stations eagerly embraced. Every time a song crossed over into another radio format, the artist's exposure increased exponentially, with the record sales following close behind. It was tricky work, because normally these remixes bore little resemblance to the original version of the song, and artists who were highly attached to their work could be polarized by the final result. Nevertheless, Atlantic demanded and generally got contractual permission to do remixes without the approval of the artist. It would cost fifty thousand dollars for Candyman 95's work, and pushing three different singles instead of one would triple those expenses as well. But this was the kind of firepower that Atlantic had, the kind that the staff of Dove exercised only in their dreams.

"I want a marketing meeting called for next Tuesday, and arrange to have Harold Murphy from Dove there as well. We'll bring the entire staff up to date on what an Andrew Miracle is at that time and decide on a plan of attack. Meanwhile, I want our people to get together with Dove's PR staff immediately to start the presses working."

Karl had listened dutifully and hadn't spoken a word. He gave Thomasson the respect he demanded, which was roughly that due a supreme court justice in session. Thomasson dismissed him and then left his office for other matters, feeling his power go before him.

John was in a good mood. The news from Harold about Atlantic was excellent. Harold had kept Thomasson apprised of every piece of news in Andrew's career on a moment-by-moment basis, hoping to build enough momentum for Michael to come on board with the complete package for Andrew. It appeared that Thomasson was convinced that Andrew had enough momentum to justify revving up the entire Atlantic machine for him. It was difficult to overestimate the impact of this decision: by comparison, the Dove marketing department would fit in one small corner of the Atlantic offices of the Nashville branch alone. Their network of salesmen, radio promoters, and public relations people combined with the prestige of major label involvement gave Andrew marketing clout far beyond the level of any artist restricted to the gospel market alone. Atlantic could steamroll Andrew into new markets with the force of its manpower and capital. Keeping Michael Thomasson happy became a major priority for the entire team, because a happy Michael Thomasson was a check-writing Michael Thomasson, and the deep pockets of Atlantic Records would make all the difference in the world.

John had arranged to meet with Michael and Harold as soon as the contracts were signed, and the three of them rapidly formulated a strategy for capitalizing on Andrew's rising popularity. They each believed that a kind of energy was forming behind Andrew and that if they acted upon it quickly, they could vault him past the preliminary stages of his career into instant stardom.

The meeting took place in the luxurious conference room at Atlantic Records. As John entered, he couldn't resist a coveting glance at the dozens of gold and platinum records lining the wood walls of the room. There would soon be one more, he thought, if everything went according to plan.

Harold had already arrived, and Michael kept the two of them waiting a few minutes. When he opened the door and entered, walking his careful, upright walk, he was smiling and obviously in good humor. He greeted the other men like a president meets visiting functionaries, with a calculating politeness and largesse that effectively communicates the power structure to everyone present.

"Gentlemen, welcome," he began, shaking hands and gesturing for the two to take their seats. He remained standing.

"I want to congratulate you both. You have accomplished a great deal in a very short time. That's what we wanted to see. You've done well." Van Grimes felt flushed, as if he had been praised by a parent. "I think you will be pleased with the result of that hard work. You've shown that Andrew understands what we're trying to accomplish here, and that was key to me. Our enthusiasm is high. I'm ready to come on board in a big way."

"Great," Harold said, smiling brightly. Van Grimes chuckled softly to himself. If things went as planned, Harold's opinions of anything would grow increasingly less significant, and everyone in the room knew it. "We intend to promote Andrew as one of our own," Thomasson went on. "Videos, print, TV, the whole shot. I want you both to know that as of today, Andrew Miracle is a priority at Atlantic Records." He reached for a small phone on the conference table. "Sweetheart, would you bring the refreshments in, please?" He smiled again, a toothy smile, his eyes bright. "I propose a toast." The door opened, and a pretty young secretary wheeled in a table with a bottle of champagne on ice. "Thank you, dear," Thomasson said as she was leaving, and proceeded to pop the cork on the bottle. He poured three glasses, and handed one to Harold and John.

"To Andrew Miracle," he said as the others stood. His tone was firm, like a general's. "To Andrew Miracle, our newest star."

21

In what seemed like a remarkably short time, the Darren McCloud tour ended. In spite of all his doubts, Andrew's homecoming with Carolyn had been a good one. He loved her; all the complexities in the world didn't change that, and being with her made things seem simpler. He resolved with her to leave the poster-Andrew behind, and for now, at least, he seemed able to do so. They had eaten dinner together at her place that first night home, and there had been a sweet, comfortable affection between them. It was as if they both wanted to go back in time to when Andrew had just arrived, and by willing it, they were for the moment able to achieve it.

Back in Nashville, Andrew found his mood had lightened. The ambiguities of concert performance were behind him for the moment. But directly ahead lay the marketing plan of Atlantic Records.

Meetings started during the last week of the tour, and Andrew arrived in Nashville to find that a great deal was already in motion with the Atlantic people. His conversations with John about a future in which Atlantic was involved were like fairyland fables; John's eyes danced with pleasure as he described the workings of a machine as powerful as ten Dove Records, all focused on the success of Andrew and his recording.

To his surprise, Andrew found himself enthralled by the possibilities that Atlantic brought to the table. The enthusiasm of everyone at Dove and at van Grimes's office was evident. Andrew had merely to enter a room to sense his importance to the business being conducted. More and more, he never had to wait for a previous conversation to end before he spoke; on the contrary, conversations ended with his arrival automatically, and he became the instantaneous focus of attention. There was no point in denying that it felt good. It felt better than good. With Atlantic on board, there was no way to estimate how far his power might grow.

The focal point of the Atlantic marketing campaign was to immediately produce and distribute a video for "Lost Without You." Andrew surprised himself by being fairly comfortable with the idea of being filmed; he had lost much of his initial uneasiness about being in front of people. Since he left Rose Hill, he had been photographed countless times and had performed in front of over a hundred thousand people.

Accompanied by John, he eagerly met with the Atlantic representatives. He was flattered that they had taken such an interest in him. They seemed to him in some ways similar to the people at Dove, but with an important difference: they were clearly comfortable working in a larger domain, and they talked of spending and making huge sums of money in matter-of-fact tones. To his astonishment, he found that they exhibited a subtle but unmistakable condescension to the Dove personnel in meetings, even to Harold and Laurence. From that time forward, Andrew began to regard the two key players of Dove somewhat differently; they had always been on a kind of pedestal to him, men of the world, unapproachable by merit of their experience and position. Now, he saw that there was always a bigger pool with bigger sharks swimming in it, sharks that eclipsed the fish in the Dove pool as surely as the great whites in the Atlantic could eat the little sharks at Sea World. Their sophisticated detachment, previously so intimidating and influential, suddenly appeared to him as ersatz; a mere copy of the power and prestige of the Atlantic people working on the video.

Adding to this impression was the subtle deference with which Harold interacted with Michael Thomasson and the other Atlantic personnel. It was clear that Harold wanted things to go smoothly, and he let Atlantic drive most of the decisions about the emerging marketing plan.

Shane MacMillian, known on the set as Mac, was the director assigned to the video shoot. Mac came with an impressive track record, and his power was obvious from the first meeting. His videos were routinely seen on MTV and VH-1; in fact, having his name on the project assured it an instant viewing and positive momentum with the programmers of the major video outlets. He had directed successful videos for several major pop stars, videos that in a measurable way had made those artists' careers.

Mac was surprisingly young to wield so much power. He looked to be about twenty, but Andrew later learned that he was in fact twenty-six—still quite young to be given so much responsibility. His youth added to his legend and gave him the arrogance of a successful prodigy. His success had allowed him to elevate his pretensions to the status of an artiste. In reality, he had found his way into music videos from the world of advertising. He had been making television commercials when his work was spotted by a record executive who recognized it as youthful, risky, and a good match for one of the artists on his label. Despite emerging from such mundane beginnings, MacMillian regarded himself as a sort of Fellini of the music world, each video a personal expression of his involvement with the music. He always assumed and generally received complete creative control of his projects.

Andrew wasn't surprised that the video had already been in large measure designed and planned before his initial meeting. He accepted this momentum as *de rigueur* to his new life. When he and John met with Mac to discuss the layout, it was more like dictation than a meeting of the minds. MacMillian swept into the Atlantic offices like a young movie star of a previous, glamorous age. He reeked of California: sandy brown hair, a perfect tan, light blue eyes, brown eyelashes that looked manicured, a slender but athletic build, all clothed in astronomically expensive and studiously, perfectly tattered clothing. He wore three earrings in his left ear, and had a small, brass-plated viewfinder tied to a gold chain around his neck, enabling him to see the world through the eye of a movie camera at all times.

Andrew and John entered the room that Atlantic had set aside for their meeting to find a standing MacMillian in mid-sentence with Karl Hunter. "Okay," MacMillian was saying, in a high, penetrating voice, "it's about style, it's about searching, it's about loneliness." He paused thoughtfully a moment. "Lonelinesssss," he intoned again, stretching the word out slowly, weighing it as he spoke. He gave a far-away look, as if he, above all people, knew what it meant to be truly lonely.

Karl rose as Andrew and John entered and introduced the pair to MacMillian. Mac was effusively polite, but he seemed to be maintaining his stream-of-consciousness monologue in his mind even as he said hello. Before Andrew was seated he was continuing with his thoughts.

"We shoot tomorrow, and everything is ready. The video is half performance footage, half concept footage."

Andrew sat quite still, having well learned that speaking up too early labeled him as naive. He listened attentively and silently as Mac laid out the format and the scenes for the shoot. Nevertheless, the longer MacMillian went on, the more amazed Andrew was. Mac seemed to be speaking a foreign language, half artsy mumbo-jumbo, half technical jargon of a highly specific nature.

After some time, John interceded.

"Maybe you need to explain things a bit more from the beginning, Mac."

MacMillian looked up as if disturbed from a trance.

"Yes, fine. Day one is performance footage. We'll shoot Andrew and the actors performing the song dozens of times, filming from different angles. That will take all or most of day one."

"Actors?" asked Andrew.

"Of course," MacMillian answered simply. "We have created a video band for you that suits your look."

Andrew was surprised. "What's wrong with my band?" he asked. "I just assumed they would be there with me. And anyway, what's my look? John, what's he talking about?"

MacMillian looked amused. "Never assume anything," he said. "Not in this business called show. And for this video, your look is . . . lonelinesssss." MacMillian once again stretched the word out for an extra second as he said it.

Andrew blinked but said nothing. He read John's face, who looked calm and happy. MacMillian was on a roll, and continued without waiting for a response.

"Day two, we shoot the concept part of the video. Don't be nervous," he directed to Andrew. "I know you're new at this, and I will ask very little of you in the way of acting. We're just putting you in some situations."

Andrew was apprehensive. "What kind of situations?" he asked.

"Situations of lonelinessssss," answered MacMillian dreamily. Incredibly, this seemed to satisfy John. Andrew wasn't as sure.

"Pardon me, uh, Mac," he began tentatively, "but I'm not sure what you mean by that. I wonder if you could be more clear. After all, I'm the one that has to do it."

MacMillian responded with the kind of studied impatience that comes with a great deal of practice. It was as if he had worked on a set of indignant responses and had perfected them, like a movie star with a reputation for being difficult.

"You are searching," he said, his voice the perfect balance of patient teacher and condescending older brother. "You are lost, *n'est-ce pas?* You will be by the water, in a motel room, walking alone downtown, all lonely places. All lost places."

"I see."

"Yes," MacMillian breathed. "So you are lost. You have been kidding yourself for much too long. So you come to the climax." MacMillian pulled a large manila folder from his leather briefcase.

"You are lost, you see. 'Lost without you.' All through the video you have been searching, searching. You look out into the distance, searching for what you must find. Then, you see her."

"Her?" asked Andrew, surprised. "What do you mean, her?"

"I mean," MacMillian said dramatically, *"her."*

As he spoke, Mac pulled a photograph of a stunningly beautiful model out of his folder. She was tall, with dark brown hair and eyes, high cheekbones, and an aura of sensuality behind her open face. Andrew had never see anyone like her, not even in a photograph. He stared, speechless.

"This is Renee Costa, gentlemen, and you may all resume normal breathing." Mac laughed easily, as one who finds himself perfectly comfortable around people and situations that others find unnerving.

"I selected Renee especially for you, Andrew," he said. "Michael made it clear that you are a clean-cut artist—he made a real point of telling me that. 'Mac,' he said, 'I want Andrew respected on this thing. This is *not* going to be sleazy rock video.'" The others, excepting Andrew, laughed heartily. MacMillian had just done a very convincing imitation of Michael Thomasson, and in view of Thomasson's power at Atlantic seeing him imitated was a rare experience. MacMillian smiled, confident of his position.

"Renee has a very special quality, gentlemen."

"I'll say," van Grimes breathed.

"She has what I call smoldering innocence."

Andrew stared at the picture. MacMillian was right. Her

face was remarkably open, like a woman who is naive and inexperienced, young and untroubled. At the same time, an untamed quality exuded from her, promising a latent but eager sexuality. Andrew wondered where Mac had found a girl who created such a carefully balanced impression.

"Is that something she learns," van Grimes asked, "or are women born with that?"

"Renee is a natural," MacMillian answered at his dreamiest.

"I still don't see how she enters in," Andrew persisted. "It's not her that I'm searching for."

For the first time, Mac looked genuinely surprised. "What do you mean, it's not her? I mean, of course it's not *her*, she's a symbol, you know?"

Andrew turned expectantly to van Grimes. John was occupied, fingering the photograph.

"What I'm saying is that it's not a woman at all that I'm looking for," Andrew said. "It's *God* I'm looking for."

MacMillian's face betrayed a flash of surprised recognition. "God?" he sputtered.

"That's right," Andrew told him. He glanced again at John, who, upon hearing the word *God,* had gotten wind of the fact that something important was happening. Van Grimes eyed Andrew carefully.

"Yes," John agreed tentatively, "that's right, Mac. It's about God, you see. That's who Andrew has been searching for." As he spoke, he kept his eyes on Andrew, reading his face.

MacMillian paused, considering. "Interesting," he said softly, pausing again. Then, quite decisively, and Andrew thought, even jovially, he added, "But hardly practical."

Andrew was annoyed. "What do you mean, not practical? I don't see what that has to do with it. You're talking about my song. The song is about something. I thought that was what the video was about. It was to bring the song to life."

Karl, whom Andrew had almost forgotten, chuckled to

himself quietly. Andrew glared at him in response, forcing
him to speak.

"Andrew," he said, with the familiar sound of condescension that was becoming profoundly irritating to Andrew,
the sound of a teacher explaining simple arithmetic for the
twentieth time to a slow child, "music videos aren't about
the song. They're about *selling the record.*"

"I don't understand," Andrew ventured. He hated to feel
stupid, especially about his own project. He wanted to understand and be a part of the sophistication he was surrounded with. Nevertheless, he pressed forward. "I mean
you have to tell the story of the song, don't you?"

"Sure," Karl answered lightly. "You tell the story. But you
have to *sell the record.* Let me put it this way: It's not *tell
the story, sell the record. It's sell the record, tell the story.* Get
it? Selling the record comes first."

"Okay. But what does that have to do with ending up lost
without some girl?"

Before Karl could answer, there was a soft knock on the
door. Without waiting for a response, it opened, and Michael
Thomasson walked in the room, followed by Renee Costa.
Intuitively, Andrew stood, and the others were close behind.
Thomasson, confident power rising from him like a vapor,
walked to the head of the table. Smiling, he introduced
Renee.

In person, she was, if anything, more beautiful than her
photograph. She moved with a languid fluidity, and her face,
the perfect combination of pouty guilt and youthful innocence, had the effect of drawing one into it, as if by staring,
one could discover its secret.

"Gentlemen, I would like you all to meet Renee Costa."
Thomasson was remarkably composed, as if he were introducing his sister. Nevertheless, Andrew detected an amused
smile creeping from Thomasson's lips. He gestured toward
Andrew. "I brought her here especially to meet you, An-

drew," he said silkily. "I thought you two would want to establish a . . . rapport."

Van Grimes, Karl, and Andrew all mumbled hellos, but MacMillian danced to her side and hugged her familiarly. "Hello, darling," he said, squeezing her around the neck, and kissing her cheek with a European faux kiss. "You've arrived just in time," he added, giving Andrew a sulky look. Andrew was standing awkwardly, feeling undone in the presence of this beautiful woman, who, he felt, was at that moment staring effortlessly into his soul.

Thomasson looked around the room briefly, taking stock of the situation. "I sense that there's some problem under discussion?" he asked, easily. No one spoke right away in response, and Andrew felt like a schoolboy caught cheating on an exam rather than a grown man standing up for a principle.

Karl finally spoke up. "Just a small misunderstanding, Michael," he said. "Andrew and Mac are having a little discussion about his video."

"I see," Thomasson said. He seemed unperturbed. "Sit down and tell me about it, Andrew."

Andrew took his seat and considered his response. While he was thinking, Renee took the chair Michael proffered her and sat quietly looking at Andrew. It was unnerving. Andrew wanted to stand up for himself, but he had no desire to be the butt of a joke around someone like Renee Costa.

"I guess what I want to say," he began, "is that Mr. MacMillian has sort of got the wrong idea about my song."

"What idea is that?" Thomasson asked, looking at him intently.

"The idea that I'm looking for a . . . a girl." Andrew finished the sentence faintly. It made him feel oddly self-conscious to be referring to a girl with the girl herself in the room.

"Ah," said Thomasson, relaxing in his chair. "And what are you looking for?"

For some reason, the question was difficult to answer under the present circumstances. Nevertheless, Andrew resolved to speak up and said, quite clearly and resolutely, "God."

MacMillian exhaled audibly, as if Andrew, by answering Thomasson's question, had convicted himself of a crime and there was no point in continuing. Thomasson, however, acted as if nothing important was transpiring, certainly nothing that couldn't easily be resolved in a few minutes. He next spoke to Andrew in a more intimate tone, like an understanding parent.

"I see your problem, Andrew. You want the video to be about your search for God, and you feel compromised by the appearance of Miss Costa in the video."

Andrew sat considering. It would have been much easier if Michael had chosen some other way to express himself. He felt validated for the first time by Thomasson's statement, however, and after a moment, he ventured a relieved, "That's right."

Thomasson sat still in the silence that followed. All eyes were on him. "I respect that," he said quietly. "I respect where you're coming from, Andrew. Let's find a compromise where we can both be happy."

Andrew looked up hopefully. "I'd like that," he said politely. "I'd like very much for us both to be happy."

"Good," smiled Thomasson. "Very good. I'm sure we can solve this problem easily. Now let me explain to you what our bottom line is, and then we'll go from there, okay?"

"Okay."

"Fine. For starters, we don't make music videos to create works of art. I say this in deference to you, of course, Mac. You are a true artist." MacMillian inclined his head slightly. "Although we are fortunate to employ the considerable talents of people such as yourself and Mr. MacMillian, we nevertheless are not in the business of creating works of art.

The budget for making videos, Andrew, comes directly out of the marketing budget for a record. You need to think of it in that light, and you will understand our point. It is an advertisement, nothing more. Of course, we try to give our groups the cache and seriousness of high art where it is appropriate to their image, but even in that there is an element of salesmanship, you see. Their success depends upon their artistic statements because they appeal to that kind of crowd. But we never, never confuse ourselves about the purpose of what we're doing, Andrew. Is that clear so far?"

"I suppose so," Andrew replied.

"That's fine, then. So you see, a video is like a print ad or a radio spot. It's a commercial, and like all commercials, it has only one purpose, and that is to sell the record. If it doesn't sell the record, we have no purpose in making it because videos are very expensive and they can only be justified as a marketing expense to increase sales. That is its *raison d'être*, its reason for existence. No increased sales, no video. Indeed, there would be no point in it."

"I see," Andrew said hesitantly.

"Yes, so you see, we operate within these confines. We must find solutions that fit those confines. Now, I must say, a video from a major emerging pop star about a quest for God does not, I think, quite fit that scenario. I mean, from Bob Dylan, possibly, but I remind you that Dylan is history commercially." Karl and MacMillian murmured quiet assents. "So. Here we are. You have written a huge hit song, which to you is about a search for God. I am deeply respectful of that. I'm only asking you to respect my needs, as well. Can you do that?"

Andrew felt dazed, as if he were confronting a talented lawyer on the witness stand. "I suppose I can," he answered. "But where does that leave us? So far you've only talked about your side."

"Of course. I just wanted you to see where we're coming from, Andrew. Now, how about this? Suppose you find Renee," he said, gesturing inclusively to the model, "and the two of you go off together into the distance, searching for God?"

"How will anybody know that it's God I'm searching for?" Andrew asked.

"Exactly!" burst MacMillian, ignoring Andrew. "You have something there, Michael. I like it. They find each other just like before. But then, they go off together to find God. I'm seeing light. I'm seeing the two of them, arm in arm, walking toward the light, a light in the sky. It's deeply spiritual, actually. I see that. Deeply."

Thomasson smiled and opened his arms. "You see, Andrew, we have no problem at all. You meet Renee, which pleases us, and you go towards the light, which pleases you. I especially like the light part, Mac. It's just like you."

Andrew sat thinking. He had to admit that Thomasson had heard him out. What he had said about videos just being advertising hadn't really occurred to him. Maybe this was the solution. Nevertheless, he didn't understand why the presence of Renee meant so much to the commercial success of the record. "I'm wondering something, Mr. Thomasson."

"Please, call me Michael," Thomasson offered.

"Sorry. Michael. Anyway, I'm wondering why my being with Renee makes so much difference. Why is it so crucial?"

Thomasson smiled. "It establishes you as desirable, Andrew. Think about it. Maybe you knew some girl in school you didn't think much about. Then one day you saw her with two or three good-looking guys paying a lot of attention to her. Suddenly, you began to wonder about her, right? That's the principle at work here. Any man with someone like Renee has something going for him. Otherwise, she wouldn't be there. Isn't that right, Renee?" Renee smiled a silent, inscrutable smile. "That's why rock stars always have beautiful women in their videos, Andrew. They become more desirable because they're with the models. It's Advertising 101."

With that, Thomasson stood, and the others stood with him. "I've enjoyed our talk, Andrew. It's good to work with an artist of integrity who is willing to stand up for what's important. It sets you apart." Thomasson held out his hand to Renee, who took it and stood beside him. "John, could I talk to you outside a moment? It won't take a second."

John started like a schoolboy called on to see the principal. "Of course, Michael," he said, and he followed the pair out the door.

John closed the door behind him to find Thomasson already walking down the hall toward his office. Following sheepishly behind, he entered Thomasson's office behind him.

"Leave us just a moment, would you, Renee? I just need to have a word with John." Renee glided silently out of the office, closing the door behind her.

Thomasson took his seat, and sat quietly a moment. When he spoke, his voice was as impenetrable as crystal. "John, I want to clarify something here. That little song and dance was for Andrew's benefit. I am under no obligation to do it again."

John felt Thomasson's sudden change in tone like a rap on the knuckles from a schoolteacher. "What do you mean?" he asked.

"I mean I am under no contractual obligation to clear artistic directions with you or Andrew or anybody else in the marketing of this record. It's our money, and it's our decision. If I want to make a video of Andrew Miracle walking a dog, I can do it because that's what our contract says I can do."

"I understand."

"I'm relieved. I don't like discord. I hope that everything is under control now. Just work with your artist and explain things so that everything runs smoothly. That's what I like."

John smiled mechanically, willing his face to show calm. "Of course, Michael. I don't expect any more problems."

"I'm delighted to hear that, John. And now, if you'll be so kind as to send in Ms. Costa, we have some pressing matters that demand my attention. It's so nice to be able to depend on you in this."

22

The two days spent making the video were a fascinating, tiring blur for Andrew, and they left him exhausted, both mentally and physically. Each work day was over fifteen hours long; he had lip-synced the song over forty times the first day for the concert footage, and the second day of dramatic filming proved to be even more demanding.

MacMillian was a master of light—the use of light more than anything else determines the look of any video—and he had painstakingly created a work that wrapped Andrew in a bright cloud of mystical impermanence, highlighting him and trailing from his limbs like thin, lit clouds. Mac had been fascinated by Andrew's eyes, for he correctly identified the disquiet and movement within them; he laboriously shot closeups of Andrew's face under varying conditions until he found at last the combinations that brought out the hazel color, and in that special light, they seemed the eyes of a lonely poet—intelligent and hungry.

The theme of loneliness that Mac had picked for the shoot had been artfully realized. There were subtleties that wove a careful story of unrequited solitude throughout the song: a glance into the distance; an extraordinary sunset; a riderless horse, whinnying and neighing into the wind; a wooden floor strewn with broken glass and roses. Through it all Andrew danced, carefully positioned, his eyes meticulously lit, his makeup retouched every ten minutes, his wardrobe as Mac instructed for each scene. The music brought the pictures to life, and the pictures, the music; it seemed that the two reached out together to the viewer, spinning a dream.

At the climax, the moment of greatest visual longing and tenderness, Renee materialized from a silvery mist, her extraordinary hair lit from behind, giving her an unearthly halo. She came to Andrew as if drawn by his power; her perfect face showing pure surrender, they met and gazed into each other's eyes. Together, they walked into the haze before them. Far off in the distance, the sky was illumined by an unearthly light, a celestial power that called them toward it. As the song faded, so too they faded, gradually vaporizing in the distant, growing brilliance.

The mood of the Atlantic and Dove teams was high: it appeared as though MacMillian had lived up to his considerable reputation once again, and the raw footage was sent for editing with very high expectations. For Andrew, however, the conclusion of the video shoot brought with it a much needed break in the flow of activity. He had worked nonstop, and he felt stretched inside, as if far too little of him was being asked to do far too much. The pressures of van Grimes's accelerated schedule had taken their toll, and he was badly in need of a rest. Far more important, he felt he needed a reconnecting with home. He looked forward to the break with pleasure: three solid weeks at the farm, and if the late February weather in Kansas left something to be desired, it didn't bother him. He was used to the seasons in the plains.

Reports from home had piqued his interest. He had it from several sources that the town was buzzing in anticipation of his homecoming, and indeed viewed it as a kind of triumphant return from foreign wars. If Cy Mathews had gotten his way, the mayor would have declared it "The Year of Andrew Miracle."

Of course, there was the problem of being separated from Carolyn. On the surface, she had accepted the idea of his long trip home with surprising ease. He knew that it was hurting her as much as it did him, however, for they were in that phase of love in which each person possesses the other, and a separation is like a tearing apart. They were together the evening before he left, trying to make it feel like any other night, studiously avoiding talking about the coming day and what it would mean.

After dinner, Andrew lounged on the couch in his apartment, watching Carolyn from behind as she sat on the floor in front of him. He liked to watch her when she wasn't aware of him, like now, as she absentmindedly turned the pages of a magazine. He thought he loved her most when they weren't really trying to be good together—when they were just being themselves, doing something, anything, together. Their relationship still felt new, and he still delighted in just seeing her brush her hair back casually or make a face at the TV. In spite of the awkwardness that his career forced on them at times, having a woman in his life like this—on his own, living in his own place—was turning out to be sweeter than anything he could have anticipated. It was one thing to think about in the abstract, and God knew that he had thought about it, endlessly, when he was alone out in the fields. But it was quite another to actually see her, to watch her slide in her socks across the hardwood floor, grinning, or to see her face, concentrating hard, running after an errant Frisbee thrown in the park. He thought he would never tire of watching her in the midst of the mundane in her life, washing their cars together out on the driveway, or glimpsing her shape through a cotton print dress.

Lately, as his fame grew, their relationship had frayed, but they had soldiered on, fueled by love and fear to stay together. For Carolyn, Andrew's trip home held a hope: the hope that he would recover himself, find his center, and reemerge onto the music scene with his uncluttered innocence intact. For Andrew, the trip home was less complex—he just wanted to be there, to feel the earth beneath his feet again, to embrace his mother—but even in his enthusiasm he knew that it might seem different to him now, after seeing so much of life beyond its narrow borders. But he held those thoughts at bay, letting the excitement of going home speak for itself in him and not thinking too deeply about it. When the evening ended, Andrew left with a forced smile and a promise to write.

Andrew was quiet on the flight, nodding politely as he entered the plane but choosing not to engage in lengthy conversation with any fellow passengers. He was full of anticipation because at home, at least, he could be himself. There was no confusion about which Andrew he was in Rose Hill. There he was just the son of Franklin Miracle, the boy with the gift.

The plane touched down in Wichita in the early afternoon. He peered out the window as the plane taxied. The grass was brown and gray, and the workmen on trucks wore heavy coats and gloves. Wichita looked desolate and much colder than Nashville.

He disembarked expecting to see his mother waiting for him to drive him the forty-five minutes from the airport to Rose Hill. She was there, but she was far from alone; to his utter surprise, Cy Mathews was there as well, standing with a handful of neighbors noisily waving homemade welcome home banners. As he came through the jetway he was surrounded by well-wishers, and he felt a dozen slaps on the back as he greeted them.

Mathews was in high style, beaming and cheerleading the little group, energetically scattering *welcome homes* and *we missed you, boys* across him. It wasn't the kind of homecoming he had imagined; he realized, of course, that he had acquired a kind of celebrity in the last several months, but without knowing it he had held Rose Hill and all that life apart from his recent reality, unspoiled, untouched by van Grimes and the rest. It was disappointing to see that the poster-Andrew had preceded him home, planting his image in the minds of all his friends. He had never imagined that people from back home would make the drive all the way in to Wichita just to see somebody that was on his way back to Rose Hill anyway. It was one more new sensation, taking its place in an increasingly long line of new feelings. But mostly he regretted not having the moment alone with his mother that he had anticipated; she deferred in crowds, and he knew the tender greeting they had saved for each other would have to wait. Nevertheless, he hugged her lightly and kissed her on the cheek, saying, "Missed you." It was enough for then, and she grabbed his arm and let him lead her down the long corridor back to the baggage claim area.

Mathews had brought the group in the church van, and they all piled in together with Andrew's luggage for the trip home. It was then that the questions started. Each person in the group seemed to know a different detail of what had happened to him in Nashville and was determined to share it with the group. Occasionally, they referred to him in the third person, as if he wasn't there, with statements like "Andrew's new single is coming out next month, you know," or, "Andrew's going to be playing this Sunday at church." But Andrew knew that gratitude was important, and he resolved to politely answer all their questions and to try to let his heart be touched by this new outpouring of good will towards him.

The van pulled up to the Miracle home, and Andrew and his mother got out. There was a round of hearty good-byes, and with promises to visit soon, the van pulled out, leaving a trail of gravel dust behind it.

It was cold, but Andrew didn't care. He stood in the front yard and looked around him, turning in a circle to take it all in. The end of winter wasn't the farm's prettiest time, but the desolation always awakened a poetic loneliness in him from which some of his best songs had emerged. Ever since he had realized that, he had considered winter his friend. The plains seemed to stretch just a little bit further when they were covered with a light, unbroken dusting of snow. His mother let him look, not hurrying him into the house. After a few moments Andrew turned and grabbed his bags, smiling at his mother as they went inside.

"It looks the same," he said, sounding relieved. The music business didn't have the power to change the earth, it seemed. Alison smiled at her son. "Not exactly the same," she said. "There's new fence, and we're leasing a lot of ground this year for grazing."

Andrew's interest perked up. "No kidding? What's that all about? We never leased land."

"It's easier than farming, especially with you gone. It's working out well this year. We've got around two hundred head grazing where the wheat was last year."

Andrew looked crestfallen. "You mean there's not going to be wheat next year?"

"Maybe, maybe not. Right now, I'd say no. The grazing pays the bills, and that's all I need around here. I'm not sure I feel like taking the risk right now."

Andrew pondered the Miracle farm without wheat. There had always been wheat, as long as he could remember. It was a marker, a constant in his life that seemed to represent much more than a crop to him. "That seems sad," he said, slowly. It was clearly his mother's decision, however. He was gone, and the farm was hers to run. It wouldn't do to second guess her without being around to make the decision work.

Alison looked out the picture window of the family room at the crackling, cold ground. This time of year it seemed especially forbidding, and the idea that anything could grow out of its frost seemed a distant possibility. Nevertheless, it was only a matter of weeks before tractors would break through the crust and plant for the year, burying tens of millions of wheat kernels in the ground like so many sleeping soldiers, waiting for nature's orders. Just then, she found she missed Franklin a great deal. His good nature and optimism had always been enough for her to count on.

"Well," she said, changing the subject and turning back to her son, "let me see you, Andrew Miracle." She reached out, holding him at arm's length, looking him up and down, appraising him with a mother's eye.

Andrew let her look, smiling back at her. "What do you think?" he asked.

His mother smiled. "I think my son's home," she answered simply.

That night they had talked deep into the evening, perched in comfortable chairs in the living room, the drapes pulled back to look out at the moonlight on the plains. There had been so much Rose Hill news to catch up on. There had been a handful of marriages and a few illnesses since Andrew had left. Christ's Kingdom had been struggling, and attendance, as he had been told, was down—not hopelessly but a solid twenty percent. Mathews had been plodding on, preaching and encouraging his flock as always, but Andrew's departure had left a hole there that had never been filled. His return for a concert had been heralded for weeks and much anticipated by the town.

After some time, Alison looked her son squarely in the eye and said, "I guess we could talk a long time about Rose Hill, Andrew. But I want to know about you. Tell me."

"Tell you what?"

His mother considered a moment. There were many things she had wondered, living alone on the farm for the first time. One thing, however, had consistently pushed to the front of her mind. "Tell me about Carolyn," she said, her expression open and expectant.

Andrew smiled. Of all the subjects his mother could have picked, this was the one he was most looking forward to talking about. "You'd like her," he said, knowing that the simple statement bestowed a world of worth on Carolyn.

"Would I?" his mother responded, interested. "I'm glad. Tell me what I would like about her."

"Not because she's like you," Andrew began, and then he corrected himself, "or rather, she is like you, only different."

Andrew's mother looked at her son with a combination of satisfaction and curiosity. She had never seen Andrew, her youngest, in love. It was long overdue, and she was glad. All the same, Carolyn wasn't a local girl, and she knew that entanglements could take Andrew even farther away from her.

"She's a city girl, but she's none the worse," Andrew went on.

Alison nodded knowingly. "Good," she said.

"She's got a sweetness that reminds me of you, but she talks a lot more." Andrew laughed. "A lot more."

"Nothing wrong with that," his mother answered thoughtfully. "I should have spoken up a good deal more than I did. Wish I could have, too."

"Anyway, she's pretty—brunette, brown eyes, not too slim—I never liked that. But most of all, she sees things."

"Such as?"

"Stuff about me. That's where she's the most like you, I guess. She sees things in me."

Alison seemed pleased. "Tell me what she sees."

"She asks the right questions, you know? I can tell when she looks at me that whatever's happening on the surface is only a part of what she's seeing. She thinks about things. She's happy, too. That's something else I like about her. She's happy." In making this last statement, Andrew was hiding something; he knew that Carolyn's anxiety had been growing lately, but there was no way to talk about that without bringing up the reasons why. He wondered if his mother would detect this distinction in his voice, but she relaxed, content in his description.

There was much more to say, and in the course of a happy evening they said it to each other. Andrew talked of the tour, and the remarkable response he had received. His mother listened with great intensity and pride to what he said, asking him about the people he had met and the places he had seen. They each found a particular pleasure in the story of his success; for him, feeling like a son who has done well and even surpassed expectations, and for her, the joy in seeing her boy's talent recognized and celebrated. They laughed a great deal that night, and Andrew had no desire to dampen that evening or any other by expressing reservations about the path he had chosen; here at home, he found even more than the usual reasons to forge ahead and ask no questions. He had wanted to talk far into the night, but his mother had seemed tired, and they had both gone to sleep by eleven. He wondered if she was overworked in his absence. She seemed to lack her usual energy, and though she listened with interest, she had sat quite still through the evening, as if she were conserving her strength.

Saturday morning dawned with a cold, dry crispness. The wind is never completely still in the plains. Often, it slows to a trickle, resting, its immense power stilled. It never completely stops, however, as if by stopping it would die and never return. Instead, it creeps across the packed earth, nibbling instead of biting with winter.

Andrew awoke late, his internal clock changed by touring and drawn curtains. He pulled on his clothes and stumbled down the stairs to find Cy Mathews sitting at the breakfast table, contentedly munching fresh bread and eggs and chatting amiably with his mother.

"Hello, pastor," he said, taking Mathews' outstretched hand. Mathews was a furry ball of motion at the sight of him. Andrew deflected Mathews's effusive greeting with a practiced ease, and sat down to the sight of his mother setting a full plate before him.

"My boy, my boy," Mathews began, "the star returns. You're up late, boy. City life made you soft?"

For some reason, Mathews's familiarity was oddly irritating. Nevertheless, Andrew responded with a smile. "I guess so, pastor. City folks don't get up with the cows."

"Guess not, boy, guess not."

Mathews looked Andrew up and down thoughtfully but said nothing. Andrew had the distinct feeling he was being x-rayed. "Andrew, we're all looking forward to Sunday. I've got the word out, and we expect to be packed."

"I'm glad, pastor," Andrew said. He knew better than to comment on the lower attendance the church had been experiencing. It was odd to think that simply by his presence he could now ensure the church would be filled to capacity. Who, after all, were they coming to hear?

"Now Andrew," Mathews bubbled on, "we want to make this a special occasion, something out of the ordinary. After all, you're a big star now."

Andrew let Mathews's assessment pass unnoticed. "I was kind of hoping we could keep things the same. What did you have in mind?" he asked.

"The same? For a real recording star? No, we're talking about a real concert, Drew. We'll just give you the whole show. We've built this thing up to really be something special."

Inevitably, the contrast between what Mathews meant and what Andrew had experienced on the Darren McCloud tour came to mind. Andrew thought back to the huge halls he had recently played in, halls packed with six months' worth of Sundays at Christ's Kingdom in a single night. The lighting system alone was probably worth the equivalent of an entire wing of the church. Van Grimes had been right, he thought. The numbers spoke for themselves. Andrew smiled indulgently at Pastor Mathews.

"That would be lovely, pastor," he said evenly. He was experiencing an odd, and unforeseen sensation: although he had been missing the intimate ministry of his old performances, now that he was home he found them small and their importance a bit trumped-up. The very most the small sanctuary could hold was around three hundred and fifty people; that typically amounted to one section of the kind of halls he had been playing. If he looked at it that way, there was really very little point to spending an evening with so few. He put those thoughts out of his mind, however, and smiled and accepted the invitation without protest. He smiled to himself: his fee was already five thousand dollars, but according to John, it was only days away from doubling to ten thousand dollars a night. Ten thousand dollars. That much money could probably run Christ's Kingdom for two months. He wondered what Cy Mathews would think if he realized he was asking Andrew for a ten-thousand-dollar favor. He resolved to say nothing about it, but even in this he found his pride caressed; the waiving of his fee turned playing a concert into an extraordinary act of largesse to the church, certainly the largest single gift of the year. His silence about the matter helped Mathews save face and proved to Andrew that he was still in touch with what mattered.

Saturday was a quiet day at the farm. Andrew puttered around aimlessly, pleased that he was still able to enjoy the place so much. He fired up his father's truck and rambled far out into the stubbled fields, the windows up tight and the heat on. It was cold in Kansas, made worse by the wind that ceaselessly swept across the terrain. After a half hour or so he turned back, lured by hunger for lunch. As he arrived back at the big white wooden gate that led from the fields into the back yard, he was surprised to see his mother's Chevy was gone, but he thought little of it. He checked his watch: a little after noon. He imagined that she must have gone to the store.

His mother's absence gave him a good opportunity to do something he had been wanting to do for a long time; he decided to drive over to the Sunset Retirement Home, and see all the old ones there. Even when he was feeling most detached and withdrawn, their faces never entirely lost their power to warm him and bring him back. They were helpless, and in the world of conspicuous, hazardous power in which he now found himself, they seemed sweetly above it all, blameless and safe.

He knew he had been right to come the moment he entered the home, swinging the big metal doors open and walking in, looking for friends. Gladys Crawford, a large black nurse, lit up when she spied him, and she shouted his name out loud. The others quickly got wind of his arrival, and soon he was walking among them again, touching them and being touched as well.

They were old. Their leathery skin was thick and lined, even for the women, and their faces broke into crinkly smiles like rubbery Play-doh, sweet and fragile. He saw them all: the Newmans, still sharing a room, holding hands as always; Eleanor Grier and Miss Tucker, who never married; old man Carr, curmudgeonly and stern—they were all there, rustling softly in the subdued energy of old age. Andrew could tell in a moment that here there was no poster-self, no image to shout down. Here, he could whisper or even, in the sweetest of possibilities, be silent.

There were a few to round up in wheelchairs, and a tiny number were stuck in their beds like planted trees—for them, the doors were flung open, open to hear the music that had been so much missing. Gladys saw to them all. The piano was rolled out, and Andrew noted with satisfaction that it still had not been tuned—it would have been a shock if it had, like seeing the house in which you grew up freshly painted a different color. He pulled up a metal folding chair, opened the squeaky keyboard, and motioned them all to come in close. They did come in, a chair against his own to his left, metal on metal, old Mrs. Ingham's knees sticking out of her resplendent purple dressing gown, pressing in on his own leg. They crowded in a circle, and a couple of the more fit ones stood behind the piano, leaning on it. He felt a hand on his shoulder, and looking up, he saw Lloyd Bartlett, every day of ninety, shouting out of his hardness of hearing that it was about time he had got back and requesting "Melancholy Baby." Andrew gave a laugh and banged it out as loud as he could, staring old Bartlett down as he did.

He played the hymns, of course: "Standing on the Promises," "In the Garden," "Love Lifted Me," and a dozen more. The sad hymns were sad, the praise songs lifted the roof, and the sweet ones hurt. Their voices were unearthly, full of creaks and wavers like ghosts. It was then that he thought of her, up to now having been preoccupied with so much of his own joy, and he asked about her—the woman in so much pain, the one who was the most alone, clinging to God. Gladys, looking dignified in her starched white nurse's uniform, stood near him and looked him in the eye.

"Mrs. Harvey's gone, boy," she said in a voice that she had used to make many such pronouncements in her years at the home. "She's gone on home, and her back don't hurt her anymore."

There were murmurs but no tears, and Andrew choked his own back, turned silently to the piano, and kept on playing.

It was much later when he returned. As he pulled the truck into the barn, he heard the crunch of gravel on the driveway, but it wasn't the familiar sound of his mother's car. It was a deeper, rumbling sound. He hopped out of the truck, and turning the corner of the barn, he saw to his surprise the pastor's huge old four-door Oldsmobile parked at an angle next to the house, looming like a mastodon from an earlier age. The pastor was sitting in the front seat, alone, seemingly deep in thought. Andrew approached from behind the car, and Mathews didn't see or hear him as he did so. Andrew's curiosity was aroused: Mathews had just been there yesterday morning, and if there had been some detail to discuss about Sunday, he could just as easily have called. The idea of surprising him seemed oddly appealing, so Andrew walked quietly up to the car, keeping out of sight. As he silently covered the last few feet to the window, however, he noticed that Mathews's eyes were closed, and his lips were moving. It was apparent that the pastor was praying.

Andrew tried to move quickly back and away from the pastor's line of sight, but his jerky motion attracted Mathews's attention, and he swung his head around rapidly, looking, Andrew felt, even more shocked than he had anticipated. Mathews's face settled back down after another moment to an unusually grave expression, but after a second moment, he assumed his normal, smiling visage. Andrew stared, because it seemed somehow that Mathews had almost willed his happy expression, and that by considerable exertion.

Mathews opened the door with an energetic motion and smiling brightly, greeted Andrew. "Andrew, my boy. You gave me a start. Out and about on this cold day? Fine, fine. Does you good, doesn't it?"

Andrew reached out and shook Mathews's hand, and the two turned towards the house, bending their heads in the cold wind.

"Didn't expect to see you out here today," Andrew began, but then he stopped himself. He found himself unaccountably curious about this surprise visit, and didn't want to push too hard. If Mathews had something special on his mind, he might have a way he wanted to bring it up. Andrew decided to take it easy.

"No, no, just thought I'd stop by," Mathews said. "Thought we might take a walk, but the cold's come on, hasn't it?"

"Yeah, it has. Want to come on in? Mom's not here."

The pastor opened the screen door to the back of the Miracle house, and Andrew followed him inside. "Yes, I know Alison's not here," Mathews said. "I thought it would give us a chance to have a chat."

For some reason, Andrew felt a chill with the pastor's words, but he didn't show it. Instead, he simply followed Mathews across the vinyl floor to the kitchen table, and took the seat opposite him. Mathews was clearly uncomfortable, in spite of his familiarity with the Miracle family: a telltale fleck of perspiration began to form on his forehead, a sure sign that Andrew had long ago recognized as nervousness in the man. Mathews was rumbling about in his seat, taking his time to get comfortable. Andrew sat silently, waiting.

"Andrew, my boy," Mathews began, after several moments of readjusting his body to the wooden frame of his chair, "do you know where your mother is?"

Andrew didn't know. She hadn't mentioned that she would be leaving. He had gone out into the fields, he explained, and she had been gone when he returned. He hadn't thought much about it. "Why do you ask?"

Mathews sighed and gave a knowing nod of his head. "I didn't think you would. I'm not surprised. That's like her, you know."

"Like what? What are you driving at?" Now he was making Andrew nervous.

"Andrew, your mother is in Wichita, at the doctor."

The words went into Andrew like a knife. "You better tell me what this is all about. Right now," he demanded.

"It's not serious, at least I don't know that it is. It's hard to tell with Alison. She's a hardheaded woman, your mother."

"What is this, Cy?" Andrew interrupted impatiently.

Mathews motioned him to calm down and listen. "I'm taking a big risk talking to you about this, Andrew, because

I'm stepping into your family's business. I do so with fear and trembling because I know that your mother is going to give me fits when she hears about it. But I prayed about it, and I think this is right. Besides, I know Franklin would want me to handle it this way. You're no child anymore, and she's just plain wrong about this thing, even though she's keeping silent for your benefit."

"My benefit? How could my mother be sick and not tell me for my benefit? I want to know what's going on, Cy. Everything."

Mathews wiped his forehead and rubbed his eyes. He looked like he'd been doing a lot of thinking. "Well, here goes. Your mother started feeling unusually tired about two months ago."

"Two months!" Andrew blurted. "This has been going on for two months, and I was never told anything about it?"

"I don't know for sure what *this* is, Andrew. Nobody's sure. All we know is that Alison started feeling run down a while back, and then it got a bit worse, so she went to Wichita to see a doctor at Wesley Hospital."

"And the doctor said what?"

"That's where it's complicated, you see. And I'm sure that's why she didn't say anything to you at the time. Didn't want to bother you or upset you over what was probably going to turn out to be nothing. You were on tour. There was nothing you could do but worry anyhow."

Andrew thought back. If she had gotten sick during the McCloud tour, that meant that it had been going on since the middle of January, at least.

"Anyhow," Mathews went on, "the thing is we're not sure that it is nothing, now. It seems to be getting a little worse, and she's had some pain in her chest."

"Pain in her chest? What does that mean?"

"I'm not sure, Andrew. That's what she's in Wichita to find out. The doctor wouldn't tell her what was going on over the phone. He wanted her to come on in. That's probably not a good sign."

Andrew sat back in the chair, stunned. He had been so preoccupied with himself that he had missed every warning sign. Home reminded him of compromises he didn't want to think about, so he didn't call very often and when he did, his calls seemed to have an artificial quality. All this time real life had been going right on around him, behind his back. It hadn't cared at all about his career.

"Why did you wait so long to tell me?" he asked after a long moment of silence. "Why didn't you tell me right away, as soon as you even suspected anything?"

Mathews grimaced, as if stretched painfully between two opposing forces. "I wanted to, but I felt I had to respect your mother's wishes. Even now, she wanted to wait until she knew for sure. But the last few days I've known in my heart that it was going to be bad news, and I wanted to give you the chance to prepare yourself. I thought if you had a chance to think things over before she got home, you wouldn't be so hard on her, Drew."

Andrew looked at his disheveled pastor. Since turning forty he had started to put on weight, and now, nearly fifty and wedged into a wooden kitchen chair, he had all the sophisticated charm of an old alley cat. Andrew loved him just then, however, like he had never loved him before. Cy Mathews was a friend that he could depend on. That made him solid gold.

"I understand, pastor," Andrew said gratefully. "You just wanted to be loyal to us both. But you did the right thing in coming out here today, and I'll never forget you for it."

Mathews reached across the table and put his hand on Andrew's arm. "I'll be praying, Drew. I better leave so I'm not here when your mother comes home. You'll want to have that time just the two of you. But I'm just a phone call away."

Andrew nodded and rose. Mathews heaved his way out

of his chair and went to the door with Andrew. "See you, son," he said, pushing the swinging screen door open. He walked through, and it slammed shut behind him as he made his way up the gravel pathway to his car. The sound of the door echoed off the barn and slammed again a split second later in Andrew's ear, a final, cold emphasis.

For the rest of the afternoon Andrew sat silently, waiting for his mother to return. Once the phone had rung, and with his heart in his mouth, he had leapt up to answer it. The call had been for Alison from a neighbor, however, and he had been forced to make polite small talk for several minutes before he could extricate himself from the call. Then he had taken his seat again, rigidly waiting for the sound of tires on the gravel outside.

It was nearly five when he heard it. He started to attention, and then sat motionless as the car approached the house, slowed, and finally stopped. He counted seconds in the stillness, waiting for the car door to open. Five, six, seven. Still nothing. Eleven, twelve. Finally, a metallic sound, a long pause, and a door not slammed but gently closed. Soft footsteps on the gravel, getting louder as they drew near. Andrew looked up to see his mother silhouetted against the bright light of the sun setting behind the window. When he could make out her features clearly, she stood looking at him through the screen and glass of the two doors. As soon as their eyes met, Alison knew that Cy had come and gone and that Andrew knew more than she had wanted him to know.

At last Alison opened the door and came inside. "Is it bad?" he asked, knowing full well the answer. She stood before Andrew across the kitchen, her face beautiful and resolute.

"Yes."

At the sound of her voice, Andrew stood and rushed to

her, folding her in his arms and holding her, his eyes welling with tears. She held her hands before her face in tiny fists and leaned on him. For her, there were no tears. She merely shook a little when she exhaled, each breath a little quake. Andrew held her, his chest tight with fear. She had been so strong, ever since he could remember. She had worked the farm, cooked ten thousand meals, and buried a husband. She had seemed as eternal as the weather.

Andrew led his mother to the table, and sat her down. Taking the seat opposite, he faced her and looked at her for a moment, trying to assess the seriousness of the situation. After a long, terrible silence, he simply asked, "What did the doctor say?"

When she answered, her voice was slightly shaking. "There is a spot on my lung." She looked down, tearing her eyes away from Andrew's. She looked almost ashamed. Nevertheless, when she spoke again, she had steadied her voice. "Actually, it's more than a spot. It's quite large. Apparently, I've had it for some time." Suddenly, she looked up, but not at Andrew. Instead, she swung her head slowly around, as if taking stock of her home, mentally calculating the work to be done. After a moment, her shoulders seemed to slump slightly, and she trembled for an instant.

Andrew felt numb, as if that part of his brain that allowed him to feel had surrendered to this news, disconnecting itself in the face of it. His instinct to resist took the place of his emotions. "How do we fight it?" he asked. "What do we do?"

His mother smiled a thin smile and looked back down at the table. Her face was drawn, and some of the strength seemed to have already drained out of it. "It seems that there is very little fighting to do, dear," she answered vaguely. "This thing has already spread into the rest of me." She was almost humble, quiet and resigned. But she looked invaded, as if a thief had come and ransacked the house of her body. She seemed fragile and unsure of herself.

Andrew stared at his mother, his heart imploding. He was searching for words, but could find none. They sat together in the silence for a while, hurting together.

Life had gone right on, imperious and demanding. It had no regard for his career. It had drawn no distinction between the famous and the obscure. "We can fight this," he said softly, to the table. His voice was barely a whisper, and it didn't have the power to change what was. "How could this have happened?" he asked the air.

At those words, his mother smiled her grim little smile again, and reached out to take her son's hand. "We don't get that answered, Drew. Your father and I worked a lot with the farm chemicals, and the doctor thought there might be something in that. The pesticides back then were different. Folks didn't know much about what caused things back then. I must have breathed a lot of it in those years. Maybe it would have got your father, too, if he had lived long enough. But I could see the doctor was just guessing. No one ever knows, really. There is destiny in this, Drew," she added gently. "I know it, inside. The doctor told me he could give me a bit more time, but it was a horror what he wanted to put me through for it." She paused and looked away, out the window. For a moment, she looked like his mother again, strong and dignified. "I won't give it the satisfaction." Then she looked back at him. "The doctor wants me to go into Wesley Hospital tomorrow, but I wouldn't go, not tomorrow."

"You've got to go," Andrew protested. "You've got to do what the doctor says. Maybe there's an answer to this. You can't just give up like that."

"I'll go," his mother answered, and then more softly she repeated, "I'll go. But not tomorrow. I'll go in my time. Monday morning."

"What's Monday morning? Why delay a moment when time is so important?" Andrew was feeling frantic, wanting to take some kind of action. His mother's detached calm angered him.

Alison looked around the room. "There's still things to do here," she answered. She was trembling, but her voice was still incongruously calm. "While I have my strength. I have almost got the end tables refinished in the living room. I want to finish them. They're so beautiful, you know. Your father made them, of course. They are beautiful." She was eerily repeating herself, but she nevertheless sounded resolute. "Saturday is the first of March. The weatherman says it's turning warmer, much warmer. I've got flowers to plant. It may be pushing things a bit, but I've had them in the ground that early before. They might make it."

Andrew was incredulous. "You're staying out of the hospital to plant bulbs?" he cried. "Mom, you've got to go to the hospital tonight. Let's not even wait until tomorrow. I want to talk to the doctor as soon as possible." He sat shaking, maddened by his mother's calmness.

"Son, you've got to listen to me," she said. "There's a lot of things this doctor talked about, and I'm not going to let him do any of them to me. I might, if they had a chance of helping me. But I could tell that they don't. I could see it in his eyes, and I could hear it in his voice. I'm not going to mortgage this farm and let him into my body to cut me up and fill me full of radiation when it's not going to help anything. Anyhow, it's not just the bulbs and things. I'm going to church on Sunday. I'm going to hear my boy play." She seemed to come back to herself for a moment.

"I'm not playing on Sunday, Mom," Andrew said bitterly, "not now."

His mother looked at him sternly for a moment, but suddenly her face softened, and she seemed not to reprimand, but to implore. "Yes, you will, Drew. You will do as I say. Please do. I want to plant my hyacinths and irises and things. And I want to hear you play on Sunday." She was pleading now. It was hard to watch in someone so strong. "I want to hear my boy," she repeated, as if she were speaking to someone else. Her hands were clasped as if in supplication, but he could see the tension in them; the blood vessels stood out in her wrists.

Andrew stared blankly. He knew he would give in to his mother. "All right," he numbly acquiesced. "Monday morning. Then we'll see what we can do."

"That's it, then," his mother said. She sounded relieved but also defeated, and her words held a chill.

Andrew played the concert as she had asked, but it was nothing like the original plan. He insisted that Mathews put a stop to all the extra attention that the performance was to receive, and he asked him to preach as usual. No one would mention his mother's condition until later, after she had gone to Wichita.

After a short sermon, Andrew stood and walked to the old Bluthner. He sat silent a moment, listening, grateful for the stillness of the church. The extraordinary pomp and drama of his touring performances had made his gift elusive, difficult to find. It had been silent within him for so long, he feared he had grown deaf. He suffered a moment of dread, for he had always assumed that back at the church he would regain it again. For some time, he heard nothing. Then, he felt it stirring, gentle but audible. He played as he used to, sharing it all and hiding nothing of his sorrow and anger. The music was a prayer between himself and God, an accusation, a plea, and an unraveling. His mother watched and listened, not in any place of honor but sitting up straight and proud in her usual wooden pew. Her back was a rail, and while Andrew played, she seemed herself again. She was in fact already weaker, but whether the weakness came from the illness itself or from the fear of it, Andrew wasn't sure. She sat after the playing ended until Andrew came over to her, and they walked out of the church together. She took his arm, and she must have looked like she did years ago with Franklin by her side.

In the end, God was merciful. Alison Miracle never had to endure the worst of her illness. She was never cut open.

She was never violated by that medicine which sometimes gives life but always robs dignity. Weakened by her invader, she caught pneumonia during her second week at the hospital, and she succumbed to it, seeing it as her deliverance from so much that was hateful. Andrew's brother had returned, and the two of them sat in vigil beside her each day. She slipped away quickly, unable to resist the crawling infection. She was laid to rest beside Franklin, the common gravestone etched at last with her name beside his.

Some days after the funeral, when all the family and friends had left, Andrew stood in the garden, alone. It had turned warm as predicted, and he wore a light jacket as he stared out into the fields. The garden looked dead, in the way that perennials have when they are out of season: brown, dry, and fragile. But he saw where the dirt had been recently tilled, a row of fifteen or so spring bulbs that his mother had buried in earth the day before his concert. Like his father, she had planted until the end.

His brother and the extended family had worked hard in the days after the funeral, and there were only a few more details to work out before he left. The estate was resolved, and the Inghams across the road had agreed to look after the farm for now, until a permanent solution could be found. The farm would not be sold; that was certain. Wheat would be planted, to Andrew's great relief. Mr. Ingham had agreed to lease the land and split the proceeds with the brothers. At least for now, Andrew knew he would leave with the farm in good, experienced hands.

The morning he returned to Nashville, he shut the farm up methodically, packing up the few remaining things that needed storing and locking the doors behind him. He gave the key to Mrs. Ingham, and Pastor Mathews drove him to the airport. As the big Oldsmobile pulled out of the Ingham's driveway, Andrew didn't look at the Miracle farm. The two men were quiet as they rode, but he felt some comfort with the only real pastor he had ever had sitting beside him as they drove. But there had been a rending, the healing of which he could not foresee.

The pastor had hugged him hard at the airline gate, saying little. He had earned the right to be silent, had stood by the Miracle family for more than twenty years. Then, with a jolt into the air of burning fire, Andrew numbly returned to the life he had left.

23

Andrew returned to Nashville to the expressions of very genuine sympathy. John and the staffs at both Atlantic and Dove had gone out of their way to tell him how much they felt his loss; Helen and Mark, especially, had taken him aside on many occasions to let him know they stood by him. Michael Thomasson had sent flowers to the funeral personally. Carolyn had offered to come down immediately, but Andrew had deferred, begging her not to take it personally; with his brother gone all those years he felt he was the man of the family, at least as far as the farm was concerned, and he had so much to take care of during those days. It wasn't the way he wanted her to see the farm. When and if she truly entered that world, he wanted her to come to it with wonder and joy. He knew that all that might be lost now, but still he clung to his hope that it might be so, and for this and other reasons he asked her to stay away.

Eventually, John began to ask him about working again, and Andrew understood. He knew that his loss could never really become someone else's, and he didn't expect it to be so. He had lived already through his father's death and through the shock of seeing the world continue on indifferently afterward. That time, he had been stunned, secretly believing that the world would cease to turn until, secure in his healing, he gave it leave. But it had not been so, and he had learned not to expect it.

Still, there were days he felt he couldn't bear his loss, and he walked the streets of his neighborhood in the cool March air, sometimes with Carolyn but more often alone. His mother's death increased his sense of isolation; he felt like a stranger as he walked, his steps following a string that led through the busy lives of active, interconnected people. Living people.

For two solid weeks John eased off, letting Andrew defer any responsibilities when he felt he needed to. But inevitably, each day John asked a little more of him, and he did his best to comply. While the real Andrew Miracle was undergoing a painful tragedy, the fact remained that the poster-Andrew was in the midst of a carefully timed career explosion that had required an enormous amount of work to create. The groundwork had been laid, and the time had come for an enormous, profitable payoff: John had carefully tested the waters, and had determined that the time was right for Andrew to headline his own triumphant tour.

For John, a major tour for Andrew was the culmination of a dream. In his mind, it was the reward for paying his dues with Heaven's Voices, and he embraced it with a kind of fierce joy. He reveled in every detail of the tour, fascinated and obsessed with it. Where Heaven's Voices stayed in homes, often played for love offerings, and traveled in a worn-out bus, Andrew's tour would have all the accoutrements of fame and power.

The poster-Andrew was white hot, and van Grimes was committed to establishing him as the fastest rising star in the music business, gospel or otherwise. He made contact with the top booking agency in Nashville, and they set forty-one dates, concentrating on the major markets in the eastern United States.

Van Grimes pushed his power to the limit, extracting high guarantees and heavy percentages across the board. He had waited a long time to have that kind of clout, and now he wielded it like a mace. There was money to be made on Andrew, and everybody knew it. If you wanted a piece of the action, you had to play by John's rules.

The mood at both Dove and Atlantic was approaching a carnival atmosphere. Everyone involved could smell success, almost palpably. Andrew's momentum in the marketplace had achieved a kind of synergy, feeding on itself. The coming tour would impel his career well into the next record, and by then he would be a major star.

Andrew embraced it all as best as he could. His work was his only connection to the people in his life, other than Carolyn. Inevitably, conversations with others revolved around the tour or other pressing aspects of business, and he felt the loss of personal connection keenly. Even Carolyn, he admitted, had come into his life through van Grimes. He needed her now, but he found himself wishing that they could have met in a different way, maybe in a restaurant, or at the park. It wasn't fair to feel that way, he knew. For the most part, he was grateful just to have her. He didn't reprimand himself for his thoughts, however; he was still mourning, and he had already learned once that a broken heart doesn't think clearly.

There had been some genuine comfort between Andrew and Carolyn when he had first arrived home, and at the time the loss of his mother superseded the concerns of the immediate future. They were content to relate on that level, and it was good just to forget about business and be together. As the tour approached, however, the peace between them became more and more elusive; they both found it a strain to maintain the sweetness between them. At first, he had thought that the impending separation was the cause of the difficulties between them. Often, to his consternation, he would catch her watching him, and he thought he could detect a bit of sadness in her at those times. But there was another, less definable quality in her then, as well—she was compassionate, certainly, but there was something else that felt to him coldly like sympathy. It was disconcerting, and he was impatient with it. More and more, he avoided open conflict with her by holding himself at a distance just beyond the place he used to let her touch.

There were no real fights between them, and they went through the days more or less mechanically, as if pushing the levers of a machine that they both knew how to run. But the kinship, the almost supernatural acceptance that they had found in each other, was slowly coming apart.

Just as the many forces brought to bear on the marketing of the poster-Andrew intersected with this tour, so the forces working within Andrew's own mind converged, speaking to him, shouting, whispering, cutting off any retreat. Every day that brought the tour closer brought Andrew an increased sense of pressure and expectation. When at last the tour left Nashville, he began it searching for redemption and the happiness he had expected to come with it. In a very real way, the tour was the fruition of all the difficult decisions he had made in the last year, and as such he demanded from it a kind of emotional payoff. Getting to that point had cost him a lot, and he wanted it to be worth the price. He had changed the lyric of "Lost Without You." He had agreed to the video concept. He had permitted himself to be remade for public consumption, threatening the fragile power of his gift. Each decision had been made believing the implicit promise that it would all make sense in the end.

Nevertheless, he found to his dismay that his attitude was becoming increasingly querulous and exacting. Little things that went wrong set him off inside, and although he resisted it, his temper became increasingly demonstrative.

To his surprise, the more demanding and difficult he became, the more he realized his freedom to do so was absolute. He was accountable to no one, because the security of everyone on the tour depended on nothing more than a word from him. He was a kind of emperor of the tour, and the crew merely scurried harder to please him as he became more difficult. This deference, in particular, he hated: to be set free from the mutual give and take of normal relationships set him adrift, rather than liberated him. But though he detested it, his power was intoxicating. More than once he had ordered a crew member about, chillingly fascinated by his absolute authority.

No one spoke against him at any time, for any reason. In each city he was treated with delighted, overstated good will. If he returned it, the people he met beamed delightedly, as if knighted at court. If he returned antipathy instead, the objects of his scorn merely bowed and scraped to regain his favor.

The fiction of his infallibility was kept alive by one thing: money. Andrew's responsibility began and ended with doing a great show, and everything else he did was tolerated, even celebrated. As a result, he found himself picking the shows apart, paranoid about certain aspects of his performance. If everything depended upon the show, then the show must be perfect. It was the tenuous glue that held them all together. There was only one unforgivable sin: to resist the momentum that pushed him forward and to jeopardize the flow of success that rippled out from him to all who depended upon him.

At the beginning of the tour, he had held out the hope that he might be able to find the gift again, as he had back in Kansas. Thwarted in finding meaning in the external, he hoped to find it again within. It had been the gift, after all, that had brought him to the church to play each week. It had been the gift that covered the little congregation and ushered in the Spirit. It had been the gift, he knew, that God had used to minister to the tiny world in which He had first dropped him. But it seemed that the poster-Andrew had no way to reach it. The bigger the poster-Andrew became the more distant the gift seemed, until gradually he gave up searching and worked the crowd as he had learned. The audience, to his confusion, continued to respond as if he had offered them something real, and their excitement, more than anything else, made him doubt his ambivalent feelings. No one, whether on or off the tour, acted as if anything was wrong. Andrew began once again to believe that they must all be right.

Each night he stood before the crowds, a Pinocchio, his decisions hanging above him, working the strings. Each night before the last song he took the microphone, and lit by two hundred and fifty thousand dollars worth of lighting equipment, talked about honesty and sincerity before God. Then he would sing his biggest hit once more, and with the audience in exultant, expensively crafted hero worship, he would walk offstage to his waiting limousine and ride away to his hotel suite.

When he spoke into the silence of the concert halls, he could hear the echo of his voice, an unearthly power reflecting his words back on himself. He couldn't escape that echo. In an enormous, still auditorium, a word spoken was a word impossible to take back. It shot out across space, hit concrete and came back to him, hard and ineluctable.

"The secret of finding God," he heard himself say, his voice reflected and flattened by concrete, "is to be absolutely real. The secret of finding God is to reveal everything to Him and to bring it before Him in humility. Don't hide. He knows it all, and He is waiting to hear from you. There is no secret that is intolerable to Him. He will love you through it." Then, he would spin on his heel, his jacket flowing around him, and walk toward the fifteen-foot letters spelling out his name. On cue, the band would kick powerfully into "Lost Without You," the crowd would scream on command, and with tears, many would raise their hands and begin to sway to the song. It was extraordinary, what he saw. It was the thing he had wanted longer than anything else, even before he wanted God. He had it, now, in a darker shade than he had dreamed of, but he had it. He could see it in their eyes, as they sang together: they loved him.

He had, of course, received dozens of proposals of marriage. Letters by the hundreds were pouring in to the Dove offices, and many were from young girls, complete with photographs and long, heartfelt explanations that God had told them that they were meant to be with him. Some of the letters were touching; others had the flat, penetrating tone of obsession. All were stunning to him—to be the object even of obsession is something—and he insisted that each be one answered.

His mail was far too voluminous for him to handle himself, however, and in the beginning, this task fell painfully to Carolyn. The irony of answering these bizarre love letters was not lost on her; often she had read the scrawled writing, and a shiver would run down her spine, though from fear or simple jealousy she couldn't be sure. He was a superman in these letters, and she read them, wide-eyed, wondering if the writers in their monomaniacal intensity saw something she was missing in him. She had the real Andrew to compare to the Andrew of their letters, and her thoughts careened inside her head in an effort to reconcile the two men living within her. It was too easy, she knew, to call the writers crazy. Some were close to the edge, but many were far more subtle, and too forthcoming, as well. They revealed an eerie truthfulness about themselves in their writing that sometimes left her crying. Soon, Carolyn convinced van Grimes that her time was better spent doing other things. In fact, the sheer volume of mail increased to the point that an intern had to be brought in to exclusively answer it, and she worked long hours each day to finish the job.

Every week brought more triumphant news from Atlantic and Dove, and the mood of the team in Nashville was high. Andrew's album was certified gold, signifying five hundred thousand sales in the United States. Atlantic continued to push marketing dollars toward the record, sensing a groundswell of interest in Andrew and wanting to capital-ize on it. The effect of the video in particular had been gratifying and instantaneous—it had translated directly into sales.

In fact, the video for "Lost Without You" made Andrew a star. Indeed, that was its only reason for existence: Shane MacMillian had crafted a four-and-a-half-minute film in which every frame was meticulously calculated to create an Andrew Miracle infinitely desirable, microscopically per-fected, and mystically unattainable. With the coming of the video, public awareness of Andrew increased exponentially, pushing him out of the gospel world into the pop main-stream. The lake that they had all been swimming in had been overwhelming to Andrew when he had first arrived; now every day revealed that the oceans of people interested in and buying pop music easily drowned the Christian music market. When after five weeks "Lost Without You" topped the MTV charts and the Contemporary Hit radio charts nationally, Andrew had been seen or heard by over thirty-five million people in the United States alone. The video established him as a pop star with serious financial potential, a name to watch and to take seriously.

Upon no one was the effect of the video more pronounced than on Andrew himself. It was an already powerful thing to be experiencing his new life through his own eyes, but to watch his poster-self from a distance was perhaps the oddest thing to have happened so far in his journey.

He was in the fourth week of his tour when the video went number one. On that day he found himself in front of the television in his hotel room, staring blankly at the screen. His career was flying. Everything was perfect. Nevertheless, he felt once again the now familiar distance between himself and what was happening around him. He wanted to push through that distance and submerge himself in the love he read in those letters and stay there forever. But that love was elusive: sometimes, on stage, it seemed real, and he possessed it; at other times, it seemed to slip through his fingers. He was powerless to control it—a glance at a band member or at Graham standing offstage, and he was himself again, a thousand miles away from the adoration, feeling foolish to be the object of so much unqualified adulation. Once again he felt guilty for his ingratitude, but he was powerless against it now. Everything seemed so different now than when he had sat in van Grimes's office that first time, longing to play his songs and let God's spirit move in the audience.

On the day of his video triumph, he sat blankly staring at the screen, waiting for his clip to come on MTV. They played it at least once every hour, so he knew he wouldn't have to wait long. After several minutes, the poster-Andrew appeared once again on the screen, tracing perfectly for the hundredth time every move that Mac had designed for him. The figure on the screen never changed; he was locked in an endlessly repeated loop, each performance identical to the last, and to the next. A hundred years from now, Andrew would still be twenty years old, would still be lost and lonely, would still light up with just the right exhilarated expression when Renee stepped from the mist to surrender herself to him one more time. For some reason, this scene was intolerable to him: his real reaction to meeting her had been the breathless nervousness that a man who considers himself ordinary always feels in the presence of remarkable beauty. He had stammered. He had felt his gaze fall, unable to meet hers. He had stared surreptitiously at her perfect cheekbones, at her absurdly thick and shiny hair. He had felt like a schoolboy, assuming the silence of a child caught in a crush on a teacher. Yet the poster-Andrew had accepted her unequivocal yielding as if it were his right and destiny. Her face in the video revealed unmistakably that she had been longing for him, missing him, and searching for him. She could never be satisfied until she found the poster-Andrew, her true love. It only took looking at her to know that an ordinary man could never interest her. She was reserved for the poster-Andrew, and he for her. The poster-Andrew had been waiting for her, expected her, took her into his arms, and comforted her loneliness. All was well. After a station break, they would find each other all over again.

He couldn't wait. He popped a tape of his video into a portable VCR and watched himself going through the motions over and over again. From where he sat in front of the TV he could see himself in a mirror on the wall. His eyes went back and forth from the television screen to the mirror, as if comparing two similar but distinct twins for identifying marks. His face betrayed a wealth of changing emotions: at one point, he laughed out loud, as if the perfect character on the screen were making some jest. Each time his eyes drifted back to the mirror, however, his face was troubled, as if the perfect Andrew was mocking him and his imperfections.

The phone rang, rousing him from his thoughts. It was van Grimes, calling to celebrate. "We're number one, Drew!" he cried. "Number one in the country! Can you believe it?"

The sound of van Grimes's voice brought Andrew back to himself. He shook his head, waking from a dream, and walked with the phone to the other side of the room. "It is incredible," he answered flatly, hating to have to act more excited than he was. John had worked hard and deserved his exultation. It was a great accomplishment. "You did a great job, John," he said, trying to sound earnest. "I appreciate it."

"Everything worked out perfect, Drew. Hey, I meant to tell you, everybody in the office was watching when MTV declared it number one. You'll never guess what the VJ said when she introduced it."

"What's that?"

"She's counting down the top five, right, and she says, 'And the new number one, Andrew Miracle's very *spiritual* video, 'Lost Without You.' *Spiritual*, she says, Drew! So that's really coming across in the clip. I think the Lord is really going to use this thing."

"That's great, John," Andrew answered, trying to sound upbeat. He found himself wondering just what *spiritual* meant. He wondered if people thinking of joining Baha'i would see his video and think, *Yes! I have to join! The world is a very spiritual place!* But maybe John was right. You can't beat people over the head with Jesus. Turns 'em off, and then they don't hear. God brings them in little by little, and He can use anything.

"There's more good news, Drew," van Grimes went on, interrupting Andrew's thoughts.

"What's going on, John?"

"What's going on, my friend, is the Candyman 95 re-mixes."

Andrew knew the story on the remixes, at least theoreti-cally. Van Grimes had presented the plan as a *fait accompli,* as if Atlantic had bestowed a gift on Andrew. Candyman 95 was going to remix "Lost Without You" for three other radio formats, and create a mix for dance clubs as well. Andrew's apprehension about the remixes was considerable. The idea that someone with the name Candyman 95 was going to remake a song of such personal intensity was disturbing to him. "What's the deal with this, John?" he asked, sounding concerned. "Who is this guy, and what's he going to do with my song?"

"He's going to make you a pile of dough, my friend," answered John. "He's going to get your song on stations that wouldn't touch it the way it is. He's going to get your song played in dance clubs. He's going to sell a lot of units."

"But what's going to happen to the song? That song was a gift, John." He paused. "It's already been changed," he added, his voice not concealing his disappointment. "You know it's been changed once before."

"Nothing's going to happen, Drew. You worry to much. Besides, it's Thomasson's call," John added.

"What do you mean?"

"I mean Thomasson can do whatever he wants," he answered matter-of-factly.

"Are you saying that we have to go along?"

"That's right. It's standard—the labels can remix without artist permission, by and large. At least for artists in your position. But I think you're missing the point, Andrew. We *want* to go along. The guy is the top man in the business. Just having his name on the remixes gets them played. Thomasson is paying you a terrific compliment by bringing in the ace for your project."

"So you don't think he'll do too much to it."

"Nah," van Grimes reassured him. "He'll just punch it up a little, make it strut for the R&B stations and the dance clubs, you know. Nothing serious."

Andrew felt tired. He didn't have the energy for a new confrontation, especially one that van Grimes had made clear he couldn't win. There seemed little point in arguing when the result was a foregone conclusion. He was locked in before he even started. "I don't like it, John," he said. "But it seems that doesn't matter much."

For once, van Grimes made no attempt to conceal his irritation. "I have to tell you, Drew, I get a pain in my side when I hear you talk like this. These people are busting their chops to get your career to happen, and all I hear is complaints."

Andrew stared at the phone, startled. There was something new in John's voice, as if a veil had been torn aside and something hidden was being revealed. Perhaps the time for polite accommodation was ending. "I'm sorry, John," Andrew replied, surprising himself with his own terse voice. "I'm not used to my music being considered the property of everyone else. It's an odd feeling, seeing it thrown to the winds like this."

"The winds, my friend, are where the money is. Or maybe you picture yourself back in Rose Hill again, playing to a couple hundred country bumpkins." John's voice was fraying, and it was becoming apparent that he was having difficulty keeping his temper. Then, he seemed to break. "Look, let's just cut the crap, Andrew," he said, releasing his anger. "You've been resisting this thing from the beginning. What's bugging you? Do you have some problem with how we're handling things for you? Things not going well enough for you? Making a little too much money? Getting a little too successful? What's your point?"

Andrew sat as still as a statue, thinking hard. Maybe it was time to let things go, once and for all. The awe in which he had held John and all the others had kept him silent, but his own heart and mind had never been quiet; he had internalized so much, and he wanted to release it.

"Listen, John," he said earnestly. "This is important. I don't completely understand it yet myself. I just see the beginning of it. But it's like there's two of me, you know? There's the me that I know, the one that just got off the plane from Rose Hill. It seems like a long time ago, but I still think I know that guy pretty well. At least, I remember him. He's a regular guy in some ways, but he's got this music to share. This gift. Then there's the one that I hear about when everybody talks about the record and the career. That Andrew's *fantastic*. He's a genius, a star. I have no idea who that Andrew is. And the scary thing is that I really have to *be* him. I have to perform and travel and give interviews all that. What if everybody suddenly decides I'm just a boring kid from Kansas? What if I say something stupid and make a jerk out of myself? They can build me up, but I still know exactly who I am."

There was a silence on the phone. When John spoke, his voice had less edge to it. "Is that what this is? A crisis of confidence? Look, you have nothing to worry about. You've done great up 'til now, and you'll do great from here on out. Like I said, you worry too much."

"I don't know, John," Andrew answered. "Some of it's a lack of confidence, sure, but that's not all of it. I don't think I'd have a problem just being myself. It's the poster-Andrew that I can't be. Nobody could ever be that person. And in the context of my ministry, there's something disturbing about that."

"You're blowing this way out of proportion, Andrew. We never said you were perfect. You never said it, either. You've been truthful from the beginning."

"It doesn't seem to matter what words come out of my mouth," Andrew argued, "if the image of me that's been created overwhelms those words. I can't say it any plainer than this: how can it be right for me to *know* that I can't be the person that I'm presented as? How can that be right?"

"Look, Drew, I know what you mean, but marketing is an essential ingredient in this business. You must understand that. It's an occupational hazard, all this hype. You really can be yourself through this. Just hold on to what you know. Naturally there's some pressure to hype you, but it's just the excitement about your project. Stay true to yourself, and you'll be fine."

Andrew exhaled deeply, slumping slightly in his hotel chair. When he spoke again, his voice had lost a good deal of its steel. "So you think I can do this."

"Oh, yeah, I'm a big believer in Andrew Miracle," John answered, his voice suddenly soothing.

Andrew sat quietly holding the phone, for the first time wondering which Andrew John believed in. He knew better than to ask. But he realized now that the more the distinction between the real Andrew and the public Andrew grew, the more he would be asking himself questions like that. He wanted to minimize that distance and keep his life simple.

But how could he do it when there was so much momentum in the opposite direction? There was a lot of work to be done, and it seemed that the better everyone did it, the more confusing things would become. It was a competitive marketplace, and there was little room for the ordinary. Helen had said it best: Who did he think would buy a record from a guy who was full of doubts?

He sat thinking, still holding the phone. But something his father had said to him long ago had been coming back to him lately, and in a flash it rumbled once again through him. His father hadn't been a terribly religious man, but he had a rock-solid bottom line that others respected. One day, when Andrew was about ten years old, they had been riding fence in the pickup, looking for breaks to repair. Andrew had just accepted Christ as his Savior at the church the Sunday before, and he was curious about things. As they bounced along in the truck, Andrew had asked his father what his favorite verse in the Bible was. Franklin slowed the truck down, and pulled over next to the fence to stop. He looked right at Andrew and said, "Book of John, verse three and thirty." By this he had meant the thirtieth verse of the third chapter. Even at ten years old, Andrew knew that his father didn't spend a lot of time reading the Bible, and he was impressed that he had received an answer so quickly.

"What does it say?" he asked.

Andrew's father had smiled. "Look it up, boy."

With that, he had pulled the truck back out into the field, and the two didn't speak of it again. That night, however, Andrew had pulled his father's big Bible off the bookshelf and looked the verse up. It contained only seven words.

"He must increase, but I must decrease."

Now, more than ten years later, Andrew heard the words again in his memory, and they gave him pause. There was a mystery there he couldn't quite understand. How could those words refer to the poster-Andrew? How could he decrease, and be lifted up at the same time? For a moment, he wondered if the verse could apply to his real self and exempt his poster-self. He rejected the idea outright. In the end, there could only be one of him. But how could he have his image professionally maintained by a staff of people and have that verse come true? And if the verse couldn't be true for him, what was he doing? He tried for a moment to imagine John the Baptist with a press agent. But John had gone out to the desert, and the people destined to hear him had found him there, including Christ Himself. Of course, John hadn't been in business—in business with many other people, each with a personal stake in how successful the business was. Suddenly, he was aware of the silence, and he shook his head, coming back to himself. He could hear John breathing through the phone. "You know who I find myself thinking about lately?" Andrew asked, his voice strange and distant.

"Who?" John answered cautiously. The long silence had made him wary. The flash of anger between them had been as big a surprise to him as it had been to Andrew, and he couldn't tell if Andrew was about to capitulate or to explode once again. But when Andrew answered, his voice was eerily calm and resigned. "I've been thinking about the chair stackers," he said.

"Who?"

"The chair stackers. You know, the guys who stack chairs after church. Back home, I mean."

"Just tell me what on earth you're talking about," John pleaded, exasperated. "We have the number one video in the country, and you want to talk about stacking chairs?"

"Yeah, I do. It seems important to me, now. More important than anything in the world. Just listen. Sunday evenings, we would meet in a fellowship hall. After the service, every one of the chairs would have to be stacked up and moved out. The pastor would end up his sermon, and then he'd say, 'We'd love some volunteers to help stack up the chairs after the service.' The same four or five people always did it."

"In my church we never had to stack chairs."

"Okay, but it doesn't have to be that, necessarily. It could be anything, see? It's like the three or four ladies that make the food for Wednesday night dinner. Or the people that always say yes when the church has a clean-up day, you know, where they mow the grass and paint the building and stuff like that. It's all those people who never get any recognition but without whom the church would cease to exist."

John was troubled by Andrew's remarks. He didn't know where this was heading. Nevertheless, the sudden calm in Andrew's voice had quieted his own anger, and in spite of himself he couldn't help remembering the faces of the older women in his church back in Illinois, the ones who had been quietly faithful through a generation of church-going. He wondered where those old ladies were now. He didn't know if they were alive or dead. It was hard to stay angry when he thought about them.

"Yes, I know who you mean," he answered quietly. "What about them? What do they have to do with us?"

"Just this," Andrew replied, surprising himself with the emotion in his voice. "Nobody knows who those people are. They just serve. I get the feeling that in the big scheme of things, they wouldn't feel like what they did was that important, you know? I mean compared to what I'm doing right now. They wouldn't even dream of comparing. They stay in the background. I mean they don't just stand up and say, 'Hey, I stack chairs better than anybody in the world,' you know? They don't say, 'I have a special gift for stacking chairs, a gift to the world.' They just stack the chairs, or clean a bathroom, or bake bread for somebody. They pick up stray hymnals or visit a hospital room. They sit in a pew and pray for somebody else in the service. You know something, John? I'm thinking more and more about those people, and I'm starting to envy them."

"I appreciate that they do wonderful things, but why would you envy them?" John asked. "Not everybody is called to stack chairs. You have a different gift, Andrew. Your life is extraordinary right now. You're living a dream."

Andrew paused a moment, considering. "I envy them because I'm beginning to suspect that they're the ones."

"The ones?" John asked.

"Yeah, the ones. They think that in the grand scheme of things, what they do is small change. But maybe to God, they are kings and princes. Maybe to God, they are ruling the earth already. Maybe He looks down from heaven and sees them lighting the darkness more than anybody else in the world. Maybe God looks at what we're doing and says 'big deal,' and it turns out that the guy who's playing a beat-up piano for a prison mission is a star in heaven. Him and all those old ladies baking bread and cleaning bathrooms. And not a press agent among them."

Now it was John's turn to be silent. He was thinking about things he hadn't thought about in a long time. To his consternation, he couldn't get the image of his eighth grade Sunday school teacher out of his mind. He hadn't thought about him for years. He felt a sense of warmth come over him, remembering when his life was far less complicated and his friendships had a quality different from what they had now. He wanted to embrace that memory. For a moment, he thought he might. But the feeling lasted only a short while; it was too late for all that now. He was committed. He had a staff, a mortgage, and plans, the biggest of plans. When at last he spoke, his voice was brittle, and not a trace of the sound of his past lingered in it.

"What do you want me to do, Andrew, just call up Harold and Thomasson and everybody else and say 'Sorry, Andrew's had an epiphany and he thinks this whole thing is a big mistake for him—hope it's not inconvenient'? Are you nuts? If you had any sense, you'd realize that if God wasn't in this thing, there would be no way that it would be so blessed. You have the number one video in the country, and you're complaining. This isn't spirituality, for God's sake, it's just ingratitude!"

Andrew shivered, stung by John's words. That was the last impression he wanted to leave. The anger drained from him, and his voice was full of conciliation. "No, John, that's not it. It's not ingratitude at all. I appreciate what you've done for me, and that goes for everyone. I know full well that without everyone else's work, I wouldn't be anywhere. And I'm not saying that the whole thing is some kind of scam. I'm just saying that it's a hard fit for me. Just me."

"That's just great, kid, 'cause you're the 'me' that happens to be in the hot seat here. This isn't some metaphysical discussion, my friend. This is reality. And the reality is that you are committed, with everybody else, to do your level best to make the belief that everybody has had in you worth their while. There's no direction but forward. Now there's only one thing I want to hear from you, Andrew, and that's the simple statement that you are on board and one hundred percent behind this tour and everything else that you have been indescribably fortunate to experience."

Andrew slumped, beaten down by van Grimes's argument. He was right, of course. Without his realizing it, the poster-Andrew had grown in power and importance to the point that he couldn't be shut off. He was, in effect, already bigger than the real Andrew, and his appetite demanded constant feeding. He was like King Kong, larger than life, and the trainers and feeders all depended on a good show. Otherwise, chaos.

"All right, John," he breathed. "I just wanted to let you know how I was feeling. Maybe you're right. Maybe I'm just ungrateful."

"Got that right," van Grimes answered. He had the kid on the ropes, and he needed to teach him a lesson. "I don't want to hear this kind of talk again, Andrew, and no matter what happens I don't want Harold or anybody at Atlantic to hear it. It's imperative that those folks know that we are a hundred percent ready to play ball. This is a tricky business, and it can vanish as quick as it comes."

With a click of the phone, John was gone. Andrew comforted himself with his manager's last statement. *It can vanish,* he had said, *as quick as it comes.*

24

John glanced at his watch surreptitiously as Laurence Hill droned on. This must be the meeting to end all meetings. Three and a half hours, and still no sign of ending. He looked around the room. Laurence. Harold. Helen. Mark Haffner. Once Laurence got wound up, he could talk. Numbers. Demographics. Credit terms to retailers. He had a million things he could run on about. But right now, only one thing mattered: Andrew Miracle's star was bright and getting brighter, and he was exclusively represented by the John van Grimes Agency. The tour had only a little over a week to go, and the remaining nights were all sellouts. John listened another few minutes and finally cleared his throat. "Laurence," he said, "your command of detail is . . . overwhelming. I wonder if I can just interject something?"

Hill stopped in mid-sentence, his business monotone having run over the front of van Grimes's statement for several words. "All right, John," he said, giving van Grimes a look that mixed outward tolerance and inner loathing. "You have something to add on the subject of cassette tape costs?"

Van Grimes smiled indulgently. With Atlantic's signing on, his relations with Dove had taken on a decidedly less critical nature, and everyone in the room knew it. The big dog had come to hunt, and the little dogs got out of the way. Dove made a small amount of money on every record that Atlantic sold, of course, but the fact remained that with the huge success of the video of "Lost Without You," the action on Andrew Miracle had shifted out of Christian bookstores and right into mainstream retailers—outlets that Dove records couldn't get into with a crowbar.

"I willingly defer to you on the subject of rising tape costs, Laurence," van Grimes said. "You're the expert. Unfortunately, I have to leave in a few moments, and I have exciting news, news that I had to share with all of you before I left." The staff at Dove perked up, brought to life from Laurence's numbing speech. "I just got off the phone before coming here with the director of talent for 'The Barry Rosenberg Show.' Andrew is scheduled next week."

Van Grimes noted the immediate response in the room with satisfaction. Barry Rosenberg was the preeminent late night talk show host, and his show was the number-one rated program of its kind in America. He had made the careers of dozens of stars. For a new artist to get on was a major *coup*.

"We all know the terrific success that Andrew's tour has been," John continued. "The last date on the tour is next Saturday, and every date until then is a sellout. We're meeting in LA on the following Monday to do some press work and glad-hand the West Coast office of Atlantic. I wanted to take advantage of the Rosenberg thing to leverage into some things. Andrew's on the show Friday. He's doing 'Lost Without You,' and I have a promise he'll get to do the couch." It was a major accomplishment for Andrew; Rosenberg had to like you if you were going to get to the couch, especially if you were a newcomer. If Andrew came off well, the other talk shows would follow suit with no problems.

"Outstanding, John, outstanding," Harold said. "How did you pull it off?"

"Actually, Harold, Karl Hunter at Atlantic called the talent director, a guy named Stefan Green, and Green called me." John kept his face neutral, but inside he was enjoying himself. He took pleasure playing Dove and Atlantic off each other. Everyone in the Dove office knew that access to major Hollywood media was something that they simply could not provide. But it didn't hurt to remind them from time to time. Kept them honest.

"Glad to hear it, John," Harold said. "That's the kind of thing we hoped for with this Atlantic thing."

John let a smile creep out. Harold was playing it like he should, going with the flow and letting his people feel like a part of things, even though they were becoming increasingly irrelevant. "Exactly, Harold. I'm sure we're all very excited."

"Any worries about Andrew?" Laurence spoke up.

"What do you mean?" John asked.

"Doing TV."

John stared. Hill must be the most blunt man he had ever met. "No, Laurence, Andrew is up to the task. I anticipate no problems at all. He's come through like a champ so far, and he knows the score."

Hill's mouth crept into a scowl, but he mastered it, reassuming his neutral visage. He then gave Harold a furtive, questioning look. Harold nodded almost imperceptibly in response, and Laurence squared himself toward John.

"We've been hearing things, John," Laurence said. "I suppose this Rosenberg thing is as good a time as any to bring it up."

John stiffened. A recalcitrant, confrontational Hill was not on his agenda. "What do you mean, you've been hearing things?" he asked. "What kind of things?"

"From the local salesmen, John," Laurence answered flatly. "The regional reps that are meeting with Andrew out on the tour. We're a little concerned."

"Why don't you just come out and say what you're driving at?"

"All right, John. Here it is. We're hearing some negative things on Andrew. On his state of mind."

Van Grimes's face hardened. "There is nothing in the world wrong with Andrew's mind," he said with carefully measured hostility. "He is absolutely under control."

"Yes," interjected Harold, "but whose control? We hear that he's depressed. The shows are going okay, but our peo-

ple who meet with him say he's down, John. Really down.
And we hear he's become a bit of a tyrant—getting on the
crew like he never did before." Murphy gestured vaguely,
and his voice took on a dreamy, distant quality. "I'd have to
say I'm personally disappointed by that. It happens to so
many, but I'd hoped that Andrew would be different. He
was so . . . so fresh."

"I'm telling you that there is no problem with Andrew,"
van Grimes replied evenly.

"We'd hate to see him not at his best if he's going on na-
tional television, John," Harold offered. "You understand."

Van Grimes smiled grimly to himself. He understood, all
right. This wasn't about Andrew. It was about power. Hill
and Murphy were letting him know that his personal power
began and ended with a happy, productive Andrew. If Andrew lost his touch, the John van Grimes Agency would be
back to booking Heaven's Voices so fast he wouldn't know
what hit him.

"Andrew is fine," John said, curtailing his anger and giving in to the game. He gave his voice a calm, soothing
quality. "He's just tired. After all, we've been working him
hard. It was difficult timing, what with the tour following
on the heels of his mother's death. That took a toll. After
the TV show, we'll see that he gets a good, long rest."

Hill emitted a guttural assent but said nothing. John rose
with a smile, effectively ending the meeting. He had received their slap on the wrist, but he wasn't going to lie
down and die. As long as Andrew produced, everything
would be fine. Power was flowing, moving away from Harold
and Laurence and toward Michael Thomasson and, with
Andrew's rising star, toward John as well. It was not an
unpleasant feeling. Time to take a last shot.

"I've enjoyed this, my friends," he said cheerfully. "I hate
to run, but there's a great deal to arrange, and I promised

a few people I'd meet with them before the day is done. I'll
be in touch."

Carolyn slipped on her pale green angora sweater with
a tight-lipped, brave smile. It was already too warm to wear
it, and May days had a way of actually getting hot in Nashville by late afternoon. But she wanted to wear it one last
time. It was Andrew's favorite. She closed her eyes and let
her mind drift a moment, but then she shook her head and
turned back to dressing. She would wear the sweater. But
she couldn't really let herself think about how relaxed and
easy they had been together in the beginning, about how
he had stared at her, wide-eyed, when she had worn the
sweater for him the first time. All that was hurting too much.

Their nightly phone calls had been especially hard lately.
After several weeks of separation, they had lost their center,
and it seemed like two voices were dating, not two whole
people. Andrew had been evasive, cutting short their conversations. When they didn't see each other for so long, she
began to wonder exactly who it was she was dating. The
glue of their relationship had always been their vulnerability
with each other, the fact that they had no secrets. She saw
that openness fading; Andrew seemed to be hiding behind
an exterior, becoming more and more remote. She was afraid,
watching something beautiful in a person shrivel and die.

Then, the oddest, saddest thought of all came to her. The
tour was ending, and she realized that she didn't want him
to come home. Funny, she hadn't dreamed she would ever
feel that way, wanting the tour to stay out on the road and
delay the day that Andrew would return. Not that she wasn't
missing him; she missed him all day long, and she often
caught herself looking at his picture at her desk—not one
of the glossy press pictures sent out to fans by the hundreds
but a simple, happy one she had taken of him on a picnic
during those first weeks together. A big mutt had run free

from his master and jumped up on Andrew's lap, and she had caught him there with her camera, the dog's tongue lolling out and Andrew smiling. She liked to think of him like that. More and more, when she thought about him, it wasn't in the real life in which they found themselves, but in a fantasy life—simpler, and without so many complicated arguments and questions. So a part of her didn't want the tour to end. When the tour came back, she wouldn't be able to dream like that anymore. Real life came back with him, and a lot of questions would find answers, once and for all.

She knew that they couldn't go on the way they were for much longer. They had tasted something so rare and penetrating that going through the motions just hurt too much. Every bad day or bad phone call hurt more because Carolyn compared it to the sweetness of their early time together. Once Andrew returned, they would have to face what they had lost head on, and move on from there.

Carolyn pushed all that out of her mind once again, finished dressing, and drove to work. John had hinted on a big job waiting for her there, and she mentally steeled herself to concentrate on the task at hand. She couldn't afford to daydream as much as she had been. John was making contact with some other big-name artists, looking to expand his business and become a major player in the entertainment industry. The company had really outgrown its staff, and now, when so much depended on everything being accomplished with utmost professionalism, they discovered that there was more to do than they could handle. John would have to hire more staff, but he was waiting to land a big name to finance the expansion. Carolyn knew some of the stars John was pursuing; her boss was thinking big, and with Andrew's momentum behind him, he just might pull it off.

She had just arrived and poured herself a cup of coffee when van Grimes called her into his office to discuss the day's agenda. She set the cup down on her desk, mentally braced herself, and went in.

Van Grimes seemed a bit more nervous than usual, she thought. He had changed, subtly but unmistakably, in the last few months. She had first begun to notice it in his clothing—he had always dressed superbly, but gradually, it became evident that he was spending extraordinary sums on tailored coats and suits. He rarely seemed to repeat himself, appearing each morning in another tasteful, precisely fitted outfit. At the same time, however, it seemed that the more perfectly attired he became, the more perceptible his inner fraying. His easy, smooth style had gradually deteriorated, and a repertoire of quick, jerky motions that seemed to take an effort to control began to surface. It had taken some time before Carolyn put the two phenomena together: his external dress and internal state of mind seemed to be traveling along opposite vectors, so that given enough time, he would become the most perfectly dressed madman in the world.

"Carolyn," he said, "I've got a critical job for you. Highest priority." As he spoke, his voice slightly cracked.

"Of course, John," Carolyn answered. Oddly, the more nervous and frazzled he became, the more unnaturally calm and still she became, as if their souls were in a strange, connected, zero-sum game.

"Good," said van Grimes. "Here's the drill. I've got some big clients coming in here in a few days. The biggest. You know all about that. They're going to have one question in their mind. That question is: What are you going to do for me if I sign my enormous career to the John van Grimes Agency?"

"I understand."

"Right. They're going to take a hard look at every detail of how we've handled this Andrew Miracle thing. So I want you to go back over Andrew's entire career to this point and create a killer presentation on everything we've done for him."

"What do you mean?"

"I mean press clippings, reviews, advertisements, interviews, press kits, everything. I want to show these new guys that when I go to work for somebody, things happen."

"And this presentation would be for me to give?" she asked.

"Of course not. I give the presentation. You prepare it."

"I understand. When do you need it?"

"Pronto, please. ASAP. It's Friday now, so let's have it on my desk Monday morning. The tour's over tomorrow, and I fly out to meet Andrew first thing next week for press work and the Rosenberg show. I'd like to have it in hand for that— I'm meeting some top people while we're out on the coast."

Carolyn nodded, smiled her brave little smile again, and went back to her desk to work.

It was no easy task accumulating the massive amount of material associated with Andrew's relatively short career. With van Grimes, Dove, and Atlantic all working hard to promote him, an extraordinary amount of press and publicity had been generated for such a young artist. She decided to go about it methodically, working chronologically from the time he had arrived in Nashville.

All morning she went through press clippings, press kits, and photographs of Andrew's first few months in Nashville. The contract-signing photos, in particular, caught her attention; he had been in town less than a week, and he was smiling, his face open and untroubled. She smiled at his tousled, short hair, and his slightly frumpy clothes. But even in the photograph she could see something in his eyes, life and vitality and anticipation. There was something sad in seeing the picture now.

She ate lunch alone, grabbing a take-out sandwich and sitting quietly, almost serenely, at her desk. Every hour took her further through Andrew's career, and gradually the pictures of him changed. They were superb and he was beautiful, or rather beautified, but already, it was harder to find the person she loved underneath the gloss. By afternoon she had moved into his first tour, and she read the interviews he had given to local newspapers, noting how much more professional and ultimately, predictable, they became as the tour progressed. She uncovered a tour poster, Mark and Helen's work over at Dove. A Miracle is Coming, it blared, and it showed Andrew in one of his most romantic poses. She cataloged it all: photos from concerts in his stage clothes, the gold record, the sold-out concerts.

As the afternoon wore on, she glanced more and more at the early pictures, and at her little snapshot taken at the park. At one point she began to tremble slightly, but she quickly mastered herself, and once again assumed her quiet, still demeanor. She was just about to pack her things up and go home when she saw them.

Peeking out from a stack of magazine articles was a set of Mark's first two posters—the ones he had presented at the album release party. She pulled one out, and stared at it for a long time. She read it to herself several times, like a prayer.

Andrew Miracle is like no other friend you have.
He's a friend who's seeking the heart of God.
He's seeking your heart, too.

Andrew Miracle
is
Lost Without You

She read the words over and over, realizing that they meant something quite different to her now than what Mark had intended. They were personal now. She closed her eyes and sat silently, breathing softly. Her lips moved without a sound for a time, and when she opened her eyes, she smiled. It wasn't her thin, brave smile. It was the first peaceful, resolved smile she had had in a long time.

She picked up a copy of Andrew's tour schedule. The Cleveland concert was at the Convention Center music hall.

She picked up the phone and pushed the button to speed-dial the travel agency the office used, spoke into the receiver for a short while, and hung up.

The next morning, she drove to the airport and boarded a plane.

25

Andrew rode to the concert hall in Cleveland in a poor state of mind. The remix was wrong, all wrong. What did Candyman 95 know about his music? Thinking about it had kept him awake, and he hadn't slept well. He was tired, and the limousine had picked him up almost twenty minutes late at the hotel. That meant the sound check would be rushed, and he hated that. It put him on edge, knowing things might not be sorted out for him to hear well on stage. One thing he had resolved: if he couldn't hear properly, the evening was a washout. He must speak to John about it once again. There really was no reason why things couldn't be organized better. Why should he have to wait in the lobby for twenty minutes when he could be sleeping comfortably in his room?

The black limousine pulled into the underground service garage and parked in between the familiar semitrailers that hauled the stage equipment. Andrew smiled at the memory of how impressed he had been with the setup of Heaven's Voices back in Rose Hill. Their modest little stage and lights would fit on one corner of the layout he was using tonight. That night seemed like years ago. Funny how your perspective changes, how you grow and mature, he thought. This was the big time. *He* was big time. He opened the door without speaking to the driver, grabbed his shoulder bag, and walked across the gray concrete floor towards the stage entrance.

It always struck Andrew how drab and industrial the great concert halls were behind their thin veneer of luxury and occasion. Where the audience was allowed, they possessed an ornamental quality that added to the excitement of the event. But underneath all the trappings even the best halls in the world were nothing but glorified loading docks, built for maximum efficiency and little else. In their bowels, they all looked remarkably the same. The moment in the sun for each artist was rendered as short as possible by design, and Andrew realized there was nothing special about his appearance there for the stage hands and technicians. He was interchangeable, and a new artist would be unloading his trappings of fame within hours of Andrew's departure.

Andrew picked his way through the trucks and forklifts to the stage door. A stocky woman wearing a blue, official-looking jacket sat at a desk just inside. She wore a large, laminated badge that said "Hall Security," with the name DORIS printed in bold letters underneath. She motioned for him to sign in. Andrew took the clipboard and wrote his name and filled in the time of day. He turned to walk through the inner door, but she raised her hand to stop him.

"Is there a problem?" asked Andrew abruptly.

The security guard slowly spun the clipboard around on the desk and stared at Andrew's name.

"I need to check your name against the list," she replied. "Andrew Miracle?" She looked up at Andrew, skeptically.

"That's right," he shot back. "Andrew Miracle."

The guard opened a drawer of her desk and pulled out a spiral notebook. Attached to it was one of Andrew's back-stage passes. She flipped through several pages and finally settled on the day's date. The book was filled with the names of previous artists and approved guests for each event at the hall, names now irrelevant to her.

"Well, I see your name here sure enough," she said, "But I don't see no pass. This here's the official pass for tonight. You got one?"

Andrew couldn't believe what he was hearing.

"Look, uh . . . Doris," he said, peering at the name on her

badge conspicuously. "Take a look at the pass you have in your hand. What does it say?"

Doris plucked the badge from the front of the notebook and held it up in front of her. She said nothing.

"The pass, Doris, says 'Andrew Miracle—Lost Without You Tour.' I am Andrew Miracle. I'm the artist performing in your lovely little hall tonight. I don't have a pass, Doris, because I don't need one. Okay?"

Andrew strode over to the inner door and pulled at the handle. It was locked. He turned in exasperation and looked back at Doris. She picked up a pen, and methodically placed a checkmark beside Andrew's name on the backstage list. Then she pushed a button underneath her desk to release the lock on the inner door. Andrew heard a buzzer and felt the door move slightly in his grip. He pulled open the door and strode in.

"Dolt," he muttered. "All these guards, they're on a power trip."

After wandering around in the catacombs of the hall for a few minutes, he finally ran into Graham, who greeted him cheerfully.

"How's it going, Andrew? Get here from the hotel okay?"

"Yeah, twenty minutes late," Andrew answered. "We ready for sound check?"

"You bet," Graham replied. "Let me show you to the dressing room, and you can drop your bag off and get situated."

"Forget it, Graham. I'd rather get sound check out of the way first. Let's go to the stage."

Graham led Andrew through the long halls to a door marked ENTRANCE—STAGE LEFT. Andrew pushed open the door, and they entered the backstage world of ropes, pulleys, lighting trusses, stage supports, and trap doors. He walked straight up to the center of the stage, where a piano tuner was putting the finishing touches on his Steinway. All around the stage workmen were moving busily, taping down cables and checking equipment. Up in the lighting truss, two men were hanging precariously, positioning Vari-lites. The members of his band were playing an old sixties tune, but when they saw Andrew, they stopped immediately and called out their hellos. This was what it was all about, thought Andrew. Showtime.

The tuner packed up his tools as Andrew approached, waiting off to the side of the piano for the okay that the tuning job was acceptable. Andrew motioned for silence, and the band members called to the workmen to ease off for a moment. After the cacophony of stagehands working and musicians running through their parts, the silence was striking in the huge hall. It seemed to throw its own echo out into the rows of empty chairs. Andrew looked around, satisfied, and sat before the piano.

He played several notes individually, leaning forward, caressing each key. He loved this instrument, and no matter what else had changed in his life, this remained: the sound of a superb, perfectly tuned piano ringing out into the darkness, splitting the silence of a three-thousand-seat hall. It was an anchor, a mooring for him. At that moment, a spotlight operator at the back of the balcony opened his light on a tight focus, directly on Andrew. He was illuminated, and the spotlight cut a visible path four hundred feet long from one end of the hall to the other.

Andrew counted off a song, and the band went through it with him, adjusting amplifiers, getting comfortable playing in a new environment. Satisfied, he told the band to relax, and headed back to the catacombs to find his dressing room. He needed to call John.

Thirty minutes later, around six-thirty, Carolyn landed at Cleveland Airport. As she walked down the airport corridor, she stopped in the bathroom to freshen up after the flight. What she saw staring back in the mirror gave her a start. She looked awful. Her eyes were red and puffy from lack of sleep. She bit her lip, and tried to pull her hair back the way Andrew liked it, but it wouldn't cooperate. She looked at her dress and was sure she should have worn something else, maybe the black one he had commented on. This one never seemed to hang right on her. She turned in front of the mirror, hating what she saw, feeling useless. For some reason she was starting to cry now, ruining her makeup. She leaned over the sink, holding it with both hands, crying harder, feeling herself losing control. She grimaced, trying to master herself. But then it was gone, and she was sobbing, feeling lost in an airport bathroom a long way from home.

Andrew was talking on Graham's mobile phone with John when she arrived at his dressing room forty-five minutes later. She tried one more time to pull herself together, knocked briefly on the door, and let herself in. Andrew looked up from his call, surprised, and motioned her to sit down. Carolyn walked to the other side of the room, and tried to look happy. John was explaining the remix to Andrew, and they were obviously disagreeing.

"Andrew," said John, "this is opening a whole new world for you. I mean, who could have imagined that your music would be getting played in dance clubs. It's a completely new market."

"Look, John, I don't care what you say, when I heard that remix I panicked. The only thing left of my song was the vocal and one piano part. It was like a completely different thing. I hate dance music, and now I have a single out there that *is* dance music."

"Andrew," John answered, "you're not getting the point here. These people have never heard your stuff. They've never heard of Andrew Miracle. They have nothing to do with your existing fans; they're a whole new horizon. The fans you have will listen to the contemporary hit mix and love it. The new fans will hear the dance remix in every dance club in America and love that. And they will buy the record, Andrew, and even buy the dance single. Do you understand me?"

"I understand it's not the song I wrote, John. I understand

that people are hearing a song with my name on it that I had nothing to do with."

"Andrew, be reasonable. It's not like this is unusual. This is standard procedure, man. I don't think you realize the magnitude of what is happening here. Everything, and I mean everything, depends on momentum. You have it, the label loves you, and you win. You lose it, and the label hates you, and you lose. You're deciding your future here, Andrew."

"What do you mean? How greedy are they?" he complained. "The record's already an enormous success, John. What do they want from me?"

"Andrew, the remix has been out for a week, and we've already sold thirty-five thousand singles. Your album is going up to number six in next week's *Billboard*. Atlantic is freaking out, and they're talking about pumping in another major dose of promotion money behind you. The net effect of this is that you could easily sell another hundred-fifty thousand singles, maybe three hundred thousand more albums. Which makes your price go up another five grand a night. Which gets you on Arsenio. Which gets you in *People* magazine. Which sells another two hundred thousand records. You follow me? You wanna turn that off, Andrew? Are you kidding me?"

Andrew was silent, thinking over what John was saying. Once again, he felt his power base slipping away. Decisions, even artistic ones, were being made by people who wore suits, and who had never even met him. People with their own plans. He felt helpless.

"John, I understand what you're saying. I don't want Atlantic to feel like I'm not playing ball. But that song has a special meaning to me. It's the reason I'm supposed to be out here doing this. I didn't picture people picking each other up in dance clubs to it when I wrote it. Can't they do whatever it is they're doing to some other song?"

"Andrew, career hit songs don't grow on trees. You will be making money off this song for the rest of your life. And so will Atlantic, and so will I. The people working at Atlantic want raises too, Andrew. They've got kids. They've got mortgages. The salesmen want bonuses. Maybe they want to take a nice vacation this year. You're telling them no? You're gonna decide that for all of them? For your artistic integrity? The decision's out of your hands, Andrew."

Andrew slumped in his chair, confused, and beaten. "Okay," he said at last, and clicked off the phone.

Carolyn straightened herself up and forced a smile on her face. She wanted to reach out to Andrew and comfort him, to make everything better. As soon as she saw him, however, she realized that she was powerless to do so. Andrew was fighting a battle within himself, and no one could fight it for him. She immediately began to regret having come. She felt like a voyeur at a private destruction. Nevertheless, she loved Andrew, and moved by some instinctive, compassionate force she rose, crossed the dressing room, and put her hand on his shoulder. Andrew looked up at her, tired frustration in his eyes. Curiously, he didn't comment on her surprise arrival, but merely started talking as if they were continuing some ongoing conversation.

"That was John," he said, his voice fatigued. "It seems that thanks to Candyman 95, you can now pick up girls in dance clubs to 'Lost Without You.' You can't imagine what a joy that is to me." Andrew leaned back in his chair, full of resignation. "We've been down a long road together, haven't we, Carolyn?" She stepped in front of him, and he took her hand, accepting the fact that she had come to him without comment. "I wonder what we would have said to each other that day when I landed at Nashville and you picked me up if we had known how bumpy that road was going to be?"

Carolyn closed her eyes and stood before him, thinking of that day, of how perfect and innocent it had been. They had driven with the top down, the wind rushing past their faces, and she had felt like a princess showing a visiting knight her kingdom. If she could have gone back in time, she would have kept on driving with him, straight back to Rose Hill and the little church in which he had been so vital. She would have stayed there with him; they would be walking hand in hand across the wheat and listening to the wind tonight instead of crying together in the bowels of a concert hall.

"I just wanted to be myself, you know?" Andrew said, his voice tortured. "I had no idea what an incredibly hard thing that is to do. I thought it was simple. How stupid of me."

"I don't think so, Drew," Carolyn said softly. Somehow, seeing him so vulnerable and defeated comforted her. She hadn't expected that. But he had been so hard and distant lately that watching his inner defenses crash down gave her an odd hope, a hope that they could find each other again. There was a chance that the Andrew she had met over a year ago would rise out of the rubble and they would find a small but sincere life together somewhere. "I don't think you were stupid at all," she said. "I think, even after everything that's happened, that you're on the path of your destiny, somehow. At least I hope so."

"That's what John said. He was big on destiny. I think he meant something different, though."

"It doesn't matter what he meant. I just think it's true. Maybe that's all I came to say, and just to stand by you in this. But I have to tell you something."

"I don't have much energy, but I'm listening."

"Good. I flew hundreds of miles to tell you one thing, and I didn't realize what it was myself until this moment." Carolyn paused, letting her thoughts settle. She released his hand and walked slightly away from him. Something was dawning inside of her, something she hadn't anticipated.

"What is it?" Andrew asked, fearing a blow.

"I've been sad, too, and I know why now. It's because I miss Andrew Miracle."

"What do you mean, Carolyn? I'm right here."

"No, you're not. You look like Andrew Miracle, sort of, but you're not him. I don't know where he is. I thought maybe I would fly out here and find him for you, but I see now that's impossible. If anyone finds him, you will. But I can tell you that I love the real Andrew Miracle and that I miss him, miss him terribly. I need him. And I think he needs me, too."

Andrew sat, tears welling in his eyes. Carolyn, by contrast, had seemed to find a sudden inner strength and stood tall and dignified. "I see something, Andrew," she said, her voice surprisingly firm. "I thought I would come out here and help you discover yourself again. I was ready to do that. Now I see how pointless that is."

Andrew slumped. "What do you mean, pointless?"

"I don't mean that you can't do it, if that's what you think," Carolyn answered. "I just mean that you will have to do it on your own. I see that now. The more I think about it, the more I realize how much deciding you've let other people do for you. It's time for you to decide who Andrew Miracle is, once and for all. Nobody can do it but you. I love him, and I miss him. I'm hoping and praying that the Andrew I love will come back to love me, too. That's up to you, if you can find him again."

Andrew sat silently, processing as much as he could. Carolyn had found her center again, and he now knew that it was up to him to find his. He could no longer blame anyone else for his misery. After a moment, a sturdy knock sounded, harsh on the metal door to his dressing room. The door opened, and Graham stepped brightly in; he was stopped cold by the sight of Andrew in tears.

"Sorry, Andrew, but it's time. I hate to barge in, but it's time for places."

Andrew wiped his face and breathed heavily. "All right, Graham. I'll be there in a minute." Graham glanced at Carolyn, nodded and quietly closed the door behind him. Andrew could hear the increasing noise from without as the moment for the show to begin neared and people assumed their positions and shouted instructions to each other. He rose, wiped his tears again, and looked into the mirror. It was not a pretty reflection. As if in sudden defiance, he decided not to fix his hair or wash his face, but to walk out on stage exactly as he looked. If he had to go through the circus one more night, at least he would reserve this bit of honesty for himself. He smiled grimly as he thought how the first few rows would react to his appearance.

"I've got to go," he said, turning to Carolyn. She stood a few feet away, calm now, and he loved her through his torment. He would have to find a way to get back to himself on his own now, and if he didn't, he knew they would have nothing between them again. He was afraid but glad, because it seemed a risk worth taking to have something that real and unaffected.

"I'm going home, Andrew," Carolyn said. "I know its ridiculous, flying out here and turning around and going home, but I know it's what's right. I'm glad I came. I could have waited for you to come home, but somehow I knew that I had to do it now, right now. There wasn't a moment to lose. I needed to tell you, face to face, that I want the real you back. I love that person, and I need him. I needed to tell you that you are the only one that can find him. I don't want to get in the way of that."

"But maybe you could help me."

"I don't think so. Anyway, I don't want you to do it for me. I want you to do it for you."

Andrew rose, the pressure of time upon him. He wanted to reach out to her, but he couldn't. He was torn in half.

"Andrew Miracle is not dead," he said, half a prayer and half a declaration. With those words, he turned and walked out the door, onto the stage.

Andrew stood woodenly listening to his guitar player scream out a solo on his instrument. There had been surprised looks on the faces of his band members when he had appeared, hair disheveled, eyes swollen and red from crying, but they had performed like professionals and played with the usual intensity and enthusiasm. In many ways, it was a night like any other night. But inside, Andrew was going through a thousand questions in his mind, retracing his steps through a hundred tiny decisions that had seemed logical, even inevitable, at the time. Those decisions had brought him here, to the brink of losing himself.

Secrets, he thought to himself, blocking out the blaring guitar from his mind. He had been talking about secrets and truth during this whole wild ride. He had spoken enough platitudes about honesty to last a lifetime, enough to suffocate him. He looked out on the sea of faces swaying to the beat of his song, unsure who had betrayed whom. Both he and the audience had a stake in this fiction, he thought. But it was time to sing again, and once more he picked up the mike and sang, lifting up his hands, moving his body for emphasis, the crushing weight of expectation continuing to move his hands and legs like a nameless puppeteer.

The song ended, and it was time for him to talk. It was ironic, now; in the beginning, John had forced him to pare down his speaking time, saying, "People don't come to hear you talk. Besides, you're no preacher anyway. Just get up there and do the songs. That's what people paid their money for." Lately, however, Andrew had been limiting himself more stringently than even John had felt necessary, shortening his talk to the bare minimum. It was easier that way, just going through the motions and letting the poster-Andrew win without argument.

Tonight was, if anything, harder than usual. Carolyn's visit still resonated inside him. He felt he had reached his limit in living up to other people's expectations, but the expectations were still there, just as strong as ever.

Andrew took the mike and stood quietly a moment in the spotlights. His band was silent behind him, prepared to hear the same short speech about truth he always gave. In the stillness, several whistles came piercing out of the darkness, accompanied by sporadic clapping. It was hard to concentrate. Andrew moved a few inches to the left, and he felt the spotlights move precisely with him, three rails of light converging on him from hundreds of feet away. He walked to the front edge of the stage, feeling the lights move with him. He had the desire to see the faces of just a few of the thousands of people in the hall, to reach off the stage and touch them, talk to them, tell them about the farm and Mrs. Harvey and his father—and above all, to tell them what he had been feeling ever since his journey had begun. In the stillness, a female voice, clear but shrill rang out from high above and to the left: "I love you, Andrew!" There was some laughter and a few moments of scattered clapping, and then, from several directions, voices shouting, "I love you, I love you, Andrew Miracle!"

Andrew recoiled from the voices, and backed away from the edge of the stage. He had to go on. The crowd was getting restless.

"I'm here tonight because I love Jesus," he began, as he did every night, and the crowd erupted into applause. "I'm here to tell you all the secret of your life with God. The secret is: Have no secrets. Be honest in everything with Him. That's the secret." More applause, and several more *I love you!*'s rippled toward him from the corners of the auditorium. He looked behind him at the backdrop suspended there, his name spelled out in enormous letters fifteen feet high. Andrew Miracle, only more so. "That's the secret," he repeated mechanically, his back to the audience. He knew the next words by rote, but he couldn't bring himself to say them again. Turning, he peered out into the darkness, blinded by the spotlights. He saw Carolyn in his mind, standing before him, crying but determined. He saw himself, alone in his apartment with his press clippings, wanting to believe that he really was the poster-Andrew. He had had enough. He took a deep breath.

"The thing is," he began uncertainly, "I don't really know what I'm doing out here. I'm not sure I make sense to myself anymore." The crowd, sensing something amiss, began growing quiet, an uneasy stillness settling on it. "I had a vision . . ." Andrew's voice trailed off a moment. He stood, looking down, speaking slowly, more to himself than to the large audience before him. "I had a vision," he began again, "and I don't know what it means now." He gestured back to the huge letters. "I don't know who that person is, the one you all came to see. The fifteen-foot-high Andrew. I've tried as hard as I can to be that person. I just don't know who I am anymore, the real me. I came into this thing wanting to be real. That's what I wanted more than anything, because that's what I thought I was called to say. Be real. The trouble is, I don't know what real is, anymore." He paused a long moment. There was now a deadly quiet in the hall. "I just don't think this is it." Andrew and the audience faced each other in silence for nearly a full minute. Then, he shrugged, and stared up to the highest seats. "That's all I wanted to say. That's all I know right now. If I figure anything else out, I'll let you know."

Andrew turned and walked slowly back toward the band. A murmur began to rise up from the audience, but without a word, Andrew silently counted off the last song of the concert, the song everyone had been waiting for. "Lost Without You." The band played the introduction, but instead of the normal rush of applause from the audience at the start of the song, there was an uncomfortable silence. The powerful introduction faded away into the familiar chords of the keyboard, and Andrew took the microphone from the stand and stood alone on the stage. He closed his eyes and began to sing.

Lost without You
And I'm
Lost without You
When I call Your name
That's when I remember,
Yeah, I remember,
That I'm lost without You.

The song ended, and scattered, uncertain applause briefly sounded and then rapidly trailed away. Andrew turned and replaced the microphone in its stand, the hall now virtually silent. "Thank you," he said, his voice booming across the hushed, concrete expanse. His words echoed across the auditorium, repeating and then dying out into quiet once more. Andrew turned and walked off the stage. The lights came on, and immediately the din of thousands of people talking and clambering to their feet filled the air.

An hour after the concert ended, Andrew sat alone in his dressing room, calculating the cost of what he had just done. He had changed from his Napoleonic stage outfit into his street clothes, and had stuffed his personal effects into the shoulder bag that Michael Thomasson had given him. The bag was one of the perks of his association with the powerful executive. It was made of expensive black leather and said *Atlantic Records* on the side. Now, he sat alone, having given instructions to the security guard standing outside his door that he was not to be disturbed. He had thrown a large stone into the water with what he had done, and he knew that it would not be long before the ripples from that stone would catch up to him.

Maybe it wasn't too late. Maybe he could just pretend nothing had happened, and shake off his doubts one more time. Was it still possible to live up to everyone's expectations? His heart was sinking; he was deathly afraid of what he had started. Powerful men were counting on him, and they would not be pleased. He wondered what retribution he might face.

In spite of his fears, he had to acknowledge that there had been a release when he stopped the show and spoke the truth about himself. Even as his heart beat faster in apprehension of the consequences of what he had done, it dawned on him that for one night, he hadn't lied. That counted for something. How much, he needed to find out. The weight of expectation was still very heavy, and playing mind games with himself didn't make it less.

There was nothing more to be done there in the dressing room. He rose, searching for a jacket, but the only one in the room was an Andrew Miracle tour jacket. Reluctantly, he put it on, and grabbing the bag, he walked out into the hall.

As always after a show, the backstage area was full of noisy activity. The crew was in the process of tearing down and loading up the elaborate stage equipment that traveled with the tour. As Andrew entered the area, however, the animated talking quieted immediately. Andrew stood just off stage a moment, looking at the workmen. They continued their jobs, but without speaking or looking up at him. A palpable embarrassment hung in the air because of what he had done, accompanied by a lingering uneasiness over what he might do next. Andrew stood a moment watching them and then turned to walk back to the limousine.

On an impulse, he decided to walk to the hotel. After all, it was only about four blocks away, and the idea of the limousine was suddenly distasteful. He made his way to the edge of the stage and, swinging his legs down over the side, let himself down to the main floor. He picked his way through the seats, heading toward an exit sign. As he did so, he noticed a little girl standing quietly off to the side. It was evident that she was waiting, and had been for the whole hour after the concert on the chance that Andrew would appear. His first thought was to dart out a side door, avoiding the little girl. How could he possibly deal with another adoring fan tonight, especially one as naive as she must be?

Seeing Andrew, the girl started to attention and looked quickly to her right. Following her eyes, Andrew saw a woman sitting some distance away. The girl gave the woman an imploring look, and receiving a nod of approval, smiled brightly and began to walk timidly toward Andrew.

It was impossible to leave now without speaking to the girl, so Andrew stood waiting for her, his head full of thoughts about what had happened that night. The closer the girl came to him, the slower she moved. About fifteen feet away from him, she stopped altogether.

Andrew stood rooted to the spot, for some reason unable to respond. The two stared at each other for a moment, neither speaking or moving. What was behind the little girl's eyes Andrew couldn't guess. She was about twelve, with short brown hair curled behind her ears and big brown eyes peering unblinkingly into Andrew's. She wore a pretty little floral print dress that peeked out from under a red coat. She was carrying something in her hand, holding it quite carefully.

At last, Andrew smiled at her. His problems weren't hers, and she deserved his kindness after waiting so long. Seeing his smile, she walked lightly forward on little high heels until she stood directly in front of him. She appeared to be holding some kind of box made of paper, but she was hiding most of it behind a fold in her coat. At last, she pulled it out and timidly held it up towards Andrew.

Andrew started. The little girl was holding a perfect origami church made of folded papers. She had evidently collected several flyers of upcoming concerts, and knitting them carefully together with a series of folds, she had constructed a beautiful little New England church, complete with a steeple. It was white, the white of the backs of the concert flyers, and it looked as fragile and lovely in her hand as anything he had ever seen.

"That's beautiful," Andrew whispered. "Did you make that?"

"Yes," the little girl said, holding it up higher to him in an offering. "It's for your ministry."

Andrew carefully took the paper church from her, puzzled by her words. "What do you mean, sweetheart, for the ministry?" He held the church and suddenly realized that it was heavier than he had expected. He looked down, and saw that there was a little slot in the top, like a piggy bank. Looking down the narrow hole, he could see several coins in the bottom, lying on the floor of the paper church.

"It's for your ministry," the girl repeated. Andrew stood staring down the narrow slot, looking at the coins. There were a few pennies, a nickel, and one shiny quarter. After a moment he closed his eyes, holding the gift. Three thousand tickets had been sold that night, at twenty-two dollars per. Sixty-six thousand gross. He opened his eyes, and looked down at the little girl. "Thank you," he said softly. "Thank you so much." With those words the girl came suddenly to attention, like a doe surprised by a sudden sound. She swept her coat around her, and ran off to her mother. Andrew stared after her like a man who has taken a knife wound, but stoically refuses to show it. Turning, he made his way alone out of the hall and into the night air of Cleveland.

26

The phone was ringing. It was late, and van Grimes had been asleep at least an hour. He groped in the darkness for the light on his nightstand. Got it. He squinted in the sudden brightness, breathing heavily and still waking up. He picked up his watch. One-thirty. This had better be important.

"Mr. van Grimes, this is Graham." John forced himself to attention. Graham was a good man, and he wouldn't call if something wasn't wrong. He knew better than to waste his time.

"I'm here, Graham."

There was an awkward silence for a moment. Just as van Grimes was about to speak, however, Graham went on. "I thought I should call you, even though it's late. I think we have a little problem."

"All right, Graham. What is it?"

"It's Andrew."

Van Grimes sat up in bed, now fully awake. "Is he all right?" he asked. "Has there been an accident?"

"No, no, nothing like that. It's hard to describe."

"Let's hear it, Graham. Don't beat around the bush." Van Grimes heard Graham sigh through the phone.

"This isn't really my place, sir, and that's what makes it a little hard. I just try to do my job and keep things running smoothly. But I think Andrew had a . . . a little breakdown tonight."

Van Grimes's heart began beating like a machine. Not now. Everything was in place for the planned expansion of the agency. There was the Rosenberg show in Hollywood, then the meetings with the other artists back in Nashville. Andrew couldn't be falling apart. "What do you mean, a breakdown? What happened? Start at the beginning."

"Well, all I know is that Carolyn was out here, and—"

"Carolyn? What was she doing there?"

"I don't know, sir. I don't make that my business. I just know Andrew's been more and more moody lately, and tonight she just showed up before the concert. She had her pass, and she went on backstage. I didn't even see her until I opened Andrew's dressing room door to call for places and saw her in there. They were both really upset."

Van Grimes fumed. If Carolyn had done something to disrupt the delicate balance of Andrew's frame of mind she would be fired, looking back at Nashville from a thousand miles away. "So what happened?" he demanded. "Was she bothering him, or what?"

"I don't know, sir," Graham answered. "At first I was glad to see her, because I thought maybe she would cheer Andrew up. But I don't really know what happened in there. All I know is that she left, she didn't stay for the show at all. That struck me as odd, since she had to fly up here and everything. Why would she do that and not stay? Anyway, Andrew came out for the show and I thought everything would be okay. He was wood on stage, but lately he's been that way. I just kind of ignored it and hoped things would get better. But then, he kind of lost it."

Van Grimes was squirming on his bed, his face red with fear and anger. "What do you mean, he lost it?"

"He just—lost it. He got to the end of the show, where he talks for a minute, you know? Anyway, he just took the microphone and doesn't say anything for a long time. It was kind of creepy. Then he starts talking about how nothing makes sense to him anymore. He didn't know who he is, or why he's doing this concert, stuff like that. It was like a graveyard out there. So he goes on like that for a few minutes, and then he just blows off the audience and counts off the last tune. They do the song, he walks off stage, that's it. I've never seen anything like it."

Van Grimes sat stunned, trying to think. How serious was this? Was it a one off, or was Andrew really coming apart? Their phone call earlier that night had been a rough one, and Andrew had sounded depressed. He had laid into him pretty hard on the remix thing. There was a lot of press to do while they were in LA. Could Andrew last through the Rosenberg show, or had he completely lost it? Would he just get on a plane and go back to Rose Hill? One thing was for sure: John needed to get to Andrew himself, right now.

"All right, Graham, I appreciate the call. You did the right thing. I'll be there tomorrow. You'll be in Cleveland all day tomorrow, right?"

"That's right, Mr. van Grimes. We're staying in Cleveland and coming home Monday morning."

"Good. I'll be there by two tomorrow afternoon. Don't tell Andrew I'm coming. If he knows, he'll just work himself up with all the stuff he wants to tell me. Just let everything be normal. I'll handle it."

"I understand, Mr. van Grimes."

27

Carolyn spent the flight home thinking about the last few months with Andrew. She felt her sense of self returning, and every mile closer to home strengthened her resolve. She loved Andrew more than anything, but she knew it was the real Andrew she wanted, not the imaginary creation she had encountered lately. She had taken a great risk, but it felt good to her. The love that she and Andrew had was worth risking a lot to save.

She was quitting van Grimes, that was certain. She would resign Monday morning, effective immediately. She didn't know what kind of life she would find afterwards, but it didn't matter as long as it was real. If Andrew made the break as well, they would do it together. If he didn't, she had to accept that and go on. But no matter what, she would no longer play a part in his destruction: working at van Grimes's office had made her feel like she was a part of the problem, and that was intolerable.

Early the next morning, she rose and drove to van Grimes's office. The building was usually empty all day Sunday, but she didn't want to take any risks of running into him. It was better to get there early. It would take a good hour to collect her personal effects, and she had an idea that when van Grimes read her resignation, he would throw her out and her things after her. This was her chance to take a moment and say good-bye to the last few years of work properly, in her own time.

She let herself in with her key and disabled the alarm. The office was dark, but she didn't turn on a light. She didn't want to attract the attention of a well-intentioned policeman.

It wouldn't look good if she broke down and cried in a situation like that. There was sadness, certainly; this had been her only job since arriving in Nashville, and in a way, the office had seemed like home to her. She picked her way back toward her office, and closing the door after her, switched on the light. Quickly, she collected her things in a large box that had held promotional materials on Andrew. Handling each one for only a second, she arranged her little photographs and personal papers neatly in the box, stopping only once to regain her composure when it seemed certain that the tears would come. She held them back, however, and continued packing until she had finished.

Looking at the nearly empty room, she said good-bye to a great deal in that moment. Before she left, however, there was one important errand to be done: there were some personal notes she wanted to retrieve from Andrew's file in the work room.

She left the door to her office open to help her navigate, and switched on the light in the office work room. Several large filing cabinets were located on one side of the room, but in spite of the darkness she selected the correct one easily; she had made innumerable trips there during the last several months to add or take away papers in Andrew's personal file. Andrew's drawer was directly below van Grimes's private files, which were kept locked and for which she had no key. She opened Andrew's drawer and began leafing through the thick packet of papers, fingering them as she went through them. Concert reviews, record reviews, letters from fans selected for press releases. Some memos she had written Andrew in the early weeks of his journey. His first photos from Mickey's shoot. She knew she would never be a part of Andrew's career again, if he continued on his present course. She had worked hard for him, and she extended herself the grace of feeling her loss.

Carolyn went through the papers methodically, looking for the four or five things most personally associated with her that she could either photocopy or take outright if they were no longer needed. She had no sense of guilt; she had worked as hard as anyone on Andrew's career, and she wasn't willing to walk away from so much without anything to remember it by. Reaching far back into the cabinet, her hand struck a little box. She had been in the file innumerable times and had never felt it before. Curious, she stood on tiptoe and retrieved it. As she did so, the file drawer above the one in which she was working moved slightly, and she understood: the box had originally been placed at the rear of the file above, and over time it had fallen down bit by bit when the upper drawer was pulled out. At last, it had worked its way clear of the upper drawer entirely and fallen down into the space between.

Carolyn pulled the box out and held it in her hand. It had a combination on it, and was shut fast. Having it created something of a dilemma, because she had no legitimate access to John's private files. Nevertheless, the box had aroused her curiosity. She pressed the lock mechanism sideways and was surprised that it popped open; the combination had been left at its correct setting. Evidently John hadn't bothered with resetting it each time, content to trust the locked filing cabinet alone.

Carolyn lifted the lid of the box, surprised to find inside several papers with Andrew's name on them. In spite of her ambivalence, she pulled up a chair and began to flip through them. Some were of little account, but her eye was drawn to a check deposit: it was from Dove Records to John personally, in the amount of forty thousand dollars. The large amount of the payment gave Carolyn a shock, but she noted especially the date: September third. That would have been just about the time Andrew arrived in Nashville. How could he have already been generating such substantial income? Attached to the receipt was a handwritten note:

John:

Thanks for all your help in solidifying the Andrew Miracle deal. We know this forty grand is money well spent. Will hear from you soon.

Laurence

Carolyn stared at the note, uncomprehending. This was certainly money outside Andrew's deal, because she made those bank deposits herself into the company account. She had no record of this transaction, however. The note struck her as somehow dubious—the wording of Laurence's message seemed to carry a hidden meaning. She thought for a moment and impulsively took the note to the copy machine. She ran a copy, and went back to the box. Inside were several other papers that had little meaning for her and one other item of greater interest: a copy of Andrew's management contract.

Her curiosity further aroused, she glanced through the document. It was surprisingly long, but it took only a few minutes for her to digest its meaning. Andrew had signed away virtually every potential income source he could ever have for the next several years to van Grimes. John had a percentage of anything Andrew did over which money changed hands. When her eyes landed on exactly what that percentage was, however, she stared. Van Grimes had contracted a flat fifty percent of Andrew's gross income. On top of that, he had liberal freedom to deduct the expenses of managing Andrew's career out of Andrew's share, protecting his own. This was news: she had made only the gross deposits before the money was split with the agency's artists; John insisted on handling the money from that point on. This had struck her as curious, but now she saw why. A fifty percent split was over three times the standard management percentage, and in Andrew's case, the difference resulting in hundreds of thousands of dollars of extra income for van Grimes.

Carolyn sat with the papers in her hands. Andrew had been absolutely at van Grimes's mercy in the negotiation, and John had known it. He had gone for the jugular, and struck gold. For all Andrew knew, the terms of his agreement were fair, even generous. It was obvious he had no idea how unfair the contract actually was. She shuddered, rose again, walked straight over to the copy machine, and copied the contract page by page. She knew that she was entering a dubious area legally, but she was resolved to go forward. If worse came to worst, she could claim access to the papers on Andrew's behalf, certain that he would back her up. The main thing was to get in touch with Andrew and then to take the contract to a good lawyer and see if anything could be done about it. She had in her possession two documents, the ultimate meaning of which she could only guess. She was resolved to find out, however, and no matter what, Andrew was entitled to know what he had gotten into.

Quickly she packed up the papers and rearranged Andrew's file. She tried for a few minutes to reach up and replace the box in the drawer above, but it was futile. In the end, she just put it at the back of Andrew's drawer and closed it. Van Grimes would find out sooner or later, and she doubted she could be in worse trouble with him than she already was. She looked at her watch. Nine-fifty. Maybe she could get home and get Andrew on the phone. Now, above all, he had the right to know everything. At any rate, she knew she was through with van Grimes forever.

28

Andrew slept fitfully that night after his concert. He had instructed the front desk to hold all calls to his room, with no exceptions. Very late he fell at last into a deep sleep, but he awakened early, the face of the little girl with the paper church floating before his eyes. He was feeling restless, needing to occupy himself with something else. When his eyes opened to yet another duplication of a faceless hotel room, however, his spirits sank. He briefly considered calling Carolyn but decided against it. She had made herself clear, and he respected her for it. There was no point in repeating it all over again. He had his own decision to make. It wouldn't help to hear the reproach or even worse, the sympathy, in her voice. So he rose, showered, dressed in the still room, and slipped out the door without calling Graham to let him know he was going out.

He had no destination, but felt an uneasy desire to get out on his own. That was what was so difficult to manage anymore. It used to be so good to hop in his father's old pickup and just drive, windows down and the radio blaring. The fields would pass by, and the familiar landmarks of nearby farms would stream across his windows like an old, favorite movie. The loss of that freedom he had never anticipated—nor how much he would miss it. The fast-paced schedule and endless list of unfamiliar cities conspired against that kind of liberty, however. He never drove anywhere now. He was merely moved from one location to another, and then the spotlight was turned on.

His first idea had been to get some breakfast in the coffee shop, but even that seemed distasteful; he couldn't face one more insipid, cautious, restaurant-cooked meal. Besides, he had no desire to run into anyone from the band or crew—he was in no mood to explain things that he didn't understand himself. He allowed himself to wonder for a moment what his mother would have made for breakfast that morning, but he quickly let his thoughts move on. He wasn't sure he could afford luxurious, nostalgic trips in his mind back to Rose Hill any longer. That kind of thinking had become too painful.

Suddenly a plan dawned on him. It was Sunday. He had, he realized, nothing whatever to do. With the flight to LA not scheduled until Monday morning, there was no reason he couldn't slip out on his own and get away from the madness for a while. That was what he needed. With a sudden sense of purpose, he walked briskly toward the concierge's stand, which, to his consternation, was unoccupied. Frustrated, he strode to the front desk and engaged the clerk, proclaiming,

"I need a car."

A young lady was working there, and she smiled broadly at the sight of him. It was the smile of flattery, of people who felt like hearing his record on the radio made them special friends. He hated the sight of it.

"You're Andrew Miracle," she said brightly. "I love your song."

"Thank you," he answered tersely. "I need to rent a car." He wished he could have been more gentle, but he found he no longer had much patience. He knew it was unfair but he had been so surrounded with sycophants he didn't seem able to be kind anymore.

"I see," the girl answered with a hurt formality. "When would you need the car?"

"As soon as possible."

"Well, since it's Sunday, that's a little difficult. But if you'll wait just a moment, I'll see what I can do for you."

"Thank you," he said, forcing the edge off his voice. "I

appreciate that." Andrew took a seat and glanced impatiently through the Sunday newspaper for about ten minutes while the desk agent called rental companies in between answering the phone. After some time, he heard his name being called.

"Mr. Miracle, I think I have something worked out for you." Andrew rose, and walked quickly back over to the front desk.

"There is an airport rental agency that can have a car delivered here in thirty minutes."

"Marvelous," said Andrew. "I'll wait in the lobby."

About forty minutes later a nondescript four-door sedan pulled into the hotel driveway. He had no trouble identifying it as the rental car. It was plain, had blackwall tires, and was spotlessly clean. He filled out the paperwork and with barely a word sped out of the hotel parking lot into the light flow of traffic. He had no destination and that suited him perfectly.

Andrew drove down a large four-lane thoroughfare for some time, enjoying himself, he felt, for the first time in weeks. There had been a surprising cold snap and he rolled down the window and put his arm on the sill enjoying the bracing wind. He spied a freeway entrance to his right, and on an impulse suddenly pulled over hard, speeding up the on-ramp onto the busy highway. He noted with satisfaction that it headed straight out of town—in fact, he was already approaching the outskirts of the city.

In fifteen minutes the signs of urban life had begun to wane, and he began to see the first fields and homesteads of country life. By the time he had driven twenty miles there was nothing left to tell him that Cleveland sprawled behind him. He was back in his element now, and he drank in the long, plowed fields passing by on his right and left. The planting was largely finished, but this far north there wasn't much to show for it; the plants looked small and nondescript from the highway. He used to love to walk through young plants at home, carefully making his way through the green shoots as he tromped along. That was a solitude, surely, but a good solitude, a solitude of belonging somewhere and having a past connected to the present. It felt nothing like the isolation he experienced in the endless days of touring. He drove on, willing himself to forget about grosses and concerts and record charts.

He drove on for an hour or more, and when he began to see the roadside signs of an approaching city he turned off, taking a small, two-lane blacktop east into the countryside. The road was a comfort to him. It looked a lot like home, with its wide fields passing one after another, black dirt plowed up, clumped and fertile, like bulging banks of life. Andrew knew that sun, tilling, and rain would turn every one of them into squares of moving, living color.

He drove on for another half hour or so, occasionally passing through a small town, smiling at the mom-and-pop stores, all dutifully closed for business on Sunday. Nothing was open in these country towns, and that was the way it should be. It was already after ten, and the parking lots of churches were full of pickups and Chevys. He began, in spite of himself, to think about church back home. Cy Mathews would be locked in his study now, putting the finishing touches on another barn-burner. Services there began at ten thirty, and the crowd would already be filing in for the comfortable chitchat that always preceded a Sunday service. It was a powerful memory, and he allowed himself to feel the pang of nostalgia that came with it instead of forcing it down as he had learned to do so habitually. It hurt him that things hadn't gone well there since he left. Why hadn't God filled the gap? Andrew had always assumed that when he left, God would raise someone else up to take his place. But the church had dwindled, slowly but inexorably heading down to a half-full house of diehards that would probably attend every Sunday even if Jesus came back and they were left behind.

The blacktop was wonderfully smooth, and his car rode peacefully, almost serenely, gliding on endlessly toward the rural skyline. He let his eyes fall on the farthest points, scanning the horizon for the pleasure of the unobstructed view. He spied a simple white steeple in the haze, a good two miles away across the flat fields surrounding him. It was indistinct for some time, but even at that distance he could make it out against the blue of the sky, a white finger pointing upward out of the dark earth. As he approached, it gradually grew clear, and eventually he could see the detail of it, an unadorned wooden spike raised to the King of kings. It was in need of paint, not badly, but enough to notice. There was no bell. It stood atop a small, white church that was just beginning its Sunday services. Without thinking, he pulled into the gravel parking lot, listening to the sound of his tires as they ran over the pebbles and stones.

The church had, improbably, several simple but lovely stained glass windows, six in a row along the side of the building. The building itself was frame, its sides rising in whitewashed wooden planks up to a high twenty-foot roof where they slanted together in classic form. At the front the steeple rose, standing atop a square, ventilated box. There was not a soul to be seen outside. He looked out his open windows up and down the street, but no cars were passing, and no one was walking on the clean sidewalks of the little town. Either everyone was in the little church, or those that didn't attend stayed well out of sight until the service ended.

Andrew sat in the car, listening to the quiet breeze that flowed through the trees just beyond the parking lot. The weather was growing colder, but he wasn't ready to move on. Instinctively, he got out of the car to move around. His feet crunched on the cold gravel as he walked. He moved towards the church, drawn to it. As he approached, he listened but could hear nothing inside.

At last, he resolved to enter the building. He hoped he wouldn't be recognized here, so far out of the mainstream.

Surely this little church had yet to be reached by the message of Andrew Miracle. He opened the front door slightly, which led directly into the sanctuary itself. He winced, but the congregation was rising to its feet, preparing to sing a hymn. A few heads turned as he entered, but in the natural commotion he was able to slip gratefully into a back row with minimum disturbance. Thankfully, no one gave him a second glance, and he stood and sang with everyone else a few verses of the hymn, and took his seat anonymously afterward. Then, he saw her.

She was sitting quietly while the organ played, her auburn hair framing her face too thickly, like a reddish-brown winter collar. She was no longer a young woman. Her eyes were deep set and indistinguishable, dark drops in a pale, freckled face. There was weather there, forty or more summers and winters leaving their marks on her skin like the tiny lines in a dried, fallen leaf.

Andrew watched her during the offering as she smoothed her dress uncomfortably, sitting up front on the dais with the pastor, turning inward under the light of so many eyes. He watched as well during the prayer that followed, his lone face upturned to see. She seemed to sit in order to take up the smallest possible space, as if she had no right to be seated in any place of honor. At one point, she began bending her wrist gently backward and forward, her fingers extended in a nervous but oddly graceful motion.

The morning prayer ended, and without introduction she rose soundlessly and walked deliberately to the center of the dais, hiding herself behind the pastor's podium. A simple, pale blue cotton dress flowed down over her, concealing her shape. She did not quite stand erect at the podium, although she was clearly capable of it. Instead, she leaned far forward over the podium, placing her elbows onto the large oak stand, her hands firmly clasped before her. Her eyes were almost hidden beneath the bangs of auburn hair, and she peered out from under them at the congregation. Her face was hidden under shadows of hair. Nevertheless, Andrew felt somehow that she was aware of him and that she was looking at him.

There was no spotlight. There was no fanfare of any kind. There was just a woman, having already left behind her youth, leaning against a simple oak pulpit in a small country church. There was no accompanist. The quiet of that moment seemed to deepen as she stood, and she looked for a moment as if she were listening. Then she opened her mouth, and her voice poured gently and simply out into the wooden hall. Hers was not a voice of training and lessons, but it had the kind of pure, untroubled beauty that sings a baby to sleep, or comforts a wounded soldier. Every trial she had suffered and every victory she had won was there, clear and audible. She sang slowly, leaning forward, looking from under that hair into the small crowd, singing high and plaintive, each word like a sermon. Her voice was old wood and new honey, and though there was sorrow in it, it was the very sound of peace. Her mouth opened, and these words poured out like a graceful waterfall:

Fairest Lord Jesus, Ruler of all nature,
O Thou of God and man the Son;

Andrew was already crying,

Thee will I cherish, Thee will I honor,
Thou, my soul's glory and crown;

and he suddenly heard others around him, affected as he was,

Fair are the flowers, Robed in the blooming garb of spring;

and then right through the wall around his heart, she sang:

Jesus is fairer, Jesus is purer;

now raising her voice, singing more strongly, and incredibly, even more slowly,

Jesus shines brighter;

and he stopped hearing with his ears, and the verses flowed together into one,

Glory and honor, praise, adoration,
Now and forevermore be Thine!

and Andrew was weeping, the wall fracturing a bit more with every word that this nameless servant of God wept onto the throne of the Almighty.

He covered his eyes in the silence as she finished. The singer stood at the podium, listening or perhaps waiting, but after a moment she turned and made her way off the dais onto the main floor. Andrew looked up, staring at her as she passed by, but to his surprise she did not take her seat as the pastor rose to begin the sermon. Silently, she moved on past the rows and out a side door, vanishing out into a dim hallway beyond, disappearing at last into the dark.

Andrew didn't hear the sermon that followed. The voice of the singer was still resonating inside him, and there was no room for more words. There hadn't been a single spotlight. There was no band. There was no stage, just a simple pulpit. No one had paid a cent to get in, and no one had been paid to perform. There was no expensive speaker system to enhance the sound. There was just Jesus; He had called them together that day, and the singer had said yes to that call and offered up a pleasing sacrifice unto the Lord. It was right. It was altogether good. It was a long way from his own life. In that moment, he knew what he had to do. It would be hard at best, and possibly no one, including Carolyn, would understand. But he had to do it. He couldn't face any more little girls with humble offerings, little children with no concept of the size and scope of his career. He couldn't face any more losing battles with John or Harold. Above all, he couldn't face anymore spotlights. There were real people who needed him, and they were waiting.

29

V an Grimes checked into Andrew's hotel grateful he wasn't getting his blood pressure checked that day. His hand was shaking as he signed in, and he had to willfully steady his nerves to keep his voice calm as he asked the desk clerk if she knew whether Andrew was in his room. All the same, he was glad he had decided to come immediately; the clerk explained that Andrew had left that morning with a rental car, and had not made clear when he would return. Van Grimes felt a shot of fear run down his back. His imagination began to run wild with ideas of what Andrew might be doing at that moment, including simply driving that rental car all the way back to Kansas.

Van Grimes took the elevator up to his floor and made his way to his room with his thoughts racing. He had asked for the room next to Andrew's. He wanted to be able to hear the door open in case Andrew returned and didn't let anyone know. Once inside his room there was little he could do. He talked briefly to Graham on the phone, but there was nothing more he could add: part of the problem, after all, was that Andrew had been growing more and more distant, and he had never been in the habit of letting Graham into his thoughts anyway. All Graham could do was relate once more the events he had seen, and at last van Grimes had to satisfy himself with sitting and waiting for Andrew to return.

Those hours were long ones for John. He had so much to lose. He played back the last few months in his mind over and over, trying to see where Andrew had begun to reach the crisis point. Andrew had certainly expressed his con-

cerns, but it had always seemed possible to handle him. Out
on the road, however, his artist was left more often with his
own thoughts. And, of course, there was the matter of Carolyn: it was no secret that their relationship was deteriorat-
ing, but if in fact she proved to be the cause of Andrew's
breakdown, van Grimes would have to think long and hard
of the best way to punish her.

Andrew had brought in nearly half a million dollars for
van Grimes in the last year, but the money wasn't the only
thing he had to lose. For the first time, he had felt like a
player, a voice to be reckoned with in the industry. He had
his pick of new talent now, and he saw his management
company exploding in the coming year. There was Michael
Thomasson, too—there had been an almost esoteric pleasure in dealing face to face with him again, in being the
person who Thomasson had to go through to get to Atlantic's newest superstar. He pictured himself explaining to
Thomasson and the others that he couldn't control his artist
and that everything had gone up in smoke. He grimaced
and his head twitched fitfully, as if casting the image away.

Van Grimes thought back to Heaven's Voices. Drudge-
work. He couldn't go back to that, not now, not after running
with the big dogs. How could he step and fetch with idiotic
ministers obsessed with not having drum sets in their sanc-
tuaries? How could he regress into selling kids on going out
on the road for no money? It was unthinkable.

Everything depended on getting to Andrew before he did
anything foolish and permanent. Damage containment was
the top priority.

The hours dragged by. Van Grimes was afraid to turn the
TV on for fear he wouldn't hear Andrew return, and at last
he resorted to propping his door open with a Kleenex box
to ensure he wouldn't miss him. The hallway was busy, and
van Grimes found himself, heart in his mouth, glancing up
every minute or so as a shadow passed quickly by his door.

Around six-thirty that evening he realized he was hungry.

He made his way down to the lobby, fighting down an irrational fear that Andrew would come up one elevator at the moment he was going down in the other; his anxiety was rising, rather than diminishing, as the time clicked on and Andrew still failed to appear.

Van Grimes asked for a table with a view of the lobby. The side doors to the hotel were beyond his vision, but there was no helping that, and he couldn't bear to be alone in his room anymore. If Andrew returned and took the drastic step of checking out of the hotel on his own, he would have to go to the front desk to do it, so van Grimes felt he could risk a meal in the little coffee shop adjacent to the lobby.

There was a lot of time to think as he ate, and he found himself oddly drawn back in time, not to Andrew's arrival in Nashville but back to Rose Hill itself, to the first time he heard the kid play and to the disconcerting breakfast the next morning at the farm. He remembered Andrew's unaffected face at the church as he strove with the demons in his music, and he felt once again the pull of the Spirit in the face of so much honest searching. He saw Alison speaking with dignity and emotion about her dead husband, of the simplicity and sincerity of his life and work. That had knocked him off center, he admitted. But it hadn't been that hard to drown out the humble, emotional words of Andrew's mother in the face of the momentum of his own life. One foot had followed another because, he realized, the cost of stopping even to think was too high to bear. He had cast his lot long ago, and lacked the courage to wipe out so many hard years of effort in a discovery that his premise was somehow flawed. It was impossible. Even now, as Alison's words flashed through his mind, he shut them out; and it was easy, in the face of so much fear, to do so.

Andrew sat quietly eating a sandwich in a roadside café somewhere south of Cleveland. He looked at his watch.

Seven-thirty. He would need to head back soon, if indeed he was going back. For a part of him, nothing appealed so much in that moment as to go straight back to Rose Hill and let van Grimes and the rest sort it out. But even as he toyed with the idea, he knew in his heart he wouldn't do that. There was too much of his father in him, and he had to find a way to resolve his problems once and for all.

Problems. Andrew smiled grimly to himself as he sat in the run-down diner. There were a lot of people who would trade problems with him, he knew. Money rolling in, although he still had no idea how much. Fame. Videos. Tours. But all the money and fame in the world still boiled down to this: he had been called to minister honestly, and, he was realizing at last, to minister intimately. The fragility of that kind of communication didn't, in his case at least, seem able to weather the power of the poster-Andrew. He had seen real ministry in others, artists who had managed to forge a hard-won balance between art, finance, and the gospel. But for him, it didn't—it couldn't—work. There was a message in the very existence of the poster-Andrew that overwhelmed any words that the real one might say. The fifteen-foot letters and perfect photographs had a volume that tender piano playing and straight talk couldn't drown out.

Seeing the woman in the church had made up his mind, but there still remained the issue of what exactly to do, of how best to move forward. He was no closer to answering that question, but he had decided one thing: he would no longer lie, and he would no longer allow the poster-Andrew to lie on his behalf. He downed the last of his Coke and rose to pay the check. There were times when the only answer was to march forward and find the answers when they were found. He would do what he could, but he would lie no more.

The rental car was dusty and dirty now as he swung open the door and took the wheel. He had chosen back roads, even following some dirt roads, content to wander until he hit another highway. It was dark now, and he switched on the headlights as he sat in the car, engine idling. The windshield was covered with bugs and dust, and the car looked well and truly used in the neon light from the blinking restaurant sign.

The waitress gave him directions back to the main highway, and Andrew had no trouble making his way back to Cleveland. All the same, he was a good two hours out, and it would be nearly ten by the time he arrived. He revved the engine as he rolled up onto the freeway entrance ramp and drove at a rapid clip back toward the city.

An hour and a half later the urban sprawl began to appear, and he found his mood deflated somewhat. He couldn't pretend he was just driving aimlessly anymore. He was definitely on his way back: back to his life, and to the host of confrontations that waited there for him like small, ticking bombs.

Andrew pulled into the hotel around nine forty-five, and parked the car far away from the entrance. He stood beside the car a moment, looking at the hotel from forty yards away, musing on what the next few days would bring. He had press to do in Los Angeles starting tomorrow, but it could be canceled if necessary without too much effort. "The Barry Rosenberg Show" was something else. That would be the first moment of truth, possibly the first of many. He had a feeling that he had to follow through with the show; that somehow, it might be a redemption for him. He confirmed his resolve once again and crossed the parking lot slowly, looking up at the stars fighting to be seen through the perpetual city glare.

Van Grimes was tired. His nerves were shot, and he was beginning to fear the worst. Andrew had been gone all day, and he had called no one to reveal his whereabouts. The hours of waiting in the silence of the hotel room had numbed

John somewhat, and he felt sleep creeping over him as the clock passed nine.

Sometime later, he started to wakefulness. He had heard a door, that much was certain. He opened his eyes in the dark, listening. He was right: a lock was turning, then the door opened; a pause, and the door closed solidly. It was Andrew. Heart racing, John reached for the light and pulled on his shoes. This confrontation, he realized, had been a long time coming, almost from the moment they had met. Now, at last, it had arrived.

Van Grimes waited a few moments, trying to gather his thoughts. After several minutes, he let himself quietly out of his room and stood before Andrew's door thinking. He had tried out in his mind many approaches, and none seemed surefire. Impulsively, he reached out and rapped abruptly on the door. A few seconds passed, and the door opened.

"Hello, Andrew," van Grimes said, his voice eerily calm. "I thought it best if I came on out now, instead of meeting you in California. Can I come in?"

Andrew stared at van Grimes a while, and then shrugged his shoulders for John to enter. He shouldn't have been surprised, he realized. John was bound to have heard about what happened, and having heard, he was certain to respond. They might as well get it over with.

Andrew started toward the bed to sit, but suddenly thought better of it and took the lone straight-backed chair. He had learned something of the tactics of personal warfare from van Grimes, and he smiled to himself as van Grimes was forced to perch uncomfortably on the edge of the bed. It wasn't a position of power.

"So you've come," Andrew said. "I'm glad. It's past time we talked."

"Yes, Drew. You've behaved foolishly, but I think we can work things out. I hope we can."

Andrew smiled. He felt strangely liberated. He had a

sense of destiny now, a feeling that he had to worry about one thing only and then let the drama play out around him as it would. He would lie no more, and he would let no one lie for him. After that, his life would be what it would. In that realization, van Grimes seemed suddenly powerless to influence him. Perhaps, he thought, he had at last found the bottom line that his father had depended on so much.

Van Grimes noted Andrew's smile disconcertedly. The two of them had experienced their differences, but each time John had always been able to convince Andrew to see things his way. He merely explained the facts of life to him until Andrew gave in. But Andrew had never, ever smiled during one of their arguments. Something was different. He would have to proceed cautiously. He decided to begin with a fatherly, intimate tone.

"You've created a bit of a mess, Drew," van Grimes began. "I'm afraid I'm going to have to clean up that mess. Before we go any further, I want to be sure that there won't be any more messes. Whatever got into you last night needs to stop right there."

Andrew listened, unmoved. "What kind of mess would you say I made, John?" he asked.

"You didn't have the right to do what you did last night, Andrew. Those people paid good money to see you. You let them down."

"They paid to see a show, did they?" Andrew asked.

"That's right, Drew. They paid to see a show."

Andrew paused for a moment, taking in once again John's standard argument. After a few seconds, he answered, "I don't think so."

"I beg your pardon?" John retorted, his voice rising slightly. "What do you mean? It's obvious they expected a show."

"I'll tell you what I think, John," Andrew said, his voice surprisingly calm. "I think they were brought in there on the premise of ministry and worship, and the show was to sell me."

"What's the difference?" John asked. "People have the right to expect a show when they pay good money. What's wrong with that?"

"What's wrong with it, John, is this." Andrew reached behind his chair and picked up the little paper church he had received from the girl the night before.

John stared at the slightly crumpled structure as if he were seeing something from another planet. "What's that?" he demanded. "You're telling me that a paper building is what's wrong with what you've been doing?"

Andrew held the church gently in his hands, thinking back to the expression on the face of the little girl who had given it to him. "A young girl gave this to me last night after the concert, John. She was maybe ten, twelve years old."

"So?"

"She said it was for my ministry. Yeah, I know. I didn't understand it either, at first. Then, I saw that she had put some coins in it, just a few, maybe thirty-five cents altogether. It was like the widow's mite, though. I could tell the money meant a lot to her."

Van Grimes shifted uncomfortably on the bed. The conversation was not going like he had hoped, not at all. How could he fight on these terms? What did this little girl's gift have to do with things falling apart at the seams? "Look, Andrew," he said, "it's a touching gift, but we've got to sort through some things here."

"I know that, John," Andrew interrupted. "I see that very clearly, maybe the clearest since I first got to Nashville. I did the math, John, and we did over sixty thousand dollars gross last night."

"So?" John said again.

"So she doesn't get it, John. She doesn't understand that

this is a money-making machine. She thinks that this is about spreading the gospel and ministry."

"Look, Andrew, it's complicated. It's really about both. It's a gray area. You can't expect a ten-year-old kid to understand that."

Andrew closed his eyes and saw himself back in Rose Hill, playing for his church. There had been nothing to explain there. Suddenly, he opened his eyes. "You know what, John?" he said. "I've figured something out. I found my bottom line." In the midst of all the conflict, he felt like laughing. "Here's the thing, John. If I can't explain it to that little girl, I don't want to do it." He smiled, and a weight seemed to fall from him. "You're wrong, John. You're just wrong. She's the one who *does* have to understand. Didn't Jesus say to suffer the little children to come unto him? It's so obvious! Where did she get the idea that it was about ministry, John? She got it from us, from you and me, and Dove, and everybody else! 'The soul of an artist who is a burning flame,' John, that's what we said about me. 'The voice of a man who is sold out to God.' What a load of crap!"

John was taken aback. Dove's marketing campaign had been pure genius, and was an unmitigated success. "You're losing your mind, Andrew. The only thing I see here is an ungrateful kid from nowhere who God is showering blessings on in a way I've never seen before. You can't handle success, Andrew! Everything we've done has worked out perfectly. What do you expect me to do, shut down everything we worked so hard to accomplish just because some kid gives you a little church?"

Andrew smiled. "No, John, that's the best part of it all. I don't expect you to do a thing. Believe it or not, this has nothing to do with you. You will have to find your own path. I made that mistake, you see. I depended on too many others to make my path for me, and I'm sorry for it now. I can't tell you a thing about your next move, or mine, for that matter. I only know I'm through lying. I'm going to live my conscience."

"I see," van Grimes said, his voice sarcastic. "So living your conscience means you walk off shows and let people down. Very nice."

"No, John, I don't think you get it yet. Living my conscience means not lying to people in the first place. I was called by God to minister the gospel with my music. I had a message: be honest and God will find you there. That's what my gift was all about. It comes down to this: I can't claim to be a minister of the gospel and manipulate people into worshiping me at the same time. I don't want to bring people the gospel under false pretenses. I am not the person that they've been led to think I am. They've been told a hundred subtle, unmistakable lies about me, and all for one single purpose: to get a few of their dollars out of their pockets and into ours. I can't do it anymore."

"Are you actually saying that the whole Christian music industry is wrong? How can you be so arrogant and judgmental? It's unbelievable! You haven't been in Nashville a year, and yet you stand in judgment on everyone!"

"That's not what I'm saying, John. This has nothing to do with the whole Christian music industry. It has to do with me. I have to do what's right for me. The main thing in my whole Christian life is to get more and more real with God, every day. I can't do it in this life, John. I can't get real with God with my name before my eyes in fifteen-foot letters. I can't get real with God when people I don't know are shouting that they love me to the stage. Who do they love, John? They don't know the first thing about me! They love what they've been sold, and I'm through selling."

Van Grimes moved to the chair trying to process the last several minutes. He had come in ready to work his will on Andrew one more time, but the situation had rapidly gotten out of control; indeed, he had never been in control from the moment they began talking. His head was filling with unbidden thoughts, making it difficult to concentrate. Nevertheless, he knew that he had one trump card, one power play that was impossible to answer. Playing that card had significant consequences: once laid down, the fiction of mutual trust would never be believed in again. If he used that power and forced Andrew's hand to that extent, Andrew would never be more than a slave to him, and a lot of both of their dreams would die. Van Grimes sat struggling within himself for a while, searching for an alternative. He didn't want to do it. But even as he told himself he didn't want to, he knew that he would do it. Unless he was willing to walk away from the biggest gold mine he was ever likely to find, he had no choice.

"You and I have signed contracts, Andrew," he began slowly, his voice as brittle as ice. "You are under some legal constraints to perform your side of the bargain."

Andrew sighed. He had known, somehow, it would come to this. He had to accept it. He would follow his bottom line where it led him, and accept the consequences without complaining. No one had forced him to sign those contracts. "All right, John. Which means?" he asked.

"Which means I have legal recourse if you choose to undermine our work together. You will be in breach of our contract, not to mention Dove's."

"What do you mean exactly, legal recourse?"

"In short, I will sue you. I have done a great deal of work for you, Andrew, and I'm quite confident that any court in the land will see this my way. Before I found you, I remind you that you were a nobody playing in a tiny church in nowhere town. You were nothing, small change. It is through my hard work that you got everything you have. If you purposefully undermine that, I will have no choice but to hold you fully accountable for the loss. It would be substantial. If you force me, you'll end up in a court of law explaining all about your convictions to a judge."

Andrew rose from his chair. He had no desire to break

any contracts, but he had, he realized, no real idea what his contract meant in the first place. There was, as well, some truth in what van Grimes was saying; John had worked hard, and this was a blow to him. It all depended on what side of the argument one looked at. Andrew knew that he couldn't remain a part of what had been happening, but John had a legitimate interest in the decision as well. All the same, Andrew didn't feel trapped in the old way; his mind was made up, and he would have to work things out however he could. He could never go back.

"All right, John. You do what you have to do. I won't fight you. If we can't work out some accommodation, I'll live with the consequences. I don't want you to be hurt by this."

Even as Andrew was finishing his sentence, the phone rang. Andrew turned quickly on his heel, feeling irritated. He had given explicit instructions not to be disturbed. He looked at his watch. It was nearly ten-thirty.

"Hello?" he said, his tone abrupt. "I had asked for my calls to be held."

"I'm sorry, Mr. Miracle," a voice answered apologetically. "I have a note here to that effect, but the young lady was very insistent. She's been calling all day. I didn't put her through, but I thought I should let you know she was calling. She's on hold."

"Who is it?"

"Carolyn Hemphill."

30

In view of his highly successful practice, Greg Breyton's legal offices were quite understated. There was a sparse functionality to the appointments that surprised his clients—having represented many of the biggest names in the entertainment business, he could certainly have afforded the kind of lavish surroundings favored by younger, far less eminent attorneys in trendy Brentwood. Breyton, by contrast, preferred to stay in small, unassuming rooms on Music Row, and found the exterior display of wealth a distraction from the business at hand: winning cases for clients.

Breyton returned to his conference room leading a solemn-looking John van Grimes. The attorney's figure was essentially that of a walking brick; he was a square, solid man with sturdy legs and a stoic, unflinching face that revealed nothing about the interior of the man. His suit, indifferently tailored, was nevertheless so perfectly pressed that it actually creaked when he walked.

As Breyton entered with van Grimes in tow, Andrew and Carolyn rose automatically. Breyton gestured curtly for them to sit down; he had business to do, and he didn't want his clients to express the slightest conciliation.

A lot had happened in the last few days. John and Andrew hadn't seen each other since that night in Cleveland; Carolyn's phone call had seen to that. Andrew had listened to her attentively, keeping his face calm and unreadable as she told him the suspicions she had about the deal with Dove and the usurious terms of his contract. He had said very little in the five-minute conversation, doing nothing to reveal to van Grimes the content of the call or who it was from.

He had revealed nothing to either party, and as the call went on John had stared at him with impatience growing toward anger. Andrew had only offered a short series of "yes," and "uh-huh" until Carolyn had finished; then he closed the conversation with a calm, "I appreciate your calling. It means a great deal to me." With those words, he had hung up the phone and looked van Grimes straight in the eye. "Our conversation is at an end, John. I will speak to you again in Nashville." His voice had carried such finality and force that van Grimes had been momentarily stunned; nevertheless, he naturally raised several minutes of sputtering protest. Andrew, however, was immovable. He had flatly refused to continue any discussion of any kind, and in the end van Grimes had no choice but to retreat to his own room, his plan in shambles.

As John took his seat, Andrew looked him over with a mixture of sympathy and concern. He didn't look good. He had a haunted look that was a surprise, all the more shocking in the man that Andrew had once found so elegant. Now they sat face to face once more, with a lawyer between them. The whole history of the two men hung between them, visceral and hot to the touch.

Van Grimes felt cold; Breyton kept the conference room like an icebox. John tried to compose his face with his usual practiced ease but failed; he saw Breyton's reaction of disgust in the corner of his eye, and so he lost his power. He felt off center. To his own dismay, he made no attempt to seize control of the meeting from the outset and waited quietly for Breyton's opening move.

"We're here today, Mr. van Grimes," Breyton began, "to effect a dismemberment and dissolution of an ill-conceived and improper agreement." Breyton lingered over the words *dismemberment and dissolution* like a hungry python over a field mouse. His voice was a deep baritone, full of weighty authority. "I received a phone call three days ago from someone, a friend to the correspondent, Mr. Andrew Miracle.

What this person told me disturbed me very much. After consultation, I have elected to represent Mr. Miracle."

Van Grimes felt a chill at the lawyer's words. He had suspected as much as soon as he had received the call from Breyton's secretary arranging the meeting. Breyton was regarding him with a wilting, unwavering stare. There seemed no room under the lawyer's eyes for movement or explanation. Breyton would obviously be a formidable cross-examiner to a hostile witness in a court of law. Nevertheless, he had no intention of being a completely willing sacrifice—a sacrifice on the altar of Andrew's self-righteousness, he felt. The fact remained that Andrew had been nothing without him. He had created Andrew Miracle. Even now, he held out the hope that he could control the damage and emerge intact. He resolved to make a strong opening statement, something to even the playing field. "I think you had better come to the point, Mr. Breyton," he said. "I'm a busy man. I have things to do, not the least of which is to manage the tattered remains of Andrew's career."

To van Grimes's dismay, his opening words left Breyton unmoved. He didn't so much as blink. "In deference to your busy schedule," Breyton responded, his implacable voice shedding van Grimes's attack like a pebble off a Sphinx, "we will proceed directly to the matter at hand. I have in my possession two profoundly disturbing documents." Breyton first removed a copy of Andrew's contract from a folder on the conference table. He handled it like soiled tissue. "This, of course, is a copy of Andrew's management contract with the John van Grimes Agency."

"Where did you get that?" Van Grimes demanded. "I never gave Andrew that copy!"

"Are you saying that the artist doesn't have a right to a copy of his own contract?" Breyton asked, his voice infuriatingly solid and immutable.

"Of course not," van Grimes answered. "He didn't have a copy because he never asked me for one."

"That does not surprise me, Mr. van Grimes. Andrew didn't ask for a lot of things, unfortunately. He didn't know any better. That, however, will soon be rectified."

"You still haven't answered my question," van Grimes said lamely. "How did you get that contract? I have a right to know." Suddenly, a light came on in his mind. "You!" he spat at Carolyn. "You called the lawyer! You betrayed me into this mess!"

Carolyn flinched, not so much from her former boss's accusation, but with the sheer pain of watching a man she once thought so powerful and masterly self-destruct before her eyes. She began to speak, but Breyton, unemotional, stopped her with a gesture. "Your rights, Mr. van Grimes, are going to play an increasingly diminished role in these proceedings. However, I see no point in hiding it. I can confirm to you that Ms. Hemphill is the source of this document."

"She's a robber!" Van Grimes nearly shouted. "I never gave her permission to take it, and besides, it was in my locked filing cabinet."

"Ms. Hemphill was acting on behalf of Mr. Miracle," Breyton replied. "He has an indisputable right to the document. She was retrieving the document for him, acting as an agent of your office."

"What about the locked filing cabinet? Was she breaking into my personal files as an agent of my office?"

"Ms. Hemphill has related to me the exact circumstances of her obtaining the document. Certain of those circumstances could be construed as . . . unusual," Breyton said, casting a look of mild reproach toward Carolyn. "It would be a fascinating interchange in a court of law to determine whether or not she would be found culpable for her actions. I think not. However, there are exigencies of law, and there are exigencies of real life. I would say that your interest is served in paying close attention to the most practical side of your own dilemma, Mr. van Grimes. Now is not the time for you to be drawn aside by outside considerations. Your attention to your own situation must be unwavering."

"What situation?" John demanded. "What is this? I'm incensed that that document was, in my opinion, stolen from my office. But what of it? It's a legal contract."

For the first time, Breyton smiled. There was a tiny, but unmistakable movement in his mouth, as if a stone had moved under its own power. "That is where you are wrong, Mr. van Grimes. Are you aware of the legal concept of fraud?"

"Obviously."

"My client has informed me that you represented this contract as an industry standard—even better than an industry standard. That, Mr. van Grimes, was a lie."

Van Grimes shuddered a little in his chair. He had passed over so many indiscretions that he had learned to avoid listening to his own guilt. It was torment sitting opposite such an imposing, unrelenting judge. "I took Andrew from nowhere," he began lamely, and trailed off. "I made him what he is." These last words were whispered in a voice of a hurt, unappreciated child.

"You did not make copies of his contract available to your client, Mr. van Grimes. Could it be because you did not want that contract seen by anyone else? Anyone who could reveal its unfair content?" Breyton was detached, authoritative, and unrelenting. He had no intention of easing up on his adversary until there was total victory. "Also, there is this." The lawyer reached into the folder and pulled out a photocopy of the forty-thousand-dollar receipt. At the sight of it, van Grimes flushed, his face red and angry.

"That's the last straw!" he shouted. "That is my private property. I was robbed!"

"You were not *robbed*, Mr. van Grimes. It may be possible that your privacy was invaded. However, in my opinion Ms. Hemphill acted quite rightly, and within the confines of the law. The box containing the documents was found in her own, unlocked file drawer, which she had authority to access. She had a key to the office and permission to enter on weekends. Indeed, she had done so many times at your own request. She finds a document which she suspects may indicate criminal wrongdoing. Not wishing to be part of a crime and in order to protect her own legal culpability, she comes to me and seeks my advice. I discuss the matter with my client, and he explains the conditions under which all of these contracts were signed. I see evidence of a payment, of which my client has no knowledge, for forty thousand dollars. The word that comes to my mind, Mr. van Grimes, is collusion. Collusion to defraud."

"This is intolerable! I got a forty-thousand-dollar finder's fee from Dove. What of it? It doesn't prove a thing! You're all blowing smoke!"

"The smoke you see is because there is a fire, Mr. van Grimes. A very hot fire."

Van Grimes sat rigid in his chair. He was alive with fear. "What do you people want from me?" he demanded. "Why are you all against me?"

Andrew sighed heavily and began to reach across the table to John. Breyton took his hand and stopped him. "What my client wants, Mr. van Grimes, is in fact far less than he deserves. He has proposed a settlement that is unaccountably lenient. I have advised him against it, but he is adamant that you not be unduly punished unless absolutely necessary. I confess I don't know where his reservoir of compassion comes from in this matter."

Van Grimes looked over at Andrew, momentarily encouraged. Andrew looked pained, and clearly in some emotional distress.

"So what does this all boil down to?" van Grimes asked.

"My client is claiming that this contract is invalid. He wants this contract null and void. He wants to leave this room today with a signed legal document stating that you relinquish all claims forever of breach of contract against him. He has proposed, as well, terms of financial settlement."

Van Grimes looked at Andrew. His gold mine. His key to the big time. Now, it was all crumbling around him. He wanted to protect everything he had built. He began to speak, but Breyton cut him off.

"Before you answer, let me add one thing. My client is maintaining this contract is void and illegal. You could, of course, elect to resist, and countersue him for breach of contract. I can assure you that in that event, I will insist that my client receive a jury trial. Now, let me paint you a picture: I want you to imagine all of us in a courtroom, as I disclose the terms of this management contract to the court. As I reveal that it was represented as fair and even generous. As I expose it, point by point, as usurious and unfair. As I explain that my client never received an executed copy. As I delve into the meaning of this forty-thousand-dollar payment, and the dubious note attached. As I call witness after witness, each of which is a well known and influential member of the music community in this town. A community in which you would never again be able to get a meeting. I repeat, Mr. van Grimes: there are exigencies of law, and there are exigencies of real life. I urge you to look at your situation from a practical point of view. No matter what happened, you could scarcely remain unscathed."

Van Grimes sat heavily in his chair, like a boxer returning to his corner after a particularly brutal round. His shoulders slumped, and his breathing was audible. He was trapped. He looked up momentarily to Andrew and Carolyn, scanning their faces for a sign of explanation. Then he looked back down again, his face blank. "What are the terms of voiding this contract?" he whispered, his voice flat and lifeless.

Incredibly, Breyton's voice did not soften even in victory. He had never raised his voice or berated van Grimes in the whole of the meeting; his voice continued through everything to be the stony, unwavering sound of unchallenged power. The lawyer reached into his folder a third time, and pulled out a simple, one page document. "This paper formally voids your management contract, and ends any financial dealings of any kind, including any future claims you may have to my client's income. It spells out, as well, the terms of settlement regarding income already earned. First, as regarding concert income, against my strongest advice, he is asking for none of it."

Van Grimes raised his head, as if looking for a secret left hook when offered a hand up from the floor. "I beg your pardon," he said meekly. "He wants none of it? None?"

"That's correct," Breyton said, his voice for the first time betraying a momentary irritation. "He will not be dissuaded on this. He wants you to have all of it."

Andrew sat forward, and putting his hand on Breyton's arm to preempt any restraining action on his part, decided to speak at last. "Believe it or not, John, I don't hate you. I don't want to punish you, I just want this to end. I want you to have the money. It means so much more to you, anyway. I don't even know how much there is, really. It doesn't matter."

Breyton looked pained, but went on. "I trust you will find that satisfactory." He looked at van Grimes with irony. "Nevertheless, that leaves the question of writing royalties and royalties from record sales, both present and future. It is the wish of my client that those funds be put into a trust, to be divided evenly between two recipients: First, the Christ's Kingdom Assembly of Rose Hill, Kansas, and second, the Sunset Retirement Home of the same city."

Andrew smiled. "It looks like Cy will be getting a new building after all, doesn't it, John?" he said, his voice clear and untroubled. He was feeling lighter than he had since, well, he couldn't remember when. Carolyn reached over and grabbed his hand. The two smiled at each other peacefully a moment, and Andrew's face was happy when he returned his attention to van Grimes.

Carolyn had a look of serenity and tranquillity on her face as well. "And don't forget old Mr. Bartlett, Andrew," she said. "And all the rest at the home. They're about to get the surprise of their lives."

Van Grimes boggled. He was being offered a way out with over a quarter of a million dollars in his pocket. "And you want nothing for yourselves?" he asked uncertainly. "Nothing at all?"

"That's right, Mr. van Grimes," Breyton answered. "Nothing. Any expenses that have been incurred on behalf of my client will, of course, be paid by you. His living expenses and his legal fees. We are preparing a comprehensive list. That is the extent of your responsibility." Breyton pushed the contract over to van Grimes's side of the table. John stared at it, the irony soaking into him. Only a short while ago the tables had been reversed. He had been the one handing over contracts to be signed. Now, Andrew, armed with Breyton, was calling the shots and making the deal. Breyton pushed a pen across the table and sat waiting, his arms crossed. *Time to cut my losses,* van Grimes thought. *Time to move on. This thing is dead, my friends. History.* He picked up the pen, and signed the paper.

"There's only one commitment under our existing agreement that I'll have to cancel," van Grimes said. "We were scheduled to do 'The Barry Rosenberg Show' in two days time."

"That appearance will go on as scheduled," Breyton replied matter-of-factly. "There is no change of plans regarding that appearance."

"What are you talking about?" Van Grimes answered. "Our deal's over. I'm canceling the TV show."

"On the contrary, Mr. van Grimes. You have signed away any legal power to represent my client to the entertainment industry. If you even pick up a phone to call 'The Barry

Rosenberg Show,' I will sue you instantly. My client has a personal reason to appear on the show, and he has made it clear to me that above all things, that is his capital demand. The final details of his appearance are being handled by his acting agent."

"His acting agent?" van Grimes demanded. "And who might that be?"

Carolyn smiled, and stood. "I think our meeting is over, John," she said. "I appreciate your time."

31

The flight to Los Angeles was heaven. In a moment of pique, Breyton had booked them first class tickets, deciding impishly to bill van Grimes for the cost in his final accounting. It made the trip sweeter, and they lolled about in the big chairs like children at Christmas.

There was, at last, peace between them. And peace upon them as well, if their faces were any indication: Carolyn leaned against Andrew for the first hour, and he happily put his arm around her, playing with her hair and feeling truly content for the first time in months. It was the old contentment come back, the solid feeling of being on the plains.

They had held hands all the way across the prairie, looking down at the flatlands as they rolled endlessly by beneath them. Andrew roused Carolyn from her peaceful quiet as they crossed Arkansas, and they watched as the hills flattened out into crisscrossed square fields of earth colors in Oklahoma.

They were guessing what crops lay beneath them from seven miles high, when Carolyn said, "I still want to hear that sound, Drew."

"What's that?" Andrew asked, drawn out of his thoughts.

"The wind. The wind in the wheat."

Andrew smiled, shot back by her words to nearly a year earlier, standing in an ocean of gold. "You will, sweetheart," he answered, "you will."

Carolyn spoke softly after that of the farm, and Andrew knew that she was in fact speaking of their hopes for their future, a future away from Nashville and the madness. For some time now they had been considering being together forever, sometimes talking to each other but more often each alone with their thoughts. Andrew had wanted it from nearly the beginning, but then the madness had come, and that drove everything else before it, pushing thoughts of true contentment out of his mind. But even when things had been at their worst, his need brought him back time and again to thoughts of her; thoughts of a life they might make together full of reality and acceptance. There was so much to do back home, but for a long time it seemed unlikely that Carolyn would want to make those tasks her own. Now, it seemed, she was letting him know in her own way that she wanted her life to be anywhere he was, if only it could be real and honest.

There remained, of course, the question of his career. He still held a contract with Dove, and they could, if pushed, want him to continue to make records. But he doubted that Dove would want a war with him. There was the matter of the forty-thousand-dollar check, if necessary. All the same, the idea of going on recording wasn't unthinkable—it just had to be on his terms, terms of honesty and genuine expression. Atlantic loomed as well, but their contract was simply to distribute one record at a time, so they held no real claim on his future. They might pressure Dove to find a way to control him, but there was no way to predict that. In the meantime, there were much more important things to think about: a private, musical homecoming for the folks at the Sunset Retirement Home, with all the dear ones circled around the spinet and singing, Carolyn handing out the cookies and the compassion to each one of them, and a dozen Sundays to play for church services in genuine worship to the living Christ. There was a crop to bring in, if the neighbors hadn't already taken care of it in remembrance of his mother, and Franklin as well. As the plane flew on to Los Angeles, Andrew found himself hoping that there had been rain at the farm and that the harvest would be delayed a bit; he would like to perch up on top of the combine one more time, riding high and his face turned to the cooling wind and the setting sun.

When the plane landed they disembarked, collected their luggage, and soon found their contact from "The Barry Rosenberg Show." A little dark-haired man in a chauffeur's suit was holding a sign reading "Mr. Miracle," and whether from Andrew's notoriety or the unlikely name, quite a few eyes were on them as they made themselves known to the driver. He politely escorted them to the waiting car, drove them to town, and checked them into two rooms in Ma Maison, a trendy hotel near the television studio.

After a brief rest, the little man reappeared and drove the pair to the studio where Rosenberg taped his show. The black stretch limousine glided past the security gates and came to a stop inside the heavily protected back lot of the facility. They had enjoyed the limousine ride; its pretensions no longer held any power over them.

The backstage doors opened into a world of hectic, boisterous activity. Andrew and Carolyn stood unnoticed on the edge of the chaos for several moments, until a professional-looking young woman spotted them and walked briskly towards them.

"I'm Andrew. Andrew Miracle," Andrew said, not at all self-consciously. "This is my manager, Carolyn Hemphill."

The young lady broke into an instant, professional smile. "Oh, of course you are. I'm sorry I didn't recognize you earlier. We're so delighted to have you on the show. I'm Katy Thomas, an assistant producer on the show. Let me show you to your dressing room, and then we'll go over a few things."

Katy led them to a dressing room with a big yellow star on the door. Andrew's name had been printed on a strip of cardboard and placed in a slot on top of the star, giving the sign an odd, transient quality for something designed to bestow so much status. Once inside, Katy quickly went over the details of Andrew's performance. He would perform solo, with only a piano. Afterwards, Barry would invite Andrew over to the couch for from three to five minutes of interview.

The show had allotted fifteen minutes for Andrew to rehearse his song on stage, giving the stage crew the chance to light him and check microphones. Everything went smoothly, and in what seemed like only seconds, Andrew was excused to his dressing room for the hour wait before airtime.

He and Carolyn left the dressing room door open for most of that time, watching all the activity as the show approached its taping. For Andrew, especially, it was enjoyable: he couldn't help wondering what the experience would have been like had van Grimes been there instead of Carolyn, and he was grateful that things had worked out the way they had. John would have been nervously pacing, going over what Andrew was to say word for word, making it hard to relax. Carolyn, on the other hand, was a quiet support to him; he had only to look at her to settle his nerves. There was a quality of mutual peace between them that doesn't always come with love.

Carolyn had picked out a beautiful, simple outfit for Andrew to wear. He was grateful, knowing better than to trust his own small-town taste but avoiding the kind of flashy overstatements that van Grimes favored. He felt comfortable, and he was ready when the time came to go to the green room to wait.

Before they left, Andrew took Carolyn's hand and closed the door to the dressing room. "Let's pray," he said simply, and the two bowed their heads, standing inside the metal door that opened into the world of big time television. Their dressing room became a little alcove of serenity, and they paused there a moment to collect themselves.

"Father," Andrew prayed, "a lot of things have been done in Your name over the last year, and I doubt You recognized some of them as Your handiwork. I've dressed up in thousand-dollar outfits in Your name. I've signed my auto-graph in Your name. I've made some people rich in Your name. They always told me the same thing, Lord: do this, and then you can tell people about Christ. Well, I suppose this is it. This must be what everybody was talking about. Just grant me the grace and the composure to do it and do it right. Maybe, in some simple way, I can redeem some of this. Amen." Carolyn squeezed his hand, and they walked out together into the energized atmosphere beyond the door.

The green room wasn't actually green at all but a nonde-script eggshell, with a clean but worn gray carpet. A large television monitor hung on one wall, so those waiting to go on could watch the program in progress. Comfortable chairs and couches were scattered around the monitor, and a table of the kind of light snacks and drinks calculated to make people feel important and taken care of occupied the wall opposite the television. Andrew was surprised at how crowded the room was; it seemed that the other three guests scheduled to appear that night each had brought small ar-mies of hangers-on, attractive people with expensive clothes and detached, bored attitudes. As Andrew entered, he felt analyzed and assessed; in this world, the magnitude of his fame was his calling card and reason for being. Their gaze held no power over him. He knew that once he said his piece on the show, there was every likelihood that he was about to step out of their world forever, and these few mo-ments of borrowed significance would make little difference to him in the future. He smiled as he imagined them all with little fame-o-meters hung around their necks, with a number one through ten attached. He glanced around the room. A famous actor, scheduled to go on first. About an eight, Andrew guessed. A comedienne, nervously concen-trating in a chair, whom Andrew had never heard of. Look-ing for her big break, Andrew thought. Give her a two. A television actor, hot for the moment from a popular series.

Seven, but it needed maintenance. Last, himself. Give me a five, Andrew thought to himself, smiling. Soon to be a zero.

Andrew was scheduled third of the four guests. He watched the first two on the program with interest, and his nerves arced upward slightly as the time approached for him to go on. Nevertheless, he felt an odd distance from the proceedings, as if he were watching them from outside himself.

At last, the second guest wrapped up and Rosenberg went to commercial. This was it. The door opened, and a crew member entered asking for Andrew. Andrew stood, kissed Carolyn on the cheek as if he were going for a drive, and followed the man down the short hallway to the set.

As Andrew entered the stage, the program was still off the air; there was another minute or two of commercial. There was some light applause as he took his seat behind the piano, and he waved politely in response to being recognized. Then, in what seemed like only an instant, the stage manager was counting down the seconds before coming back to the program.

"Five! Four! Three! Two!" he called, and signaling "one" silently with his hands, the applause started, and the show was back.

Rosenberg was the undisputed king of late night talk shows. He had reigned supreme for several years, and his style was as smooth and familiar as a best friend's. He looked up into the camera with a relaxed smile. What was for his guests a harrowing experience with enormous impact on their careers was for him just another segment. With a practiced and thoroughly affected energy, he introduced Andrew to the seventeen million people that would watch the program that night when it aired.

"Ladies and gentlemen, I know you've all been hearing about my next guest. He's very, very hot right now. His hit song, 'Lost Without You,' spent six weeks at the number one spot in the country, and he's here to do it for us tonight.

Let's hear it, ladies and gentlemen! Andrew Miracle! Andrew Miracle, ladies and gentlemen!"

The crowd applauded, but Andrew heard little of it. Even as Rosenberg was introducing him, Andrew was slipping into a cocoon of silence, searching for the music inside him. Eyes closed, he felt the heat of the lights come up on him, and he started to play. The piano was perfect, the monitor was perfect, and the moment was perfect. Andrew sang to the Lord, and like those days back at Christ's Kingdom, the others were lucky bystanders to a moment of worship. This time, he would sing the song as it was meant to be sung:

> Lost without You, Jesus,
> Lost without You, and I'm
> Lost without You, Jesus,
> Lost without You.
> And when I hear Your name
> That's when I remember,
> Yeah, I remember,
> That I'm lost without You.

Each time he sang the word *Jesus,* he smiled, a lost piece of himself returning. If all the compromises had been made to draw people toward Christ, then let them hear the Name, he thought. Let them hear it from coast to coast.

Andrew finished, and he was greeted with muted applause. No one had ever heard the song that way before, and there was understandable confusion. Even as his last chord rang out to silence, however, The Barry Rosenberg Band kicked into a high energy music cue to cover his walk across the stage to the interview area.

Rosenberg rose and greeted Andrew with his usual enthusiasm, hiding his concern. Nobody had told him there was going to be a gospel song on the program. He had seen the video like most of America, and there had been nothing there to indicate that the song had an overtly Christian message. As Andrew seated himself, Rosenberg hurriedly glanced over his question cards; there appeared to be nothing at all there about religion. He decided to forge ahead with the questions written before him. "Great job, Andrew," he said, his voice full of welcome. "Great to have you."

"Thank you, Barry," Andrew answered. Gratefully, he felt calm, and happy. There didn't seem to be any nerves. He had, after all, nothing to lose; he had given it all up on his own.

Rosenberg leaned forward on his chair and turned slightly to face Andrew. "Andrew, it says here you were discovered out in Kansas, in the middle of nowhere. I think that's a great story. Should I picture you out there milking cows and writing songs?"

Andrew smiled with shy politeness. "That's right, except the part about the cows. No cows. But I am from the smallest town you can imagine. Population fifteen hundred."

"You're kidding." Rosenberg's face was a contortion of overstated amusement.

"That's right," Andrew went on. "Rose Hill, Kansas. That's my home."

"And here you are, riding the top of the charts. What a phenomenon. I love this story. How on earth did you get discovered?"

Andrew smiled. This was his chance. "Believe it or not, I was playing in church."

"In church?" Rosenberg replied, laughing. This was familiar, comfortable territory for him. Many of the biggest names in pop and R&B music had church choir backgrounds. "There's a lot of great singing in the churches, isn't there?" he asked.

"Yes, there is. There's something beautiful about singing in a church. That's where I love to play the most, I think. I'm going to be playing there a lot more, now, I imagine."

"Great. I'm sure you can play about anywhere you want,

the way things are going. Now tell us about your hit song. It's number one on the pop charts, isn't it? Fantastic."

"Yes, it is. That's why I want to thank you so much."

Rosenberg looked puzzled. "Thank me? Whatever for?"

"For giving me this chance to come on the air and sing it the way it was meant to be sung. I don't know if I'll ever happen to be on television again."

Rosenberg studied Andrew quizzically. His last few responses had been mildly disturbing, but he knew better than to be drawn into something uncomfortable for the audience, and he had continued on as if nothing had happened. Now, however, his guest had ended on a down note. Rosenberg didn't like down notes. It made people change the channel. "Don't be silly," he said lightly, "you'll be on television all the time, with this big hit record. Just wait and see. Now tell us about that song. I've seen the video. Rough work, huh, posing with that incredible girl. Stunning. I imagine you hated that part, right?" A few members of the audience hooted, and Rosenberg raised his eyes dramatically, saying, "Come on, come on, you people have dirty minds." Smiling conspiratorially, he turned back to Andrew.

"Yes," Andrew said, "her name is Renee Costa. She's a very beautiful woman. There's an interesting story behind all that, if I have a second."

"Sure. Love to hear it." Rosenberg was grinning. He loved this kind of stuff. Hopefully, the kid would wise up and give him something juicy.

"Well, it so happens that I wrote that song to God. I wrote it out in the fields one day, when I was really searching and longing for God. He had seemed so far away. I don't know if you've ever felt like that, where God seems so far away? You know what I mean?"

Rosenberg forced a smile. He was beginning to think it might be time to wrap this thing up. "Uh, sure, I guess we all feel like that sometimes," he said, glancing across Andrew to his stage manager with a telling look. *Looks like it might be time to move on, fellas. Watch me.*

"I felt, that day," Andrew went on, "that Jesus had really heard me crying out to Him, heard me for the first time in a long while. Or maybe it was just that I was able to hear Him again," he said thoughtfully. "Yes, that must be it. Anyway, on that day everything sort of clicked. I realized that without my Lord, I'm lost. Sensing Him near me again made me realize how lost I am without Him. So I wrote the song about it."

Rosenberg was frowning, scarcely concealing his displeasure. He didn't like Jesus talk. God talk, okay in small doses, spiritual talk, even better, especially if it didn't have a name. Got people off his back. Jesus talk, he hated. Nothing personal, it just turned the audience off. Too preachy. He'd give the kid five seconds to change gears. Otherwise, aloha. Business was business.

"Anyway," Andrew went on, "I got talked into changing all that to make it look like I was searching for this girl, you know? They gave me a bunch of reasons, but I'm sorry I did it." Andrew looked into the camera, ignoring Rosenberg. "So this gives me a chance to tell everybody what it's really about. It's really about Jesus, and how much I love Him and how much I need Him. How I can't make it without Him. So I can't tell you how much I appreciate getting to come on and say this."

Rosenberg made himself smile, but it was an effort. He hated preaching on his show. Wrong place for it. "That's great, Andrew. Great story. I'm a hundred percent behind you on the whole, you know, religion thing. Love it. So, listen, thanks for coming, and we'll be right back after this."

The band roared into action once again, and the show went to commercial. As the show cleared, Andrew reached out to shake Rosenberg's hand good-bye, but the host was already gone, walking off stage for a quick puff or two on his cigar. Andrew sat silently a moment, looking around him, taking in the limelight of fame and glory one last time. After a few seconds, he stood, and as he did so a crew member walked briskly up to him, shook his hand mechanically, and escorted him quickly off the stage. It was over. Andrew walked off stage into the arms of Carolyn, who was smiling, her eyes bright and happy.

Later that night, almost two thousand miles away, Michael Thomasson flicked a button on his remote control, and the image of "The Barry Rosenberg Show" flipped away into black. He leaned back on the pillows of his bed. Mathematical calculations flickered silently behind his eyes for a moment, and then he sighed. "The kid's history," he muttered. "What a waste. He had a good thing going. We made a pile, but there was a lot more there."

"What's that, darling?" a female voice whispered near his ear.

"Nothing," he answered calmly. "That was absolutely nothing." With that pronouncement, he turned and kissed Renee Costa good night.

32

In the end, it was surprisingly easy to say good-bye to it all. It took less than five days to wrap up everything and get packed. For Carolyn, there was more to say farewell to, and therefore more to miss; to give her the closure she needed, the two drove around Nashville late in those last few afternoons, saying good-bye to favorite haunts and memories one by one. But nothing stuck hard in her heart, and even for her there was much more joy than sadness. She knew that the time had come to leave.

By the last night, everything was ready, the trailer packed, the arrangements completed. The two took their last meal together in Carolyn's empty apartment, on the last two place-settings to go in the last box. They were happy; they spoke of Rose Hill, and the old folks, and even of Franklin and Alison. It was a quiet time, and they never forgot it. They were knitting the past and the future together, making sense of it all.

They finished dinner and packed the remaining kitchen things away, sealing the box with tape that gave everything a final, locked-down feeling. Andrew reached across the box and kissed her. "Come with me," he said.

Smiling and curious, she took his hand and followed him out the door. This final night was a gift: cool crystal air and the moon hanging low, dark orange suspended in black. It had rained, but the clouds had vanished now and only the dark concrete of the streets was left glistening and wet, reflecting the streetlamps. Andrew led Carolyn down the sidewalk toward the street, but she soon realized his car wasn't there. For a moment, she stood confused. Then she understood. "The truck!" she laughed. "Your father's truck!"

Andrew put his hand on the fender. "I knew you'd recognize it from all the stories. I had it brought up. I'm leaving that car behind that John gave me. I don't want it anymore. He can have it with the rest of it. I want to drive out of town in Dad's truck."

"I love it. Wait a minute!" she exclaimed, looking around. "Where's my car?"

"On its way to Rose Hill, I imagine."

"What are you talking about, silly? What's going on?"

"Well, the poor guy that brought Dad's truck up had to get home, didn't he?" Andrew laughed. "I confess. I planned everything. We drive out in Dad's truck, and we ride together. You'll be with me, the whole way."

Carolyn squeezed his hand, and taking it in her own, ran both their hands along the hood. With his strong fingers wrapped around her own, they traced the lines of the fender. The truck was gleaming, cleaned and polished like a mirror. "You know I love you," she said.

"I do know," he said, smiling. "And I love you, too." He kissed her again and said, "Come on. One more adventure. The last one."

"But where to?" she asked.

"You'll see." He opened the door of the truck for her, swinging the wide door on its hinges and closing it after her. She sat high up on the bench seat and watched him as he walked around the front. He got in, and started the old truck up. It rumbled instantly to a start and settled down to a soothing purr.

"Let's go," he said.

The old chapel on Vanderbilt campus was nearly in sight before Carolyn realized that it was their destination. "What a dear you are, Drew," she cried. "This is perfect. It makes everything make sense, doesn't it?"

"I thought so. This is where it all began. You and me."

Carolyn sat in the truck, content to let Andrew walk

around and open her door. There was a formality to every-thing between them then, and they both understood it to be an important time worth doing right. This last night together in Nashville was like a special gift, and even the wrapping was to be perfect.

Andrew led the way to the secret brick. It moved like before, and he slid it out, revealing the hidden key. "I have it," he whispered, and they passed silently into the little chapel.

"Church," he breathed, standing in the center aisle, the dim street light filtering in through the stained glass win-dows, darkest purple, crimson, and blue. "Church." He said it again, as if pronouncing a blessing. They picked their way once more down the aisle to the great piano at the front. She took her place beside him on the bench, and Andrew once more began to play. It was like a fire, and the music flickered and danced in the dimness long into the night.

33

The next morning Andrew drove the truck over to Carolyn's apartment for the last time. His own place was settled, and he had greeted the new tenants even as he walked to the truck on his way out. He wished them well, turned and smiled at the apartment, looked up and down the street, and drove off without looking back.

He arrived at Carolyn's ten minutes later and was pleased to see the last few boxes sitting outside the propped open door, ready to be thrown into the trailer. She was as anxious to get moving as he was.

She greeted him with a hug, and with a sense of finality and contentment they packed down the boxes and secured the trailer with a padlock. Andrew rattled the lock in his hand and, satisfied, came to stand by Carolyn. The two gazed back at her apartment, where so many memories interconnected. Home-cooked dinners. Falling in love. Hard talks about Andrew's career.

"Any regrets?" asked Andrew, after a time.

"No, not really. I went by John's office this morning, just to say good-bye."

Andrew grimaced, remembering his own ordeal. "What was that like?" he asked.

Carolyn smiled. "It was good, it was good. I called ahead, so I knew he would be gone. It wasn't as hard as I thought. I wished every one of them well, and I really meant it. I hope they become as big as their dreams."

"You won't wish you were a part of it?"

"No. It's fine for them. But it doesn't work for me anymore, somehow. Besides," she said, looking up at him, "my place is with you now."

Andrew gently took her hand and held it for a moment, hearing her words ricochet inside him until they had touched every surface of his heart. The woman he most loved in the world had said them.

Without speaking he strapped down a tarp over the pickup bed, and checked for the third time the hitch on the trailer. There was no point waiting any longer. The two walked to each side of the truck, and looking at each other across the roof, they seemed to speak without words to each other, constructing a private secret; a secret about the past. Then, as if on cue, they turned and opened their doors simultaneously. Once inside, Andrew pulled her close across the long bench seat and eased the truck and trailer out into the street, leaving her apartment behind.

They had resolved to drive straight through, and the miles drifted by in a timeless stream. Their heads were full of each other, of old dreams and new dreams, of old friends and new ones still to be made. They never turned the radio on. They used the silence to grow closer, each quiet mile drowning out the noise of the last months of conflict. There had been many hurts, and many miles were needed. They were still healing each other.

When night came they stopped to eat, and they spoke quietly to each other about little things, like a funny roadside sign or a pretty homestead they had seen earlier. It was not a time for deep talking, but for releasing, and letting damaged roots grow back, stronger than before. It was a time for falling back in love.

Sleep tugged at them near Tulsa, and Andrew pulled the truck into a rest stop, gliding to a halt in the moonlight. There, they slept in each other's arms for a few hours until the sun began to rise, finally rousing as the brightening sunlight filtered gradually into their closed eyes. Andrew shook off sleep, and smoothed the hair back from Carolyn's face, kissing her forehead. She rustled awake but stayed close to him. He started the truck, the smooth, deep rumble of the engine an indefinable comfort to him, reintroducing him to the sounds of home.

The miles flowed by and the sun rose across the windshield, burning off dew and high clouds as it passed. Mile followed quiet mile. There was a sense of finality when they passed the Kansas state line; a barrier had been crossed, and they began to feel keenly that each moment brought them closer to a new life. They arrived in Rose Hill at around eleven that morning, and Andrew had no doubt in his mind where he would go first. Carolyn wisely said nothing but snuggled contentedly under his arm. She knew what was in Andrew's mind, and she knew that it was what she wanted as well. Every mile brought her closer to what had long ago become her heart's desire. There were many ways that their love could be consummated, many roads that would lead with the force of inevitability to the same sacred place. Some of them were long, and full of ceremony. But for both of them now, there could be only the most direct road.

Andrew found Cy Mathews at home, as he knew he would. He parked the truck in the gravel driveway, and led Carolyn by the hand to the front steps. He knocked firmly on the wood-framed screen door and turned to face Carolyn as they waited, holding her still with his eyes.

They heard Mathews before they saw him, a loud rustling coming through the door from within the house. Andrew smiled, picturing Mathews rumbling from one end of the house to the other, probably pulling on a shirt as he did so.

It was an even more disheveled Cy Mathews than usual who flung open the door a moment later, exclaiming a welcome for Andrew that would have roused the neighbors, if he had had any.

"Andrew, my boy," he fairly shouted, "you've come back! For a nice long visit too, I hope. You're missed, boy, you're missed! But wait a moment! Who is this lovely woman you have with you?" and he smiled knowingly.

Andrew smiled back, the spirit of Franklin and ancestors he had never known awake within him.

"This is Carolyn Hemphill, and I love her. Pastor, you have a job to do."

Mathews held his arms open wide and enfolded Carolyn in them, like a father.

"Come in, come in. Carolyn, I'm sure you'll want to freshen up a bit, my dear," he said. "My wife Lois is in the back, and she'll show you where."

He opened the door for them, and closed it tightly behind them. When it opened again, Andrew and Carolyn were husband and wife.

There are two speeds that life is lived and can be observed, and never was that fact more clear than when afternoon turned to evening on the Miracle farm. One speed is obvious; the other, hidden. By the most apparent—and therefore the most suspect—standard, city life appears to move much faster than life in the country. Cities appear to be awash in frantic motion as people rush from place to place, wrapping their fragile skins and bones with steel automobiles and jet aircraft, enabling them to split asunder a wind that would tear an unprotected man apart. But burning fuel can only push a man in metal so fast, and when that pace is still found to be too slow, a city man electrifies himself. He makes himself a single stream of electrons, a tiny, infinitesimal disturbance of subatomic particles able to pass through the wind even faster, leaving no wake. He beams himself through space, thus trespassing through heaven, and his tinyness fills the air. He travels so rapidly that he becomes omnipresent. He can be seen in China and America and Africa and the North Pole all at the same instant of time, a quality once thought to be the exclusive domain of the divine. He is like a tiny god.

By contrast, life on a farm seems to crawl rather than to run. Cattle take a day to roam a half section of land, and a man can run as fast as a tractor if that tractor is pulling a harrow buried in earth. Plants move, but they have to die to do it; seeds blow a few feet in the wind, and summer squash need a season or two to take over an untended garden, doomed to push through soil rather than fly through air. But even the silliest country man knows that the true speed of life is not measured in miles an hour, and that he does not end at his fingertips.

It's on this hidden level that many from the country find that city life moves far too slowly for them. Indeed, to the wisest country folk, the city appears to have stopped moving entirely. The thousands of clanging sounds in a large metropolis coalesce inevitably into one, static gong that never gets louder or softer, higher or lower. Its timbre never changes. Night never comes to the city. Darkness is banished, and it remains perpetually lit in the numb glare of a single, never-ending day. Cities never wake or sleep. There is no climax or denouement. Like a science experiment, the tiny, fractious motions within them have become so rapid and so small that they no longer appear to be moving at all, and so city life is reduced to a single, unchanging sameness. That's why country people have no use for cities. Cities move too slowly for them, and after an initial flush of shock, they soon find themselves insufferably bored.

Andrew had spent far too long in cities, and now he was leaning against a strip of wooden fence, trying to bring his own speed back up to the velocity of what was happening around him. The sun was setting, and he knew that in the ten or twelve minutes of remaining light far more things would happen than he could possibly absorb. The light would reflect off the heads of several million shoots of blue stem grass, each completely individual in shape, floating between four and six feet high in the air on waving, blue-green stalks. The sun and earth were hurtling through space, twisting geometry and refraction, bringing darkness with them. The wind was moving the blue-stem reflectors into infinite patterns second by second, never to be precisely repeated until the end of the world. When light mixes with wind and earth, the speed is multiplied until it dazzles the soul.

Above him, twin ballets of flight were careening. A large flock of swallows pirouetted through the air, a hundred wings beating separately yet locked together by some unexplainable extrasensory perception. They reeled suddenly about three hundred feet in front of him and, changing direction a score of times in a handful of seconds, they passed low and beside him, so that for one or two fleeting moments he could hear the whir of their dark wings. Meanwhile, several dozen large purple dragonflies jerkily hovered and dipped over the pond, shrieking through the air like pilotless helicopters, dipping, rising, darting in every direction.

To the world of color a minute was an eternity, as the clouds covered and uncovered the lowering sun, shooting purples and oranges and reds across pale, darkening, blue. The music of night had started, and the uncountable insects within Andrew's hearing were singing now, every second revealing a complexity and depth of song beyond knowing.

Above him the red still battled violently with the blue, covering more and more of the sky, until the black came from nowhere and threatened in less than two minutes to silence the battle. It would take the heat and light of a screaming sun to break its hold. And all this was only a trifle of those minutes; the shimmering of silver maple leaves in their millions and the impossible skating across the pond by the hundreds of water bugs never entered Andrew's mind because he was only a man, and even a few acres at sunset is more than a man can take in, and he could see a hundred or more as he watched the last of the light give in to the dark.

As he stilled the cacophony in his soul, he began at last to hear again, and to sense the other speed of life. He was able once more to feel the slow in the world, the inexorable passing of seasons. A year had passed since Andrew's vision had turned his life upside down, and now fall was revealing itself once again across the farms of Kansas in the twilight. The fields were in the last throes of birthing their crop and would soon be settling down for a long, renewing sleep under a blanket of white winter snow. But for now, the evening winds that blew across the ripe fields near the Miracle homestead were still speaking of autumn, leaving a cool trail of whispering across the tops of plants, rippling the pond toward the east wall of the house. The sun was cooling, its light turning a darker, deeper red as it sank, preparing to vanish into the golden sea of wheat that leaned forward to receive it one more night. Nashville, and everything that came with it, was already becoming a memory, and what had seemed recently so present and frantically important now felt cloaked in a haze, indistinct. It seemed that as the sun set, Nashville was setting, and van Grimes was setting, and all the others—the photographers, the interviewers, and the faceless, adoring fans—all setting, following the sun into the gentle, ripe sea surrounding the farm. He was content to let it all set, to let all those concerns fade away into the past. Nashville was behind him now. The faces of so many were fading, and their voices with them, as if Someone had an enormous volume control and was gradually turning them all down. As the sound of the voices diminished, he could begin to hear within himself again the eternal sounds, the sounds beyond time that have no beginning or ending and whose quietness renders them inaudible, lost behind the crash of living.

There was so much work to do, he realized, work for the Kingdom. He could never do it all, of course. The fields of Rose Hill offered more opportunity to harvest for the Lord than one lifetime could ever hope to uncover. There were church services to play for. There were widows to comfort, widowed and orphaned and left to die at the Sunrise Retirement Home. There were the prisons of unhappy families all around him, waiting for the Truth to set them free, one hard day at a time. There were tables to build. There was a woman waiting inside the Miracle house for him to love, and soon, he prayed, a family to raise up. He would have to listen hard to walk that road, and the sounds of living would have to be turned down low to hear his way through.

As he stood leaning against the fence he began to listen once more with that part of him that had been deafened by the grandeur of his own life. He began to hear a murmuring, distant as a coming dream. It could never be heard in the city, for even in the stillness of the prairie it could easily have been missed.

"Andrew," it whispered, soft as rustling leaves from behind a door, "you are love." His words had come back to him now, near the end of things, or near the beginning. But now they meant something different to him. He understood in that moment that the murmuring was a prophecy, one tiny part of the great laughter echoing back. Every life was a tiny stream leading into that great river of final, victorious laughter. It echoed back from the end of the story, saying: "You are love when you do love. You do love when you are love." Now Andrew realized that there was much to do, and therefore much to become. The One who had begun a good work was able to finish it. It would take one whole life and death, but one day Andrew would be conformed to His image.

Andrew had to wonder at the long roads that God would take a man down, only to return him, changed but back home at the end of it all. He had wanted God to do something great with his life, to achieve a great work. He had prayed for a great destiny. The works of home had seemed small and limited. But at last he was learning the meaning of greatness. He was learning that there was more love in a single act of kindness than in hearing his name cheered by thousands. He was learning the quietness of God and that numbers cannot impress the Infinite. He was learning how to decrease, so that One might increase. Here in the quiet, he could hear his father, and his father's Father, again.

The sun disappeared. Night had truly come. Before he turned away and headed to the lights of the house, however, he thought once more of Alison and Franklin, his mother

and father. He saw his mother pulling back the cloth to
show John the table his father had built, dignity shining in
her eyes. He saw her painting the base of the old, creaky
windmill, and planting flowers around it, spreading beauty
with her hands. And he saw his father, sweat glistening on
his forehead, swinging a hammer on a stubborn slat of
wooden fence. He saw him, too, pulling the truck over to
quote his favorite verse. Lastly, he saw his mother and father
together again, walking hand in hand over the rise in the
road to the north, vanishing over its crest. With that image
in his mind, he turned back to the house at last, peace in
his eyes. There was much to become, and so there was
much to do.

Andrew crossed the broad lawn leading to the back of
the house, stepped up onto the porch, and quietly let himself
in through the screen door. He heard Carolyn setting the
table, but he passed without speaking through the other side
of the kitchen into the living room and took his father's seat,
the big chair that Franklin used to fill in the evenings. It was
his now.

He felt again the comfort of home, of chairs that fit him,
of pictures and mirrors, of the smell of the wood stacked
and burning within the big fireplace, smoke curling up the
chimney and sneaking out into the cool air above. He sat
quite still and content, the arms of the chair reaching out
to hold him, the patterned fabric of its back touching every
inch of his own. He sat, eyes open, feeling the passing of
minutes and seconds transform themselves once again into
the changing of seasons—and of lives. Gradually he was
moving back into the other kind of time, into what is left of
the world in which clocks have no second hands and the
actions of great-grandfathers are remembered.

This had been his mother's house, for Franklin had built
it and given it to her. She may have passed on in her turn
to the Father, but still she was visible everywhere: outside
the house, the impatiens and crocus were dead, but the

daffodils, tulips, and azaleas were clinging to their glory and would reappear every year thereafter, gentle reminders of the woman who planted them. She was inside the house as well, surrounding Andrew with herself. But this house was his to give to Carolyn now, and he knew that as time passed it would change and become her own expression. These days of feeling so very much of the past in the present would only last a little while longer. There was no security from change, not even here at the Miracle house that had stood for so many years. Franklin had died, and Alison had died as well. One day, he knew, he would die also. In the meantime Carolyn had come, and she would spread her influence over the house as surely as his mother had done. But it was a good influence, and he was content. God was in the changes, and they were not to be feared. God had brought him full circle, and he was lucky enough to have a place to come back to. There was no place, not even in Kansas, that could hide from change entirely.

Carolyn was now busy in the kitchen, and he could hear her working, the muted sounds of dinner being prepared coming from around the corner. He smiled to himself and settled in even deeper into the easy chair. He felt himself drifting toward sleep, and he didn't resist it. His eyes were already half closed, and the television was softly humming its electronic lullaby. The obsessions of such a short time ago seemed absurd and remote here, in the real world, his real world. Limousines, hotel suites, arguments about billing and creative control—it had all seemed so important then, the most important things in the world. He could see himself, red-faced and arguing, standing toe-to-toe with van Grimes or an unfortunate bellhop, determined to get what he wanted. It seemed that the primary emotions of those last weeks had been to feel underappreciated and misunderstood.

Andrew gently moved in his seat, looking far off into the distance beyond the television into the pattern of the wallpaper. Dimly, he saw the face of van Grimes, smiling and talking as always, never silent. With a start, he realized that he actually was seeing van Grimes, seeing him being interviewed on the television before him. He snapped to attention and picked up the remote control to turn up the volume. An entertainment program was on, and to his amazement, the face of John van Grimes was speaking, saying something about an exciting new development in gospel music. Andrew was still trying to pick up the thread of the interview when the picture changed, showing van Grimes with his arm around a young man with a bright, sensitive face. The young face was about twenty years old and possessed penetrating blue eyes. He was holding up a contract, and van Grimes was explaining that this young man was about to enter the music world with an explosion the likes of which had never been heard before. Then the two were shaking hands, and he could see the faces of Laurence Hill and Harold Murphy moving into the foreground to stand with them. It dawned on Andrew that this was a new protégé, a new talent to instantly slide into the space left by his own departure. Andrew smiled grimly. If he had imagined that his personal drama would upset the machine that had manufactured him in the first place, he was clearly mistaken. Van Grimes had an untroubled expression on his face, and he was slapping the young man on the back enthusiastically. The new protégé had the face of an angel, and he was looking at van Grimes beatifically. Andrew pushed the mute button, silencing the screen. The face of John van Grimes kept on speaking for a moment, electronically stilled. Andrew continued to watch his mouth moving. Van Grimes was looking straight into the camera. His lips moved, and Andrew could read them. These were the words that the lips said: "Eat 'em up, kid."

Andrew leaned back into the chair and pushed the off button. The image of van Grimes flipped away into dark green, then black. Andrew closed his eyes, exhaling deeply.

He sat in silence a moment, and uncoiling himself, rose to his feet. Turning lights out as he crossed the room, he walked to his beloved piano and pulled the black bench out. He sat in the dusk, opened the keyboard, and laid his hands across the keys.

He let single, pure tones ring out, one after another, feeling them and hearing them as if for the first time. Each note filled the great room to capacity, and he began to listen to the music gathering inside him. As he played, he saw old Mrs. Harvey in his mind, bent over and stuck in her wheelchair. He saw her singing, lips moving breathlessly, the sound of her voice falling from her mouth. For the very first time, it didn't make him sad. Amazing Grace. It was alive in that nursing home, alive for ninety minutes every Tuesday night. It was alive when he played "Melancholy Baby" for Mr. Bartlett. It was alive when he helped the staff roll the old spinet piano out into the recreation room, clearing the card tables out of the way and setting up the chairs in a big circle, each turned to face the music, to face the gift. He saw his Sunday school class, clapping and singing, the Amazing Grace alive on their faces, singing beautifully loud and out of tune. And there was Sunday service, the congregation packed into the sanctuary, singing the songs he had written for them. He could see the plump face of Pastor Mathews, mouth open and singing for all he was worth.

He heard a rustling; Carolyn was quietly opening the shutters as he played, swinging them out and open, letting the music out into the fields and into the night. Silently she passed from room to room, and as each window opened, he played louder, and when at last she flung open the front double doors, he was playing almost flat out, joyously, feeling the weight and depth of every chord sent out from the Miracle house into the darkness. He could see her now out on the porch in the light spilling out from the house, see her sitting in the rocking chair, perfectly framed in the center of the doorway with her back to the house. Her hair fell down over the back of the chair, and the night breeze rustled through it and mingled with the music as it swept past her. Amazing Grace was alive on her face, too, if he could have seen it, as she sat there staring straight out into the dark, back erect, the strength of Alison and generations and the farm and the past flowing into her. Andrew pounded out his joy and his sadness until the two became one, and the music and the Amazing Grace took them both away.

About the Author

Reed Arvin is a record producer, composer of television post-scores, arranger, keyboard player, and author. He holds a bachelor's degree from the University of North Texas and a master's degree from the University of Miami.

Reed has produced ten number-one songs, and he has been nominated for two Dove Awards. His television post-scores include work for KCAL Los Angeles, WCBS New York, Shell Oil, Atari, CNN and many others. He is the winner of the International Mobius Award of Excellence for the best television post-score of 1991. He was an adjudicator of the 1992 Emmy Awards.

Additionally, Reed has toured extensively with Amy Grant, Barbara Mandrell, and Michael W. Smith. *The Wind in the Wheat* is his first novel.

By late afternoon, the sides of the sarcophagus were fully exposed. They stood two-and-a-half feet high and were of the same limestone as the lid. Attractive rosettes had been cut into both of the long sides of the sarcophagus, and small seven-branch candlesticks into the two ends, the *menorah* symbol.

But it was not the art that transfixed the three as they knelt before the stone coffin at the most awesome moment of their professional lives. It was the inscription. Jon had uncovered the first lettering in midafternoon but left it enshrined in dirt caking until the sides had been fully cleared. Then he had taken a camel's-hair brush and gently dusted off the inscription. It had two-inch lettering, it was in two languages, and it would evoke the first flourish from the trumpets of destiny.

> *Here lies Joseph of Arimathea*
> *son of Asher*
> *Member of the Council*
> *His memory be blessed*
> *Peace*